Praise for Steve Erickson and

"Audacious, ravishing, *Our Ecstatic Days* steadily ders. As devastating and touching as only our boldest, most enduring novels can be."

—Robert Polito, *Bomb*

"As unique and vital and pure a voice as American fiction has produced. *Our Ecstatic Days* is a remarkable consolidation of Steve Erickson's strengths . . . more like music, like a lucid dream—like a masterpiece."

—Jonathan Lethem

"One of the most important writers of his generation. Against Erickson's work, most new fiction reads like it was written by stenographers."

—Kevin Bicknell, *Atlanta Journal Constitution*

"*Our Ecstatic Days* makes good on the promise of its title. The sentences swoosh into the ether as the characters acknowledge a reality that compels their awe."

—Christopher Byrd, *American Prospect*

"A cult genius . . . *Our Ecstatic Days* continues Erickson's tradition of fearlessly racing across bridges of form and content that others thought were still being constructed. Dive into its lake of longing and lyricism."

—Chris Roberts, *Uncut*

"Brilliant . . . a singular, sweeping fever-dream of a novel. Maybe the great writer of our time."

—J. Rentilly, *Pages*

"The only authentic American surrealist."

—Greil Marcus

ALSO BY STEVE ERICKSON

The Sea Came In At Midnight

American Nomad

Amnesiascope

Arc d'X

Leap Year

Tours of the Black Clock

Rubicon Beach

Days Between Stations

Our Ecstatic Days

STEVE ERICKSON

SIMON & SCHUSTER PAPERBACKS

New York   London   Toronto   Sydney

SIMON & SCHUSTER PAPERBACKS
Rockefeller Center
1230 Avenue of the Americas
New York, NY 10020

SIMON & SCHUSTER and colophon are registered trademarks of Simon & Schuster, Inc.

For information about special discounts for bulk purchases, please contact Simon & Schuster Special Sales at 1-800-456-6798 or business@simonandschuster.com

Manufactured in the United States of America

10   9   8   7   6   5   4   3   2   1

Library of Congress Control Number for the hardcover edition: 2005295980

ISBN-13: 978-0-7432-6472-3

ISBN-13: 978-0-7432-8510-0 (Pbk)

Parts of this novel originally appeared in different form in *Conjuctions*. I wish to also thank the MacDowell Colony for their generous hospitality and support.

for Lori and Miles

If there's a higher light
        let it shine on me
        let it shine on me
                through the trees. . .

'cause I know this sea wants to carry me
it's a sweet, sweet sound she sings
        for my release. . .

under the opal moon
        the world seems right to me

and all that I can say I feel is peace

and oh, the dark night wind
        is calling out for me

**an obscure pop song of the
early Twenty-First Century**

. . . for beauty is nothing
but the beginning of terror
        we can just barely endure

Rilke

2004

Sometimes I'm paralyzed

by my love for him. He calls
me from his bed in the middle of the night and, you know, I can't
resist. It's the way he calls, not sleepy or frightened or crying,
but determined and aware and awake. . . .

Mama?

and I can hear the question mark so insistent it isn't a question. . .
it would break my heart not to answer.

In my heart he opens the door to this vast terrain of fear.
It's a fear stretching out beyond these young years of mine when
mortality is supposed to be so inconceivable. How have mothers
down through the ages survived their love for their kids? The
thought of his mortality is abysmal to me. . . .

One afternoon we were at the fair down by the lakeside,
and a vendor had in captivity one of the owls that have invaded
the city ever since the lake first appeared three years ago. She
was explaining to some other mom's kid how, far up in the sky,
the owl can hear a human heartbeat, and even at that very minute
I thought to myself this owl could hear Kirk's little heart as I stood
there holding him in my arms. Could it hear his heart when he

was still inside me three years ago? Was that my first betrayal of my boy — his birth, exposing him to the peril of owls that hear heartbeats? Every night I wait for the sun to set before writing this, there it goes now, slipping down

   behind the San Vicente Bridge that

     crosses the lake to the northwest, I see it from my window. . . sun goes down, sky goes dark, lake goes black, and owls swoop across the rising moon like leaves blown loose from some phantasmagoric tree twisting up out of the ground

  and my voice rises from the crypt of my consciousness shaking words off like topsoil. Kirk and I are bonded by a cord of blood that runs from his heart to my thighs. Menstrual waves crash against the inner beach of my belly.

There was this song from

*before he was born, I heard
it on a bus riding Pacific Coast Highway south, blacksea glittering
in the sun like gun metal, he was tumbling around and around
inside me like he did, thrashing in the cradle of me. . . and it came
out of a small radio across the aisle a row behind me, an older
man, college professor-type in a brown corduroy coat gazing out
my side of the bus at the sea. It was hot through the window but
I liked it after all those cold pregnant months in Tokyo. . . . I heard
it just once, a strange little song with distant Moorish drums and a
dreamy Middle Eastern melody and soft spanish horns in the back,
and a woman singing in a turn-of-the-century voice. . . but not this
century. Last century. Maybe all turn-of-the-century voices are
the same, pure, floating, lost. Like it could as easily have been the
voice of either 1920s Paris or bright shimmery twenty-first-century
Reykjavik. Spanish horns hypnotized me, the singer's voice
transported me*

> if there's a higher light
> let it shine on me. . .
> through the trees

and hearing it just that once, I never forgot it
'cause I know this sea
wants to carry me
it's a sweet, sweet sound she sings
for my release. . .

Later after the college professor got off the bus with his radio and the bus continued onward, I went on singing it to myself if there's a higher light *sang it to myself just as much not to forget it as anything, and inside me* let it shine on me *inside Kirk stopped thrashing, listening. I knew he was listening. Later, after he was born, I would ask if he remembered me singing it to him, and he said he did. Maybe he did, maybe he didn't. But I would sing it to him before going to sleep, by the window of our apartment, while the nightwind came in off the lake.*

Started this journal in Tokyo, stopped when I thought I miscarried him, then started again after I got back to L.A. . . . that was around the time the lake first appeared, that mid-September three years ago after Kirk was born. Of course it was already there before that, before anyone realized it was ever going to turn into an actual lake, the center near where Hollywood Boulevard used to meet Laurel Canyon Boulevard, nothing more than a puddle the morning it first bubbled up, no one thinking anything about it until however long it was before it cut the canyon off from the rest of the city. . . .

Since the city was in the middle of one of its usual droughts, a lake that appeared from nowhere and kept getting bigger ought to have been a little suspicious — but I guess that's easy to say in retrospect. "What's that old machinery out there in the water?" the writer down the hall asked me not that long ago, staring in the distance out his window, and I said, "Pumps from when they tried to drain it. . . "

As usual Kirk was busy demolishing the guy's apartment, sitting over in the corner pulling the tape out of a video. "Hey!" I yelled. He stopped long enough to gauge whether this admonition was to be taken any more seriously than any of the others, before returning to the task at hand. "Hey!" I said again, "stop!"

Over by the window, the writer glanced at Kirk unfazed. "When did they try to drain it?"

"I guess when it didn't, you know, just go away on its own. . . evaporate or whatever. . . . " As I snatched Kirk up in my arms, he lunged for the video he had just disemboweled, squalling Mine! "No one had figured out yet it was filling up from a hole in the bottom. . . .Knock it off!"

"They ever figure out whether the water was coming from the sea?"

. . . no it wasn't coming from the sea. . . by then, the edge of the lake had just reached south of Sunset Boulevard. A few weeks later it was almost all the way to Fountain Avenue, which meant it was only a couple of blocks from our old hotel here at the top of what's now called the St Jim Peninsula, named after a very fancy hotel up on the Strip I can still see from my window. Kirk and I used to sit watching it during feeding right after he was born, lavender and magenta kliegs on the walls and the Ether Bar where young glam Hollywood drank tequila martinis. But as the lake overtook Sunset, you could see the kliegs go out and darkness move up floor

by floor until

it was all dead.

Doc says it would have gone anyway of its own volition. Rotted by decadence from the bottom up. . . as close as I've ever heard her come to sounding judgmental about anything, and the only time I've ever heard her sound almost glad to see a building die. In the old rundown hotel here where Kirk and I live, some on the first floor have already started moving out. Sometime in that first year, when the city would send boats out to the center of the lake, sending divers down to figure out where the lake was coming from, they referred to it in the newspaper and on the radio as "lake zero" — as in, you know, ground zero. And then at some point it got shortened to Lake Z or, sometimes, Lake Zed.

You'll spend your whole

life," *Doc said when*
I told her this dream I had, "making peace with your own true
nature. . . "

. . . *whatever* that *means. In the dream I was on the banks*
of what was once Laurel Avenue, near the old 1930s apartment
where F. Scott Fitzgerald lived when he was writing movies. . .
I was lying there hypnotically fixed on the center of the lake. . . .

Lying there in my dream I was suddenly aware of my
own womb predating me. Aware of my womb being older than I. . .
down inside I could hear historical rumors

little spasms of collective memory rippling outward
up to my lungs and

down to my thighs. . . it infuriated me. It seemed so typical. . .
after all, do men's dicks predate them? In my dream I rejected it,
this part of me that was my son's first home. . . and then in a surge
of guilt I rejected him. *And then realized, in the dream, he wasn't*
there. I sprang up from where I was, looking around frantically,
from the water in front of me to the trees on the banks behind me

. . . and opened my eyes to find myself sitting up in my bed, in the grip of this maternal dread I can't ignore. . . .

    I never dreamed at all the first seventeen/eighteen years of my life. . . slipping into the womb of the night every time I slept . . . dark, still, swaddled in the unseen, the unlistened. Waking every morning knowing I had tumbled down this wormhole of the unconscious into some void, feeling a little more nuts every morning I woke like I spent the night drifting in the black, farther and farther from the mothership of who I am, barely twinkling stars of all my impulses all around me. Feeling even when I was awake that I was really still out there, floating. . . .Crazy, when I was young, just to have any dream at all, and doing some crazy crazy things in the night to find one. But I never dreamed until that night in Tokyo that I lost him, electric icicle of him melting out of me between my legs onto my fingertips. Then he was back later that morning, I felt his return, my little unborn man who himself had been cut loose in space the night before, drifting far away until somehow, in a burst of embryonic will, he swam back through the tide of Nada in a cosmic breaststroke. . . .

    . . . and since then I dream all the time. Almost never remember the dreams but I know they were there the night before, I can feel them like I felt him that morning he was conceived again inside me, good dreams, bad dreams, mostly dreams that aren't so certain of themselves. My kind of dreams, in other words.

    I used to be fucking fearless, you should know that about me. None of this terror I have all the time now means anything if you don't know that. Ran away from home at sixteen, traveling with this weird religious-suicide cult for a while, moving down to L.A. and getting into all kinds of situations just blindly, sometimes out of desperation but sometimes because I didn't have enough sense to be afraid. Lived by wits and recklessness. Went to Tokyo the same way. . . . I was the most fearless person I've ever known. Not a better one and definitely not a smarter one, but. . . not only didn't I know there was all that fear behind that door in myself, I didn't know there was a door. Everything was about me. . .

and then you have a kid and not only isn't everything about you
anymore, in some way too hard to explain, it never was. . . .

  No doubt about it my Kierkegaard's my little wildman.
Runs around the apartment naked with his flapdoodle sticking
straight out and his treasured balloons flying along behind him,
one string in each hand. . . . Before I had him I had this idea
babies were amorphous lumps of human clay that take distinct
shape only over time. But he was half-wildman half-zenbaby
right out of the chute. . . before, actually. The weeks after I got
back from Tokyo where I worked for a year as a memory girl
in Kabuki-cho
                 we would go down to the lake which at that time
was still small enough you could walk around all of it in ten
minutes except the part cut off by the Hollywood Hills, and
                      we would sit watching the water and,
other than when I would sing to him. . . if there's a higher light,
let it shine. . . it was the only time he settled down inside me,
mesmerized by the lake beyond my belly. First days after he was
born, when the lake started spreading west down what was then
the Strip, we would watch it together from the window of our
room while he lay in my arms, and I would think he was asleep
and then I would look to see his eyes open and calm, gazing at
the lake and — I swear — smiling.
                    Big Agua
he started calling it when he turned two, having picked up the
baby-spanish I don't know where, same place he learned to call
the moon luna. . . .

  The lake was starting to get a lot of attention then,
sightseers coming and going, city officials and geological experts
standing around scratching their heads. The first year everyone
was kind of enchanted by it, however much disruption it caused
schedules and traffic and bus lines. That's when the gondolas and
rowboats came out, sailing in and out of the red light that poured
over the hills like a tide of fire bursting the levee of the sun.
Charred palms stitched the horizon. A makeshift harbor was built

*over by the flooded Chateau X hotel. Parasols were in fashion
that autumn, women walking the lakeshore with them, twirling
them from their boats so on Saturdays this panorama of spinning
colored spheres floated above the surface of the lake and in its
reflection. . . . Balloons! Kirk would point when he saw the
parasols. While I lay on the grass reading, he would blow bubbles
from a bubblewand I bought him. . . so we blew bubbles together,
watching them float to the grass where those that didn't pop would
settle like dew. He would smash them with his foot. "Smash the
bubbles!" I would cry, and he would smash them, "Pap," and then
I felt funny, it seemed wrong to encourage him to smash something
as delicate as a bubble*

pap, pap, pap

*he would go. One afternoon he blew a particularly large bubble
and said out of nowhere, "This one's for my daddy," and it caught
my breath. . . he had never mentioned his father before*

this one's for my daddy

*and the bubble slowly tumbled down through the air before us like
a little spinning glass world, and when it landed, it didn't pop and
he didn't smash it but watched it there on the grass for a long time
until it finally popped on its own. . . .*

     *My kid's beautiful. What else is a mom going to say, right?
except that my kid really* is *beautiful. . . the minute he was born
they held him up for me to look at slackjawed, stupefied — me, not
him. . . . "This child is beautiful," the nurse assured me the next
day in some wonder, and I had finally come out of my fog enough
to crack, "Yeah, but you tell all the moms that," and she glanced
quickly over both shoulders to see whatever other mother might be
listening in the bed next to mine before she whispered back, "Well,
yes, I do. But this child is* beautiful*" . . . and so he is. Which he
certainly didn't get from his mother or father, so go figure. He's
a throwback to someone I can't even begin to know, never having
known either my own mother or father. . . . Don't know where
he got the hair that shines brilliant in the sun or the sea-green
eyes flecked with amber, or the sanguine mouth of a mad monk.*

People's attraction to him is remarkable. . . when he was younger I would push him in the stroller around the lake and people would gawk like there was something slightly supernatural about him, and not just little old grandmothers either. "Hey, cute kid, man!" some tattooed skinhead sociopath would interrupt his mayhem long enough to stop and exclaim.

It worries me he's this beautiful. . . not only that some stranger could try to snatch him away, but also for how life might let him get away with too much, given how he's a wily schemer too, already determined to run the show, musical in his self-assured insubordination. "Nooooooooo please," he demurs my commands in a lilting singsong voice. Silent defiance comes into his eyes, there isn't even the slightest submission in him. At the age of three he gives orders all the time, "Do this please! do that please!" — a very polite *dictator. "La-la!" he orders at night when I'm putting him to sleep, Il Duce's way of telling me he wants me to sing to him. "More la-la please!" means Keep singing. "Bigger la-la please!" means, Sing louder.*

Who's the boss here, wildman? I ask, and he narrows his eyes for a minute looking in mine, calculating the question, before he points at me and says with a big smile

You *are*

because he knows, you see, he's already figured out that's the right answer, even if he doesn't believe it for two seconds. . . .

. . . but I decided he might turn out OK one afternoon he was playing with Valerie's kid Parker, the only other child in the hotel, about eight months younger than Kirk — black, deaf and mute, and Valerie is another single mom who works a tedious job answering telephones for the city, so sometimes to help her out I'll take Parker for a few hours if I'm free. On weekends she and I and the two kids go down to the lake where they play together. . . and this one afternoon I saw it. . . Valerie saw it too. . . .

It wasn't a big deal. Kirk and Parker each sat in their folding chairs with balloons we had gotten them tied to their

*wrists, Kirk a yellow one and Parker a blue one, and Parker
pulled the string on his only to watch it float up and out over the
water. . . it was a minute before he realized it wasn't coming back.
Then he tried to cry, which was much more terrible than any
actual little-kid cry because it was a cry no one could hear. . . he
was wracked by the futility of cries he can't voice and balloons
that don't return. No matter how much Valerie tried to comfort
him, he was inconsolable, until Kirk got up from his chair, walked
over, pulled the string of his own balloon from his wrist and
handed it to Parker. Parker took the balloon and stopped crying.*

     *Maybe other three-year-olds do things like this all the
time, what do I know? but I was under the distinct impression that
empathy was something we don't learn until five or six. For a
while neither Valerie nor I said anything. Kirk went back to his
chair and sat down and watched the lake. . . .*

     *I used to be a notorious smart-ass. . . well, notorious to
myself anyway. Always with the smart answer. . . but I'm not
that smart anymore. There's no great revelation in having a kid
. . . you think you're going to be transformed, you'll somehow
become a more substantial human being. . . but there's no change
in me I can tell other than all the new ways I've become afraid.
I can't tell that parenthood has made me a whit wiser or less
trivial, or older except in the ways I'm not ready to be older. . . .*

     *. . . all I know is the meaning of myself begins and ends
with my boy, where I didn't know there even was a meaning
before. All I know is he's the shore of the lake of my life where
before maybe I knew there was a lake out there somewhere but
had no clue where. It doesn't mean there's nothing of me. There's
always been a* me *there, I know that. But it means he's the single
lit lantern on the road to Me, dangling from the branch of
experience that overhangs my night of doubt.*

     *These are the memoirs of Kristin Blumenthal, L.A. single
mom, former Kabuki-cho memory girl. In July I'll be twenty-two.*

When I returned to L.A. from

Tokyo before he was born,
*I went to see an obstetrician for a sonogram, and they looked at
the screen a long time and finally said, "There's two."*
Two?
"Yes."
Twins?
"Uh. . . yes. We think."
You think?
"Yes."
*Or: there was one. . . and a female shadow. The shadow
of resurrection? Burned into my womb like bombs over Japan
burning shadows into walls? So on his birthday out came Kirk
and we all waited for the other, waited and waited, doctors and
nurses peering up into me and looking at each other and kind
of shrugging like, Well, where is she? What's she waiting for,
trumpets? "I guess we'll settle for one," the doctor finally
announced jauntily, when she didn't appear.*
*But ever since, not all the time but now and then, I feel
her there inside me, Kirk's little sister Brontë. Is she being willful?*

Is she just shy? Does she know something the rest of us don't, and is taking refuge? She tumbles around inside me at night until she hears me thinking about her, and then rests in a way Kirk never rested, listening, considering options, waiting for her moment. . . .

Over the last few months, more and more people have moved out of the first floor of the Hotel Hamblin where I rent a room for Kirk and myself on a more or less permanent basis, until there's no one down there but the manager and a nomadic halfdog halfwolf that wanders in and out of the hotel scrounging for something to eat. As the lake gets bigger, the power starts going out in parts of the city, you can tell that the lights in the faraway windows on the other side are lanterns and candles from their pinpoint flickering in the wind off the water, like fireflies hovering against the black hills of the distant shore. Soon the city started rewriting all the addresses. Without over-explaining it here, each new address has two parts, one fixing its place on the lake's perimeter and the other its distance from the lake's center . . . for instance the Hamblin is PSW47/V180, which means it's 470 yards west of the southernmost point on the lake's edge, and 1,800 yards from the center. . . and of course as these addresses get bigger, they render the earlier addresses obsolete. PSW47/V170 doesn't exist anymore, it's now under water. L.A. is a city of drowning addresses.

At first people wondered: if the P was for "perimeter" and the SW for "southwest," then what was "V" for? If the V part of the address was the distance from the center of the lake, why wasn't it a "C" address, or M for "middle" or B for "bull's-eye"? It turned out that V was for "vortex," and when that got out, everyone kind of freaked. A rather poor choice of words, vortex. . . *leave it to a bureaucrat to get poetic at exactly the wrong moment. Vortex sounds like a drain. It gives the impression not only something's coming up from the hole at the bottom of the lake, but something's going down too. . . .*

Not that long ago I got a letter addressed to Kristin B, and I assumed it was for me until I opened it, My beautiful K *it began and right then and there I knew he had the wrong girl,* labial jewel, riverine rapture *and so on and so forth in that vein, for the first few letters anyway, until they became more bitter, ecstasy replaced by bile as one letter after another went unanswered.* Soon the letters started coming every day, each more furious and desperate than the last, and each enclosing a small piece of an old photo which I stuck to our hotel wall with the other pieces, waiting for the complete portrait to fall into place. . . .

Of course as each letter became more tormented, it occurred to me to write and put him out of his misery. I felt guiltier and guiltier reading them. . . I mean, I had no excuses after the first one. After the first one it was pretty obvious the letters weren't for me. But there was no return address and I guess it never occurred to him they might be going to the wrong person, and soon it became pretty obvious to me he's what I've always called a point-misser. Everyone misses the point now and then but some people are just born missing the point. It never occurred to him there might be any other possible reason his labial jewel *wasn't answering. His desire was so grand and uncompromising he would rather assume she was rejecting him than that something as banal as the incompetence of the postal service could be at fault. Some part of him wanted to judge her monstrously, some part of him wanted to be a martyr for* cunnilingus *instead of a prisoner of chance.*

There was something else about the letters, something clandestine, subterranean: The lake, *he finally wrote in one,* is coming for me, *and the second I read it, I saw him somewhere out there in the city barricaded away, building an ark maybe.* In China they would have found me by now. *I don't know how long it was, at least fifteen or twenty letters, before I finally noticed they weren't actually addressed to PSW47/V180, but V170.*

When I saw this, I grabbed up Kirk — at the moment busy trying to demolish my carefully constructed jigsaw of little pieces of the correspondent's photo attached to the wall — and ran up the stairs to the Hamblin rooftop, where a panoramic view of the lake

*stretches all the way from Hollywood in the east to the San Vicente
Bridge in the west. There out in the water, about a thousand yards
away on a more or less straight line from us to the center of the
lake, rose an old abandoned apartment building like my own. . .
and I knew right away it was PSW47/V170 where she lived,
waiting for his letters to come floating up to her window in bottles,
maybe. It was dusk, light failing at our backs, and only after Kirk
and I stood there a while watching the black of the water meet the
black of the hills beyond, darkness slowly swallowing up V170
in the distance, did a light flicker in one of its faraway windows,
clear as could be since every other window was dark. And just like
I knew that was her address, when that light appeared I knew it
was her, and she was still out there, waiting for him.*

When I can leave Kirk with
Valerie here in the hotel a
few hours, I cobble together what jobs I can, including the one
with Doc and the one for the writer down the hall. . . .
. . . desperate over-the-hill novelist who checked in for a
few days in order to finish this screenplay he saw as his last best
chance to salvage a career. . . he wound up staying a week and
then two and then a month and now he's been here almost a year.
The screenplay never gets finished and meanwhile his wife and
daughter who live on the other side of the city come see him like
relatives visiting an inmate. The little girl is about Kirk's age,
long gold hair, and sometimes when the reunion is over and
there's this tearful clutching between the writer and his wife,
the little girl stands in the hallway staring at Kirk and he stares
back at her. Two little kids, little boy and little girl, just stand
there staring at each other wordlessly, they don't play, they don't
fight. During these times I stay as inconspicuous as possible
because I don't want Mrs. Over-the-Hill-Novelist to get the wrong
idea. "I miss my little girl," he whispers later. Since it would
seem he can check out of the hotel anytime he wants and go home,
it's hard to figure.

Day after day, night after night, he sits in his room gazing morosely at his blank computer screen drinking tequila and watching old movies stacked up in the corner. He stares out his window at the growing lake and talks about missing his little girl, and he never answers except to a secret knock, while bellmen slip notes under his door wondering when he's going to check out. I've read some of his script and maybe I'm wrong but I've begun thinking the main character, a chick punk singer, sounds a little like me. It isn't the best movie but I'm certain there have been worse. I think his big problem is he hasn't the slightest idea how to write women characters, but he looks completely baffled when you try and tell him this. "What do you mean?" he says.

"What do I mean? I mean every female character is a stripper or porn star or sex slave."

He's thunderstruck. "Are you sure?"

"Yes I'm sure."

He ponders this a while more. "What about Tara Spectaculara?"

"Tara Spectaculara? The amazonian motorcycle mistress with the huge tits? The one in the black leather jacket that's. . . how did you put it?" — flipping through the script — ". . . 'unzipped so far it threatens the space-time continuum'?"

"Uh," he's thinking furiously, "well, these characters," he finally clears his throat, "are just, uh, you know. . . they're just the. . . forbidden iconography of the male psyche. . . ."

"Oh, well then. In that case. 'Forbidden iconography of the male psyche,' that's OK then. Stupid me, I thought this Tara was just your basic male wangie."

"Male what?"

"Wangie."

"I don't know what that is."

"Yes you do." Talk about a point-misser! This guy is a serial *point-misser. Anyway he got this idea of passing me off as the writer of the script, that's the way his mind works, and an even better example of how his mind works is he's saddled me with the*

nom de plume "Lulu Blu," who apparently was some kind of woman pornographer back in the Eighties — which you would think kind of proves my whole argument. He's convinced *Hollywood isn't going to have any interest in failed literary-type novelists, better if a script filled with male wangies about motorcycle mistresses and rocker babes, submitted to guy-studio-execs with their own male-wangies, is written by a twenty-two-year-old punkette who would be expected to have special credibility on the subject of motorcycle mistresses and rocker babes since undoubtedly I live with a harem of them and we all have sex together all the time, which of course is the biggest male wangie of all. So for a while one of my jobs has been to run around town sitting sullenly in Century City offices listening to why I'm being turned down — which is to say why* he's *being turned down — and I guess I have to admit on some level I must find this guy just pathetic enough to feel bad for him, since I keep doing it even though it's obviously never going to pay me anything, my five percent of the script contingent on someone actually buying it. . . .*

    I don't know much about the movie business but it seems obvious to me they have a problem. "Looks like you have a problem," *I mumble to this one studio guy in his office one afternoon with the lake sloshing through the doorway. Throughout the whole floor they've set up little footbridges from this desk to that, and after a while the ultimate status power-move by a ruthless studio boss isn't the lunchtime blowjob by the personal assistant of either gender but rather commanding an associate producer to swim to his suite on the double rather than walk the little planks now reserved for the elite of a Hollywood that no longer exists.* "This?" *the executive sneers,* "this isn't a problem. Are you kidding?* Sound — *now that was a problem.* Cinemascope. Television. *We survived all that," this guy, maybe five years older than I tops, shakes his finger at me, "long before your time. What's this? A little fucking water," contemptuously waving his* *hand at the tide lapping at the ankles of the anxious secretary in the corner.*

At the beginning, the lake was banked on the north side of the Strip, but then the dam there broke and the water cut most of the city in two, and before they built the San Vicente Bridge all the east-west bus routes had to detour down to Venice Boulevard before turning back up the peninsula formed by the La Cienega and Crescent rivers. It screwed up my other part-time job and the couple of times I was late I could tell Doc was annoyed, which was mortifying given she's a fount of patience, one of those people you never want to let down. Truth is I've never quite figured out what I contribute to her work except to take the patient's various atmospheric readings and hand her whatever instruments she needs. Last time I think her irritation was aggravated by the fact that the diagnosis hadn't gone so well and she was breaking the news to the habitants just as I got there, breathless from having run the half mile from the bus.

"It's dying," she had just told them. . . they were still standing on the front lawn arm in arm, looking at the terminal house stunned. I think because there's something so calm and deep about Doc, people find this kind of bluntness easier to accept . . . there's a manner about even her most ominous prognosis that says both: This is the way it is; and I'm sorry. The habitants can tell she feels for them and I can tell it too, watching her move through the sick house from room to room in a bubble of stillness, running her fingers along the walls and the doorframes and the windowsills, pressing the side of her face against the plaster listening. When she does this, her lined face glows with the flash of both twilight and dawn at the same time. . . OK, I'm getting carried away. OK, you can tell I'm a little in love with her. Her eyes older than her face and her smile younger, her hair lost between the auburn of yesterday and the silver of tomorrow, serenity woven in the air around her like a glistening web. Truth is, this job isn't much more lucrative than trying to peddle

Jainlight's script for him, but I do it because I covet my time with her. Sometimes at night, I dream she's my mom I never knew.

There's a sadness about Doc, something she brought with her when she came out to L.A. from New York a couple of years back, not long after the lake appeared. Or maybe it's just from listening to all these sick buildings, however fatalistic she tries to be about it. She presses her face against the wall and closes her eyes, listening to the fading life of the house. . . I finally asked what it is she hears and that was when she told me about the music. Female voices singing, inside the walls, songs of. . . once I saw a tear run down her cheek. But, what makes a house die? I ask, and she shrugs, "Well," in that voice you can sometimes barely make out, "as with people, it isn't always easy to say. I just know it's slipping away. I can hear it in the walls, it sings to me. I hear death spreading through the baseboards or in the ceilings, sometimes it's just old age. Sometimes it's something unbearably sad the house never recovers from, an untimely death, the end of a marriage, an act of violence, something only the house knows, something only the house has seen, a betrayal the house absorbs while shielding the habitants from it. Sometimes when a house dies, it's an act of sacrifice."

But what happens when the house can't stand its secrets anymore? that's what I want to know. What happens when the house starts telling the secrets back because it can't bear to bear them. Maybe Jainlight down the hall can't finish his script because the walls of the Hamblin constantly hum in his head the secrets of girlfriends and mistresses that producers and studio chiefs kept here back in the early part of the last century. . . . A few nights after Doc said this, Valerie was working a night shift and Parker was staying over, sleeping in Kirk's room when I heard "Mama?" with that insistent question mark I can't resist, emphatic as a period. There was something different about it this time, though, he was whispering it, and when it was obvious he wasn't going to go back to sleep on his own, I went to him. He was standing in his crib in the dark, hair white in the moon through his window. *"Mama," he whispered again, and pointed at Parker lying in the crib Valerie brought up from their apartment.*

Flailing in the air, Parker's hands formed strange half-patterns while there twitched in his sleeping face a whimper he couldn't say. Alarmed in his three-year-old way, Kirk reached up his arms to me and I picked him up and held him a while, but then after watching Parker a few more minutes he strained to get down, so I set him on the floor and together we continued to watch Parker's hands fluttering in the air before him.

I finally realized Parker was dreaming. He was "talking" in his sleep. I looked around at the dark room, shadows throbbing with secrets of abandonment. Kirk stood there with his hand in mine "listening" to Parker's dream of lost daddies, before he went to Parker and placed his palm on the younger boy's brow. Immediately calmed by Kirk's touch, Parker dropped his arms to his sides and slept.

For a while Kierkegaard howls
on buses and in coffee
shops, *Owoooooh! like the coyotes we hear in the hills at night.*
Owoooooh, owoooooh over and over until it's driving me nuts and
I tell him to shut up with the howling already. But sometimes when
I'm putting him to sleep, I howl with him very softly. . . he puts his
ear against my tummy and listens to Brontë his sister still inside
me and howls quietly to her, all our howls getting quieter until he
howls himself to sleep.

He has his own way of seeing things, there's no doubt
about that, depending on whatever fantasia he lives in at the
moment. Up on top of the Hamblin, as dark falls he explains how
the clouds are flying igloos and the lights in the hills are the
night-robots that come out when the day-robots go back in their
cage in the sun. We're riding on the bus together looking out
the window and I'm thinking about some meeting I've got that
afternoon with a producer in my Lulu Blu incarnation and Kirk
is driving me nuts with the howling and the endless questions
he asks about this and that. It's a strange overcast day and the

sunlight is shining through the clouds in a strange way and, out of the blue, my three-year-old says, "It's the face of God."

    He has a toy he calls Monkeyman, a small plastic gorilla in a red spaceman suit and space helmet that he takes into the bath, to bed, on the bus, clutching it in his hand at all times. Sometimes hours go by and I see Kirk has had Monkeyman in his hand the whole time, has never let go of it even once, has never set it down anywhere for a second, has never even stuck it in his pocket. There's even a song that goes with Monkeyman, an old rock and roll song from before I was born that we heard on the radio with a woman singing spacemonkey, *it goes,* sign of the time. *At night Kirk clutches Monkeyman in his sleep like it's this talisman-thing, and only after sleep has come over him does his hand slowly open and let go.*

    Then in the middle of the night he wakes and realizes he doesn't have the monkey. He starts crying and I have to look through all the bedding and under the crib and around the floor. Or sometimes in the night if Kirk has a bad dream and I go get him from his crib and take him into my bed in the other room, he'll still be holding on to it, and I'll hear this plop on the floor behind me as I'm carrying him from one room to the next and I'll know he's dropped it, and I go back and find it so I'll have it to give to him when he wakes up wondering where it is. Not long ago Kirk named the red monkey Kirk, except when he says it, it comes out Kulk.

    I read him this book called I Am a Little Monkey. *There's one part where the mommy monkey cleans the little monkey by picking the bugs off him like monkeys do, and every time I get to that part I pinch him all over like I'm picking the bugs off him. Now whenever I get to that part of the book Kirk scampers to the other side of my bed with Kulk to get away, knowing what's coming. Are you a monkey? I say and he says, "No I'm not a monkey!" Are you a boy? and he answers, "Yes I'm a boy!"*

*except last time. Last time I said, Are you a boy? and he said,
"No please!" and puzzled I said then what are you? and he
answered*

I'm a Bright Light.

*What are the odds? I mean: ever, you know? what are the odds.
Whole populations unleashed in a stream of semen, whole Indias
exploding in my womb. . . so what are the odds what kind of kid
you'll wind up with? How many millions of sperm are there in the
white whisper of a cock, and if one happens to meet up with the
waiting egg, it's one kind of kid, and if another, then it's another.
Conceive at ten o'clock and you get a psycho. Conceive at 10:01
and you get a Bright Light.*

*He calls any darkness "night-time." Goes into a dark
room, it's "night-time," checks the apartment for pockets of
night-time everywhere, peering into closets declaring "night-time"
then moving onto the next. He goes through my desk, pulling open
each drawer and gazing into it one after the other.* Night-time,
night-time. *Watching over his shoulder and pondering Kulk's
silhouette on the wall behind him, he says, "God made Kulk,"
dancing it in his fingers in front of my eyes for a while before
adding, "but He made his shadow first."*

*Since the lake, there's been an epidemic of dying houses
all over town. . . Doc sees all of them. Consumptive houses,
malaria houses, alzheimer houses, heart-attack houses. Houses
with tumors growing out of the attic or the bedroom windows or
the family rooms. Dying faster than Doc can pronounce them
terminal, and you see it mostly when the sun goes down and there
are black patches in the hills and skyline where once were lights
. . . an urbanological mourning, a city bound and gagged in the
black memorial armbands of lightless windows and doors.*

*One late afternoon, out on the shores of Laurel Cove
where it first appeared, not far from where we saw the owls the
afternoon at the fair, I was walking with Kirk holding his hand,
and we heard music coming out of the lake. First it was only
a shred of a melody and then there was another, two melodies*

interweaving, and then suddenly there was a flood of them,
an outburst so loud Kirk put his hands over his ears. The music
was accompanied by a light, first a small glowing string and then
another, and then a mass of them, each melody snaking its way
outward from a place in the lake just above its source, until the
whole lake was shimmering with light and music, melody-snakes
wiggling their way out into the city. I kept looking around to see
if anyone else was out there to hear it and see it like we did, but
we were alone for a minute, like everyone in the city had vanished.
And although at first I thought it was the sound of all the songs
of dying buildings escaping from the walls that held them, all the
female voices that Doc always heard, it was more like they were
coming from deep under the water. Like they had broken through
from whatever was on the other side of that hole at the bottom
from where the lake had come.

When I was a kid back on the little island where I grew
up in the Sacramento delta, the sound of the radio was the sound
of tourists who came and left, sound of freedom and desertion. . .
all the strangers who could come to the little Chinese ghost town
where I was a prisoner and then leave on the ferry the next day.
Sometimes Kirk and I find a song on the radio that we sing
together, there was one by this chick band from the late Nineties,
guitars going off like terrorist bombs and girls singing dum dum
da dee dee dum dum da dum doo! All the little babies go, Oh! oh!
I want to! *and for some reason this one underground station*
played it a lot for a couple weeks, and every time at the chorus
Kirk and I would jump up from the bed and shout at each other,
"All the little babies go, Oh! oh! I want to!"

Like me when I was a kid, Kirk used to never cry, he only
started lately. I think somehow he got it in his head the music
is the sound of freedom and desertion and that I'm going to
disappear. I go in the next room and he gets it in his head I'll
never come back. Suddenly he's wailing for me, and it's just
lately I've realized that, as much as anything else, his call of
"Mama?" in the middle of the night is nothing more or less

than to make certain I'm still here, that I haven't vanished from his life. I don't know where he got this idea he would be left all alone in the world. I wrack my brain trying to figure what I might have done that made him think this, but I can't think of anything, and I wonder if it's like his premature empathy — a sense that, sooner or later, everything goes away.

After Kirk was a year old, the lake had gotten big enough there was a fog off the water in the mornings and evenings that climbed the Hollywood moors and wound through the city. A big chunk of the hills broke off and tumbled down into the lake and onto its shore, including a huge rock as big as a house that landed near where Kirk and I would blow bubbles. Of course I couldn't get it out of my head, what might have happened if we had been there when this monster rock came crashing down. I'm haunted by such possibilities hour on the hour. Kirk always likes to throw rocks in the lake so I told him to go throw this one. He looked at it with suspicion, then surmounting his doubt went over and put his hands on the towering rock and pushed with all his might while I laughed. "Too big," he finally announced solemnly, his spirit far bigger than the rest of him, far bigger than I.

I'm not a religious person but after Kirk was born I started praying. Every night, "Dear God do whatever you want to me but don't let anything bad happen to my boy." I think about all the stuff I've done, running way from "home" — such as it was, my drunken uncle who ran the town bar — the lies I told, guys I fucked in their sleep to suck out their dreams with my thighs and carry them off splashing inside me. I tally it all up and it occurs to me if God wants to punish me then my prayers have given him a pretty good hint how to go about it. And now God's just one more Predator out there I have to protect my kid from.

Around the time Kirk was eighteen months old, the city finally sent some divers down into the lake to try and figure out what was in the hole at the bottom. This got a lot of attention, half the city there watching the divers in their black wetsuits slip over the side of the boat and disappear and then come back up.

Every time they came back up there seemed to be much conferring back and forth with various officials on the boat. Everyone figured there would be some kind of press conference or announcement at the end. But there was no announcement, instead everyone on the boat immediately hurried to their cars and drove off — pretty quickly it seemed to me. Since then, no city officials come to the lake anymore, but for a week or so afterward everyone else who had been at the lake would stand staring at the water, like some answer would come floating up any minute. . . .

I don't know so much about science or higher math, but in the more complicated equations I always assume there must be a wildness factor somewhere. . . or maybe that's what math tries to avoid. I guess maybe math and science are about factoring out the chaos not factoring it in, determining a definite value for everything. Math and science don't allow for the possibility of true chaos, only for an unknown order that calls itself chaos. I mean, if that butterfly flapping his wings in South America twenty years ago really did cause the toaster to burn my English muffin this morning, that isn't randomness, that's cause-and-effect of a truly cosmic kind, the exact opposite of chaos.

My kid has his own way with numbers, his own mathematics. "How many bites of that cereal have you had?" I ask him, trying to get him to eat his breakfast, and his eyes narrow in that thoughtful calculating way they do: "Forty," he answers. He doesn't even know what forty is. You have not had forty bites, I say, and he thinks some more and says, "Seven." You've eaten seven bites? I ask, dubious, and he thinks some more very carefully before announcing, "Twenty-one." The three-year-old poet in him likes the sound of forty and seven and twenty-one, and adds and subtracts them accordingly, dividing night-robots in the hills by the size of the moon, adding the number of day-robots in the cage of the sun squared, figuring the wondrous equations of his little existence.

He's the chaos factor in the equation of my existence, the thing that makes true the math of my days. For a while it made me nuts, his havoc, and then it finally occurred to me that like chaos in science, Kirk's chaos is an unknown order, his havoc a rearrangement of the world in a way that marks his entrances into it and his exits from it. Like I've done since I was a kid myself, on the wall of our apartment I tack articles about things that fascinate me and pictures of things that inspire me, and I tacked up the little pieces of the photo that my correspondent was sending his lover, the other Kristin across the lake, trying to assemble them into the whole, not knowing how many more fragments might be to come. The morning I got what turned out to be the last letter, Kirk took all the pieces off the wall and stuck them back in different places, completely upsetting my very meticulous efforts. I screamed at him about it for ten minutes. Then, feeling shitty, I dressed him and we grabbed the bus to the San Vicente Bridge, and crossed to the other side and walked over to the lake, hand in hand, and sat on a small beach below the hills where I fell asleep in the sun, I don't know how long. . .

    I woke with a start. Woke in complete panic that I had dozed off with Kirk sitting there in the sand six fatal feet from the water. But there he was just hunkered down in the sand by the water in that way he sits sometimes, not on his butt but in a crouch, studying the view in front of him, and only when my brain assured itself he was OK did I realize he was peeling one page after another from my Proust and throwing them in the lake, and I almost started screaming at him again. Instead I walked over and just sat with him, our feet in the water, the two of us together watching the pages of the book float out, little paper boats with sails made of reverie.

    K, beautiful betrayer, *begins the last letter,* Mao of my desire, killer of my trust. Were I to have foreseen this silence from you all those years ago in that murderous moment that made me so anonymously famous, then I could have stood up to nothing, rather I would have accepted the chains of the passionless, the defeated, the tyrannized, the hopeless. . . . What do you suppose I saw in the barrel of that gun rolling toward me if not your face?

What do you suppose made me brave? What do you suppose was
the mouth of freedom I longed to kiss if not yours? Do you really
think I did it just to thrill the world? In that last moment before
I slipped into the confessional of history, forever pulling its curtain
closed behind my innocence, before I dropped through the century
so as to make my way to you over the years, I heard in my ears the
melody of your sixteen-year-old dreams — something ageless and
haunted by however many voices have hummed it — and which
on that morning drowned out every scream of danger: I peered in
the hole of the gun before me and saw your legs open to me; and
so leaned forward to taste your promise there. Stepped to the right
so there could be no eluding my fate, stepped to the left so there
could be no eluding your whisper of love, clutching in my fist your
yellow dress that the world took for a banner of freedom. Begged
for destiny to flatten me against the Square beneath my feet.
Begged for the explosion of the gun in whose smoke was written
the way you belonged to me. . . . Bitch. Whore. History's fucking
tourist. Why don't you write me? How can you not write me?
How can you not answer! With the passage of time have I become
merely *quaint,* as my photo recedes into the world's nostalgia?
Please. . . love me and I will redeem the ways I have become
passé. Love me and I will service you night and day on the
tiananmen of our appetites. Love me and in a moment I will
ruthlessly trade the word *freedom* on the tip of my tongue for the
opiate drop of your release. Love me and I will take on the lake
for you, I will take on the world for you, again. . . .

    *Enclosed with the letter were the two last pieces of the
photo, one small round orb of black, one small orb of white — the
eyes of his portrait, each a different color. But when I put all the
other pieces on the wall in some semblance of what I had before
Kirk scrambled them that morning, and then added the two eyes,
his face still didn't come together except as a crazy abstraction.
I kept rearranging the pieces, this way and that. Sometimes they
formed a cracked vase, sometimes a cloud passing before the
moon, sometimes a flower floating above the sea, each of the*

images somehow off, straining for a cohesion the pieces didn't believe, until I fell asleep again and woke to find once more that Kirk had taken all the pieces down and put them back in his own way. He was adding the two eyes just about the time I opened my own.

Except they weren't eyes. One was the hole of the barrel of a gun on a military tank, sitting on a flat paved open space. Behind it was a second tank, with a third behind that and a fourth behind that. The other was the back of the dark head of the tiny man standing ramrod straight in front of the tanks, arms at his sides, holding in one hand a pale cloth.

A pretty famous picture, I guess, from not that long ago in the last century. But I was very little at the time so it wasn't something I knew all that much about, and I couldn't help feeling disappointed that I had put so much time and energy into coming up with only a man blocking a line of tanks, in the same way that, over the years, the man himself had become bitter about having dared and risked so much, only so now love could forsake him.

L*ater that same night after*

*I went to sleep, I was
awakened by music. When I stuck my head out the window, I saw
that Zed Lake, onxy in the moonlight, was singing, all these tunes
snaking in and out of each other, a whole time of tunes, a century
of them, old ones and ones I had never heard before, songs that
had escaped from the* other side, *glowing and slithering through
the water. I knew if I had been down at the water's edge
I could have reached in and touched one, and that musical notes
would have glittered on my fingertips like tiny stars.*

*The melody-snakes were gone when Kirk woke crying an
hour later, looking for Kulk his red monkeyman. Exhausted, I went
into his room and shook out all the bedsheets, lowered myself on
my hands and knees to look for it. "Well where did you last have
it?" I said, even though I had seen him holding it like he always
did, one hand a fist as I was shoving it through the sleeve of his
pajamas. We looked all over the apartment, high and low. I say
we but it was really me looking and Kirk directing me. "There
under the couch please," he would suggest very helpfully, "maybe
behind the door." Pointing here and there, reclined on his chair*

like it was a throne, he just needed a slave to fan him and drop grapes in his mouth.

When and how did he make me so fucking tender, that's what I want to know. It wasn't when he was inside me, I remember when he was inside me. He just took me over at some point. And don't tell me all moms are like this, because that couldn't be further from the point. It couldn't be further. I mean certainly I always figured I would be an OK mom, taking care of him and so on. . . but when did he get to me? Tenderness. That's a new one. I don't think I like it, no not much. I don't think so. I want to be a tough chick again.

A few nights ago the lake reached the Hamblin, and we woke the next morning to find the water up the steps of the eastern entrance. Surveying the lake from our window, Kirk quietly announced, "The water-robots are here." Then the next morning the wolf that's been living in the building paddled through the door into the flooded first floor from somewhere outside and then paddled back out, frantically looking for a place to beach himself. Bobbing in the lake outside the hotel was a silver gondola that shone in the sunlight like a bullet. . . it belongs to the hotel manager, he's prepared I guess. Yesterday morning water filled the first-floor corridor and the gondola drifted up and down the hall. Down the hall in Jainlight's apartment, the TV reception flickers in and out. . . later in the day when Kirk and I knocked, he wasn't there. Inside, the TV was on, piles of pages by the computer, stacks of videos on the floor, tequila bottles, everything in its usual dishevelment. But he was nowhere to be seen.

Lately, the last week or so Kirk's cries of "Mama" in the night have turned into wails of "Mama where are you?" desperate, wracked, forlorn. His insecurity has found a wider vocabulary. . . does he really not know where I am? Does he really suppose I'm not right beyond his door? "Mama, come back," as if he's already learned how a little boy's cries can go unanswered forever, as if he's known it from the beginning, from before the beginning, insisting like his still unborn twin sister

I'm not going anywhere, *as the sac of the womb around him
burst. In the mornings he'll be calling from his room, and I get
up from bed and go to his door and knock playfully: "It's me,"
he answers. In case I'm not certain. In case I might think it's
some other kid who's taken his place, who I might mistake for
my own.
     I've been having this dream. In the dream I look out the
window and the lake approaches like a swarm, and I close all the
windows, pull the shades, lock the door, and there's the rumble
of music, the loudest watersong ever, it grows and soon invades
us, seeps into the apartment, comes in under the door and through
the cracks in the window. . . and then everything explodes.
Everything explodes with water and I would expect to be swept
under myself; but I'm not, it's taunting me. Roars in on a black
wave, the lake, and roars right past me, dismissive of me, wanting
me to watch, wanting me to see it take him. And I watch. And
it takes him.
     I notice now that when Kirk talks, he uses his hands,
like the night Parker "talked" in his sleep. Did he immediately
grasp within the strange patterns of Parker's hands their secret
language, and become fluent? He sleeps in my lap and his hair
smells like tall dry grass, I put my face in it and breathe it and
listen to the coyotes in the distant dark hills. Stubborn stoic
Kirk, won't be shamed or cajoled into emotion. I see him
self-consciously suppress his small smile that gets more and
more rare, as if having already learned to find his joy suspect.
With every passing day I worry he retreats farther into his
three-year-old heart even as he talks more and more with his
hands. . . but then in the dark, just as I think he's about to fall
asleep, suddenly he clutches my arm and won't let go, both of
his arms around mine, an outburst of need under the cover of
darkness. After a while there's that body-shudder of him tumbling
into sleep, and then I whisper in his ear*

your mama loves you

even if he's asleep and doesn't hear, because even if he doesn't hear, I figure he hears. *I whisper it in his ear and figure it makes its way to his brain, and some day years from now when he needs it, it will float up to the surface of his memory and open itself like a time capsule, with the message he especially needs most at that moment. And he'll find, to his surprise, he heard it after all.*

Now that the lake has reached the hotel, some things seem urgent in a way I don't really understand. There have been no more letters from my correspondent. Once Kirk put the pieces of the photo together, he didn't mix them up anymore but now sits on the floor silently looking at the tiny figure of the man in the Square. If just once more I had seen the other Kristin's light in her window, I wouldn't have involved Doc at all, and I don't know whether it's that Doc is so wise that nothing surprises her or that incredulity just isn't in her repertoire of responses. . . but when I showed her the photo, she didn't say anything. She just looked at it a long time, at one point lifting a finger like she might touch it and glean something, before pulling back her hand like it was too sacred. When she finally spoke, it wasn't until we were out on the lake, halfway to the deserted building, after I begged her to sail out there with me. "Are you certain which window is hers?" was all she said, and of course I wasn't certain at all, I just thought we would figure it out when we got there.

I had talked her into going out there with me, and the whole way I kept watching the lake to see if maybe the Hamblin manager had sent the zedcops after us to retrieve his gondola, or if Kirk was still watching our journey across the Big Agua from the Hamblin roof with Valerie and Parker. I hoped he had stopped crying. There aren't many people out on the lake anymore. . . . As it's gotten bigger, it seems to have lost its charm. There have been accidents, people who sailed out and haven't been seen again. Soon I had to take over at the oars when the lake was too deep for the pole. It took us a little more than half an hour to get to the abandoned apartment building that was once just a

ten-minute walk away, and then we had to sail around it to dock
the gondola somewhere it wouldn't drift off. Finally we sailed in
through the building's garage, now flooded with only a few feet
between the water and the ceiling. There were stairs where once
had been a furnace room. We were able to get out where the water
met the stairs and drag the gondola up the steps.

Out on the water I had started to tell Doc everything about
the letters I had been getting, but she raised her hand to stop me,
like too much information would only prejudice a diagnosis.
Truthfully I'm not certain we ever would have known which was
K's room if not for. . . well, if it hadn't been obvious. I had only
seen the light in her window in the dark from a distance, when it
isn't that easy to count windows or floors, and from far away
outside a building you think that you can kind of guess where
something is, and then you get inside and it isn't so clear. We kept
going through one deserted room after another trying to find it
before late afternoon turned to twilight, and then we found it and
even Doc was impressed for once.

It was my room, or a version of it. Articles tacked to the
walls if not the same articles, books on the shelves with a lot of the
same titles as mine, same Proust and Kierkegaard and Dickinson
and the Brontës except now mildewed, mixed in with a lot of books
in what I guess was Chinese, there was the same photo — except
not in pieces — of her lover as a young student standing before the
tanks. There was a child's bedroom except it was that of an older
child, about ten with a small bed instead of a crib, animé posters
instead of small plastic monkeys. . . and no sooner do we step into
the room than Doc staggers a little from the dirge in her ears,
catching herself against the door with one hand and holding her
forehead with the other.

From up over the hills in the far west come the first wave
of owls, still far away enough that their shadows on my back
skitter up my spine like small black spiders. Reflexively I turn to
face the sun through the window, squinting for sight of them and
looking to my own building on the other side of the lake, hoping

Valerie has scurried Kirk to safety. For a while Doc seems frozen where she stands. With a kind of hesitation I've never seen in her, she lays her hands on the walls and moves through the apartment slowly, from the far doorway that already darkens with night into the part of it blood-red with sunset, like she's melting into the decomposed smear of the dead day, hands spreading out away from her until it's like she's scorched to the wall, face burned in the plaster.

She doesn't make any sound at all for a minute. Then I hear this cry — at first I think it's coming from the room itself — and she drops to the floor. The grief on her face is. . . it's like her face is trying to catch up to it, eyes and mouth so stricken they're incapable of tears or sound, and, well, I just wish I didn't see it. God only knows what terrible song she heard coming out of that room, and I just wish I hadn't seen it, because some last shred of trust in me shatters when I see her fall apart like this, some small capacity for faith I didn't even know I still had, until this moment when I know I don't have it anymore. Doc the quietly indomitable, who tends to sick and dying houses with the kind of resolve where strength trumps sympathy every time, lies at my feet waiting for whatever she's sensed in this room to recede just far enough away that she can finally lower all her defenses against it and break down.

Just standing there I don't know whether I feel more terrified or betrayed, because this isn't my role with Doc, to comfort her. It's her role to comfort me, and I can't even bring myself to go near her. All I can do is crouch on the floor studying her from somewhere near the new sea level, the best I can offer is eye contact, if she wants it. She never tells me what the walls sing. She never tells me what she heard in the yawn of the floor beneath her. What's the matter with you! is all I can finally scream at her out on the lake, after waiting almost an hour in that room for Doc to get herself together or for the other Kristin to show, which we both know isn't going to happen, until finally it starts to get dark enough that I know we have to get back to the gondola if we're

*going to find our way back through the garage and across the
water. "Why are you acting like this? it's just another dead
building. . . !" I'm hysterical with disillusion. The whole trip back
across the water she doesn't look at me at all, sitting in the
gondola staring straight ahead in this blank way until all I can say
is, I depended on you, to be better and stronger and braver and
wiser than I can ever be. . . and then before the final fall of dark
she looks straight at me, the mouth once younger than the rest of
her now old, the eyes once older now ancient.*

Are you a monkey?

No!
Are you a boy?
No!
Are you a Bright Light!
No!
No? and my heart sinks. Then what are you?
. . . and with great glee. . . .
I'm Nothing!
he cries, clapping his hands together.

I'm lying naked on the

                           Laurel banks. In reality
there are no such banks anymore, they're long since underwater
but in my dream there's no lake just the banks where I lie at war
with my womb. . . .

         . . . it grows dark. We're well into the hour of the owls.
From out of the trees behind me I hear him come, I close my eyes
and wait, feel his hands on my feet and feel him lower himself to
my thighs. He puts his tongue inside me. Mao of my desire, killer
of my trust: *I feel his words make their way up inside me. At the*
moment of the most unwilling orgasm I've ever had, I grab him
by his black Chinese hair and my water breaks — am I pregnant?
— and the torrent that pours from me sweeps in its path the
Chevron at the corner of Sunset and Crescent Heights (in reality
now long gone), rushes down the street and ebbs for a minute
before streaming down the Strip. The force of it tears him from
me. Last I see him he's caught in the racing flood somewhere
down the boulevard, trying to keep his head above the water as
his arms flail frantically to grab on to something. I laugh out loud
at the sight of it. Then in the last gush here comes Brontë, finally

*ready to emerge, and I reach to catch her as she leaves me but,
slick with afterbirth, she slips from my hands, caught in an
undertow that burps her up once at Zed's center before pulling
her back down. . . .*

*I wake. I bolt upright. Because my thighs are soaked, for
a minute I'm confused, certain I've given birth to the lake. I can
still smell the dream. My heart pounds with fear. I lunge at the
white waves of the bed before me to catch my daughter I've ejected
so cruelly, all before my consciousness understands it was a dream
— but I can still smell the dream. I catch my breath in the dark to
wonder what's wrong, and look out the window by my bed and,
in the light of the moon, see the ripples of the lake below me. Then
I realize I haven't heard Kierkegaard's* Mama where are you, *his*
Mama come back, *and I stumble through the apartment from my
bed to his.*

*An amniotic fog fills the room. I can barely see him
through it. The smell of birth and the lake is overpowering. I
move through the vapor to his crib where he sleeps too soundly,
and pick him up. . . he barely stirs. In his sleep his hand grasps
for Kulk his missing spacemonkey, and his face glistens from
the fog off the lake. I take him from his room and close his door
behind me. I take him to my bed and put him on the pillow next
to mine where he goes on sleeping. I place my body like a barrier
between him and the window with the lake beyond it. I watch the
center of the lake waiting, my heart still pounds from my dream —
but now it isn't a dream:*

the lake is coming for him.

When I wake this morning,
                         the hotel is quiet. There are
no sounds in the hall, or in the rooms above or below me. Kirk
still sleeps on the pillow. . . almost always he wakes before I do.
I lean over him, inches from his face, and listen to his breathing,
watch his chest rise and fall. I get up from the bed only kind of
remembering at the last second to pull on a robe. . . the world's
never been as casual about my nakedness as I am. I walk out
in the hall and down to the writer's room, my ear at the door
listening for the sound of old movies or even the tapping on the
computer of him working. But I don't hear anything.

It's still early enough that the hall lights are on except,
I notice, in the east end of the hotel, and I realize this part of the
building has finally lost power. I go back to my room and Kirk
still sleeps on the pillow, and leaning back out the window I see
the black waters of the lake have already pushed past our hotel.
The lake extends north to the hills, just a sliver of the top of the
peninsula still dry land.

The lake is coming for my kid. In my heart, *I once wrote,*
he opens the door to this vast terrain of fear. *But now I know it's
a lake not a terrain, and that it's my fear made manifest that's
coming for him.* Sometimes I'm paralyzed by my love for him. . . .
*In the last few hours, between dream and dawn, like a thought
cast adrift waiting for me to rescue it, I've come to know in no way
I can explain that it doesn't matter where we go, it doesn't matter
how far we try to get away, the lake will keep coming for him and
that I can't be paralyzed anymore. Down in the hole of the lake,
down in the opening of the birth canal where the world broke its
water, lurks my son's doom and I must stop it. I have to shake
myself loose of the love that holds me down, and find inside me
the love that will save him. I have to go to war with the womb
of the century that would reclaim him. Hand in hand, Kirk and
I make our way downstairs to Valerie and Parker's room and
they're gone, door standing open and crib hastily ransacked, the
water only a few feet below their window.*
    *Around noon the power goes out in the rest of the hotel.
I know now that Kirk and I are the last light burning in the window
for some other mom to see from some other window in the future.
When the hotel manager's deserted silver gondola washes up on
the stairs just below our floor, I know it's a sign.*
    *In my heart my boy opens the floodgate to a vast sea of
fear; but I must close that gate. I despise myself when I look at
him at the other end of the gondola, without even a life jacket,
precarious on the lake beneath us. . . I despise the danger I subject
him to now, the danger I've given birth to that laps at our boat.
His hair shines in the sun above, and I'm amazed to see him hold
his toy monkey Kulk in its red spacesuit and space helmet. You
found it, I say, and he just nods. Looking east I'm not certain
anymore how far the lake goes, although in the distance I still see
Wilshire office complexes. Nobody else is on the lake. But where
did you find it? I say and Kirk says, Under my pillow. But I looked
there, I say, I looked there a hundred times. The afternoon passes,
we sail through the labyrinth of old Hollywood buildings that*

rise from the black water like the heads of granite fetuses the world has miscarried. Out in deeper water the black of the lake frames Kirk's head, his bright light. Scraps of wood from the disintegrating Chateau X harbor drift by. Of course it seems my wildman has no fear at all. For a minute I reassure myself that from his three-year-old perspective this all seems impossibly cool. As we follow the hills around to the northeast, the lake is still shallow enough I can push us most of the way with the pole. . . I want to push the pole please, Kirk says. He starts to stand in the gondola to take the pole and I explode with terror: Sit down! I scream at him, and he starts to cry.

He cries, and as he cries his hands start to move, start to talk the language of hands he learned from Parker. For a while I just sit there at my end of the boat, then gingerly move to him, to pull him to me for a minute and hold him. The way his fingers keep talking in the air, the way he clutches me, I know he's more afraid than I thought. Sorry wildman, I whisper in his ear over and over sorry *and I almost turn the boat back to the peninsula. . . but I know what I know, and I must do what I must do.*

La-la please, Mama
his frightened whisper matching mine, conspiratorial in our fear.
If there's a higher light
let it shine on me
and by four-thirty we circle around the bend at Laurel Canyon and push our way up the watery ravine where we once watched city divers swim to the bottom of the lake
'cause I know this sea
wants to carry me
and the sound of loons echoes around us in the growing fog even as the lake's songs have gone silent. On the banks of the lake in the wind we can see flapping the tents from the abandoned fair where one afternoon we saw up close the owl that hears human heartbeats, and where another afternoon we saw and heard the melody-snakes from the lake's source. By now the lake has taken

*most of the fairgrounds. In a long dark row the empty tents billow
and collapse, black mouths blowing out over the water.*

*We reach the lake's center. The hole at the bottom is
somewhere right below us.*

Listen to me wildman
*I say as calmly as possible, lowering myself over the side of the
gondola into the water. He's puzzled.*

Mama in Big Agua?

*Yes, Mama's going in the Big
Agua for a minute. Just for a minute,
do you understand?*

*He blinks at me in the twilight. Please don't cry, it will break my
heart. I'm already starting to shiver, and I don't want him to see
that. My teeth chatter, and I don't want him to hear that. . . .*

Why?

So it can't hurt you anymore
. . . don't ask why. . .

do you understand?
*. . . there isn't time for your whys. He nods, like he's actually
figured it out.*

Who's the boss here, wildman.
It's a minute before he answers quietly

You are.

*You have to sit here in the boat
very still. Very, very still. You have to sit
here and wait for me to come back, you
can't move at all or else you could fall in —*

No Big Agua for me.

*No, no Big Agua for you. So you sit
very still, OK?*

Yes.

And I'll be right back for you. OK?

Yes please.

I'll be gone just a minute.

Silently he watches me. He doesn't cry. He looks around us at the lake and at the sky above him in that preternatural way of his.

Night-time

he says.

I love you, Kirk.
Mama come back?
Right back.

He blinks.

Yes, please.

I look around me, and for a minute the chill of the water passes. My eyes drink in everything, they're thirsty like they know something I don't. . . the twilight is the kind of blue you see maybe once in a lifetime, maybe once. In the wind I hear the murmur of the fluttering tents on the lakeshore, and I know I have only minutes before the sky fills with owls that can hear his heart and suddenly she can hear his heart herself, its steady thump in the murmur of the tents near the water. She reaches over and takes Kirk's hand in her own and presses it, and before he can cry or try and grab her, she takes as deep a breath as she can, and down into the lake she slips.

He watches his mother disappear. Another presence whispers in his ear and instinctively his head turns, like an owl, to gaze at the shore, where he sees another young woman, not more than eighteen or nineteen years old, watching him. Kneeling at the lake's edge, she's like a sprite with long straight gold hair almost to her waist, and when she sees that he notices her, she raises her hand to wave. The little boy waves back.

Sinking, Kristin can still hear his heart. Looking up through the water one last time, she can see him leaning over the edge of the silver gondola peering down at her with his red monkey in hand, his head a shimmery sphere floating above the lake, like the parasols of autumn.

2009

Every passing day, the edge of the water rots a little more the front porch of her little house, until one morning she expects to find she's finally been swept away. Every honeymoon twilight, across the house's threshold the lake is carried by its lesbian groom the moon, with a bridal train of small dead animals, palm fronds ripped from their trees, the trash of the recently submerged: pages of paperbacks, gin bottles, old tickets from the drowned Cathode Flower nightclub that used to be right below her on the Sunset Strip, at the foot of a hillside now under water. Step out her front door at dawn into the puddles that seep up through the decking, sunlight from the lake's surface cutting a gash across her eyes, and she sees the glub glub glub of rising bubbles, and wonders from what sinking building or body.

Six months ago the lake finally stopped rising. This was what everyone had been waiting for, once it became clear the lake wasn't going to stop until it reached the ocean. Once that became clear, there was no reason not to wish the lake would just get it over with, so everyone could stop moving to higher ground. It feels to her like the foundation of the house gives way a little more every night, and it wakes her in the dark, when the dream doesn't.

Then in the days between nights' dreams, the visions come, often just after the sun sets. Through the hinge where day hangs on to night, the visions come up with the bubbles from the lake's bottom. She sits on the porch of her little house and stares at the top of the Hotel Hamblin to the southeast, that roof where sometimes at fall of dark she took him in her arms to look at the lights of faraway windows, when clouds were flying igloos and the night-robots reigned. She's vaguely aware of the boats that drift by, the way the people in them look at her and mutter to each other.

About half the top floor of the Hamblin is still above water. Once she thought about taking the silver gondola out there but couldn't really see the point, unless it was one of the two or three hundred occasions she considered slipping into the water for good, the way she should have that evening five years ago when, out on the center of the lake, she lowered herself from the gondola. So then why keep moving to higher land at all? Let some watery night take her. Night after night, hour after hour, moment after moment she sees his smile, hears his voice from the other bedroom that used to call *Mama where are you?* Five years, two months, sixteen days since she heard him say the last words she heard him say: and when she came up for air, swimming desperately up up up until she finally broke the surface of the water to gasp back her life at the very last possible second, the devastating emptiness of the gondola left her to curse for the rest of her life that last second God gave her just so that she might hear those words over and over

yes please

You Sick Fuck. Having had Your little joke with Abraham, hissing Your little amusement in his ear and finding what cowards fathers are when he didn't spit in Your face, when he didn't clutch his son close to him and say I'll go to hell first. . . when for all his supposed righteousness he couldn't even be a man when it came to protecting his child, then You moved onto mothers didn't You, because mothers were more your match, beginning with Mary. Now that was fun. Tortured her boy in the grisliest most twisted way possible before her very eyes and then had the sadistic wit to call it The Salvation of the World: so what I want to know is, was that the forbidden iconography of the divine psyche, or just the Male Wangie of all male wangies? God tries to hurt my kid, He has to go through me first. God tells me what He told Abraham, then He isn't any god that means anything to me, He isn't any god I owe anything. I kill anyone who tries to hurt my kid, any man, any woman, any god, any lake.

She's dreamed it so often, sometimes she's almost not certain it really happened. She breaks the lake's surface gasping, grabs the side of the gondola, and her soul implodes at the horror of its emptiness; for a minute she stares into the bottom of the gondola like he must be there and she just isn't seeing him. Like there's some place he could be hiding. But it's as if he was never there at all. She dives beneath the water again, thrashing around as if to catch him on his way to the bottom — but there's no one to catch, and she rises to grab the gondola once more and look frantically around her. It's only then she hears something, and looks up.

Looks up and sees him in the distance, high in the sky. Hears his voice as it gets farther away

Mama where are you?

like he would call from his crib

Mama come back

and the owl that has him in its clutches actually seems to falter a bit, confused by the burden and sound, finding Kirk bigger and noisier than the usual prey. Sometimes in her dream Kirk plummets to earth, and she wakes to a black room with the taste of *no please* on her lips.

One morning about six months ago she got up from the toilet to stare down at the blood in the bowl. She was so fascinated by the pattern that she sat on the bathroom floor studying it, circling to see it from every angle. Next month the same pattern and the month after that, and it's been the same every month since. She keeps trying to decipher this menstrual rorschach; slit between her legs is the stigmata of the full moon from which her womb telegraphs a message. A month or so back she even tried copying it down on paper before it dissolved into streaks down the white porcelain. Sometimes she lies in bed at night and sees the pattern in the dark above her, and watches baffled for hours until its mystery lulls her back to sleep.

Lately, in a city where sooner or later any kind of cult behavior becomes a fashion statement, everyone wears the blue of the lake, all the colored parasols of five years ago having given way to blue from the neck down. Everyone camouflages herself and slips alongside the water like a spy of the shoreline, disguised as a splash. Blue hat, blue shirt, coat blue except for dark shadows rippling across the buttons like riptides, or flashes of white on the thigh of the pants like the glare of the sun on the water's surface. When she rows her silver gondola on the lake wearing a brilliant red dress, the lake around her suddenly clears of all other boats, taking cover, as if she's an incoming fireball from space. As if she's a drop of blood — but is she the lake bleeding, or blood rained from the sky? She can see it in everyone's eyes, the red provocation of her, the defiant affront of her red to the blue of the lake, daring it to rise higher and seep deeper into the land.

If the lake sends back my boy, I'll wear whatever it wants, the blue garb of its Order, I'll wear blue until the day I die. If it wants I'll wear nothing and dip my naked body into its blue embrace whenever it wants me, lie nude in my silver gondola and drift wherever it drifts me. If the lake will just send me back my boy.

Until then, the only thing blue about her is her name. . . .

    . . . the writer who lived down the hall of the Hamblin having left her with Lulu Blu. . . .

    . . . and afterward she couldn't tell for certain when she stopped being Kristin; maybe it was that very moment she came up for air and saw the empty gondola. But now she's taken refuge in Lulu. She's fled from any Kristin who would leave her three-year-old son out in the middle of a lake because she had this insane idea she had to stop the lake from taking him. She fled to Lulu because she believed Kristin should have sunk back down to the bottom where she belonged, and left to someone with better wings the task of flying after that owl. So it was a kind of debased suicide, abandoning Kristin for Lulu, and now she sits on her porch at the water's edge in her red dress staring out over the lake while blue citizens drift by in their blue boats and whisper among themselves *The Madwoman in Red, whose son was abducted by owls.*

    When a woman becomes a mother, she develops this new instinct for danger. She develops this instinct for every possible disaster that awaits her child around every corner. Lulu, once called Kristin, doesn't know if five years ago her danger-instinct failed or overwhelmed all reason so that she led her son *to* danger instead of from it, so that everything she did to protect him only endangered him. Little amorphous lumps of human clay, that's what she once thought babies were; but then she found there were things about her child that had nothing to do with her, things that were his own from the beginning, from the minute he was born, perhaps from before he was born, perhaps from before he was conceived, although there was no point getting into that since no one knows anyway. Anyway, she realized, that's when you're stuck with the Soul. That's when your child becomes inescapable evidence of the cosmos, a membrane-map of the spirit, that's when God becomes a Piercing Hope or Dark Suspicion or both. Because there's nothing a mother fears more than the chaos of the world.

And then danger has won.

Then danger has won. Then fear takes a form. Detaches itself from all the things she was afraid of, the reasonable things and the stupid, and becomes its own thing, bigger than either the reasonable things or the stupid things. Grows in the pregnant heart until it's born; and then she stops being a person, then she becomes fear's walking womb.

Then her fear is bigger than her motherhood. Fear has metamorphosed into the danger it feared

and it's called a lake.

Absently she listens to the radio all the time now, the radio she listened to all the time with her son when the lake came because the music was the one thing the lake, alive with its own music, couldn't or wouldn't drown. She sits on the porch of her house while the people sail by looking at her, and she listens for a song she and Kirk sang together

all the little babies go, Oh! oh! I want to!

while sometimes the snakes of music swarming the lake coil through her house. They wind along wooden beams, pythons of melancholy English verse from before she was born, and Debussy melodies but only if Debussy had been a bossa nova guitarist in a heroin haze, brooding aquatic chamber quartets rising in the background like autumn glimpsed for the first time on the horizon of midsummer. Boas — gorgeous and dangerous — of static bursts and swoons of strings drape themselves along her window sill and slither through her house like women's voices, dusky, jazz-depraved, desperate.

The first time the lake sends her a vision, Lulu is sitting on her porch at dusk and feels a swell in the lake beneath her. It slowly rises from the water before her, a huge bubble. She gets up from the chair and walks to the edge of the porch and, as she watches, the bubble bursts to reveal a man in his forties with black hair and black beard and startling electric blue eyes, a man whose name she never knew. She lived with him when she first came to L.A. as a teenager nine years before, a kind of sexual serf servicing him when, after being abandoned by his pregnant Asian-American wife, he wasn't crashing around in a secret room at the bottom of his house where he worked day and drunken night on a huge blue calendar that completely reordered history according to the chronology and logic of apocalypse. Even now she looks back on that time dispassionately, having grown up with a practical view of her own sensuality and surviving then by whatever means she could — until one night he disappeared. She wasn't altogether certain he was even the father until Kirk was born, another candidate having been a doltish Japanese boy who jumped her one afternoon in the rain out in the Black Clock time-capsule cemetery on the west side of town, now under water, before out of the blue a lightning bolt literally left him lying next to her on the grass, life only in his erection. In the early months of her pregnancy, and particularly on the night she believed she miscarried her twins only for them to somehow become manifest again in an inexplicable resurrection, she felt Kirk and Brontë glow inside her as if with electricity — so when Kirk was born, she wouldn't have been shocked if he had been half Asian. Now as Kirk's father rises from the lake in Lulu's vision, it's only long enough for him to reach out to her, not as if asking her to save him but as if beseeching her to understand or even forgive him; and at that moment, for the first time in the eight years since she last saw him, although she's often suspected it, she knows he's dead.

Her house is drenched with the evidence of visions. She wakes in the morning to puddles by the bed, in the hallway, just inside the front door, and knows other visions came to her in the night when she was asleep. Her next vision is of her other self. Another twilight and again the lake bubbles, and again Lulu rises from her chair but not going so near the water, and from out of the lake's fountain emerges Kristin. This other self swims to the edge of the porch and, reaching up and grabbing hold of the post, looks at Lulu for a full minute with the lake glistening on her skin and her hair hanging in her face, before she sinks back into the water without a breath. She comes again three nights later. This woman Kristin who looks just like Lulu, who *is* just like Lulu, who is the woman Lulu was before she became Lulu, swims up from the bottom of the lake and breaks the surface of Lulu's nights. Lulu wakes from her bed just long enough to sit up and catch sight of

Kristin flitting around the corner of the bedroom door, before Lulu falls back to sleep; but then the next night Lulu wakes right before dawn and Kristin is sitting in the corner of the dark bedroom, naked and wet, and she says, Why did you leave me?

"I couldn't stand to be you anymore," Lulu answers, "couldn't stand to be Kristin. . . *you left him in the fucking boat in the middle of the lake.* Why did you do that, or. . . why did *we* do that. . . leave him there like that?"

Doesn't matter anymore why, Kristin answers in the corner. There's some serious point-missing going on here if you don't know that by now.

"I don't care about you or me anymore," Lulu says.

Me neither.

"All I care about is him." In the dark, she starts to cry.

Then go find him, Kristin says.

"I don't know," really crying.

Look, Kristin says, pointing to the front door that Lulu can see from the bedroom, and Lulu gets up and goes out onto the porch, and the lake is black and still and the light of the sun is just starting to pale the sky a dark dawn-blue over the east hills, and Lulu turns to stare back into the house where Kristin was a minute ago, but then she hears the lake bubbling again, although she's never had a vision at dawn, and Lulu stares into the water black with sunrise and hears from its bubble a small faraway sound and takes the telescope that hangs from the beam of the porch and looks through it down into the bubble into the funnel of the lake and what she sees in the reflection of the barely paling sky makes her pull away as if the telescope is enchanted and she doesn't trust what it shows her.

At first she thinks it's an airplane, which in itself is startling because there haven't been any airplanes in the skies of L.A. for a long time. But when she squints she sees it's not an airplane rather it's something very little, flying deep down in the sky of the bubble. She looks back into the telescope.

Il Duce, bigger now of course than when she last saw him five years ago, pointing this way and that, talking with his arms and hands, conducting his higher mathematics and dividing night-robots by day-robots, directing the aging owl that still holds him in its talons. A battalion of owls wearily follows. Go this way, go that way! happily snapping orders at them, go up, go down! with great delight while the owls appear to be, oh, a little beleaguered maybe? to her untrained eye, of course. . . what does she know from beleaguered owls? But as if they're thinking maybe this is a classic case of having bitten off more than they can chew, although she supposes just letting go of him is out of the question, against an owl's owlish nature.

She doesn't hear her Kierkegaard saying "please" either, she notices that right off. What happened to his manners I taught him, is all she can think.

Eight days she waits. Eight days she waits for another vision. Eight days she sits by the lake hour after hour, more passing boats muttering at the spectacle of her. Eight days she waits, heart slowly sinking at the idea that it was only a new dream, worse than the old. Eight days she barely moves from the porch, staring at the lake when she's not searching the skies with her telescope.

On the sixth day, as she waits she hears it, for the first and only time since she first heard it riding the bus on a stretch of Pacific Coast Highway that doesn't exist anymore. A DJ from one of the pirate radio ships broadcasting out on the lake plays it, and Lulu is a little surprised at how exactly she's remembered it, when she might have done almost anything to forget it: a snake of subtle spanish horns playing a vaguely Middle Eastern melody

>*if there's a higher light,*
>>*let it shine on me*
>>*through the trees*

and she pulls up her dress

>>*'cause I know this sea*
>>*wants to carry me*
>*it's a sweet, sweet sound she sings*
>>*for my release. . .*

and bares her thigh to it, inviting its lunge.

One night at dusk before the sun falls, the final vision comes. A black globe of water rises from the lake's surface just as the moon chases the sun into the west. "Kirk!" she calls to the bubble and in its wet wound there he is again far away, same black dot as he was the night five years ago when she saw him carried off, but distinct, unmistakable, calmly issuing directives to his chagrinned feathered squadron. Somewhere inside the periscope of the lake, for one fleeting moment she watches him fly away once more, and can almost see him waving back to her or maybe calling to her in the language of hands

>>*catch you next time Mama, but now*
>*I've got places to go, things to do. . . .*

Even when she lived in Tokyo, when the signs were everywhere, she never understood how she was the agent of chaos. Later she would tell herself Kirk was the chaos factor in her life because, pregnant with him, she would walk the streets of Tokyo and around her everything went berserk: radios went haywire, subways broke down, glass buildings shattered. Had she been as self-aware as she thought she was, she might have noted how it was that on her return to Los Angeles a lake appeared. In the early months of the new century, it was she who embodied the chaos of the coming age. Her child would only be chaos' son.

And now she sits by the lake in a state of truce. She's not certain she can actually say the lake delivered him back to her, but a deal is a deal, so she takes off her clothes and gives herself to the lake, lowers herself in the lake's waters for a while and gives the lake a chance to have her way with Lulu in the moonlight.

But Zed is too weary of all her brides, and soon Lulu climbs back up on the porch, goes inside the house and gets under the covers of her bed and in the dark tells her boy a story, the first in five years; she makes it up as she goes along, as she used to. There was a little train named Tyrone that rode through hills and across deserts and past houses and towns and over bridges until it reached the end of its track where there was a cloud raining, and just beyond the raining cloud was a rainbow. And for a long time

Tyrone was afraid to go through the rainbow to the other side where there was no track he could see, and every day he would try to work up the courage until one day he finally did. He went through the rainbow and on the other side was a tunnel, and the rainbow became a train track, with rails of green and yellow, and tracks of orange and purple. And in the meantime there was a little tugboat named Tyrone, sailing along the shore of a huge lake. . . .

But

Kirk interrupts in the dark, finger poised in correction

you said Tyrone is a train —

Yes Tyrone is a train, she answers, *but the tugboat is named Tyrone too, and he's sailing along the shore of the lake, and on the beach is a little boy named Kirk*

and she expects him to say, That's *my* name, but he doesn't, accepting this as if it makes complete sense, eyes blinking in the light of the moon off the lake beyond the bedroom window.

The boy named Kirk waves to Tyrone the Tugboat. *Tyrone the Tugboat!* he calls, *I want to sail away with you,* so Tyrone the Tugboat sails over to the beach and the boy named Kirk climbs in, and they sail out onto the lake and down the Venice Channel where the canals used to be, down to the marina where the harbor used to be, out to sea. They sail past other boats, past tropical islands, with fish and dolphins and squid swimming alongside, following a faraway cloud in the sky, and just when they reach the cloud it bursts into rain, and just beyond the rain is a rainbow, and Tyrone the Tugboat is afraid to sail into the rainbow because he doesn't know what's on the other side. But Kirk the boy gives Tyrone the courage to go on, and they sail into the rainbow and on the other side is a cave in the ocean, and inside the ocean-cave the rainbow turns into a river, with currents of green and yellow, and tides of orange and purple. They follow the rainbow river until it becomes a rainbow track, where Tyrone the Tugboat becomes Tyrone the Train, and Tyrone the Train carries the boy named Kirk deeper into the cave until finally they come out the other side of a tunnel, and together they travel over bridges and past towns and houses and across the desert and through the hills until they reach the end of the track at the shore of a huge lake, where the little boy named Kirk gets out of Tyrone the Train and runs down onto the beach just in time to see Tyrone the Tugboat sailing by; and the boy waves to Tyrone the Tugboat and calls. . . .

> *Tyrone the Tugboat! I want to sail*
> *away with you!*

Sometimes, when Lulu had almost forgotten Brontë was still there, her long unborn daughter would wake her: I'm still here. Lulu believes Brontë has come to sense that her twin brother has been gone awhile. She hopes that Brontë doesn't hate her as Lulu has come to hate herself. But after Lulu separated herself from Kristin, she was stricken by the idea that she had cast her daughter into exile as well. Now Lulu lies in the dark and howls softly to her belly, waiting for an answer.

A week after having the vision of Kierkegaard flying with the owls, Lulu sails out to Port Justine. From time to time she puts down the oars and unwraps the telescope, searching the sky for him. A western fog comes in from the sea through the Wilshire

Straits to the west. Once Justine was a billboard on La Cienega Boulevard, advertising Justine herself, a big inflatable doll of a blonde who wasn't famous for anything except being blonde and famous and bigger than anything in L.A. except her breasts, which were bigger than she was. There isn't much of Justine left anymore, most of the billboard having floated away long ago. From one upper corner of the billboard, the top of her blonde hair still blows in the wind off the water.

When Lulu casts her line at Port Justine and the Chinese dockhand pulls in her gondola, he takes her hand and she looks into his eyes and the first thing she thinks of aren't the letters she got five years ago but her hometown where she grew up, where she was still Kristin. . . tiny chinatown up in the Sacramento delta on the tiny island called Davenhall, where she was raised by her uncle in the town tavern and it was full of Chinese ghosts that the old Chinese women claimed they could see caught in the high branches of the island trees lining mainstreet. . . so Lulu has never seen a beautiful Chinese man before this moment, she didn't know there were any. . . .

. . . so beautiful that for a minute it distracts her from why she's come, which is to take her telescope and climb the rungs up alongside the billboard to the top, in order to get a better view of the distant horizon. . . it *distracts* her, the beauty of him. For a moment she betrays her quest to find her son for the distraction of the dockhand's beauty and the flash of confusion across his eyes; and then she knows it's *him*. That confusion gives him away and, who knows, maybe in turn something about her reminds him of his own Kristin — *beautiful K* — after all, even with all that labial-jewel stuff, maybe something about Lulu is just enough like his own Kristin for them to have shared a name once, for their addresses to have been crossed once, for Lulu-when-she-was-Kristin to have moved through the other's apartment once and seen all the walls that were a little like her own, for her to have felt the presence of a lost child, like hers.

Taking her hand as she steps onto the dock, he barely holds it. Rather her hand just rests in his; that's when she notices it.

She can't help looking, because she thinks at first her eyes are playing a trick on her. Lodged in the middle of his hand is a piece of rounded glass, like a monocle, or the lens of the telescope she carries. As if she could lift his hand to the sky above her and look through it for her son. With the tips of his fingers holding hers, to her astonishment she can see right through the hand's small window the dock at their feet, interrupted only by blood vessels woven through the glass like red strands. The hand is virtually useless, she realizes now; he does all the work of pulling in boats with the other one.

He sees her looking at the glass hole in his hand and lets go of her. With his good hand he ties the silver gondola to the dock.

Since the lake came, rising to the bottom of the billboard, Justine has spread out into a flotilla, a lily pad of small shops and food stands and a pay phone. A couple of petrol pumps offer the last chance for gas between the Hollywood Hills and the ghetto that's taken over the top floors of the shopping center rising from the water like a massive gray whale half a mile away. He doesn't say anything, tying her boat to the dock. "Can anyone climb up there?" and she starts to point at the last of Justine's platinum locks when she loses her footing on the dockside bobbing violently from the evening tide; he catches her arm, and she would bet he thinks she did it on purpose.

He waves at the billboard. *Be my guest.* Off his glass hand flashes a glint of the silver sun.

Lulu sticks the telescope under her arm and, clutching the rope rail, follows the footbridge that rocks and sways with the water. When she gets to the more stable scaffolding of the billboard itself, she looks back to see him still watching her. She sticks the telescope in back of her red dress where it ties and starts up the side of the billboard, and at some point looks down and the height frightens her a moment; she almost loses her grip. As far as she can tell, he doesn't flinch. But he's still watching when she gets to the top, both fascinated and hesitant, as if he's a man who never looks up but can't help himself now.

At the top of Justine, at the eye of the city's panorama, with the flooded skyscrapers of Wilshire Boulevard rising to the south and the mansion-islands of West Hollywood and Hancock Park to the north and east, and the domes of Baghdadville to the west, the wind is much stronger. There isn't really all that much to hang on to, just a narrow walkway running the length of the billboard with a small handrail — and as Lulu turns to where the fog comes in from the sea, now lit red by the setting sun meeting the red lake in a bloody swirl, there splashed across the horizon she sees it, the same dark red advertisement of her subconscious she's seen the first morning of every monthly cycle, hovering over the city. Far above the lake, for a third time she nearly loses her balance and, below, the man watching her lurches forward slightly, arms slightly outstretched as if he actually would try to catch her.

Overwhelmed by the menstrual vortex of water and fog, rocked by the red wind trying to rip her from the billboard where she clings to the flimsy rail of the walkway, she suddenly flashes back on the moment five years ago when she reached the hole at the lake's bottom, with the silver gondola above her head where

Kirk was being kidnapped by an owl. She remembers that she was already wondering how she was going to get back up to the surface before her lungs burst; she was trying not to panic. She could feel the pull of a riptide and the push of a current, the hole drawing her in and turning her back, and even now she's not really certain whether going into the hole was her idea or *its* idea; but she distinctly remembers the loss of control and that then she *did* panic: the opening didn't seem nearly big enough. But she slipped through suddenly in a dilated rush, and on the other side she was . . . she was. . . back in the lake. She had swum down into the hole and, on the other side, found herself coming back up out of the hole, swimming up toward the gondola.

At the time, and all the time since, she thought she must have just gotten confused. She assumed she just got turned around, what with currents and tides coming and going. But now up here on top of Justine, hanging on to the rail in this red wind, with her blood splattered across the sky, she suddenly knows something she didn't until now: that she wasn't confused. That she wasn't turned around. That she was pulled through the opening from one lake into another just like it, just like it in every way, every way except one, and that one difference was that on this other lake, there was another silver gondola just like on the first lake — except that this was a gondola without her son.

In the thrall of the wind and the red sky, there at the top of the billboard she feels hysteria lapping at her mind, first a small swell then rocking her harder and harder: suddenly she understands that the vision of the boy and the owls given to her by the lake has led her here to this vantage point at this place in this moment beneath this sky so that, beneath the red heavens above, she could have this revelation of another lake and, on it, her son, still waiting there even now. Understanding this with more clarity than she's ever understood anything, she feels the coming hysteria and an irresistible urgency to get off the billboard; but when she moves to climb down, the red wind threatens to blow her off, and finally all she can do is lie flat and wait. Lying flat on her back, she slips off her red dress and ties herself to the rail with it, although this is more instinctive than any kind of cool collected action: she's in a trance because, lying there flat on her back staring up at the sky and the wind, all she can think is that back through that hole at the bottom of the lake, back on the other side of that opening, on the Other Lake she left behind five years ago, her wildman is still there sitting in the gondola looking around, still trying to be brave, still waiting for his mother to come back. He's been waiting what's been five years on this side of the hole, on this lake, although who knows how long it's been on his side, five minutes or five seconds; but he sits there now waiting as it gets darker and darker, calling "Mama?" and gazing over the gondola's side. The more Lulu thinks about this up there on top of the billboard, the more she knows it to be true. Lying there in the wind beneath the endometrial sky, hysteria finally begins to recede. But the realization of what happened five years ago doesn't recede with it.

That night the red storm blows across the lake while she stands on her front porch staring east to where she left her son in the gondola five years ago, promising she would be right back. She waits for the storm to pass but it blows all night and, watching, she lashes herself to the porch with sheets from her bed as she lashed herself to Justine that afternoon with her dress; she can't bear to abandon him again. She's torn between two sons, the one she's seen flying with the owls and the one down beyond the uterus of the lake on the other side, in the gondola still waiting for her.

In the morning she wakes chilled and soaked, still bound to the porch and having slept through the rain in a blizzard of dreams, she who used to never dream. She can't be certain whether the fever that wracks her is the fever of dreams or the fever of rains, and she finally undoes all the wet saturated knots of the sheets to stumble into the house and fall on the bed. The last time she was this cold was the night five years ago she lowered herself from the gondola into the lake; and as she takes off all her wet clothes and wraps her nude body in several blankets and sleeps again, in her sleep she sees him, still waiting for her in the gondola, calling to her

Mama?

and she wakes to a bed drenched in fever. She smells the dreams like wet ash on the mattress. She sniffs the mattress up and down from the foot of the bed to the head and sometimes catches a whiff of the lake at the juncture where the fresh water meets the sea, sometimes a whiff of the wet wood of oars, and there at the mattress' northeastern quadrant is the smell of him. It's there. She had forgotten how he smelled but now, this afternoon, in the sweat of her dreams she remembers, because the wet stain of memory is there on the mattress. The mattress has become a map of her dreams and their remorse, longing, rage, desolation. For the rest of the afternoon she lies naked on the bed with her head in that one spot, one side of her face to the mattress so she can smell him, and when she falls asleep yet again, the smell of him is all she dreams. She wakes to a call

Mama?

and hears it so distinctly that for a moment she believes he's there in the house. She believes he's fallen asleep in his bed in another room and that he calls out to her like he used to back at the

Hamblin. She sits up with a start in the dark and listens, but the call doesn't come again until she falls back to sleep.

Her fever has passed but it's exhausted her. She lays back down but every time she falls asleep on the map of dreams she wakes to his call, until even in her fatigue there's nothing she can do but pull on some clothes, stumble out to the porch of the house, loosen the line of the gondola and get in slowly, wearily pushing herself with the pole east along the coastline of the Hollywood Hills to that place on the lake she last went five years ago. Although it's not much more than a mile from where she lives, she's avoided this part of the lake all these years and dreads it now.

The shoreline has changed a little since then, the lake having risen farther down what was once the Strip, now submerged. Rowing along the Hollywood cliffs she sees newly abandoned patches of the hills, empty houses and what were once chic little lanes that now disappear into water. Several members of a tribe of nomads, identifiable by their lack of either blue attire or Lulu's subversive red, run alongside the water following the gondola for a while before they give up and turn back. Around a bend in the coast she sees the spires of the old Chateau X hotel; as dusk falls she can see lit candles darting in the castle's top windows. From the top of the hill above the Chateau the sky tram erected just a few years ago launches itself out over the water, the Nichols Canyon Line that runs to the Fairfax station in the east and then to the Old Cahuenga station beyond; plunging south into the lake in the distance is the Port Justine Line that was begun but never finished. Not far from the coast there still bobs on the lake's surface the remnants of the sky tram shuttle that plummeted into the water ten months ago when the line broke, drowning nine people including two children. Forty-five minutes later the terrain becomes familiar to her in the twilight, minus the empty fair tents she so distinctly remembers as blowing on the Laurel Canyon beaches that evening that now seems like it was just a month ago, a week, an hour.

She rows to the spot; she dreads it; these are the watery coordinates of her loss and shame, and now her failure of nerve. She fears she can't go through with this and so hopes this vision is madness, that down through the dark water there is no Other Lake on the Other Side attached to this one by a common birth canal. She drifts on the spot, pulling up the oars, and sings in a cracked, unconvinced voice

if there's a higher light

hearing the hypnotizing spanish horns in her head — and for a moment she stops to lean her tired self over the side of the gondola and put her ear as close to the water's surface as the gondola will allow.

She listens for his voice.

Listens for him calling from the Other Lake on the Other Side. For a while she almost convinces herself she hears nothing, and is appalled how momentarily relieved she is, as if she would rather not have to go through whatever she has to go through to have him back; and then, confronted with her relief and guilt, and confronted with his loss all over again, she feels a despair more unnamable than she's ever felt at any moment in these five years, which she wouldn't have thought possible. Leaning over the side of the gondola, her face very close to the water so that the ends of her hair are wet, she begins to cry, tears dropping onto the surface of the lake until

Mama?

unmistakably. Oh dear God she says to herself, and then hears it again

Mama?

and she recoils from the lake. She stares at the black water his *Mama?* floating up through the dark water toward the surface like a fish. She can see it down below silvery and fluttery light, with the scales of a child's sobbing. With the waver of his voice the word flashes in and out of view; when she lunges her hand down into the lake she feels his call brush against her fingertips before slipping away. She calls back. For a moment it sticks in her throat

Kirk?

and then she watches it fall from her mouth and sink into the lake, blue and porcelain and breathless. There's a moment's silence before he answers, with that question mark so insistent it's not a question

Mama?

and then she begins rowing away. This is her great failure of nerve. Maybe it's that she can't bring herself to believe. Maybe it's that she's afraid reaching him is beyond her. . . and that's unbearable, because she's always been convinced she would do anything for him. She's always been convinced she would hurl herself off any towering building, before any roaring airplane, in any harm's way for him. When he was born, every instinct of self-interest seemed to give way to an instinct she never knew she had before she had him: the love of something bigger than the love of one's own life; and now in this moment she's failed that love.

She begins rowing very quickly from the spot, one *Mama?* after another floating up to the surface of the lake behind her, a school of his cries desperately swimming after her. Glancing over her shoulder she can see them. She begins weeping in a hysteria that keeps time with her rowing, until she's rounded the bend of the Chateau X and can't see the spot anymore behind her. She cries all the way back across the lake to her house.

That night her uterus explodes in a tantrum of blood. Hunched over the toilet she feels the presence of Kristin, her other self whom she so rejected for abandoning their son: Lulu Blu, she hears

Kristin whisper from the hallway, you're no better. Worse, actually, she goes on, I left him in the gondola that night because I was afraid for him. Now he waits on the Other Side (the century's uterus exploding in a tantrum of water) and you leave him there again, afraid for yourself. Lulu sobs no, her womb answers a red yes, she crawls back to the mattress to paint the dreams mapped there with the scarlet of her thighs.

Once not long after Kirk was born, back when she was still Kristin, she offered God a deal. Whatever good things might be in her future, she would trade them all just for her boy to be all right. She would trade them all. She would trade every minute of happiness, every minute of fulfillment, every minute of accomplishment, all those minutes for his well-being. And then when she lost him, she thought it was God answering, No. God had it in for her, and He had gotten back at her through a helpless child, Sniveling Coward that He had always been, the Neighborhood Bully who pulls the wings off angels simply to prove He can.

And then this notion occurred to her, she didn't know why. This notion occurred to her; she thought what if in fact she and God *had* make this deal — but sometime in the future? At some point in the years to come that she doesn't know, that she never can have foreseen, because it's a future that's never going to come to pass, what if God took her up on her deal and in fact they're now living out the bargain? She has been stripped of happiness, stripped of fulfillment, stripped of whatever it is she might have accomplished, so that she might be guilty, lonely, haunted by the woman she once was who now despises her: but her boy lives. Her boy waits at this very minute on another lake not so different from this one, afraid, confused, but still alive.

In her sleep she smells smoke, feels the heat.

In her sleep another song-serpent — did she leave the radio on? — hisses in from the past. In her sleep it crawls through the front door, and somewhere in the front room catches fire. Maybe because some part of her brain knows that a dream rarely has a scent (she smells the smoke) and rarely a touch (she feels the heat), she wakes. She sits up in bed slowly at first, then startled to complete consciousness by the smoke that begins to choke her. Seeing the fire, she sees herself as others have seen her, in her arrogant red dress against the blue of the lake, a red flame floating on the water. By then the fire is in the hallway where Kristin stood whispering to her a few hours before. For what seems to her an absurdly long moment, she sits on her red dreamsoaked mattress looking at the flames just beyond the door, then shakes herself from her inertia and leaps to the floor, only to realize it's too late.

Did she leave a candle burning? Did someone sail by and toss in a torch, because it was time to burn the heretic Madwoman in Red from the hills? What's that phenomenon, she thinks to herself, where people burst into flames? The house spontaneously combusts, its fuse lit at the end that curls into a house's subconscious. Was the house committing suicide in a symphony of self-immolation — an act of protest, like a Buddhist monk? She can imagine nothing to be protested unless, of course, it's her presence. Unless, of course, the house means to burn away the human mark of its disgrace.

She's beset by more responses than she can sort through in the moments the fire allows her. Somewhere in the ember-blizzard of these responses is calm; she feels it somewhere beyond the heat, before the calm is finally interrupted by a now rather ragged instinct for self-preservation, which itself transforms to panic. The daze of her sleep finally succumbs to adrenaline. She goes to the window of her bedroom only for the sill to fracture into flame, and then the curtains go up; she leaps back from them. The inferno drops to the floor on a parachute of fire, then the floor goes up in flames. Then the bed goes up. Now smoke drops her to her knees. For a thoughtless moment she reaches to one of the bed's blankets, itself engulfed, so as to cover herself, before she drops it and retreats. But there's nowhere to retreat.

Perhaps it's this that accounts for it. Perhaps it's her abject helplessness, perhaps it's that she finally has nowhere to go and so surrenders to the End. Or perhaps it has nothing to do with her, perhaps it's a fluke of nature

but the lake begins to rise

after having not risen at all in months. It now rises very suddenly and visibly, by inches.

At first she thinks the house must be sinking. As if somewhere nearby a dam burst; but there is no dam; it's a tide as mysterious as the intricate flow of her womb that manifested itself to her in the sky over Port Justine the afternoon before. Perhaps the lake comes so that it might claim Lulu before the fire can — so it has nothing to do with rescue, everything to do with possessiveness. . . but for whatever reason, the lake comes up over the edge of the front porch, comes through the front door into the front room, comes into the hallway of ghosts and into the bedroom and rises up around her feet then her ankles lapping at the flaming walls around her. It brings with it a spray, Lulu's private rain. It's now her private lake, beneath her private sky.

The lake that was her enemy. *The lake that was my fear.* The lake that was the afterbirth of her dreams. *The lake that preyed on my son.* Now comes as ally, confessor, co-conspirator, savior.

It stops about the time it gets to her waist.

She doesn't move, partly caught in the shock between the heat of the fire that's given way to the cold of the water. She keeps throwing water in her face to get the stinging of the smoke out of her eyes; she doesn't move, as if not to tempt either the lake or the house of ashes around her, until a wall suddenly gives way behind her, falling away; and she sees the lake has dropped to her thighs.

It likes her thighs and stays awhile.

Peering off in the dark where the wall has collapsed, she sees bobbing flashlights on the hillside that abutted what once was her house, and she finally dares to move toward the dark, walking up out of the water onto the new beach.

"You all right?" she hears a stranger ask in the dark, some guy she recognizes as living on the hillside above her, with his son at his elbow, only a few years older than Kirk would be now. His flashlight shines in her face until she shields her eyes with her arm. Beyond him she can now make out others on the embankment in the dark, watching: "What happened?" someone says to someone else nearby, as a woman comes up to Lulu and wraps a blanket around her. "You should get out of those clothes," the stranger with the boy suggests, and is startled when Lulu, in a daze, drops her red dress from her body to the ground; she pulls the blanket around her and stands shivering for a while.

"You have anywhere to go?" the woman who gave her the blanket asks in the dark.

Lulu stands naked in her blanket shivering. She's dazed enough she doesn't register the question at first, but studies the wreckage and looks for the gondola to see if it survived. Does she have anywhere to go? the same woman asks someone else; and in the dark Lulu sees, floating silver among the black remnants of the house, the gondola. Yes, she says. I have somewhere to go.

There's no convincing any of them, she knows, that she's not who she's always been in their eyes, the Madwoman in Red, even if she's now dropped her red dress to the mud of the new shore and stands naked in the blanket. *The world's never been as casual about my nakedness as I am.* When she turns to go back into the lake, a couple of people try to stop her — the woman who brought her the blanket, the man with his son — assuming she's in some kind of shock; as calmly as possible she explains she's quite coherent but has to retrieve the gondola. It's imperative she save the gondola. They help her pull the gondola up onto the new embankment and tie it to a tree.

They think I started the fire, she realizes, they think I meant to go up in flames with the house. Later, when they want to take her to a shelter out in the Valley, she says no I'm staying near the water, and when she looks at the lake, the lake looks back. *Are we sisters now? Lover and lover, wife and wife, wife and mistress, mistress and slave?* The lake, she's still thinking to herself hours later, sleeping on the living room floor of the woman with the blanket, *saved me tonight. . . for what? Does it have a conscience? I thought it came for my son five years ago. . . did it really take me instead, and I'm just now realizing it?* Lying in the dark she tries to remember now as clearly as she can what happened five years ago when she sank down through the water, Kirk's gondola above her head, *but I can't. Is it the same lake at all? Or was the lake that came for my son the twin sister of the lake whose shores I've known the five years since, the lake that saved me tonight? This lake* she rises from the floor in the dark of the stranger's living room and walks to the window, staring out at the night and the glitter of moonlight on the water in the distance where her house was *this lake that covets me* and Lulu somehow resists the almost overpowering compulsion to run outside the house right now and down the banks to the gondola.

For a moment she's overwhelmed. She grabs the window-sill to steady herself because she almost comprehends the huge unmeasurable love of it, the lake's sacrifice in saving her so that it could then give her up. *Saving me so I could have one more chance. . . and go back.* She whispers in the dark through the window, *You would do that for me? You would give me up so I could go back? You would do that because you love me that much, and therefore you know what it's like for me to love my son that much? You would do that for* him, *because you know what he means to* me?

For a moment there's nothing but silence, and then in the night the lake answers.

She has the almost overpowering compulsion to rush to the gondola even in the dark; and realizes that in part it's because she's afraid if she waits then she'll fail herself again, and fail her son again as she did the afternoon before. But as soon as that realization comes, it passes: she knows she won't fail again. And knowing that, she returns to her place on the floor and, against the hard wood beneath her, finally sleeps.

In her sleep, the red sky stretches across the dome of her inner lids.

When she opens her eyes, she hears voices from outside the window. She turns on her side and pushes herself up from the floor, walks to the window and looks out; the sky is ablaze with blood. All along the road, down the embankment that leads to the lake, people stand in their blue clothes looking up at the clotted clouds. She looks herself for only a minute, looks around the house for her red dress and finds it nowhere: so she steps naked from the front door and walks down the hill to the water, astounded witnesses diverted from the astounding sky by the astounding woman who passes.

As she passes, someone reaches out to her as if to help or stop her. But she isn't stopped. A crowd at the beach parts for her as she moves through them to the tree where the gondola is tied. She unties the gondola from the tree and, holding the rope in her hand, looks at the sky again to assess the storm. She pushes the gondola out in the water and gets in, and takes the pole.

The last vision the lake shows her is a vision of herself again, except she's changed places with it. This time rising from the lake and stepping from the black atrium of an underwater geyser, among the cinders of her house that still float on the lake's surface like slivers of ice from a black arctic, is Lulu; that's when the naked woman in the gondola knows she's Kristin again.

She continues to watch as the vision of Lulu slowly recedes in the distance, getting smaller and smaller with all the other people on the shore that now gets farther and farther away. Lulu raises her hand in farewell and Kristin nods in farewell back, continuing to push herself out into the water with the pole.

As she pushes the gondola by pole along the edge of the lake, people run alongside. The farther she sails, the bigger the crowd becomes, mesmerized by the spectacle of the nude woman with the pole guiding her silver gondola. After a while Kristin pushes herself beneath the inverted arc of the fallen line of the sky tram, then around the bend where the Chateau X rises up out of the water. Off to her right in the southwest she can see the Hotel Hamblin. She feels calm unlike the afternoon before when she took this same trip. Accompanying her are the melody-snakes loosed last night from her house by the fire; now homeless they slither alongside the gondola as the growing throng of observers run alongside on land. She can hear them as they brush past her, women's voices in the lake crossing her path as if daring her to cut them in two in her image, and then there's a school of them, all the voices she's heard for five years, some she didn't even know were singing to her, now slipping back and forth across her path darting across her passage as if to either clear the way or stop her, because they can't stand to lose her, not to the lake that's now her sister or lover or mother. Beneath the hemorrhaging sky, the snakes just beneath the water's surface reflect red strings of blood.

The crowd on land grows. Stragglers along the shore are caught up by the others following her, until by the time she rounds the Chateau and approaches the lake's origin there appear to be several hundred onlookers, including people who before now have never heard of the Madwoman of the Lake. No one calls or heckles, everyone is quiet. Soon Kristin puts down the pole and takes the oars to row, and as she approaches the spot she drops the oars and allows herself to drift to it, as if trusting the boat's precision more than her own. The melody-snakes that have followed her relentlessly for the last quarter of a mile have stopped at an unseen but unbreachable border, out of earshot of the past, muted into invisibility by the lake's hush. Kristin peers over the side of the boat. Zed is blacker and emptier than it's ever been. Kristin looks up for a moment at the shore of the northern Laurel Bay which is now lined with people. No one calls to stop her. In the red glare from water and sky she can just make out some people holding their hands over their eyes. It's perfectly quiet, not a voice or a song to be heard and

Wildman?

she says, leaning over the gondola. She doesn't shout it, she lets it fall from her mouth and watches it sink. It vanishes into the pitch black of the lake and she waits. Seconds pass. A minute. Another minute and another, and then, in the pitch black where she watched her question disappear, she sees the approach of its answer. Slowly it grows before her eyes, floating up to her until it breaks the surface

Mama

and she scoops it up in her hands. She cups it in her hands and sits in the gondola looking at it, as if it's a prayer and the gondola is a floating pew. She splashes her face with it and feels his voice run down her cheeks. For a moment she covers her eyes. She feels his voice dry on her face. She looks back down into the lake and now deep in the black water she sees something else, slowly floating up to her, another answer; and she reaches into the water and takes it as it breaks the surface.

In these five years she's forgotten all about it. It's a small plastic monkey in a red spacesuit with a space helmet. She thinks about that last day in the gondola five years ago, Kirk clutching in his hand the monkey he named after himself; she remembers slipping into the water and hearing his heartbeat under the water, and looking up through the water and seeing him peer over the edge of the gondola, still holding the monkeyman he called Kulk in his fingers. She remembers now the terrible emptiness of the gondola when she returned to the water's surface a minute later, the way there had been no sign of him at all, and now she looks

at the toy monkey that's come floating up to her out of the lake
and says
I'm coming
and slips her naked body, pink with the light of the red sky, over
the gondola's side.   As she slips beneath the water she thinks
maybe she hears someone on the shore finally break the silence of
the lake and shout out No! but she isn't certain about that, *that may
be in my own head. Because I also hear* if there's a higher light,
let it shine on me *but I look around for some sign of the melody
bolder than the others, having dared to swim into this forbidden
zone of the lake but I don't see it, so the song must be in my head
too. . . all the songs and all the No's are in my head. I sink.
I don't swim to the hole below, I let it pull me. I didn't even get
a good gulp of air first, I'm calm in my chest and my descent, and
feel the peace that maybe comes with drowning, once the panic
is over. . . I don't know why I don't panic. I look up and see the
gondola above me like I saw it above me the last time I went this
way, five years ago, but this time without his small head looking
over the side. As I sink there rise around me the small canyon
houses that went under when the lake first appeared, I can see
below me the sidewalks that once lined the boulevard below
me too, and around me the neighborhood where I walked years
ago pregnant not much more than a week from labor, drawn here
as I'm drawn now, only to find at my feet a black puddle where
now is the dark hole I can see through the water's murk, coming
up at me, the opening of the lake's birth canal, here it comes.
Here it comes. Too small it would seem for anyone to slip through, and yet I*

slip through anyway, drawn beyond any resistance, pushed through in a nev irth, when domination is submission and submission is domination, shaking myself loose of the love that held me down so as to find inside me the love tha

2017(2016)

ill save him, continuing down with bits of everyone I've ever been falling away from me, down down down down in what I know is my own passage, a

In his sleep, the dome of his eyelids is red, like the bloody red sky of L.A. that he remembers from nine years ago, and he hears the song like he heard it that day in the Square twenty-eight years ago.

In his dream, which he has often, he's standing there in the Square again, although it's not clear to him whether he's nineteen again, as he was then, or in his late forties, as he is now. He clutches her yellow dress in his hand — *K, beautiful betrayer* — and watches the tank roll toward him. Even looking at the famous photograph that thrilled the world, one still couldn't know how big that tank really was.

hough it's unique to me as the same passage would be unique to someone

But when he stood there in the Square that day twenty-eight years ago, watching it come closer, it rolled toward him like a huge metallic wave, followed by another behind it, and another behind that and another behind that.

Now in his dream the tank rolls toward him more like a giant stainless-steel egg, with another behind it. The rolling of the eggs always nauseates him; once he lurched from the dream running for the latrine, vomiting in the outer tunnel. Just as it was twenty-eight years ago, in the dream he knows that somewhere, along with the rest of the world, she's watching. Somewhere she's watching, was what he thought to himself on that June day, and in his dream he thinks it to himself now; and knowing this, he can die, because he's not just dying for the freedom of man, he's dying for the tyranny of love. Kristin, he whispers into the barrel of the tank's gun as though it's the opening between her legs and he's her slave again, whispering her name that curls up into her body like smoke.

In his dream, standing in the Square as the tanks roll toward him like great eggs, he hears the song as he heard it that morning. Hears it drift out from what he reasoned at the time must be, beneath the red sky, some unknown window.

else, the same but different, a passage without time, that might take a minut

For a moment in his dream he's distracted. As he did that morning, he searches for it, a melody he would hear again only once, years later.

A gust rises on the Square as mysterious as the song, as though to blow the song away, as though to blow him out of the way of the tanks: Is the gust, he wondered at the time, an ally meaning to rescue me, or a weapon of the State meaning to remove me? before he learned it was really an anarchist without conviction. He stands his ground. The tank tries to go around him, he moves to block it. The tank moves again, so does he. Was it only six minutes, as a newsmagazine reported? Of course it seemed much longer. There in the Square he's ecstatic in his terror: Try to deny me now, he says to her, as I defy the world. As happened then, he hears the melody and in his dream is just beginning to remember its source, leaning into the large gun barrel of the tank before him, when there is out of the corner of his vision a blinding flash of something, and he raises his hand to shield his eyes. At some point in the dream he sees her appear at the far end of the Square that's empty except for him and the tanks, a distant figure crossing the Square toward him.

He knows it isn't his Kristin. Rather, as she grows in the distance it's the Mistress; in his dream he vaguely knows she doesn't belong here, that she's out of time. She's dressed as

r a hundred years depending on the one being born through it, from

always, in stockings and garters and heels and a small chain belt around her waist, but the attire is more an assertion of power than a suggestion of seduction. In one hand she carries the chain leash she keeps for him, in the other her black riding crop. She has shoulder-length sandy hair; she isn't beautiful but commanding. She doesn't offer her sensuality but marshals it. As she strides toward him across the Square, her eyes locked on him never averted, not alluring but imperious, a spreading pool of black water precedes her like an honor guard. As she grows closer, the pool spreads faster and wider, seeping across the Square until it's a wet black mirror tinged with red, reflecting the sky above.

There's a cracking sound. Is it the explosion of guns, or red thunder announcing a red rain? Not the marxist red of the State. . . . A seed in the uterus of history to be washed away in the flow of the womb's rejection, he recognizes it rather as the dark rust-red of his Kristin's blood on their thighs after they have made love during her period. There's another round of explosions

and he wakes and

in the dark, as he lies on his cot, someone pounds on his door.

He sits up from the cot, holds his face in his hands. "Sir?" comes a voice from the other side of the door; Wang fumbles for the small lamp on a nearby desk. "Sir?" comes the voice again. When he turns on the light he sees the picture looming over him as always, it's everywhere, on every wall up and down the front line; a flash of rage comes over him. I took that down, he thinks to himself. Someone put it back up. In my own quarters.

The men draw inspiration from it, one of his officers explained not long ago. Well I don't draw inspiration from it, Wang had answered. They can paper the entire front with it if they want but he doesn't understand why they have to hang it in his

somewhere that was a minute ago or a hundred years ago, a passage from m

own quarters. He sees quite enough of it everywhere he goes, every headquarters, every outpost, every barracks — raised over the battlefields like the towering banners the Party used to hoist of its leaders back in his home country *so I don't see why I have to look at it in my own quarters.* Back in his home country they would have called this a "cult of personality."

No wonder I dream every night.

The pounding on the door continues. "Come in," Wang says.

The soldier comes in. "Sir," he says.

"Why is that on my wall?" Wang says.

"Sir?"

"Why is that on my wall." Wang points at the picture. "I took it down. Someone came into my quarters and put it back up after I took it down."

The young guerrilla looks at the enlarged photo. "The men draw inspiration from it, sir."

"My own quarters."

"Yes, sir. The men — "

"Yes I've heard how the men are inspired by it but I'm not inspired by it. Why don't you put up something that inspires me?"

The soldier, a kid, not much older than Wang in the photo, seems flummoxed. "Uh. . . what would that be, sir?"

He tried to get them to stop calling him "sir" since he's not an officer and in fact has no ranking at all, but that only seemed to cause more chaos among the ranks. "What's your name?"

"Parsons, sir."

"Parsons, let me ask you something."

"Sir."

"How do you know it's me?"

"Sir?"

"I said how do you know it's me," Wang points at the

wn unique chaos maybe to my own unique god, and as I slip on down through

poster. "It's almost thirty years old, this picture, blown up about a hundred times its original size. . . that man" — pointing at the lone figure before the tanks — "is a blur. . . he could be anybody. So how do you know it's me?" This is perverse, Wang thinks. Such questions just undermine the resolve of Tribulation III. . . is it Tribulation III now, he asks himself, or still Tribulation II? "Never mind," he says, his face in his hands again. "Please take it down."

The young soldier takes down the picture. He rolls it up and puts it under his arm.

Wang still sits on the cot, exhausted by his restless sleep. "So what is it?"

"Sir?"

"What did you wake me for?"

"Sir. Major Tapshaw reminds you it's a full moon tonight, sir."

"Tell him to send up the flare."

"Yes, sir."

"Give me a few minutes."

"Sir." The soldier leaves and for a while Wang sits on his cot looking at the blank square of wall where the picture was a few minutes ago. Tribulation II or Tribulation III. . . how can I be confused about such a thing? He gets up and moves to the desk and wakes the computer and turns the desk lamp off again; now there's only the light from the computer. He takes off all his clothes and for a moment stands naked before the computer before he sits, inputting his password and opening the mail. He addresses a new message, staring at it as he composes in his head.

the birth canal of the lake then I have three visions there before me in the

With his one good hand, he begins to type.

To: MistressL@aquamail.com
From: FalseMartyr@4june89.net

my Mistress,

      Your devoted possession requests the honor of subjecting himself to Your Cruel Pleasure on this night. Abjectly apologize for the short notice and duly expect to feel Your Exquisite Discipline for the impertinence. i await an answer, unworthy as ever of my humiliation, and remain Your

zen-toy

Wang looks over the message, considering the tone and double-checking the proper Upper/lower-case etiquette. He sends the message and waits to see if he receives an answer immediately, as sometimes he does, but after several minutes there's still no response. He closes the program and dresses and pulls on his coat, and opens his door to the outer tunnel that leads above ground.

      Outside his door in the tunnel, a guard snaps to attention. Like the soldier who just woke him, the guard wears the regulation lake-blue of the guerrilla insurgency as well as the blood-red beret. Hanging on the outside of the door is a picture identical to the one that was in his quarters a few minutes ago. "Guard," he says.

      "Sir," says the guard.

      "How long has this been here?" indicating the picture.

mniotic dark, or maybe more precisely two visions and a presence, with the

      "Sir?"

      "Hanging on this door. It wasn't here when I came down a few hours ago: how long has it been here?"

      "I couldn't really say, sir."

      "You couldn't really say? How long have you been standing here?"

      "Sir, I came on duty at nineteen hundred hours, sir."

"And was it here when you came on duty?"

"I don't really remember, sir."

"You don't remember?"

"No, sir."

"You don't remember whether this was on this door right in front of you when you came on duty?"

"No, sir."

"You've been staring at this door for almost two hours and you don't remember if it was here?"

"Sir. Permission to speak."

"Go ahead."

"The men draw inspiration from it, sir."

Wang's shoulders slump in defeat. He grabs the top of the poster to rip it from the door but stops himself, and instead starts up the tunnel to the surface where he can hear the shelling in the distant night and the planes of the airlift coming and going.

Guards and soldiers snap to attention as he passes. A dozen small fires dot the expanse of the campground, where guerrillas

first being of God Himself naked and erect, shackled and restrained

who don't have tents sleep on exposed cots or the ground. Major Tapshaw meets him at the end of the barricade. "It may," Tapshaw says, "be any time now."

"Transcriber?"

"Waiting for us."

"You send up the flare?"

Tapshaw hesitates.

Wang says, "Do we have to have this discussion every time?"

When Tapshaw is angry his black face grows even darker and now in the night all Wang can see of him are his eyes. "I think it's better," Wang hears the tension in the major's voice, "if one of the men takes you across the lake."

"I know you do, because we have this discussion every time."

Tapshaw turns and calls over his shoulder to a soldier who appears as though he's been waiting. "Send up the flare," Tapshaw tells him quietly. He turns back to Wang as Wang watches the guerrilla disappear toward the far rampart. "You knew you were going to wind up sending up the flare," says Wang, "so why do we have to go through this?"

"I suppose I feel the need to keep making the same point."

Together in the dark they start walking to the listening station. "I think by now I've gotten the point."

"We don't know anything about this boy. And he's. . . slow."

"We know he knows the lake better than anyone," Wang answers, "that's what we know." The two men mount the steps of the barricade, and Wang barely glances up at the sky above him for the full moon he knows is there.

lindfolded and swaddled in latex, enslaved and cuffed around His wrists and

He's a man who never looks up. Over time, the acrophobia he developed in the last fifteen years has grown only more acute; as much as possible he lives on the latitude of his dreams.

He breaks into a sweat just climbing the barricade, less than twenty feet high. This is something he hasn't told anyone; he can barely bring himself to look at the sky above him when in fact, once, in one of his aimless lives before this, he lived closer to the sky than the ground, as close to the sky as one can live without being on a mountain or in an airplane. "I hope this time," Wang says, "we're going to be able to hear something over the shelling."

"We have a recorder with the transcriber."

"I know but last time it took the recorder half the night to clean up the disk."

"This transcriber is better than the last one. Maybe she'll be able to catch parts of the transmission if the recorder doesn't." They reach the rampart where both the recorder and transcriber, waiting with recording equipment and a laptop, come to attention. "As you were," Tapshaw says; from the station can be seen the distant lights of Baghdadville in the west and the abandoned downtown skyscrapers lit by searchlights to the northeast. The sky above Wang that he can't bring himself to look at is illuminated by the flare, a star momentarily brighter than the flaming white moon. The entire L.A. bay lights up. As the flare fades and the sky becomes black again, Wang says to the transcriber, "Are we ready?" and she answers, her fingers at her keyboard; the recorder pulls at some cables. "How quickly can you clean this up and get it back to us?" Wang asks.

"Thirty minutes maybe," the recorder answers. "Turn it on

ankles, red rubber ball-gag in His mouth and awaiting His humiliation, and

now," Wang says, "so we get it all from the beginning." They wait. A wind off the lake triggers a memory in Wang and he realizes it reminds him of the gust in his dream, blowing across the Square — and now the whole dream, which he had forgotten, returns to him. He's thinking of the black water spreading across the Square when suddenly it comes from somewhere out over the lake, out of the night.

The shelling actually stops, as though the bombs are listening too. An occasional plane from Occupied Albuquerque flies by overhead.

The broadcast isn't that loud and doesn't sound that far away, maybe no more than several miles. It's over in a few minutes. For about ten seconds everything remains silent, then the shelling begins again. "You get it?" Wang says to the recorder and transcriber.

"As best I could," the young woman transcribing says, apologetic, "I didn't understand some of it. . . . "

"It's all right," Wang says, "that's what he's for," nodding at the recorder.

"I think I can get you a pretty clean copy," says the recorder.

"Make an extra one," Tapshaw tells them. "I want you both in Strategy as soon as you're ready."

He and Wang make their way back down the rampart. "Thirty minutes, Major?" Wang says, heading to his quarters; Tapshaw stops in his tracks. "Are we going to argue about the boy again?"

"Something else," says Tapshaw.

"What?"

"We can talk about it in Strategy too." Tapshaw has a funny look.

he second vision being of the Chinese man whose love letters to another

"All right. When they bring us the transmission."

"I'm bringing in our geologist too."

Our geologist? thinks Wang. "All right," and he turns and heads back down the tunnel to his quarters. The same guard is at his door and the picture is still there, but Wang is relieved to note as he enters his quarters that the blank square of wall where he had

the other picture taken down is still blank. He goes quickly to the
desk to the computer and fills in the password, but there's still no
answer to his message; he takes off his coat and lies back down on
the cot, determined not to fall asleep. He's beginning to doze,
however, when the computer wakes him. "Message," the
cybervoice calmly announces. Wang sits up and looks at the time
on the computer and realizes he's due in the strategy room; first he
checks the message box.

> To: FalseMartyr@4june89.net
> From: MistressL@aquamail.com
>
> zen-toy,
> Come at 1.
> your Mistress

Wang looks at his watch. It's almost 10:30. He'll need to leave by
11:30 to safely make it across the lake in time, assuming his
boatman responds to the flare, and Wang can never be sure about
that until he actually appears. He smiles ruefully: If that boy ever
doesn't show, I'll never live it down with Tapshaw. Wang deletes
from the computer mailbox both the new message and his own that
he sent earlier, turns off the account and the computer, pulls on his

woman named Kristin I intercepted by chance five years ago, who I then sav

coat and walks from his quarters, guard snapping to attention as he
leaves. This time he heads down the tunnel in the other direction,
deeper underground.

Wang reaches yet another tunnel that leads to a door where
two guards part for him to pass, one of them opening the door for
him. Inside, seven men and the female transcriber rise from their
seats around the table as he enters. He's a little surprised; this is at

least two more people than he expected. There are a couple of other officers besides Tapshaw plus an unfamiliar face that Wang assumes is the geologist, plus the cryptographer who always attends the post-broadcast sessions. Including the transcriber and the recorder, all of them sit around an egg-shaped table. Wang takes his seat and Tapshaw nods at the recorder who puts a disk on the sound system at the end of the room.

As the disk begins to play, Tapshaw hands another disk to Wang, who slips it in his coat pocket. The sound of the earlier broadcast is reproduced with new clarity; when it's finished the nine sit around the table pondering. "Do you want to hear it again?" Tapshaw finally asks. "All right," answers Wang, for no reason at all. The song begins again, very martial and anthemic *Blood on the T.V., ten o'clock news. / Souls are invaded, heart in a groove. / Beatin' and beatin' so outta time. / What's the mad matter with the church chimes?* "What's the matter with the what?" one of the officers says; there's the same perplexed silence as the song continues. "Church chimes," the transcriber finally answers, although she seems less than certain.

> *Humans are running, lavender room.*
> *Hoverin' liquid, move over moon for my*
> *space monkey. Sign of the time-time*

The song ends and after several speechless moments the cryptographer finally suggests, "It seems clear the 'church chimes'

orking the docks out at Port Justine with the small round monocle in his hand

are the key."

"What about the lavender room?" the young transcriber asks, immediately mortified by her temerity. Several of the men around the table glare at her. "Well it's a good question," Wang says, then asks her, "Do you have a hard copy?" and the grateful young woman hands him a copy of the transcription. He begins to rise from his seat and everyone else begins to rise with him when Tapshaw says, "There's something else."

"Oh yes."

"The other matter I mentioned."

"Yes." Wang looks at his watch; it's almost eleven. "It can't wait?"

"If you don't mind. Particularly given this transmission."

"All right."

Everyone sits again. "This is Professor Stafford," Tapshaw says.

"Professor."

"Sir." Stafford the geologist momentarily hesitates. "I'll try to be as brief as possible."

"I would appreciate it."

"One night," he begins, "about nine years ago, there was. . . a strange geological disturbance in the area."

"I was under the impression the whole last sixteen years had been a strange geological disturbance."

"Well, yes sir," the geologist says, "but this was unique even by recent standards."

"You don't have to call me sir." Sometimes he can't help it.

"Uh," the geologist looks around at the others, confused, "OK. As you know, after the lake first began to appear — as you say, sixteen years ago — within those first few years it rose very

through which could be seen the lake, who watched me climb the billboar

quickly, completely flooding most of the basin and some of the outlying valleys. After that, over the next five years or so the lake rose more slowly."

"May I interrupt?" Wang asks.

"Of course."

"Am I correct no one's ever established the reason for the lake in the first place?"

"No, sir. I mean, that's correct, sir."

Sighing heavily, Wang continues. "Or where it comes from."

"Well, we know where it comes from."

"The hole in the bottom."

"Yes."

"But beyond that, no one's ever established why a hole appeared in the city and a lake came up through it."

"That's correct."

"All right."

"One night nine years ago, the lake rose three feet — three feet and two inches by precise calculations — and fell again to exactly the level it had been, all within a matter of minutes. No one has ever accounted for it."

Wang pointedly looks at his watch and back at the professor.

"Then for eight years," the geologist continues, "up until fourteen months ago, the lake didn't move at all. Not so much as an inch. By what we've been able to determine it didn't rise or fall, it maintained exactly its same level — there weren't even the usual signs of water evaporation, seepage, displacement by natural erosion of the shoreline, any of the things that would account for the normal life of a lake."

"Well, it wouldn't seem to be your normal sort of lake."

"No, sir."

here I might lie in the red wind and gaze on a sky menstruating in tandem

"You said up until fourteen months ago."

"Yes, sir."

"What happened fourteen months ago?"

"The lake began to drain."

"It began to drain?"

"Yes."

Wang scratches his neck. "Do lakes drain?"

"Not like this. It's not your normal sort of lake, sir."

"I think I just said that."

"Yes, sir. They don't drain like this one is draining," the geologist goes on. "This one is draining the way it rose."

"Meaning?"

"Meaning it's going back where it came from."

"But we don't know where it came from."

"Well, no."

"So. . . ?"

"I mean it's returning to its source," the geologist explains.

"The source?"

"I mean it's going back down the hole."

Silence around the table. Wang finally says, "Back down the hole."

"Yes."

"And this began fourteen months ago."

"That's correct."

"This is Wilson," Tapshaw indicates another officer on his right, "in intelligence. Our operation up in Oxnard sent him down a few days ago at my request."

"Really?" says Wang. "Did you and I talk about this?"

"No."

"You requested this transfer on your own initiative?"

"'On my own initiative'?" the officer says, standing. "Yes, I certainly did."

with my own blood, and the third vision being the strange presence of a youn

"Well then," Wang says after a moment.

Everyone is tense. "Wilson," Tapshaw finally continues, "has a particular sort of expertise, having to do with theological cult phenomenology, that I thought — "

"Theological what?" Before the other man can answer Wang says, "Never mind. Go on."

"Sir," Wilson the theological cult phenomenologist begins, "have you heard of the Order of the Red?"

"Some sort of theological cult phenomenon?" says Wang.

"A religion," nods Wilson, "of several hundred followers. They set up their church nine or ten years ago out on one of the old hotel-islands in the West Hollywood part of the lagoon and then seem to have dispersed, moving inland fourteen months ago."

"Just as the lake started going down. That's what you're getting at, right?"

"And I should add, sir, before anyone knew the lake was draining, sir."

"I have a feeling," Wang says to Tapshaw, "you're going to point out this was also about the time the broadcasts began."

Tapshaw holds a small bundle wrapped in leather. He opens it and places a small object in the middle of the table.

For a while everyone sitting around the table stares at it. Something about the moment strikes Wang as absurd but he reminds himself that, more and more, he has that reaction to

oman about my own age, tiny with long straight gold hair almost to her

everything. When he reaches for the object, he's aware of the way the other people at the table surreptitiously regard his other hand, so that when the young transcriber works up the nerve to ask, "What is it?" for a moment everyone is shocked before realizing she's referring to the object Wang holds up to her.

"A religious icon," Tapshaw answers after a moment.

"It looks like a toy," she says.

"Is it a monkey?" someone says.

"In a red space suit," says Wang.

"To try and make a long story short — " Wilson begins.

"It's a little late for that, but go ahead."

" — the founders of the Order of the Red claimed to have had a vision, which they called the Epiphany of Saint Kristin, nine years ago on the morning after the lake rose and fell those several feet, during the inexplicable geological event that Professor Stafford referred to."

For a moment Wang is stunned. "Saint Kristin?" he finally says.

"Accounts have it that a disturbed young woman took a boat out to the place above the lake's source, slipped into the water and never resurfaced. Her body was never recovered. Hundreds of people saw this. It was a highly unusual day, given the phenomenon of the previous night regarding the level of the lake, as well as other meteorological occurrences."

"What meteorological occurrences?" says the geologist.

"People's recollection of that day," the intelligence officer continues, "is vivid. Everyone remembers the strange winds and a great deal of volatile storm activity, and, uh. . ." He stops for a moment. "That the sky was red."

"Her name was Kristin?" says Wang.

"The young woman reportedly sailed a silver boat almost

waist, there in the passage right beside me but going the other way, being bor

two miles along the Hollywood shoreline. Even on an overcast day, people high in the hills saw the boat on the water. Those following her from the shoreline — and there seem to have been hundreds — are consistent in their observations, such as the fact she wasn't wearing anything. We don't know much else about her except her name, that she was in approximately her mid-twenties, that there was nothing particularly remarkable about her except that she lived in the hills in a small house which she allegedly set on fire the night before."

"You don't think that's remarkable?"

"There's speculation that whatever it was that happened with the lake on that particular night triggered this woman's final collapse into some sort of dementia that led to her suicide. Apparently she was already something of a local oddity, referred to by the other people of the area as the Madwoman of the Lake, the Madwoman in Red, that sort of thing, given her refusal to conform to the blue attire of the other residents. Regional legend has it that, some years before, she abandoned her small son out on the lake at the same place she drowned herself on this particular day, setting him adrift in the same silver boat in which she returned on the day of her own death."

"If she set him adrift in the same boat," Wang says, "how did she still have it?"

"That's a good question," the intelligence officer admits. "It's a little confused."

"So a religion sprang up around this crazy woman?" asks another officer. No one at the table says anything until Wang, still studying the toy monkey in his hand — Tribulation II, or III? — says, "Well, no cult was ever inspired by anyone who was normal," wondering if he himself is the exception that proves the rule.

"At any rate," Wilson says, pointing at the toy monkey,

nto the lake that I've left behind me, expelled from the rubble and fire and

"on the morning the woman took the boat out to the spot on the lake above the source, every eyewitness has her sitting there for several moments staring at the water. Some say she appears to have been praying, but since no one was close enough to hear, we don't really know. Many of those watching that morning report seeing her reach into the water and take something from it. It may have been what you have there in your hand" — indicating the toy monkey — "but we don't really know that either. Accounts of those who saw her disembark from the shore don't mention her taking anything with her, and recall the boat as empty except for the oars and pole. No one remembers seeing her take anything from the water as she sailed along the shoreline, but of course it's possible she did and everyone just missed it. When she lowered herself into the water above the source and didn't reemerge, others sailed out to retrieve the silver boat and found in it only the toy."

Tapshaw turns to Wang. "I think the question now is what tonight's broadcast means in relation to this."

"I don't understand what bearing," says the officer who asked how it was religions spring up around psychotic young women, "any of this has on the Crusade." This reminds Wang that it's always good to include in such meetings one or two people with no imagination whatsoever; they ask the very obvious questions that force everyone to not overlook the obvious.

"Yes," Wang answers, rising from the table as everyone else stands, "I'll leave you all to ponder that very thing." He picks up the little red monkey from the table. "I'll take my icon with me," pressing it to his forehead, "and ruminate upon its mystical properties. Or play with it in my bath." Only the young female transcriber laughs; this sort of humor just confounds everyone else.

Wang smiles at her conspiratorially. He's had to teach himself that too much irony just makes everyone nervous. He slips the monkey in his pocket with the extra disk of the night's

confusion and terror and chaos of the new age's single greatest moment o

broadcast, and one of the guards opens the door for him as Wang hurries from the room up the tunnel; finally breaking into a trot, he can hear in his head the chaotic discussion that's no doubt exploded in his wake. He looks at his watch and thinks to himself, Be there. Emerging from under ground into the night and the ever-present sound of shelling, he heads for the dock down the dark embankment outside the barricades of the Tribulation compound. He glances over his shoulder to make sure Tapshaw isn't following. Be there. If i'm a little late, my Mistress will punish me, he thinks with a small thrill; but he can't be too late, or not show up at all, without jeopardizing the relationship altogether.

At the top of the embankment, at the top of the wooden steps leading down to the dock, a guard allows Wang to pass on recognition, but an officer — undoubtedly alerted by Tapshaw — presents himself as Wang starts down the steps. "Sir," the officer says to him, but Wang doesn't stop. "I can have one of the men accompany you, sir," calls the officer. Resolutely Wang continues down the steps toward the lake; when he reaches the bottom, stepping out on the wharf he sees no one. Then the boatman is there. As always he says nothing, greeting Wang only with silence, maybe a nod although it's difficult to be sure in the dark; even in the moonlight — and these assignations, like the broadcasts that trigger them, always take place during a full moon — Wang can never completely make him out, but the boy can't be any older than seventeen or eighteen, maybe younger.

Like Tapshaw and the others, Wang takes the boy's lack of verbal communication for a kind of dimwittedness. But if the boy is slow then he's the lake's idiot savant, a master of its strange currents that recently have gotten only stranger, gliding the boat among Zed's dark zones that have gotten only darker, avoiding the full moon's exposure and thus the notice of enemy search parties in the nearby hills.

orror, hurled through the birth canal of the lake in a full-force gale of ash

Then it occurs to Wang. Of course the currents have gotten stranger and the dark zones darker: the lake is draining.

Immediately the young boatman pushes the vessel out into the water with one of the oars, then at his end of the boat begins to row.

Wang watches him. The lake is draining, he almost blurts to the boy but stops himself.

More and more everything strikes him as absurd. He wonders if this is because he's fundamentally still a rationalist in a rational universe that renders the absurdities more salient, or because he's changing into an absurdist. He thinks about his dream, his defiant stand for freedom before the eyes of the world and the way in which love is bondage, the way one happily trades freedom for it. He thinks about the woman who drowned herself and wonders what she did it to be free of, what she did it to be bound to. What bearing has it on the Crusade? one of the officers asked, not an unreasonable question if for sixteen years you've ignored how the lake has had a life of its own, how from the beginning the lake has manifested its own psyche, altering the surrounding psychotopography. There wouldn't even be a Tribulation II or III if not for the lake because — although he can't remember why — he's quite certain that if not for the lake, there would never have been a Tribulation I or II. Well. It's the business of soldiers, thinks Wang, to pay attention to trees rather than forests. Distracted by forests, they can't be expected to tend to the trees.

He both warns and reassures himself the woman who

and obliteration, hurled through the opening of the lake by an Oblivion Wind

drowned couldn't have been his Kristin. While she did have a son — by another man, it was the thing that had torn them apart, as well as all his unanswered letters after he finally came to L.A. for her — they said this woman had been in her mid-twenties, and his Kristin would have been well into her thirties at the time; and although he can't quite place it, he vaguely remembers having himself seen a young woman in a brilliant red dress and flashing silver gondola sailing the lake. He's troubled by the morass of emotions he feels at this moment: relief, sorrow, grief, guilt. . . is this the only way he's to be free of her ghost? for, dead or not, she's been a ghost to him all these years anyway, for the way she's haunted him. Navigating from one dark zone of the lake to the next, never breaching the radius of moonlight that floats on the water, the boy at the other end of the boat rows so silently and invisibly it's easy for Wang to feel as though he's the sole passenger of a boat that sails itself. He pulls his coat up around his neck as the wind casts in his face a light spray, and as he makes his way toward the black silhouette of the hills under the full moon, he hears the lake's strange melodies. Glancing over the side of the boat he can see just under the water the glowing snakes that slither alongside; sometimes he can almost make out lyrics, instrumentation, musical bridges, pop hooks. As the lake drains, Wang wonders if the music will diminish or grow stronger. He wonders at what point the lake will finally become an inexorable whirlpool.

Of course he remembers the red sky, color of blood, as vividly as he dreams of it. Everyone who was in L.A. then remembers it, even a man who never looks up. For a moment he's aware the boy has stopped rowing; in this place the lake is blacker than ever, the air around them so black not even the light of a full moon penetrates it. Not even the melody-snakes glow, assuming they still accompany the boat at all, not even the hills can be seen

ontrol and its loss asserting themselves as the parameters of her new psyche

although now they're close. At this moment Wang realizes they're at the place of the lake right above the source; directly below, at this moment, the lake rushes back to wherever it came from.

At the other end of the boat, the boy says, "Night-time."

"Uh, yes," is all Wang can think to answer, "it's night time, yes." The boy has stopped rowing. In the dark they drift. Is he lost? wonders Wang in consternation. But this has happened before. Suddenly Wang hears what at first he thinks is the hooting of an owl, so close it's as though the owl is in the boat with them — but Wang remembers this from before as well, and that it's not an owl, it's the boy. The boy hoots again and then somewhere overhead the boy is answered, the night hooting back; the boy responds and then the night responds in a chorus that trails across the sky, and the boy picks up the oars and begins to row, following the sound above. In a while, as though the darkness is a fog, it parts and the spires of the flooded Chateau X suddenly appear not more than thirty or forty feet away, and the boat is surrounded by a swarm of the illuminated snakes as though the lake's on fire, a faint maelstrom of music and it shocks Wang, the largest swarm of them he's ever seen.

Something he's never thought of before occurs to him now. His mind tries to hold onto it as the boy rows them to the usual docking point around the back of the Chateau, in the grotto formed by what was originally several of the Chateau's suites, where the walls have been either deliberately knocked out or washed away by the lake. A lantern hangs over the outer archway and another shines in the distance off to the right, at the top of the stone steps that lead to a door at what was once the hotel's top floor. To the left, at the end of a granite walkway around the edge of the grotto several feet above the water, is another door with a large rusted brass ring for a doorknob; below the walkway near this door is another mass of snakes as though a star has fallen there, lighting up

just as they do for me, passing so close to me that the two of us almost brush

the water from beneath. Again a moment of elusive comprehension shoots across Wang's mind while, as always, the boy docks in the dark, at the bottom of the steps that once served as a hotel stairway. As always, sitting on the bottom step is a large basket with bread, fruit, cheese and an uncorked bottle of wine, all wrapped in a cloth.

Wang climbs out of the boat and takes the basket and turns to the boy. "Why don't you come inside," he says, "you can wait in the entryway. I'm sure it would be all right," although he isn't sure at all. The boy doesn't answer. "You'll be dry and warm and you can eat and drink there." But there's no answer and so Wang places the basket for the young boatman in the boat. "It may be a couple of hours," he says and then, "uh," unable to stop himself, "do you know, uh. . . is it Tribulation II, or III?"

"No," the boy answers in the dark, if it's an answer at all. At the top of the steps a door opens and light comes through and the boy ducks away, pushing the boat off from the makeshift landing; Wang can hear the lapping of the water from the boy's oars in the dark. Wang turns up the steps. No one is in the open lit door; when he reaches the top of the steps, stepping through the door, no one is in the entryway. Off to the left of the entryway is another single door. He goes into the dressing room behind it and takes off his clothes. There's a sink and mirror, and on the counter next to the sink a red studded collar. The dressing room serves as a transitional passage to the next chamber, and after Wang places the collar around his neck — always with some difficulty given his one useless hand — before he exits through the other door he closes his eyes and, as much as possible, pushes everything from his mind. He makes a point of never looking in the mirror, particularly after he's put on the collar. He realizes he's late tonight and can't take too much time to clear his thoughts; before

ach other as though we might be sisters, I find myself thinking at this minute,

going through the other door he hastily takes from the pocket of his coat, hanging on a hook, the disk of the evening's broadcast along with five one-hundred dollar bills. He doesn't notice that the toy monkey falls from the coat pocket to the small throw-rug at his feet.

Now on the other side of this door he's in the Mistress' lair. Candles burn. There's an end table by the wall where he knows to leave the disk and the money, there's a step up into the training space where he knows to wait, kneeling attentive and naked except for the red collar, before the large hearth of the Lair where a fire burns. Several minutes pass before he hears the steps of her high heels. "zen-toy," he finally hears her, "you're late."

"i'm sorry, Mistress."

She circles where he kneels and strikes him once with the riding crop. Then she takes the chain leash in her hand and attaches one end to his collar locking it and the other to the chain belt that hangs around her waist just above her garters and stockings. She has a pair of fur-lined handcuffs, and after she's pulled him to his feet and cuffed his hands, she turns and strides across the Lair pulling her behind him; for an hour or so he carries out her commands at the end of the leash. After a while she reclines on a leather divan before the hearth and has him massage the muscles of her calves and lower back, striking him with the riding crop when his fingers become impertinent or she feels he's enjoying it too much. At some point she blindfolds him. When an hour has passed she uncuffs him and has him lie face down on the floor where — as always in these sessions — he believes he can hear singing in the walls of the Chateau an ancient city of women, actresses and singers and models and publicists and playmates and escorts and personal secretaries and drug connections and investment bankers and systems analysts and marketing vice-presidents and studio heads-of-productions and strippers from

as though we might be lovers, as though we might be wives to each other

the Cathode Flower nightclub down the boulevard who stayed within these walls back when this was a famous hotel and left behind whispers and arguments and moans of rendezvous and seduction and merger. The Mistress repositions Wang's hands behind him and cuffs him again and beats him with the riding crop in time to the sound of the lake lapping against the walls of the Chateau outside her window. Whose zen-toy are you? she asks between blows, and he answers, my Mistress'. What is the one and only reason you exist? she says and he says, To please and amuse my Mistress. After a while she pulls him to his knees by the fur-lined cuffs around his wrists and has him kneel before her on the divan. She pours over her thighs a sepia-colored liqueur and pulls him to her by his black Chinese hair; still blindfolded he licks the liquor from her thighs and when she feels he takes too much pleasure in this she beats him with the riding crop some more. When he's drunk one thigh dry she moves his mouth to the other. Tasting her thighs and the liqueur, he's transported. Drugged by the liquor and her thighs he falls into a trance, lost, floating above a black lake like a red cloud, a sepia rain on his tongue, and although he murmurs my Mistress, my Mistress in the groan of his climax, it's the name of Kristin, the last woman before Lulu with whom — many years ago — he shared any sort of sensual moment, that fills his mind.

Spent, he sleeps naked on her floor. She covers him with a blanket but doesn't remove the collar or cuffs.

s though mistress and slave, as though mother and daughter, and then

Through the white groan of his climax, he's tumbled into a memory as potent as a vision, more than a dream. In it he can feel the movement of a train he's on, he can smell the grass from the passing Midwest farms outside his window as he smelled it once before, he can touch the flyer he holds in his hand just as he held it then. He's back in his past; he looks around him, momentarily confounded as to how he's returned here. It's years ago again, on the train that took him from the New York of chaos, where God lay in ashes, to L.A., the last city of the modern imagination, where even God and chaos could be reimagined.

In this vision on this train, it's midnight, the final days of summer. In Wang's mind his K hovers before him — *labial jewel, riverine rapture* — waiting for him in the dark distant west, in the unknown future, except back here now on this train where past and present coincide, he knows the future. He already knows he'll get to L.A. and not find her, he already knows he'll write all those letters she'll coldly ignore. The train car rattles. He likes the horizontalism of the train, the way it proceeds between ground and sky belonging to neither, although in his vision he isn't sure whether this is something he actually felt before, years ago when this first happened, or something he's only aware of now. He looks at the flyer and remembers the strange wonder he felt the first time he looked at it on this same train in this same moment: HAVE YOU SEEN ME? it reads like thousands of them then; the face on the flyer is his. His name isn't on it because no one knew his name: "I'm an Asian-American man last seen. . ." although actually he's not American. He wonders who had the flyer for him made — someone who doesn't know his name but remembered him, someone who isn't also one of the missing, as are most of those with whom he had a passing acquaintance.

There was another woman.

all the commotion of visions stops as still as time has stopped here in this place

In this memory-vision, as he considers the flyer he holds, awash in a guilt he's held at bay for many years now, he thinks about her *don't think about her* though he had met her only three times *don't think about her* she was no more than eighteen years old maybe nineteen, tiny, spritelike with long straight gold hair that hung almost to her waist. He never knew her name. Somewhere behind him he's sure there's a flyer for her as well, and tries to convince himself she's somewhere sitting staring at her flyer in the same strange, almost amused fascination with which, on this train, he stares at his. But he doesn't really believe it.

In China they would have found me by now. Even riding the train, some part of his brain can still hear the lake beyond the terrace of the Chateau X, just as he feels — from the Lair's hearth near where he sleeps — the heat of the fire that lights up the train car bright red. And then he hears it, the song he first heard that morning in the Square almost three decades before and only once since, hears it and is astonished she's singing it, his Mistress. It's the Mistress' voice and he wonders how she knows this song. He's trying to make out the words but recognizes the melody immediately, and as he listens a rivulet of red runs down the aisle of the train that he knows is menstrual blood, and forms a pattern.

In another chamber of her lair in the Chateau X that Wang has never seen, as he sleeps naked before the fire by the divan beneath the blanket with which she covered him, the dominatrix-oracle now studies the pattern on a parchment on the floor before her. As she tosses the soaked tampon into a nearby toilet and waits for the pattern to dry, she gazes for a moment at the pulsating full moon that the bathroom window so perfectly frames, then returns to the pattern and for a brief moment considers the thing that's crossed her mind that she doesn't want to consider, which is the recent ebb of her monthly flow: *Your childbearing years are numbered* rolls across her mind. Since

nd in the silvery bubble of the birth passage I feel myself caught up in the

she's had no thought of having another child, the pain of it might make no sense except that it has to do not with any child to come but the one to whom she said goodbye so long ago. The irrevocability of her body's recent monthly messages is more profound than she wants to interpret. In order not to think about it, she puts the disk that zen-toy brought her on the chamber's sound system. She already knows what she'll hear. Spacemonkey sign of the time, she murmurs to herself and turns back to the pattern of drying blood on the parchment, and lowers the lights and waits until the glow of the melody-snake's head rises from the black shadows of the floor.

On the train he sees it too. As her monthly blood forms its pattern in the aisle of the train and begins to dry, there beneath the car's dank light with midnight outside, the song he's been listening to in his Mistress' voice fades, desperate as he is to make it stay, and from the other end of the car he sees slither the luminous melody-snake along the lines of its lyric *humans are running, lavender room, hovering liquid, move over moon* into the menstrual red lattice; its tongue flickers. At this point in the climax's vision, Wang wants to flee. At this point he would forsake both love and heroism. The snake is drawn further into the pattern and becomes stuck in the blood, melody coiling and uncoiling *hovering liquid move over moon moveovermoon moveovermoonmoveovermoonmoveovermoon* struggling until it dies in awful exhaustion, tongue protruding limply from the slit of its mouth, as spent as Wang who shivers with sweat.

In his sleep he feels her tender hand on his brow. He feels a cool cloth across his face. A moment later he feels one of his wrists come free of the fur-lined handcuffs and his neck come free of the red-studded collar, and the blanket pulled up around him. He feels her take his other hand that's still cuffed; in his sleep he's vaguely aware of her running her finger over the rounded piece of

memory-stream of my own life and begin to drift in it, first returned to the

plexiglas that, almost thirty years ago now, a surgeon in the Chinese underground inserted to try and save the hand, threading the blood vessels through it even as he was unable to preserve tendon and muscle. Now in his sleep he feels the Mistress gently run her own fingers up and down the forearm that is distinctly thinner in comparison to the forearm of the other, good hand.

He opens his eyes.

She kneels beside him. The train is gone. He looks around, remembers he's lying on the floor of the Chateau X; she's blown out some of the candles so the Lair is darker than before. She kneels beside him no longer in garters or stockings but a black silk robe with a pattern of jade-tinted vines that wrap themselves around her. She helps lift him from the floor to the divan; naked he pulls the blanket closer to him, shuddering. She raises a cup of water to his mouth, then a glass of hot brandy. "Are you OK?" she says.

He nods. For a moment the two of them say nothing. She watches him but he can't quite look at her, feeling exposed and vulnerable as he always does after these sessions, until finally he says, "This time was especially. . . ."

"I know," she says. "You saw it, then?"

"Yes." He sits up, a bit revived, and she repeats the administration of water and brandy. Over on a low coffee table is the parchment she's brought in from the other chamber, now dry, a dark brown-red map with the death streak of the melody-snake, the echo of it just barely audible; she brings it to him. They study the menstrual I-Ching together. "Do you know the song?" he asks.

"New York punk-blues, apocalyptic subgenre," she says, "late 1970s. '79, '78."

"What's the 'lavender room'?" he asks.

"That's not the important part."

"The 'church chimes'?"

mall chinatown on the small island in the delta where I grew up, raised by my

Lulu reaches over, pulls the blanket away from off his shoulder and touches a small forming welt. "I struck you too hard."

"I didn't notice. Truly." He looks at her now. "You know I want you to hold back nothing."

When they look at each other like this, it's very difficult for her to believe he doesn't remember that time out at Port Justine, when he was working as a dock hand and secured her gondola. She had convinced herself that afternoon they connected in some way, particularly when, in a kind of paralysis, he watched as she climbed the billboard. At their first session more than a year ago she almost said something but didn't, since that kind of acknowledgement implicitly threatens an arrangement based on anonymity and discretion. As time passed, however, she understood that he doesn't remember her at all and it angered her, and she used and channeled that anger in her training of him: *This she thinks to herself, touching the welt is that anger. It's unprofessional she chastises herself. Anger is a betrayal of an implicit understanding of the relationship; it renders personal what's supposed to be impersonal, the objectivity of the relationship being that which both heightens the senses and clears the mind.* Yet at this point in their relationship it's difficult to maintain the impersonal; she pulls her fingers back from the wound, returning to the interpretation of the parchment. "Something is happening to the lake," she says.

"It's draining," he tells her.

He's surprised at the way the blood seems to run from her face. "What do you mean?" she says.

"I mean it's going back. Back wherever it came from."

"Here," she points to a small bright nexus on the parchment, where the last flicker of the melody-snake's tongue lapped its final drop of blood, "is the event vortex. I say 'event'

drunken uncle in the town tavern where I never knew my mother, the closes

but that doesn't necessarily mean an event in the sense of an occurrence, it may mean the revelation of something that's already existed a long time, that will manifest its existence in a way never perceived or comprehended before. Maybe something very obvious, something we've thought of in one form that in fact takes another. . . . " She shrugs. "This is vague, I know. . . . "

He's never heard her sound so. . . uncertain before. It unnerves him. "I have to take something back with me . . . something that can mean the difference between victory and defeat. . . ."

"You're not understanding, zen-toy," the Mistress says. *"This"* — pointing at the nexus — "renders your victories and defeats insignificant." Oh yes, Wang thinks to himself, that's what I'll tell them: whether we win or lose is insignificant. "You already know these answers, zen-toy. You already know these questions."

"What do you mean?" he says.

She studies him hard. His confusion sounds genuine, and she wonders if she's wrong in her suspicions; she gambles. "Who's broadcasting these messages?"

The question stuns him, given his own suspicions. Instantly and instinctively he analyzes the tone of it: is this a confession on her part? A challenge, a test? Is it just a moment of disingenuousness, when in fact this woman has always seemed anything but disingenuous? "You tell me," he replies, and the moment of truth collapses between them, each thinking the other has failed it.

Disappointed, she says, "Drink some more water," and raises the cup to him. Disappointed, he takes it and drinks. They don't say anything for a while. "When does your boat return?"

"I don't know. He may be there now."

ever came being one day when I was three years old and stood at the edge

"What do you tell them about why you come here?"

"I don't tell them anything. They don't know anything about you."

"They don't ask."

"They ask all the time. They wonder all the time. But it's part of my. . . mystique, I suppose, that I don't have to answer such questions."

"But they do know you come here."

"They don't know where I go. The boatman who brings me isn't one of them. One of the locals. . . . "

"That seems even more dangerous."

Wang stands up from the divan, a bit shaky, but steadies himself. "I've taken the liberty of offering him your hospitality, so that he might wait in the outer entryway."

"That would be OK."

"Thank you. He doesn't seem to want to anyway. It's very kind of you to leave him food and drink." Wang hesitates a moment. "I'll dress now." He staggers a bit toward the dressing room and turns; once he goes through this door, he's not to see her again until next time, so he says, "There was another song," still a little dazed.

"What?"

"Another song. Other than this one — " indicating the parchment with the blood. "It sounded like you were singing."

"You're surrounded by signs," she answers. "Ignore none of them."

He nods and enters the dark dressing room. He pulls on his clothes and coat, and exits the other door of the transitional chamber into the entryway, and then through the outer door into the bracing cool air that blows off the lake into the open Chateau grotto. Slowly he moves down the stone steps to find the boy with the boat waiting for him.

of the dock in a blue dress holding my uncle's hand, patiently watching th

For a while, on the way back, he's oblivious to everything: the night, the searchlights, the Chateau behind him, the bombs in the distance, the sound of the airlift, the boy in the boat — oblivious to everything including, he finally notices, how the glass hand that has no feeling still wears the fur-lined handcuffs she put on him, the other cuff dangling empty. Wang begins to think about what he's going to tell Tapshaw and the others; he wonders if she's becoming less certain of her interpretations or if the very notion of meaning approaches critical mass, beyond which is the void. He can't tell whether this evening undermines or reinforces a theory he's had for a while now. He's not exactly sure when he first formed this theory, although he remembers it was during one of their sessions near the end, when the white moment always seems to open up like an orifice.

If this theory is correct, that in fact she's the one who's transmitting the broadcasts, then it raises many questions, and so he's always been careful not to reveal too much. He's never actually explained to her who he is, although he knows she understands he's a man of "mystique" as he put it, of power and position, as are most of her clients who from time to time need to shed power and position and control. He's never told her of his past and she's never pried, which he's always taken to be part of her professionalism, a demonstration of her discretion and respect for his privacy; if anything, sometimes her lack of inquisitiveness gives him the feeling in fact there's nothing about him she doesn't already somehow know. He might even believe she knows him better than he knows himself, if one can live his life at odds with his own true nature. For a so-called rationalist he certainly has a lot of dreams and visions, not to mention the mystic menstrual prophecies of L.A.'s most famous bondage queen — so if she's the one broadcasting the messages, then for whom or what is she a medium? Between Wang and whom does she serve as translator

island ferry cross the river to a woman on the far other side who then didn't

and interpreter? And then suddenly out in that darkest part of the water, somewhere close to its source, he remembers how pale she went when he told her that Zed is dying, and gets it in his head that, as he is her slave for the few hours they spend together, she is the lake's.

For as long as they both have been here, Wang and the lake have lived in mutual denial, each barely acknowledging the other.

Once he might have supposed the lake could be a source of comfort to him, for the way it raised the latitude and shortened the longitude of everything: a tower becomes much smaller when half of it is underwater. The lake leveled everything for a man who never looks up, and in fact coincided neatly with his new fear since, not so long before he came to Los Angeles, back on the east coast he had been not a man afraid to look up but, to the contrary, a man who lived in the sky, riding floating boxes. Ironically, once it was the sky that offered him solace from ground-level — to be precise the ground level of city squares; ironically, once it was the ground he fled, until the day the sky betrayed him and came crashing down. When that happened he became a man caught in limbo between the sky and the ground, someone who lives looking only straight ahead in a state of hovering, for which a lake should have been perfect. But as both the mirror of the sky above and the window of the ground below, the lake became the worst of all: liquid ground, liquid sky: lake zero.

The lake is coming for me, he used to write in his letters to Kristin from the city's southern shore. The truth is he's never stopped thinking that. The truth is he thinks it even now, if he allows himself to. The lake is coming for me, to expose me for the fraud I am. There's a certain contradiction in his thinking about both the chaos he rejects and the higher order he believes is mathematically untenable: Is the lake God, he sometimes asks himself, is the lake chaos? He's never believed in God or chaos,

board the boat but rather shook her head, turned and vanished, something c

he thinks chaos is as religious a concept as God and that God is about as scientific as chaos — but sometimes he wonders. Sometimes he thinks that when he was a mathematics student his professors did their work better than he wants to believe, successfully having imprinted on his subconscious the conviction that everything is empirical after all. He always liked to think he departed from such teachings when, as a young rebel, he embraced the heresies of freedom and desire and redemption in their most truly heretical form, not as calculations of sociology or biology or some quantifiable philosophical value system but as entities unto themselves; but he's pushed from his mind, more times into the thousands than he can count, like he's pushed away every thought of the lake, every question of whether it's really possible to believe in freedom, desire or redemption if you don't believe in chaos or God — if not both, then one or the other. *The lake is coming for me.* He ignores it even as he's in the middle of it, even as his boat cuts through its water, the way one tries to ignore an old lover who's standing very conspicuously on the other side of a room just entered.

When his boat reaches the guerrilla encampment on the southern edge of the lake, Wang is surprised to note on the pylon of the dock, in the light of the full moon, the watermark of the lake from just a few hours ago when he disembarked for the Chateau. Clearly the lake has already gone down several inches. No sooner has Wang cleared the boat than the boy pushes off again, rowing back out with determination. Above him the moon erupts, a lava of light pouring from the white mouth of the cosmos' black volcano; no longer darting among the dark zones, the boy heads northwest in a straight line making remarkable time, until after a while he can see his hotel-island in the distance. He slows down as he nears the island, on his guard for marauders and pirates and stray cultists who still circle grounds they can't decide are holy or

hree-year-old could only find as baffling as it was devastating, after which I

haunted. The boy who now calls himself Kuul, a name half the language of childhood-memory and half the language of owl, has never believed the Hamblin either holy or haunted; he returned here a year ago only by some instinct he doesn't understand. Having seen the city and lake from any number of high vantage points over the course of his young life, he finds the perspective from the top of the Hamblin only a variation on that view. If it ever reminds him of when his mother brought him up here to the rooftop as a toddler, it's only for a moment more brief than his mind can grasp or wants to.

When he reaches the square brick island, he sidles the boat up to the top of what used to be the hotel's fire escape. He ties the boat and takes from it the basket of bread and fruit and cheese and wine left for him at the Chateau X. Luna completely lights up the Hamblin and he makes his way easily around the door that used to lead to the stairway inside the hotel, now completely submerged except for the top. Tucked away in an alcove formed by the rooftop door and an adjacent storage space that used to house all the hotel phone lines is an old silver gondola that stands upright like a small altar; propped up inside, resting against an assembled mass of old blankets, pillows and bits of old mattress, is a woman now somewhere in her early sixties but who seems much older. Once her eyes were older than her face but her face has caught up. Once her smile was younger but it's raced to the edge of death before the rest of her. The hair that Kuul's mother once saw as lost between the auburn of yesterday and the silver of tomorrow has long since found its way to a white amnesiascape.

Now the old woman's mind wanders its own rooms from one to the next. Kuul has no idea who this woman is. He found her here left behind on Hamblin Island following its abandonment by the Order of the Red, and for a year now has cared for her, protecting her from the rains and the wind off the lake and bringing

began to realize over the years that in my nights I never dreamed, no dream

her what food he can find. Round-luna has become a sign of bounty because he knows it means there will be a flare and he'll row the man with the hand to the Chateau and there will be a basket of food. As the boy tears off pieces of the bread and slowly feeds it to the old woman, he likes to pretend she's his mother and that he's nursing her to health. He knows she isn't his mother but she doesn't seem so very unlike who he imagines his mother might have been.

Touching it, slowly running his finger down its side, he knows this silver gondola was her boat. With his mother having slipped over the edge of this small altar and given herself to Big Agua for reasons he doesn't understand and that he only remembers in bits and fragments, it just seems fitting then that he might think of this woman who takes shelter in this gondola now as a kind of mother for whom he'll care. When he finishes feeding her the bread, he raises the wine to her mouth just enough so she won't drink too quickly, feeds her a bit of fruit and cheese and then some more wine, and when she's done and her eyes close to sleep, he lays his hand against the side of her face.

From her window on the top floor of the Chateau X, Lulu watches in the light of the full moon the boat with the two men make its way back across the lake.

She feels the blood of her womb stir to the moon's pull and backs away. *When I was pregnant sometimes at night I would*

t all until finally as a teenager dreamstarved I would prowl the small town

open the window and expose my belly to the moonlight but now thinking of her diminishing periods *I wonder if it cast a spell on me, laid some claim on what I carried inside me.* Among the moon, the sky, the lake, she doesn't know who are her allies anymore, who are her enemies. Gazing out the window, mindlessly she sings to herself an old song. *'Cause I know this sea wants to carry me.* She turns from the window back to her lair, and her heart stops.

Wrapped in the blanket that she pulled over him while he was unconscious, the man she knows as zen-toy stands naked at the other end of the room, at the door of the dressing room and the transitional passage that leads outside. "I heard another song," he says, "it sounded like you were singing."

"Uh. . . . " She tries to think what she said before. . . something about not ignoring the signs. "Yes," is all she can manage now, and then he turns and opens the door and disappears. She does notice this time, as she didn't when this same moment took place just a few minutes ago, that her fur-lined handcuffs still dangle from his wrist she forgot to set free.

She whirls around back to the window. She can still see the boat crossing the lake, with the figures of two men. She turns back to the dressing room door but no one is there. Her heart is thundering in her chest: *Have I just had an hallucination? Was it a ghost? Some strange synapse* in her mind by which something that just happened not fifteen minutes ago looped its way back into the present? She turns again to look at the boat from her window: is it a decoy, a trick, is this a plot to make her crazy. . . and if so, to what end? Now suddenly angry, purposefully she crosses the Lair to the dressing room door and flings it open to confront the ghost; but the room is empty. In two steps she's crossed to the door on the other side and out into the entryway, which is also empty.

and its tourist hotel after sundown because I heard somewhere that men hav

She crosses the entryway out onto the stone steps that lead down to the landing, but there's no one there either, the boat having already departed just as she witnessed minutes ago from her window upstairs.

She makes her way down the stone steps to the granite walkway that circles the hotel's grotto, to a small chamber she calls the Vault, its own door just a few feet above the lake and

unremarkable except for the large rusted brass ring of a doorknob.
On the walkway she stops, swallows hard. "Hello!" she calls
defiantly to someone lurking in the shadows; she takes one of the
lanterns that overhangs the steps and holds it up in front of her to
blast the shadows away. . . but no one's there. She looks at the
vault door and now makes her way to it along the narrow walkway
above the water. Still holding the lantern she futilely inspects the
brass ring as if there might be a telltale sign of someone's entrance;
she notices the glimmer at her feet of a melody-snake's glistening
residue. Casting the light of the lantern around her one more time,
she sees something else on the side of the stone steps leading down
to the landing: a fresh watermark, almost half a foot above the
lake's present level.

She throws open the vault door.

She shoves the lantern out in front of her into the dark of
the Vault. But the Vault is empty except for gleaming traces
across the floor of a nocturnal tune that's slithered away. Once
again she looks out on the landing to convince herself no one is
there, then turns and goes back into the Vault among its shelves of
disks from all the melody-snakes she's charmed and captured over
the years.

By now an archive of several thousand fills the Vault's
three small walls. Reading by lantern she finds in its place, where
it's been missing the past month, the plastic case with a spine
where long ago she printed **SPACEMONKEY**; damp, with drops of

rections when they dream and so I thought if I fucked enough of them in their

the lake smeared across its cover, clearly it's been returned just in
the past few hours, maybe the past few minutes. Months ago she
discovered the Vault was being raided and that every full moon,
after one of zen-toy's sessions, a disk was missing which, a full
moon later, would then reappear. To test her theory, last month
she pored over the collection to find exactly which one it would be
tonight; sometimes she thinks she can almost hear the broadcast

herself, south of the wind that comes down off the Hollywood moors. At best it's a distant sonic smudge in the air. If it's now obvious to her that zen-toy himself is behind the mysterious monthly broadcasts, she still doesn't understand why he would confiscate a disk, presumably on his previous visit, have it broadcast and then — replacing the original — bring a copy to her for the explanation and meaning of a song he himself chose. Was it a random selection, made by a man whom she knows in other matters is incapable of even considering the possibility of random chance? This conspiracy isn't just circular, it's labyrinthine. That it should have been this particular song only unnerves her all the more.

Now, the **SPACEMONKEY** disk having been returned tonight as expected, she pores over the archive again looking for an interruption in their order, for a slot where a disk should be but is missing, which will tell her what the next one will be on the next full moon. When she finds it, her heart stops for the second time in less than half an hour, and for a moment she wonders if, like when zen-toy reappeared in the door of the dressing room repeating the same words he had spoken upon his earlier departure only a few minutes before, the space where the song should be is a ghost.

Not that one.

She says it out loud, "No not that one," and begins looking at all the other disks that come right before and after, thinking it's just been misfiled. But it hasn't been misfiled, there's an empty

sleep I might take away with me a dream splashing in my womb, and yet whe

slot where it's supposed to be: *that* one; then she wonders if she herself took it and left it somewhere and has forgotten. She wonders if she discarded it unconsciously, in the same way she unconsciously was singing it to herself only half an hour before. She wonders if she cast it to the lake where, on breaking the surface, it turned back into a snake that quickly escaped to the water's lower depths where it came from. But she knows she hasn't discarded it. She remembers too well the decision she made to keep it in the first place, because at the time she couldn't bring herself to discard it as surely as she couldn't bring herself to hear it.

I'm stirred in a way I don't want to be. Inside I feel I'm not in control the way I'm supposed to be and now anger becomes a sense of betrayal: *he's supposed to submit to* me, *and now he's found a way to be master of events, master of my emotions.* She thinks of nine years ago out at Port Justine when he tied her gondola there, the almost arrogant, almost untouchable way he took her hand when she stepped out onto the floating dock. *This can't be coincidence that now, of all of them, this one is missing, particularly right after the last one.*

She has no idea at this moment that tonight she's far from finished with surprise and coincidence, if that's what it truly is, with the most shattering to come. Her sense of betrayal flares in part because she believes its indignation may protect her from feelings she thought sailed away in a silver gondola nine years ago. Betrayal propels her from the Vault out onto the granite walkway that leads around the crescent edge of the Chateau's grotto to the stone steps she climbs; in the entryway she closes the outer door behind her then enters the transitional dressing room that would lead her immediately to the Lair beyond if she wasn't at this moment stopped in her tracks by the sight, there on the rug at her feet, of the little red monkey she walked right past before.

still didn't dream then, not yet eighteen years old I finally left the small town

The sob bubbles up from her throat before she can swallow it. Although Kristin may have plucked it from the lake and left it in the gondola when she returned to the lake's source nine years ago, the incarnation of her called Lulu who was left behind and bid farewell to Kristin from the lakeshore that morning after the fire hasn't seen the monkey since the day fourteen years ago she left Kirk, in order to save him from being swept away by the breaking water of a pregnant malevolent century; she recognizes it instantly. She falls to her knees. Gently she picks up the toy as if it's a small body, and all promises are broken now, all bargains unmade: the bargain with God, with whom she made a pact somewhere in an abdicated future to give up her son if it meant sparing him some fate that hadn't yet come to pass; the bargain with the lake, who spared her from the flames of guilt that consumed her house if she would agree to live with the waves of guilt that flooded her past; and especially the bargain with her Other Self to whom she waved goodbye when she watched Kristin set out naked in the gondola to go back to the Other Lake. All these promises, all these bargains, made so she could live in some kind of truce and endure the only loss in human life that simply can't be endured, for all the ways one might find to go on functioning. Now her heart is broken again down to the bone of the soul. *The lake is dying, returning to where it came,* an irony too bitter to even be mere irony, since it means all of her efforts of years before to stop the lake were unnecessary and everything that effort cost her was pointless; she clutches the monkey to her as if it's *him*. She sees him before her with his sun-lit head and amber-flecked sea-green eyes and the sanguine mad-monk mouth, and pulls him to her and begs for another vision that will make her mad too, begs to be trapped in a mad vision of him and never sane again.

traveling for a while in the company of a millennial religious cult that

In his sleep, the dome of his eyelids is strewn with stars. Disoriented, he looks around for the Square, and a moment passes before he remembers.

No not here. Better the Square than here — but he *is* here, an immense rooftop spread out before him on top of the world, just inches beneath the night. A quadrant of the world lies in moonlight before him. He can see the curve of the earth in a white shimmering arc against the black of space. It's a dream he never has because he's struck a deal with his subconscious to never raise this memory although, now that he thinks of it, he wonders what his end of the bargain was ever supposed to be. Nonetheless this is his unconsciousness' betrayal: *better the Square.* In the dream he looks not for Kristin but a young woman he met only three times and who he's put out of his mind ever since one dazed night years ago back east: The Emperor of Elevators, he murmurs in his sleep, feeling the tail-end of a familiar gust blowing from a vent in a low rectangular storage hut near the rooftop's edge. He wonders if this gust is an ally meaning to rescue him, or a weapon of the State meaning to remove him, before he remembers it's an anarchist without conviction.

In his dream he crosses the building rooftop to the vent and looks deep into it. Mistress my Mistress, he whispers and hears the song and feels the gust of the Oblivion Wind in his face; and when he pulls his face away, the vent has become the gun barrel of the

earned in the nick of time meant to sacrifice me on New Year's Eve, then to

tank and he's back in the Square with the tanks rolling toward him like great eggs. He looks up and the sky is bloody red again; standing his ground, the gust dies. The tank tries to go around him, he moves to block it, and when the tank moves again so would he, to block it again, if he weren't transfixed by the song. From out of the corner of his eye, he sees a blinding flash of something and raises his hand to shield his eyes, and a moment later he's aware of the hot pain in his hand, his hand burning, the small explosion in the palm where one's fortune is told. He looks up at his hand quizzically to see a bit of red wedged in the middle, and thinking at first it's blood, he realizes he's seeing through the new hole a spot of the red sky beyond.

He hears the song, the gust rises again, and she appears at the far end of the Square that's otherwise empty but for him and the tanks, a figure walking across the Square toward him. The Mistress isn't dressed in her stockings and heels but in her black silk robe, vines the color of jade climbing up her body and binding her. When she reaches Wang, she holds a cool cloth in her hand and mops his brow.

She gently lays the other healing hand on the welt on his shoulder that she left earlier that evening with her riding crop. It's all right, he says in the dream, I don't want you to hold anything back. But. . . .

But? she says.

San Francisco with a pair of psychotic lesbian lovers I learned in the nick

But what do the broadcasts mean? he says.

What? she asks, confused.

Why do you do it? Why the broadcasts? What are they for?

Why do *I* do it? she says. I thought it was you.

Me?

Yes.
You thought it was me?
Yes.
He shakes his head. It's not you?
No.
Then. . . ? as Wang wakes suddenly in his quarters, lying on his cot in the dark. Opens his eyes, knowing that in just seconds there will be a pounding on the door.

He fumbles for the lamp on the nearby desk. Sitting on the edge of the cot he holds his face in his hands and waits; barely before the first knock has finished he says, "Come in," and there's a hesitant moment before the soldier enters.

"Sir?"
"Yes, Parsons."
The soldier is disconcerted. "Uh, yes, sir," he finally says, "that's correct, sir."
"What?"
"That's my name, sir."
"I know it's your name."
"Sir?"
"You told me earlier this evening."
"Uh, with your permission, sir."
"Yes?"
"That couldn't have been me. Sir."
"Parsons. . . " Wang says.

me meant to murder me in my sleep, finally arriving in Los Angeles where

"I mean, we've never spoken, sir."
"I want you to find something to get this off." Wang holds up his hand.

The young soldier is flummoxed, first by the glass in Wang's hand and then the Mistress' fur-lined cuff that still dangles from his wrist. "Sir. We'll get someone to file it off."
"I don't want to file it off. Find a master key of some sort."

"Yes, sir."

Wang stares straight ahead of him in the dark. "Who put that up?" he says after a moment, quietly.

"Sir?"

On the wall in front of him, where there was a blank space when he went to sleep after returning from the Chateau X, looms the inevitable image. "I said," Wang can barely spit it out between his teeth, "who put that up. Who came into my own quarters while I was sleeping and put that back up."

"Sir?"

"Did you put that up?" He's barely raising his voice.

"Me, sir?"

Wang slowly rises from the cot. "Parsons." He's so silently furious he can't quite think what to say. "Take it down," he finally tells the soldier.

"The men draw inspiration from it, sir."

"If I see it up there again, I'll have you arrested for insubordination," although he doesn't really have the authority to do that.

"Sir?" Parsons says, and a couple of miles away, out in the western darkness of the lake on the hotel-island called Hamblin, Kuul listens to a song and begins to cry. Having pulled a blanket up around the sleeping old woman and eaten some of the bread and cheese and fruit from the Chateau X, having made his way in the light of the full moon around to the storage space that holds all the

after a week of living and sleeping on the streets from Hollywood to Centur

hotel's long dead phone and power lines, as well as an old sound system the Order of the Red left behind with everything else, he's pulled a disk from his shirt, flipped off the switch to the outside speakers, and put the disk in the carrier tray.

When he presses the play button, he begins to cry and doesn't know why. But since he was a small child, music has been the sound of freedom and desertion, and although he's barely conscious of remembering this particular song, inside him it opens up a door — *if there's a higher light, let it shine on me* — that closes again before he can go through. As when he chose this song from the Chateau's archives in the first place, for reasons as mysterious to him as most choices, fingers just running along the walls of the Vault until they stopped, he hears music in silence like an owl sees in the dark; it's an instinct that's become a little more than human by now; too human for him to understand is the instinct that makes him cry now when he hears this song: *'Cause I know this sea wants to carry me / in a sweet sweet sound she sings / for my release.* He can almost hear her singing it somewhere that feels close but also like another life, a life that feels at once gone forever and at the same time just beyond the bend of the lake or maybe on the next lake over, wherever such a lake might be. Although he can barely remember her, the sound of this song makes him wrack his brain to try and figure out, as he's tried before, what he did when he was three that was so terrible it would make her leave him.

He sits slumped against the wall until it finishes. He doesn't think he can listen to it again. He knows there will be no more broadcasts, which were an accident in the first place when he discovered the sound system on the island a year before and was half way through playing something when he realized the speakers outside were on too, blaring so loudly everyone within two or three miles could hear. After that the music just became

ity to Baghdadville on the beach I responded to a personals ad from a

part of a full-moon ritual that has no particular meaning at all, at least none he knows of. He rises from the floor where he's been sitting and walks out onto the Hamblin rooftop and takes solace in the moon that floats at the end of a chain of utterly random events like a balloon at the end of a string; like letting go of a balloon, he would like to watch the moon float away for nothing but the sake of watching it float away. He hears the bombs and fly-overs in the distance and wakes the next morning with the song he doesn't want to listen to anymore still in his head, and the sky a brilliant blue, more and more rare in the Age of the Lake. Sitting up in her gondola as though it's a chariot is the old woman. She actually has a small smile on her lips as though she's expecting something to happen. Off to the edge of the Hamblin, Kuul pulls up from out of the cold lake a bottle of milk tied to some twine, and as he's pulling up the bottle he's struck by the wet trail of the water down the hotel wall: sometime in the night, the lake fell.

He's thinking about this and still hearing the song in his head while he brings the milk over to the woman and pours her a cup. She's still smiling and he smiles back at her but the song is still in his head and soon he can't resist anymore, and he goes back into the little makeshift broadcasting booth and stares at the disk player awhile before submitting to the impulse. He doublechecks to make sure the outside speakers are off

then, reconsidering — he lets go of the chain, up behind the blue sky the moon begins to rise — flicks the speakers back on, and turns up the volume.

Hesitating again, he presses the play button.

It doesn't start anything like he remembers from last night. Does it start like this? he wonders when the vocal begins

"Humans are running, lavender room. . . "

No . . . .

"Hovering liquid, move over moon. . . " No, that's not

middle-age man who had been abandoned by his pregnant Asian wife and wa

right. "For my spacemonkey. . . . " He stops the disk then presses the play button again, as if that will correct the error, then stops it again. He ejects the disk. He picks it up and looks at it, turns it over as if that will reveal an answer, turns it over and over and over and over. He puts it back in the player and plays it again, then stops and ejects it again.

He feels something so unknown to him that he's incapable of identifying it as emotional panic. He gazes around for the right disk but he knows better, he knows there is no other disk, that this is the disk he played last night and left in the player. He also knows that the song he's hearing now is the one he returned to the Vault last night when his passenger with the hand was inside the Chateau, and that yesterday's song has somehow replaced last night's, and that this is difficult to understand even for a boy who has an owl's sight for invisible music. In the tower of the Chateau X to the north, wearing her silk robe, she stops brewing her tea and cocks her head; she's been up all night crying and drinking, sitting at her divan before the dying fire, staring at the red monkey perched above the hearth, and now, almost beyond the capacity for confusion, she hears it. She goes to the window and stares out over the lake to the south. On a clear blue day when there's no wind off the hills to separate the music from her, she can hear it. She thinks to go back down to the Vault and doublecheck whether the song she found returned to the archive last night is still there. But she doesn't.

In a water-craft a couple of miles to the east, speeding toward Hamblin Island, Tapshaw says to Wang, "Do you hear that?"

Over the roar of the boat, the song is almost indistinguishable. It may be, as Wang tries to reason, amid the vertigo that buffets him now on the watery sky of the lake

oking for a pleasure-slave although he wouldn't put it in that fashion, and as

spanning out all around him, that this is his mind playing another trick on him; but sometime in the last twelve hours he's come to realize that because something is a trick of the mind doesn't mean it's not real. That the real of the remembered is no less profound than the real of the perceived. This morning, when Tapshaw asked him what Wang found out in the mysterious hours that have lately come to accompany full moons and mysterious songs, thinking a moment Wang answered, "We're surrounded by signs, ignore none of them." Now he looks at the Hamblin in the distance and his ears and mind try to filter out the sound of the boat for the sound of the song, but then he doesn't hear it anymore and isn't altogether certain he did in the first place. As well, however, he isn't altogether certain he didn't.

Kuul sees the approaching boat far away. Quickly he gathers together the old woman in order to put her in the rowboat, but intuitively rethinks this and decides instead on the gondola. Maybe he just can't imagine leaving the gondola behind. Maybe the old woman can't imagine it either. As he carefully helps her down into the gondola from the top of the hotel fire escape, he sees she's still smiling as when she woke, having known as she did sometime in the night that they would be taking this journey. Actually she's already taking it. Actually, in her mind Doc is on it now, at this moment, and has been on it for some time; making her a bed in the bottom of the gondola and laying her there as comfortably as he can, with the pole Kuul pushes them off from the island and around its corner, heading northeast toward the lake's source. Gleaming glass-white in the sunlight, the boat might almost be seen from a castle tower or, high above, a daylocked owl frantically in search of the night that's set sail without him.

In her mind, Doc has been on this journey a long time. The exact hour of its beginning is nameless but certainly she's been riding this silver gondola since that afternoon years before when

I was at the end of my rope I went to live with him in his house in th

Kristin sailed her out to a hotel not far from the Hamblin to read its walls and diagnose its mysteries. In the world outside Doc's mind it's been thirteen years but on this particular journey that sort of measure of time is meaningless and besides, the lake is drowning in itself, going back down its drain, and memory is moving backwards. Consumptive houses, malaria houses, alzheimer houses, heart-attack houses, houses with tumors growing out the

attic or the bedroom windows or the family rooms. . . Doc knew
them all once, healed them all or consoled them when they
couldn't be healed, back when she was in the business of being
strong, back when she was in the business of being indomitable. In
a city congenitally incapable of a tragic sense, she was the ultimate
citizen: she had come to Los Angeles expressly to leave all sense
of tragedy behind. In her new scheme of things she had made sure
there was no such thing as tragedy anymore, there were only life's
processes and passages, in which loss was only another fact.

She had never before diagnosed a house or room or building
dying of sorrow. Dying not of physical dissolution or even a
fatigue of body and spirit as triggered by sorrow, but of sorrow
itself. She had made herself believe sorrow beyond its logical
self-exhaustion was an illusion, a collapse of fortitude on the part
of the afflicted, a failure to surmount. This changed the afternoon
Kristin sailed her out to the flooded hotel, where the two of them
wandered through the abandoned apartment with its books and
animé posters and the same famous photo on the wall that Kristin

1ollywood Hills according to the terms of the agreement always nude which I

had on hers.
　　　There in the walls Doc heard the song of the sorrow that
can't be surmounted or endured, the sorrow that life's processes
can't process, that its passages can't pass away. She's been in the
gondola ever since. She lies in the bottom staring at the black sea
of the sky rolling by overhead, white waves of clouds; fleeing —

for the second time in her life — sorrow's song, she escaped the hotel in the silver gondola but then, in the years after, couldn't escape the gondola itself. Unable to escape the gondola itself, sometime in the night that began thirteen years ago or a thousand, she set sail back to the sorrow because she needs to face it again before she herself passes away, although why and what she'll do when she finds it she has no idea. It isn't a matter of conquering anything. She now knows this sorrow is beyond conquest. She's reconciled herself to her tragic sense she thought she left behind when she came to Los Angeles; it isn't a matter of understanding anything; the whole point of this sorrow is how its song is beyond human understanding. The whole point is how pretending to understand is conceit, presumption, hubris that calls itself insight.

So there's no human or rational reason for Doc to face this sorrow again, but she has to or feel her existence will have been one of cowardice, stupidity, cruelty that calls itself compassion. As she lies in the bottom of the gondola in the night of her mind, with the cool night breeze blowing in her face, the lake is much bigger, a vast ocean aswirl, because even here in her mind the lake is going down its drain. For a long time the young man who takes care of her has been rowing them toward the center of a black whirlpool, having left his owls far behind on land. He has amber green eyes and once light hair that's darkened with adolescence; he doesn't really look much like his mother. As they near the whirlpool they feel the churning of the black water broken by

didn't care about even if the world's never been as casual about my nakednes

white foam. Bubbles rise at the center of the whirlpool — and finally the gondola's passengers feel themselves caught in the current of the vortex and begin the long journey down to the whirlpool's center.

Pulling in the oars, gripping the sides of the boat, the boy guides them down the whirlstream as the sunken city of Los Angeles flows by behind the dark-glass curtains of the lake that rise around them — sunken palm trees and boulevards until, in the distance, at the center of the whirlpool she sees the Hotel of the Thirteen Losses. It's nothing like the hotels she's seen before in L.A., nothing like the one she visited with Lulu, it's much bigger, extending as far as she can see with glistening ebony walls, huge deserted atriums, grand forsaken lobbies; it looms larger as the gondola speeds through the big open doors

into the foyer,
up cascading
stairways and
down the long
blue corridors
into the first
room which is

the Room of the Lost Home. This is an unostentatious room. It's plain, almost barren except for purely functional furniture; but as the silver gondola slowly glides through, Doc and the boy will note — as they'll note with the twelve other rooms to come — how from different perspectives the room takes on a different appearance. In the natural course of things, loss of home is the easiest to bear, particularly if it's the voluntary loss that comes with growing up. Only from the far corner of the room

s I, wandering nakedly aimlessly up and down the stairs of the house that was

does the room's loneliness give way to desolation and then terror, not only the walls and beams of the room but all light and warmth falling away, when the loss is an act of catastrophe or when the room suddenly opens up into the
adjoining
room that

is the Room of Lost Livelihood. This includes a small sitting room of Lost Fortune, not as impressive as the Room of Lost Livelihood that's more spacious because it must encompass the loss of not only past fortune but prospective fortune as well. The sitting room of Lost Fortune, however, does have a nice big window for jumping purposes. The Room of Lost Livelihood is plush with overstuffed sofas and high-armed chairs to remind those who pass through of a graciousness of living they'll never attain. From the gondola Doc notes, however, that there's nothing practical about this room, there aren't even bare necessities, just promises that shimmer enticingly before disappearing, like the vanishing walls and light and warmth of the Room of the Lost Home.

These are the first and last rooms that will manifest themselves so materially, as is this corridor down which the gondola now sails. As terrible as

stacked against the hillside, smelling through the open windows the nearb

these rooms can be, their dim e n s i ons remain very concrete; from here on, the rooms into

which   Doc
and   the   boy
sail   in   their
gondola   have
no truly fixed
di m e n sions.
Their terror is,
in   varying
degrees,   as
profound as it
sometimes   is
illusory.   The
most   shape-
changing of all
is the Room of Lost Love. Here in the Hotel of
Thirteen Losses this is the most chameleon of
rooms. It reflects more the nature of the guest
passing through than the nature of the loss itself,
because this loss has no true nature of its own. This
room is a bombardment of hallucinations, which
isn't to say the hallucinations aren't truly
devastating, because they're revelations of the self,
a rave of the id: when Doc first sails into this room
it's nothing but a massive fireplace, with a roaring
fire; suddenly the fire is gone and the hearth

ucalyptus and smoke, standing for hours in the large windows overlooking a

becomes the cold slab of a grave. The Room of
Lost Love is never stationary. It isn't to be found in
any one permanent location of the hotel; it moves
from floor to floor, from the beginning of one
hallway to the end of another, from the penthouse to
the basement. As the gondola sails through, the
room may tend to settle, its mercurial torments

exhausted; when one has sailed far and deep enough
into the room's recesses, it may lose all
ephemerality and transform to a different space
altogether that's both the same room but a different
room, which is the Room of the Lost Mate, utterly
uninhabitable for some and a way station of sorts
for others. As the gondola leaves the Room of Lost
Love, it remains to be seen whether it will sail out
the same door it sailed in or an altogether different
exit. Something melancholy grips Doc on her
voyage through this room, and she realizes that this
is the only loss that someone might envy if she's
never known it; there is, then, perfectly contained
within the Room of Lost Love another room with
no walls at all that's the Room of the Loss of Lost
Love — the loss of never having had the experience
of losing love. Leaving the Room of Lost Love,
Doc's gondola
sails   into   a
huge ballroom
or, in fact, three ballrooms that are conjoined as one. These are
the Ballroom of Lost Faith, the Ballroom of Lost Dignity and
the Ballroom of the Lost Soul. It would be difficult to tell where
one finishes and one starts; the conjoined ballrooms are mirrored
from one end to the other and the chandeliers that hang from

strange city I didn't know and the panorama of strange little houses an

the ballroom ceiling glitter not only in the mirrors and the mirrors'
reflections of each other but off the water and off Doc's
silver gondola, so that the cumulative light is blinding.
Thus all perceptions are refracted, dazzled, suspect. What seems
to be lost faith may be a failure of will or nerve. What seems
to be lost dignity may be wounded pride or ego.   And at the
far end of the ballroom, where tides flow in from all other rooms

of the hotel and collide, and it's all the boy can do to right the gondola's course, it's often impossible to know which transgressions of behavior, integrity and conscience will drag the soul down into the undertow of the irredeemable.

So from out of the Three Ball rooms, Doc's silver gondola is drawn into two small, tran si tion al rooms linked together that, from here, provide the only passage on to the rest of the hotel. The first transitional room is the Room of Lost Youth and the second is the Room of the Lost Parent. Because both are rooms in which the traveler learns her earliest,

trange little trees and strange little cars driving up strange winding streetlit

most significant lessons in mortality, at first they appear to Doc to be the same. In both, all the furniture has been covered with sheets as on moving day — but the sheets are black rather than white, and gauzy and transparent, so the outline of the furniture beneath them can always be seen. There are two differences between the rooms: in the Room of Lost Youth there's a crack in the corner of one wall through which a gale blows, disheveling the sheets on the furniture so that sometimes the Room of Lost Youth might take the form of the Room of Lost Health, for instance, or the Room of Lost Promise — which is to say one might enter the Room of Lost Youth early in life or late, age isn't a factor, no one checks for identification at the door. It's the same with the Room of the Lost Parent, which may also be either one of the first or last rooms in

roads that seemed to drop off in midair, not finding it so disconcerting, even

the hotel one passes through; it's even possible to be born in the Room of the Lost Parent. The other difference between the two rooms is that in the Room of Lost Youth, a pillar stands in the center from floor to ceiling, while in

the Room of the Lost Parent
the pillar is gone, although its
shadow remains both night
and day cast by no apparent
light across the length of
the room and always leaving
the exit on the other side
in darkness. But there is
a navigable exit, after all;
a guest adjusts to her stay in
these rooms and sooner or
later leaves, the losses
endured if always felt.
Having sailed through these transitional rooms, then Doc's
gondola emerges in the hotel's lavish mezzanine. All this time,
sailing through the Hotel of Thirteen Losses, Doc and the boy
navigating the boat have followed a very distant melody made only
more obscure by the oceanic symphony that plays it. Doc
recognizes it. Even faint as it is she can barely stand to hear it
again, even as she knows that it's for this melody she's come here.
Now in the hotel's lavish mezzanine the song is louder; other than
a single small door at the far end of the mezzanine that leads to
either some sort of closet or pantry, before the gondola are three
sets of double-doors to three separate suites and Doc knows it's
from one of these suites the song comes. She knows she's closer

nding it reassuring, even finding I felt profoundly secure to spend my

now to the end of her search. She knows that behind one
of these three double-doors is the suite of the most unendurable
loss of all, the loss she felt that day with Kristin in
the other woman's apartment. She assumes such a room and
such a loss must be at once splendid and terrible. They sail
through the first set of double doors

into the Suite of Lost Freedom. She might expect this suite to look like a dungeon, chains hanging from the walls, shackles close to the floor, mechanisms of torture in place of a bed or chair. She would expect no windows. In fact the suite is well-appointed. It's comfortable. It's secure: the lock is on the inside of the doors, not outside. The Suite of Lost Freedom has a huge bed and love seat, and a window opens from an alcove through which blows a fresh breeze. A grand light fixture hangs from the ceiling which makes the room very bright, even happy. It not only doesn't seem such a terrible room, it's an inviting room. There's maid service, room service. Someone could very well choose to live here, particularly with someone else; behind the bed there's a secret panel although it must not be very secret if Doc knows it's there, and from the Suite of Lost Freedom to the Room of Lost Love there's a secret passage; many of the hotel's guests spend a lot of time wandering back and forth in this passage. In fact the room is filled with secret panels and secret passages to other rooms of loss, to which this suite seems eminently preferable. It isn't until Doc and the boy sit floating in the gondola for some time that she notices something: the walls are closing in. Almost imperceptibly the suite is growing

existence entirely within the walls of a space I never saw from the outside

smaller. Then she notices something else: the light above is growing dimmer. Almost imperceptibly the room grows darker. In the early moments of the suite becoming smaller and darker, the guest still has the capacity, with a word and the will, to stop the walls, to turn back up the light, if that's what she wants to do. It's almost impossible to say at exactly what point this

suite goes from being a room where one would choose
to live to a room that one must escape at all cost; and
to that end, even when the room has become very
small and dark, the far window still glows slightly, so
that even as the walls become so close as to crush
anyone between them, the possibility of escape,
however increasingly difficult, remains, and may even
become a distant promise that gives life a meaning it
never had before. For all these reasons, because there
are times when the Suite of Lost Freedom is
hospitable, even apparently civilized, where one's stay
is content, even apparently fulfilling, and because even
when the suite is at its least human, when one is
desperately trying to hold back the walls with her
hands, there's still a faint hope of escape, and it seems
clear to Doc that this isn't the most unendurable of
losses, that it can be not only endured in its
smallest measure but reversed at its greatest extreme,
that it's a loss that can bring out the best and noblest
and most inspiring in people, even to the point
where they would choose over the Suite of Lost
Freedom the very next suite over, to which Doc's
gondola now
sails, back out
into the great mezzanine and then slowly and with more difficulty

xisting as a kind of erotic furniture, of which I took a functional view having

through the next set of double-doors
into the Suite of Lost Life. Well, Doc thinks to herself,
certainly this has to be the most unendurable loss; what
loss could be greater than the loss of one's life? Isn't,
she thinks to herself, every other loss in life measured
against this one? Isn't every other loss ultimately
endured in order to avoid this one? The gondola sails

into the middle of the Suite of Lost Life — which
suddenly vanishes: the walls, the ceiling, the floors all
gone in the blink of an eye, leaving the gondola
suspended in a void of black. Then the suite suddenly
reappears, as a rounded blue chamber. Of all the suites
this is the most capricious in form and nature; and as
with the Suite of Lost Freedom and its secret passage
to the Room of Lost Love, populated by nomads
wandering between the two, the Suite of Lost Life is
riddled with secret passages to other rooms in the hotel
such as the Ballroom of Lost Faith or the Ballroom of
the Lost Soul, all with their own wandering exiles.
Whereas Doc could feel in the other rooms the
presence of hurt, walls faintly throbbing with pain,
here in the Suite of Lost Life there's nothing to be felt
at all except, when the suite assumes the incarnation of
the blue chamber, a kind of peace. And Doc realizes
that in fact the loss of one's life isn't the most
unendurable of losses, that in fact whether life's end is
a blue chamber or black void, there's nothing to be
endured at all — that in some ways this suite shouldn't
even be in the Hotel of Thirteen Losses, that the loss
of one's life is really endured by others, who are
guests of the hotel in other rooms, such as the Room
of the Lost Parent or the Room of the Lost Mate.

already decided in those young years of mine that life was a matter of tradin

So this then leaves to Doc and her pursuit of the
unendurable loss only one remaining possibility,
and that's the final suite next to this one;
and so the
silver gondola
sails back out into the grand mezzanine toward the final set of
double-doors. Doc braces herself. Lying in the bottom of the

gondola, remembering that afternoon in the apartment of the other
hotel with Kristin, she becomes afraid as the boy rows them
through the last set of double-doors

into a suite of nothing but doors, each with a mirror,
much like the mirrors of the Three Ballrooms, except
that, as the gondola passes, each mirror loses its
reflection and turns into a window, with strange faces
on the other side peering in. This is the Suite of Lost
Memory. Beyond the doors with the mirrors that turn
into windows are corridors that run to every single
other room in the hotel, because the Suite of Lost
Memory may also be the Suite of the Lost Self,
although that remains to be known. It's uncertain,
what with corridors running to the Ballroom of Lost
Dignity or the Suite of Lost Freedom, what constitutes
the self, and what of the self still exists when
self-consciousness is gone. This is why the Suite of
Lost Memory and the Ballroom of the Lost Soul aren't
the same room although they might seem the same to
those outside the windows gazing in. And it's partly
because of this unanswerable mystery that Doc, braced
for the great wave of anguish she expected from this
final suite, realizes this isn't the most unendurable loss
either, that it's a kind of death, in some ways more
profound than the body's death, and as a kind of death

n one's most valuable commodity whether it be intelligence, strength, talent,

it's something to be endured not by the one who has
lost her memory but by those around her who watch
her recede into life's horizon in the gondola of
amnesia. Now Doc is perplexed. Lying in the bottom
of the gondola adrift in this last suite, having taken this
long voyage on the lake of her mind down to the Hotel
of Thirteen Losses at the bottom of the whirlpool so as

to face what she couldn't face all those years before, she tries to remember all the suites and all the ballrooms and all the guest rooms and sitting rooms she's been through but can't, and then realizes of course she can't remember because, after all, she's in the Suite of Lost. . . well, now she can't even remember what suite she's in, but she still has enough presence of mind to lift her arm and point the way out. For a moment the boy can't remember the way, but circling the windowed doors around the perimeter of the room he finally finds the exit and rows them out of. . .

now it comes

back to her, the Suite of Lost Memory, yes. . . and out into the mezzanine, bobbing above its flooded marble floors in the whirlpool's current, where it all comes back to her and she counts the losses to herself: home, fortune, livelihood, love, faith, dignity, the soul, health, parent, freedom, life, memory. . . that's twelve. Feebly she holds up her fingers and counts them again, and wonders where in their voyage they missed a room. Bobbing there in the water, puzzled she can hear the song clearly, the song that was coming from none of the three suites, and lies there listening — "Can you hear it?" she cries out to the boy — when the boy picks up the oars and begins to row, and rows them to the far end of the mezzanine and the small single pantry door, or perhaps it's a

charisma or beauty, and so in order to survive I traded on my nakedness an

simple door to a janitor's closet, that earlier they not so much ignored as dismissed. And as they grow closer to the door, the song becomes louder. As they reach the plain unadorned door it's so distinct now it frightens her, and she's about to cry out to the boy and tell him to stop when he takes the door knob in his hand and opens it. Out of it roars a music that's more than pain, more than anguish, more than desolation, more than sorrow, more than grief. Out of it roars the greatest of all losses, the loss that can't be endured. It's not a loss that one truly survives let alone surmounts, it's not a loss that one out-exists let alone outlives; it's the loss that breaks your heart and it never mends. It never mends. It calls into question everything, so that it entails in some way all the other losses: home is lost; fortune and livelihood have no more meaning; love not only has no more meaning but becomes a kind of emotional treason; faith becomes a kind of spiritual treason; dignity becomes a joke; the soul is forever in the terminal grip of a psychic cancer; health is an affront; the loss of a parent is the perverse twin of this loss, like the reflection in the mirror of a funhouse; freedom is a curse; life is torture. Memory is worst of all. From the doorway of this tiny closet or pantry one would almost gladly flee, if possible, to the Suite of Lost Memory or, failing to reach that, perhaps even the Suite of Lost Life. This is the Unendurable Loss because it involves the one thing that one loves more than one's own life; and no meaning that one strives to give her own life, however great or good, can ever truly compensate for what's been lost, will ever be truly convincing in any scheme of things that in the heart of hearts one believes. This loss is the essence of the universe's impossibility, it's the one thing for which a benevolent God never has a persuasive answer, and which a malevolent God holds over the head of humanity. Although she wants the boy to row far away from this door as fast as he can, in the wave of music that roars out of the tiny closet

is needs, which bound him more than they bound me, particularly since many

Doc, weeping, takes hold of the sides of the gondola and summons all her strength and courage to rise from the bottom so she can look inside and face it at last. Inside the closet is nothing but a hole, the birth canal down through which rushes the lake back to wherever it came, and inside this hole Doc sees a vision of a young Asian boy maybe ten or twelve years old, unknown to her, growing up among his animé posters in the apartment Doc visited with

Kristin that one afternoon thirteen years ago, suddenly swept under by the lake and reaching for a hand too far from him, and Doc can hear the mother crying for him frantic, disbelieving, but the boy descends; and out of the hole in his place Doc sees rise the Unendurable Loss like a bubble of black air

this

is the

l o s s   o f

o n e ' s

child

At some point past Coldwater Canyon, gliding westward into the lengthening shadows of the hills, Kuul looks down at her lying in the bottom of the gondola and knows she's gone.

He's never seen death in a person before, only in owls, but the stillness is the same; it's not like sleep. The small smile she had on her face for a moment isn't there anymore. The cheeks of her face are wet — from the lake, he supposes; or some

times he was really too drunk to do anything anyway except lie in the throes of

astonishing dream maybe? He's close enough to shore that now he uses the pole to push the boat into the mist off Beverly Glen, trying to think what he'll do with her. Don't people put their dead in the ground? Or do they burn them? Do they eat them? But he has nothing with which to dig out the ground except his hands, or to start a fire, which doesn't seem a good idea anyway, and the owls leave their dead where they die, which seems more sensible than anything else. So beaching the gondola on the banks of the glen, he steps out into the mud and turns and pushes the silver boat with the old woman's body back into the water and watches it disappear back into the mist, floating back out into the western part of the lake where it will eventually become caught in the current that leads to the sea.

Except now, of course, he has no boat anymore. He'll have to get another. He looks around him at the trees and the rising hillside throttled with fog, and calls to the owls for direction. When he receives no answer, he calls again. He still receives no answer and, in his head, divides the number of shadows by the minutes of twilight, arriving for the first time in his life at the sum of zero. He begins to make his way up the hillside. For an hour as he makes his way up the hillside he calls again and again to the owls, and again and again receives no answer until he finally understands that, having crossed the experiential threshold of human death, he's now on his own.

is terrible headaches muttering his wife's name and dreaming of his unborn daughter as I rubbed his head for him, the two of us almost never conversing

2028

all except when I would whisper in his ear as he slept how ridiculous he was, how absurd he was, what with slavegirls having gone out with th

These are the memoirs of Lulu Blu, otherwise known as Mistress Lulu, the Dominatrix-Oracle of the Lake, Queen of the Zed Night, once called Kristin.

I still live in the tower of the Chateau X, I've been here almost seventeen years. I never leave anymore. Minions bring food and wine, leave it on the stone steps that disappear into the water. . . sometimes a client-submissive pays in supplies rather than cash, which doesn't count for much these days. I'm in retirement. Once my subjects numbered in the scores but now Brontë brings in the business. . . . After the Unrest moved north ten years ago and as I got older, my services as both Domme and seer

wentieth Century, and I went on living there with him then until he simply

were in less demand, except for the occasional businessman who flew in from Bangkok, Tokyo, New Delhi, but now they come for Brontë who takes them into the dungeon downstairs where I hear the wet echo of the lashing up through the vents. *Not too hard now girl* I think to myself when she lets loose a particularly sharp crack of the whip.

She's a natural.

She's a natural but you might ask, What kind of life is this for a mother to give a girl? Has my own life become such I can connect even to the people I care about only through the means and devices of domination? Dark falls as I write this, sitting by the terrace just inside the walls. . . a week ago the moon was full but tonight with the fog everything is black, none of the lake's usual lights. . . . Ever since the water level finally dropped enough to expose the rooftops of the old Strip's long-sunken shops and clubs, night-torches have burned from them forming a winding watery corridor — but there are no torches tonight, no glow or its accompanying music from the lunatiques in the canyons just over the near north hills. . . . Lately for the first time I can remember, waves have been crashing the Chateau's sides, I don't remember when it began, the crashing of waves sometime in the past months, I just woke one night to the lake pounding the Chateau and at first I thought it was an earthquake, or explosion. Waves have been crashing like an ocean shoreline, the lake has become an angry sea, furious at something and I believe it's me. Is this fury the despair of old age, rage of midlife, the cynicism of young adulthood? is the lake only in its adolescence and this is its rebellion? All these years I wondered if she was my sister or lover or bride. . . has the lake in fact been my daughter, intent on getting my attention?

A memoir I call this but that's a misnomer, truly I choose to remember as little as possible. I think as little as possible of my

vanished overnight after I discovered behind the locked door on the bottom

past, and with every night's dose of lapsinthe greater than the night before, my mind becomes more resistant to its effects until soon I'll overdose on memory or amnesia. Every night that my life sheds is one less to get through, one less link in the chain that leashes my heart like that leashing a slave's collar. Each night one more dose until finally I just slip over the line. Four months ago Brontë found me in the transitional chamber slumped on the floor,

face brushing the place where — eleven years ago? twelve — I
found his little monkey. My life has been cruel enough to give me
every now and then the hope or reassurance of some new clarity,
once a decade or so before snatching it away. . . hope on a leash
like a slave like my heart. . . but since that night eleven years ago
I've slipped toward an ending not simply out of despair but rather
as a flight to freedom, of course. But not a cry for help. Please.
Maybe Brontë tells herself I'm crying for help. She called it in on
the wireless and the ambulance-boat came with a pump so my
belly might be as empty as the rest of me. . . .

Not a cry for help. . . in a way it's just the opposite. The
only way of taking control over my life: by taunting it, flirting with
an ending. . . the only way to place life at the end of a lash as I've
so placed over the years everything and everyone I would have
submit to me — after first coming to L.A. an orphan three decades
ago and serving as the sexual serf of a man I never really knew or
understood, out of which came the only thing in my life I ever truly
loved so huge. . . at which point I had a mother's fear of the
world's chaos; and nothing is as afraid as that. Is it so bad, to have
wanted control when I never had it before? with men not so unlike
the one who fathered my son, who themselves just wanted to give
up all control for a few hours? Yes of course I've asked myself —
cracking the riding crop across their asses (they *never* touch me)
— asked myself whether in fact I was resisting their fantasies or
fulfilling them. But at that point, when domination is a kind of

oor the huge blue calendar he had made that circled its room and covered

submission and submission a kind of domination, it all gets a little
complicated.

In any event I had found some reconciliation with my life
. . . until the night I found the monkey. Found the little toy
monkey and suddenly could only wonder if it had all been a hoax
I perpetrated on myself, that vision-dream-hallucination I had of
going back back back down the hole of the lake, down down down

to where I came from a quarter of a century ago now, down down down through the hole to the Other Lake to see if he's still there in the boat, still waiting for me, still in the moment where I left him. And in fact if it was all just a vision, a dream, an hallucination, if in fact it was all just a hoax I played on myself, I can only wonder how it is I so easily accepted such a delusion, so easily abandoned my search for him in *this* life, on *this* lake, to take control, to put at the end of my lash, under the crack of my whip, my despair. Because despair, I think I heard someone say once, isn't a grief of the heart, but the soul.

And then I wondered if he was still out there, and has been all along. On *this* lake, in *these* hills, a man now, wondering why I never came to find him. . . .

I would chain myself to my bed and let the lake take me some night as it rises, if it were rising. But the lake hasn't risen for a long time. For ten years it slowly but surely sank and then suddenly stopped a year ago last spring, in remission, putting off death just a while longer. Waiting for something to happen, before it dies.

I know what it's waiting for.

People have stopped trying to understand the lake. They accept that the lake has its own logic, stranger and bigger than the rationale of tides, geology. Before even the geologists knew, those who live with the lake knew the sinking had stopped, because the Lapses stopped. . . those who live with the lake felt stop, for the

every wall and blotted out every window and flowed over onto the floor an

duration of its remission, the draining of time. Felt stop, in its pause before death, the way that every day after tomorrow was answered by another day before yesterday. Felt stop the pendulum of memory swinging ever wider as the lake drained. . . they knew because time stopped going backwards, because everything that's been *about* the lake and *of* the lake finally stopped vanishing overnight into the literal fog of memory. . . people, events,

philosophies, meanings. . . one night about six or seven years ago even the color blue vanished, no one has seen it since. Now the lake is green or gray or black. . . now somewhere out there over the water beyond the hedge of fog lurks zero-year, or zed-year. My own Lapses ended last year in a cluster. . . I woke one morning to
find myself lying not
in my bed in the Chateau but the Santa Monica hospital just a few weeks after returning from Tokyo, when I was seventeen. I was seventeen again, it was eleven-thirty at night again, the thirty-first of December again of that year, under the white explosion of delivery room lights overhead, the doctor and nurse having the same argument I remember them having over my labor that night a little less than twenty-eight years ago, about millennial arithmetic, between the calculations of my dilations and the dwindling minutes of my contractions. I looked into the white lights above me, pain shot through me. . . I was startled to be back at this moment again but not amazed of course, since this kind of thing had been happening for a while now . . . what are you doing talking about, the nurse was saying to the doctor in exasperation, "if it's tonight, or tomorrow, then what was all that hoopla a year ago about?"

"It wasn't about anything," the doctor was saying, "that's what I'm explaining to you. It was about a lot of people getting it wrong, is what it was about."

"All those people celebrating all over the world?" said the

eiling and completely reordered history to the chronology and logic of

nurse. "All those fireworks over the Eiffel Tower and Big Ben, or whatever. . . . "

Excuse me, I muttered.

". . . everyone got it wrong but you, that's what you're saying?"

"Zero isn't the number before one," the doctor lectured smugly, "zero isn't a number at all. In the case of the calendar, zero is ten, and ten comes after nine."

"Thank you, I think I know ten comes after nine."

"This is a ten-year," the doctor checked his watch, then looked at a clock on the wall, "in another hour and a half it will be a one-year, and that's the *true* beginning of it."

What's happening? I can remember saying all those years ago, when I was first here, in this moment, managing to say it between the pain. But this time *excuse me*

and the doctor stared at me

but it's all metaphor anyway

as if I was a huge talking pea-pod about to split

it's all random anyway I went on *a conceit, based on the birth of a religious philosopher who wasn't even born in the Year One but probably the Year Minus-Four or sometime around then, so it's silly to get hung up on the math of the thing when everyone else has accepted the symbolism of it*

and in a dream the doctor might have accepted such an exchange from a young girl in labor, but since this wasn't a dream, since the currents of memory and time unleashed over the years by the sinking of the lake in fact had carried me back to this actual moment, the doctor stared at me in astonishment. I think the nurse was too confused to feel vindicated. In the meantime I realized I was about to deliver him again, my boy. . . would I stop it,

apocalypse, with its dates not sequential like an ordinary calendar bu

if I could? If I could, would I choose never to have had him at all, if it would undo the next twenty-eight years? Of course not. Not even a little, not for a minute. I looked at the doctor. *Please deliver them both this time.*

"What?"

There are two. . . there's a girl. Deliver them both this time.

He looked at the nurse, the nurse looked at him. The next contraction came and when it subsided I wanted to say, Cut me open this time, to get both of them. . . but truthfully I don't know whether I managed it. When the pain of the contraction passed I was suddenly so exhausted, I felt all the forty-some years of my present, even returned as I was by the Lapse to my seventeen-year-old past. . . and I think I must have dozed a little because I opened my eyes just in time to hear the voices of the doctor and nurse fade, to hear fading in the hall of the hospital on the way to the delivery room the happy-new-years and the doctor's lone, stubborn Happy New Millennium — you're a year late, someone says; I'm not, he says, zero isn't the number before one, zero is. . . — to see the walls of the hallway fade back to the walls of the Chateau. *Cut them out* I tried to whisper before the lake carried me back to the present.

The last of the Lapses was just a few days after that. . . carried me back to a week and half before he was born. . . I was walking, pregnant to burst, along Santa Monica Boulevard, past little Italian eateries, xerox stores, travel agencies, mailbox rentals, gay fetish shops, video outlets, cappuccino stands, cars driving by, all of it as vivid as can be, in every last detail, I was singing to him in my head our little song that I had just heard for the first time a week or so before, riding a bus on Pacific Coast Highway *if there's a higher light* remember this one Kirk? almost forgetting it's all gone now, all long submerged. Then I was walking up Crescent

eefloating, far removed dates overlapping in some cases, consecutive dates

Heights toward Sunset Boulevard, looking at the old Hollywood apartments with their turrets, trees, realizing soon they would all be under water. It was as if I was wandering aimlessly, although of course I know it wasn't aimless. If it were aimless the lake and this Lapse wouldn't have brought me back to it, since it's the personally momentous remembrances the Lapses resurrect, it's the major harbors dotting the shore of life's recollection where memory docks as it's carried back in the lake's vortex. . . . I crossed Sunset and kept walking up Crescent Heights, an awful long way for a pregnant girl due to give birth any minute. . . and then at some point I stopped, there where Crescent Heights became Laurel Canyon Boulevard. . . stopped at someone's lawn and looked down at my feet and there, at the tip of my toes, it was. Nothing more than a small black puddle, not more than a few inches across. There it was, long before it seemed to just suddenly appear that September morning nine months later: chaos: there it was and I stared at it, could almost see it grow as I watched, until it was almost a foot across, and I tried to bend over to look, to peer into it and see into its source but I was so huge I couldn't. I couldn't bend over, all I could do was just stand there and watch it get a little bigger with every passing second, almost imperceptibly. I was standing in the very birth of the lake as it spread around my feet. And I turned and started walking away as fast as I could, looking over my shoulder as if it would follow me, which in a way it did and

then I blinked and

the Lapse was over, and I was back on my Chateau terrace staring out at black water almost as far as I could see. In the distance was the war ship that sailed into L.A. Bay ten years ago and dropped anchor and hasn't moved since or shown a single sign of life. . . there on the terrace I lay my hands on my belly to feel its vacancy. The next night I scored from one of my last clients some

separated by the length of the room in other cases, with apparently senseles.

of the lapsinthe that's been going around and took the first dose of the sepia-colored evilixir, adding another every night after that. . . .

Sometimes, hovering in the ether between existence and non, I talk to him. Don't know whether it's the lapsinthe talking . . . but I know it's him right away although now he would be in his late-twenties. . . there he is sitting beside me saying *Mama don't die* and maybe that's what pulls me back. Sometimes we talk about all the things I would have told him if I had had the chance, sometimes we have no idea what to talk about at all but it doesn't matter, we might talk of death or God. . . does anyone ever care so much about the notion of God, whatever she actually thinks about it, as when she has a child? Isn't it when you have a child that you really need to understand the whole business of God, the whole business of death and the soul? People get to the end of their lives and say they're not afraid of death. . . but even in the course of my many tentative suicides I'm afraid to death. To not be at least a little afraid of death you have to have no imagination whatsoever. It isn't a matter of pain, pain doesn't frighten me, of course it's the prospect of nothingness, into which will pass not only one's own life but everyone else's as I've known it. What I feel for my boy will pass into nothingness, and it's intolerable: My love for you will not die with me, I promise or plead, or fume at him in our conversations. . . but the question in his eyes remains: and I see it. I read it. Will she abandon me again? it says.

I know him right away, all these years later, in these moments when we talk near death's beach. All these years haven't changed the immediately identifiable beauty of him. All these years haven't altered the memory of how beautiful he was. . . but they've left me to wonder a terrible thing, which is whether I would have loved him quite so much if he hadn't been so beautiful. I calculate absurd impossible hypotheses, transferring his soul to the body and face of some little boy not so beautiful, then try to

melines running from top to bottom leading him to the inescapable

measure the love, testing my heart. Did my own mother not love me because I wasn't beautiful? of course I hope I see his beauty through the prism of love rather than love him through the prism of beauty, but how can I be certain? Kirk? I say to him from where I lie in this ether on the edge of life *Kirk* I reach to him, and there flashes some small confusion across his face as if he almost knows his own name but not quite; but not quite knowing, he reaches back anyway. *Night-time* he answers. . . our fingers brush. . . .

Morning now, after writing all night. . . air raid siren. Has to be a test, right? they ought to announce when they're going to have a test. . . all the gulls over the water scatter and swirl at the sound. Walk out onto my terrace, listen to the siren, watch the birds. . . . OK now: very slowly, very casually, as inconspicuously as possible, turn to look and see if they're there. . . . yes. Fuck. Why don't they go away? Why don't they leave me alone? The hillsides behind the Chateau encamped with all the people. . . are there fewer? Maybe there are fewer. Maybe they're starting to go away, maybe they're starting to give up on their lost Saint Kristin of the Lake, I thought the cult went the way of the first Lapse years ago. . . but the legend persists. "I'm not her!" I even called to some of them months ago when they sailed out here on a small flotilla, prostrated before the Chateau in their boats. Kristin wasn't a saint, I wanted to tell them, she was only a mom, the other me I sent back to undo the thing she and I did years ago, when we abandoned our son on the lake. . . .

. . . remember in my delirium thinking when they pumped me out, Did they pump out my little girl? forgetting for a minute. Forgetting first how Kristin sailed away with my daughter in her belly, when she took the boat back all those years ago, forgetting then how over the years the blood began to slow between my legs its patterns fading, dark red webs of each month becoming more

conclusion that sometime in the century, among its madmen of all kind.

unwoven until only a small red spider was left. Forgetting then how, in the month I finally didn't menstruate at all, she appeared out of the lake. . . I watched her. . . was sitting on the terrace staring out over the water under the massive full moon and there in the far distance above the lake's source, above that very place I once stepped pregnant in a strange black puddle, was a ripple, someone surfacing from nowhere, looking around and swimming toward me in the moonlight.   I just sat and watched her swim toward me.

As she got closer I stood up from where I had been sitting and peered over the terrace down into the water. . . I could hear her now in the dark below me gasping for breath, knew she was in danger of drowning from exhaustion. In the blaze of the moon | I could barely see her frantically grasping for a place to hold onto the Chateau wall. . . ever since the color blue vanished into one of the Lapses, the nights are so much darker, even when the moon shines. "Swim around!" I called, trying to direct her to the port on the other side, and then everything went quiet, and I thought she had gone under. "Hello?" There was no answer. "Hello!" I ran from the terrace to the other side of the old hotel, out through the transitional chamber to the entryway, out onto the stone steps near the Vault by the water. . . I couldn't see anyone. "Hello?" I stood there five minutes calling, the grotto empty. . . and then a face came floating up to the steps like a jellyfish, barely above the surface, and I ran down the steps and fished her out. For a while she just lay there naked on the steps long gold hair splayed around her head. I kept trying to help her up but for a while she didn't want to get up, she just wanted to lie there, so I went back into the chamber and got a blanket and came back and lay it over her, tucking it beneath her until I could coax her in.

That night she slept in the room where I used to do my readings, the I-Ching of melody-snake slithering across menstrual

mong its irrational horrors, that sometime in the last century modern

blood. I laid her out on a mat, dressed in a tattered black silk robe with jade vines crawling up her body. She slept soundly. . . but it took me a while, to fall asleep I mean, tossing and turning. . . and then I woke with a start.

I sat up from my bed in the dark.

Sat listening to the dark for a contradiction, and heard none. Got up from my bed and pulled on a robe and stumbled through the outer room, over to the other room where she slept. Suddenly I just knew, I don't know why. Suddenly it was just obvious.

"Brontë?" I said to the dark, in the doorway. When she didn't answer, I said it again. "Brontë?"

"Yes," a small voice answers.

Lulu Blu, otherwise known as Mistress Lulu, the Dominatrix-Oracle of the Lake, Queen of the Zed Night, once called Kristin, staggers where she stands, clutching her robe to her, still staring into the dark where the girl lies. "It's you," Lulu finally chokes; there's silence and Lulu says it again — "It's *you*" — and then hears from out of the dark, "Yes, I. . . I'm tired. . . ." Lulu nods, still standing in the doorway. "Sorry," the girl's voice says in the dark, "I just need to sleep," and Lulu keeps nodding, "thank you for taking me in. . . " the girl's voice in the dark barely finishes; and Lulu turns to the outer room and goes to sit on the divan before the dead fireplace. She sits for a long time before she goes back out onto the terrace, staring out in the distance at that place in the water where Kristin vanished years ago and where Brontë emerged a few hours ago. She gets cold and returns to the fireplace where she wishes there was a fire, but she's too tired and rattled to build one. She's curled up there in the divan the next morning when she wakes and sees the girl out on the terrace.

Everything in Lulu aches as she stands, pulls her robe closer to her. Brontë on the terrace, long straight gold hair almost down to her waist, is still wearing the old black silk robe with jade

apocalypse had outgrown God, and after he tried in his own craziness to mak

vines. Lulu watches her awhile before the girl notices. "Are you hungry?" asks the woman.

"Yes, please," the girl answers. She looks about nineteen, which is how long it's been since Lulu waved goodbye to Kristin in the boat and Kristin disappeared into the lake. Brontë walks in from the terrace out of the sunlight while Lulu suppresses an impulse to reach out and run a finger along her face and touch her shimmery golden hair; as though she senses this, Brontë pulls back from the other woman, feeling examined: Is she my daughter, Lulu wonders, or Kristin's, or is there a difference? Did I conceive her and Kristin deliver her, as we both carried her for all those years? Conceived with Kirk, is she his twin? Delivered years after him, is she his younger sister? Is she his half-sister, both of them of the same father but of two mothers, who used to be one?

She's petite, spritelike. She can't be five feet tall, a wraith except for breasts that, on her frame, verge on the absurd. How did such a little girl get such breasts? the mother thinks, not from me. Not classically beautiful, thinks Lulu, but much prettier than I ever was. . . did she get that from her father? She doesn't look anything like him — he had jetblack hair — but then Kirk didn't either. Am I doomed to strangers for children? Are all of them to be more of the lake than of me?

Lulu cooks some eggs while Brontë sits at the kitchen table. The younger woman doesn't say anything or seem particularly curious about the older woman, more wary than anything although suspicion doesn't agree with her: "Nice place," she finally allows at some point, to say something.

"I've lived here almost twenty years," Lulu explains. "It was a hotel once."

"Oh."

"Before the lake. Movie stars and musicians stayed here. It was famous."

ie part of the calendar, a moving date unto myself, a date he had determined

The younger woman realizes she's stumbled irrevocably into a conversation. "Were you here before the lake?" she finally asks.

She doesn't know who I am, Lulu thinks, trying to consider this in all its aspects. Or rather: I don't know what she knows: does she know what she knows? Just as well she doesn't know me as Mistress Lulu. . . but then does she know I'm her mother? Did she really return to me by sheer accident? "What's your name?"

The younger woman flushes, narrows her eyes. After a moment she says, "You know."

"Tell me."

"You know. You said it last night."

"Tell me."

After a moment the girl says, "Brontë."

Lulu turns back to the eggs on the oven. "Yes, I was here before the lake. What about you?"

"What about me?'

"Have you been here long?"

Brontë seems to meditate on the question. "No," she finally answers.

"Visiting?"

"Yeah."

Don't pry so much, Lulu tells herself now, you're prying. What were you doing in the water last night? "Family or friends here?" She puts the eggs on the table in front of the girl who begins devouring them. "Boyfriend?"

"No boyfriends," Brontë says emphatically between bites. She's sucking on slices of lemon, one after another, until it makes Lulu's mouth sour to watch her.

"You don't like boys?"

Well, not in that way, the girl thinks to herself. I like them

through his arcane and unhinged calculations but the meaning of which

all right, but not in that way. Actually I'm into girls — and I almost say it, as much for the shock value, you know? Because actually at this point I'm a bit afraid of this woman cooking me breakfast, whoever she is. I'm trying to act cool and it's true about the girls but if I were to say it, it would only be to try and perhaps intimidate her back a bit, though as I'll find out soon enough that's hardly the sort of thing that would. Intimidate her, that is. So I don't say it, and the way she keeps checking out my chest just makes me think all the more perhaps I shouldn't say it, because at this point I still can't tell about her, here I am out in this old hotel out in the middle of this lake stuck here for the moment and also, to be honest, not all that ready to leave, it seems a pretty mega place really, a terrace you can walk out and see a big part of the bay, water stretching far out to sea in the west, hills curving 'round to the north and that big battleship or whatever it is out in the distance, the one tall building that's not gone under. It's all something to see isn't it and I'll never get tired of it, so already I'm thinking I wouldn't mind so much not having to leave right away.

Even from the first the Mistress, she seems a bit off, I must say, as much as I come to love her. Naturally later I understand some of it a bit better, later clients they'll tell me there was a time not so many years ago she was the most powerful woman in the territory with an army of submissives, and then there's all the religious business going on 'round her, but I don't know what her story is this first morning except she's called me a name I'm not really sure is mine and she's checking out my chest, which I'm selfconscious about anyway. So they're a bit big. If I was taller they wouldn't seem so big. It's not really they're so big it's that the rest of me is small. My chest and height I'm selfconscious about. If it was up to me I'd like to take a bit off the front and put it on top.

Later when I get to know her better and realize it's a

emained an infuriating and impossible mystery to him and everyone else, and

mother thing with her not a lover thing, I tell her about being into women and she laughs and calls me God's little joke on the male gender. Perhaps so. The boys they do check me out and want to be with me and we all know what that's about, and I don't think it's taken me much of my life to figure that out. It's funny what I sort of remember from before and what I don't. As time goes by, some things come back to me but they're just isolated pictures in my head of a city street though not this city, a thousand shops, a thousand cars and lights and towering buildings — but it's all another lifetime. I still remember things about myself like being selfconscious, I have this sort of sense of who I am even if I don't remember the name, and for a while I confess it scares me, it seems important doesn't it, but honestly? I don't know that it's so important, if you think about it. Perhaps my name really is Brontë, it's not as though it's impossible. That night the Mistress pulled me out of the water, brought me in, gave me a place to sleep, I felt so strange about everything and awhile there in the water at the end I seriously thought I was about to drown. And when you seriously think you're about to drown, all the little chambers of your mind become one big room, all the walls between things that happened long ago and not so long ago, things you've felt badly about perhaps or things you're sorry you didn't get to do I suppose, all the walls come down and memory, it becomes this big open mezzanine, to the extent you're actually thinking any of that at all as you're trying to keep from drowning. Except at that moment, when all the little chambers of my mind opened up and all the walls came down, I couldn't see a thing, though at the time I wasn't conscious of much other than trying to stay alive. I was looking at what was revealed in that moment, and nothing was revealed. The big open mezzanine of what I remembered from my life was just dark and empty.

So I was sort of — I'm sure when I first get here I'm a bit

which I couldn't be expected to remember but which I know at this ver

hysterical, I'm sure I'm in some sort of shock. At first I don't know where I am or how I got here and I'm exhausted and scared, and lying in that strange dark room that used to be the Mistress' ceremony chamber, how do I know it's not my name when she calls me that? I still don't know. Later I actually read the books and I'm not sure which she named me after but I like Emily the best, the one about the girl who drives the boy crazy and then even when she dies she goes on driving him crazy, yes I like her best.

So I know at once the Mistress she's a bit off but I also decide she's probably all right too, and it becomes obvious it's a mother thing. She says something a couple of times that, when I think about it, seems a bit odd, we'll be talking about the business, the clients and what not, and she says in self-reproach, "What kind of life is it, for a mother to leave to her daughter?" Later after I've been here awhile and when I think she knows I won't get too put off by it, that's when she tells me how those first nights after I arrived at the Chateau she would come into the chamber while I slept on the mat, sitting and watching and even talking to me. I had no idea. I never heard anything but then I'm a *very* sound sleeper. I was talking to you, she'll say, but you were sleeping the sleep of the dead, and perhaps that's the first real memory I have of before, I can remember someone else saying that. Because that's exactly what I sleep all right, the sleep of the dead. And if the Mistress isn't in any hurry for me to leave then I'm not in any hurry to go, not back out there into the lake I came from. I love the Chateau, feel safe here, protected from the lake and after awhile I feel protected *by* the lake, from the world. I surely don't feel any great urge to go back and find out things about my life or my past or wherever I came from, to the contrary there's something a bit lovely about the feeling of starting fresh. What happened before that would make me feel I want to start fresh? Well all right that

moment here in the birth canal of the lake, as I know so many things, happened

does nag at me a bit, I do wonder, but not so much. To wonder too much about it, after all, wouldn't be starting fresh, would it?

The Chateau, there's the main room and what I come to call the ceremony room when I begin working it, where I usually sleep except the nights I sleep on the divan out before the fire listening to the sound of the lake and the feeling of the night air coming through the terrace doors — or in the dungeon downstairs.

Since it's below water the dungeon is cool all the time, in the hot months it's lovely and I sleep down there listening to the radio like the Mistress says she used to when she was 'round my age living in Tokyo — a pirate station broadcasts from a boat out in the lake. It probably makes sense to keep my private space and my working space separate but cool as it is in the dungeon I'm all the more inspired to put something into the discipline, without getting carried away naturally, then if I work up a bit of sweat I can stop and cool off, watch the beads of the lake form on the dungeon walls while the submissive writhes a bit in his shackles. Another good reason for the blindfold, you see — besides the sensory deprivation he can't see when you're taking a breather, and he gets all excited the way men do wondering what's going on, when all you're really doing is just sitting there enjoying the cool and listening to the currents of the lake against the outer walls. Any one of these days — I'll tell the client now and then — any minute these walls aren't going to hold and that lake it's going to come crashing in. I tell him this and then leave him there by himself awhile chained and naked in the dark thinking about what I said and, you know, listening for the walls to start cracking. During these little recesses the Mistress and I, we have a cup of tea out on the terrace for ten or fifteen minutes and laugh at the sound of the clanking of chains coming up from below through the vents. What a bad girl you are, the Mistress says. Sometimes when I go back, without even being able to touch himself he's gotten off just from

to be the very date when, three years old, I stood on the shore of that island

the terror, so don't tell me the boys don't like it in their own way. When I mention this to the Mistress in some amazement, she already knows all about it: the male-wangie is a thing of mystery, she just smiles.

But jeez life is lovely in these early days before the business with the Mistress' lapsinthe. I don't go ashore for three months after that first night, very contented in the Chateau,

standing on the terrace sucking those slices of lemon like I love
and dropping the yellow peels in the water below. At first, because
I know nothing about the Mistress, to me she's just an eccentric
lonely lady; I haven't heard the stories about the dominatrix-oracle
business or the Saint Kristin stories, which I don't understand
anyway or what they actually have to do with the Mistress, but
I see the people camped out on the hillside hour after hour and day
after day and week after week watching the Chateau as though
expecting a sign. Sure it's not something the Mistress ever says
much about. That is, early on it's a bit obvious she was in the
trade given the shackles on the walls downstairs and then I come
on the tool box with the ankle cuffs and fur-lined handcuffs and
riding crops and ball-gags and violet wands. I find this tiny collar
I think is for a cat or something. Well it's a collar all right but not
for any cat. So I ask her right out and she tells me right out,
though I see this look in her eye a moment like she's trying to
decide. She tells me right out and I just say no way. Not really.
Really? And here I thought she would be shocked by my liking
girls! I'm fascinated from the first. I go right past offense and
never even skirt revulsion. Something in my true nature takes to it.
Not to pain, I never want to inflict real pain and never have,
beyond a good healthy whack in the balls, naturally. The Mistress
says she never inflicted real pain either or meant to anyway; if she
struck harder than she intended and left so much as a bruise or welt
she felt bad, and there was never a drop of blood once — other

ith my uncle and gazed on that strange woman across the river, now here in

than her own, when she did the oracle business — in all the years
she did it. It's about the power isn't it, and not even so much
power over someone else as the power over your own life, and
that's what I like too, that power, I take to it right from the first and
you can make of that whatever you want. I can tell you for a fact
that as far as I know no one's ever gotten hurt, so you make of it

what you want. You can spend your whole life, the Mistress says to me one time, making peace with your own true nature.

"What?"

"Something," she says, "someone once said to me," and it's the strangest thing when she says it, I'm not even sure what it means but it unnerves me some because I know I've heard it before, that very thing, back before I came up out of the lake, like the thing about sleeping the sleep of the dead. But if domination was about the power of it for her, if it was the Mistress' true nature just to take command of her life then how is it four months ago I'm calling up an ambulance-boat on the wireless to come pump out her stomach? Unless that's her way of taking control of her life for good. So it's a complicated thing, one's true nature, isn't it. Sometime long ago something happened to her, something beyond her control, something she's not been able to escape from or explain to herself in any way that she's ever actually believed for any length of time, something that won't heal. Something no act or ritual of domination has been able to get her through no matter how hard she's tried. Something. I've come to learn things about her life but not that. I think awhile after I first come to the Chateau perhaps it's better for her, it's like she regained something, but then — I'm happy to be a daughter to her if that's what she needs. Why not. And one afternoon a few months after I've been here I say as much and I can tell right away it's the wrong thing to say, I can tell from this look on her face. This shattered look. Perhaps

the birth canal of the lake I know this and maybe should be astounded by it

it's the casual way I say it, like it doesn't mean anything either way. Now that I think about it, it's after that she begins to slip away, except for times we embrace for whatever reason, and I can feel the way she holds onto me that she's trying to come back, come back from wherever she's slipping to.

There was a man once, that much I know. That I've figured out. And for a time I thought, well then that's it isn't it, a man. He may even have been a client. I've never asked, perhaps I'm not the inquisitive sort. Perhaps I have an overly developed male-sense of privacy — that is, for a female. But whoever he was she's not seen him for a long time. Awhile, though, I thought that's what it was.

Now I don't think so.

As for the lake, well for sure there's something between the Mistress and the lake. She stands on the terrace must be hours every day and she and the lake stare each other down. The Mistress, she thinks I don't know what she's thinking, but I do. I've figured it out. The Mistress thinks the lake is waiting for her to die before it sinks any further, and I'm not going to be the one to say she's wrong. God's little joke on the male gender, that's what the Mistress says I am, and after a while it becomes clear that her god is full of such jokes, and so sometimes I wonder if the lake is God's joke on her or she's God's joke on the lake. It's almost six months later I hear the Saint Kristin legend, by then I've finally left the Chateau for an afternoon now and then, going to Port Justine for supplies and that's when I hear, when I'm out among the locals, how the Mistress is Saint Kristin's twin or Saint Kristin returned from the dead or something, I hear it but don't make much sense of it and I don't think anyone else makes sense of it or even really wants to. Four months ago when I call the ambulance-boat, well there's a commotion then on the hillsides, people skittering back and forth like forest animals smelling

ere anything was astounding or, maybe more precisely, if there was nothing

smoke. You might think a pathetic botched suicide attempt would sort of snuff the legend, what? but instead the offerings just start coming more than ever, the stone steps of the grotto laden with bread and cheese and fruit and drinking water. While the Mistress sleeps I go out on the terrace to see boats bobbing on the lake below, people standing in them staring up in anxious anticipation. She's all right, I tell them, go home. They don't move awhile.

They're still suspicious of me, perhaps more than ever, still not sure whether I'm priestess, temptress, judas, magdalene.

After a while they drift back to shore. Return to their vigil. That same afternoon I go out to the back grotto behind the Chateau to find a lone man in a boat leaving on the steps an offering of flowers. Not much good for anything, flowers, I think, but he lays them up and down the stone stairs. The tide will just take most of them, I tell him.

He looks up. He's in his mid- maybe late-twenties. That afternoon he looks up at me and his jaw drops a bit, and I see that expression I've seen before and think, Oh I'm about to become God's little joke again. But he's pretty for a boy, I'll say that for him, eyes the color of the lake and hair like owl feathers. I see him again about a week later, one twilight all by himself on the lake in his boat — what, does he live in that boat? I wonder. He's all by himself drifting out there watching the Chateau like they all watch it, except that where all the rest of them are waiting for the Mistress, I know he's waiting for me. We just look at each other and don't wave or anything, just look at each other till I go back inside, but there are more flowers on the steps the next morning except for the ones the lake has stolen, a trail of garlands leading back to him I'm sure. Then I see him a lot over the next week or so and don't pay much attention, never wave or say anything, thinking I shouldn't encourage him too much. I like the notion of men under my spell, I confess, it's the whole point of what I do,

that was not astounding, and I can't help wondering how my life might hav

but if I'm to be God's little joke then I don't want it to be any crueler than the sport of it calls for. And then I don't see him at all awhile, perhaps another week, and then he's there one night on the grotto steps again not with flowers, not delivering anything except himself. He's there as a client.

By now I've really got the business going. Twenty or thirty steady regulars, more than I can handle really, and then all the

semi's who drop in and out of the picture, and new ones showing
up fairly often and a lot of them come back. From the short time
I've been here already it seems to me nothing in L.A. ever quite
fits any sort of real pattern anyway, and this sort of work is volatile
by nature; sometimes when the fighting up north gets worse or
there's especially ominous news from back east you can almost
predict an upturn in traffic, men wanting to explore their dark sides
before the end. More often than not these are men of some power
or influence, men in control of others, men in positions of
responsibility who long to be free for an hour or two of power,
control, responsibility, free of themselves — men who want to turn
power and control and the Self over to someone else. Perhaps they
feel guilty about the way they fuck over other people all the time
and want to be fucked over by me in return as a sort of penance —
every client is different isn't he. Some have lives they need to
escape from and others have no lives at all, that is no lives of
emotional connection or intimacy, and they're the problem-ones
because then they want *me* to be their life, and I can't, can I. I just
can't. Those are the ones who start hounding me till I have to cut
them loose. You probably think they're all creeps and losers in
which case you would be in for the surprise of your life, I won't
say most of them are nice normal men because, take it from me,
there *are* no nice normal men — nice perhaps but not normal. But
some of them are actually a bit sweet — sad and messed up yes but
a bit sweet and like I told the Mistress that very first day it's not

een different had I known, how far I might have gone with him to unlock the

like I don't like men, sometimes they actually can be easier to deal
with than women because everything's so straightforward in terms
of what they want. So don't get the idea I do this because
I hate men. Perhaps back somewhere in my mystery past before
I came up out of the lake I was a cliché, you know, the molested
daughter or whatever — but I just don't think so. So before I take
on a client we'll usually talk awhile and I'll try to figure out what

his story is and why he's there and whether what he wants is something I can give him, and I make it clear then that there are things I don't do and I don't need to go into those here, just things that cross my own line of dignity if not the client's. There's humiliation and then there's humiliation. Like I said before, there's a line drawn on the discipline I'll inflict, because while it's all very amusing to blindfold and harness a naked man by his ankles and wrists and beat him awhile, it's not like I'm a sadist or something. Erotoasphyxiation, electrocution, cattle prods, I don't go in for any of that. It's all about limits isn't it, the ones you test and the ones you observe. There's a code word the client and I agree on that he'll say if things are going farther than he wants or he changes his mind about something, something besides "no" or "stop" because in such situations people say no or stop all the time without meaning it. For a while I was coming up with a different word for each client but that became confusing and I was always afraid I might forget, though I imagine I would have remembered when I heard it, but anyway now I have a one-code-fits-all policy and the word is *zed*.

But no one's said it yet.

There's no sex. Not with me, anyway. Do you get that? I'm not a hooker. The need and situation may be sexual to the client and I understand that in the submissive's own weird way I'm an object of sexual interest. At the end of the session, before releasing him, if he's been obedient and I feel he's done well in his

riddle of how every life is a millennium unto itself, of how the single smalles

training, I'll give him permission to pleasure himself if he chooses. But that's up to him, he does it without any help at all from me, though if he wants to do it in front of me I may allow him, depending. A female client, she's different, to the extent I've had any and can really tell. I confess I wouldn't mind more female clients. For a while I was a bit surprised I didn't have more but that was me being naïve, women just aren't wired that way are they. Someone else will have to explain that, I can't. Perhaps for women submission has been such a fact of life for so long that they don't have the luxury of making a game of it. I've had two female submissives but I'm not sure they count, the first was part of a couple, she and I performing for her man and while I think perhaps she liked it more than he did or more than he wanted her to, she wasn't really my type; the second wasn't really one client but several thousand, the all-female Freek Recherche that's the most famous of the movable lunatiques that take place clandestinely night to night in one canyon or the other 'round here. Which in a strange way doesn't count either. By then I had a reputation and while I usually don't like doing outcall I confess I was flattered that they came looking for me, a couple of the women putting on the fête sailing out to the Chateau and offering me the job. It would be an honor, one says to me — how do you resist that? Flattery or not I'm not sure I could have anyway.

This was the night I found out something interesting about myself. After all the days and weeks and months of wondering about my past, of wondering who I was before I came up out of the lake, this was when I found out perhaps I don't really want to know. The night of the Freek Recherche the two women come back for me and sail me over to shore and drive me in a beat-up thirty-year-old Jag through the pass in the hills to Nichols Canyon and I think I'll remember till the day I die the sight of *all those women* there by Nichols Pond that looked like it was on fire from

uman experience like losing a child can be a universe of meaning unto

the melody-snakes imported and dumped in, flashing and singing. How did they get all those snakes? Where did all those women come from? I didn't know there *were* that many women still in L.A., they had to have traveled from all the far reaches of the lagoon thousands of them, a vast memory-carnival of women dancing to the music of the snakes and drinking lapsinthe like there's no yesterday. My job is to stand on this little platform and crack my whip at the girls dancing 'round me as well as the blindfolded man fastened naked to the spinning wheel behind me 'sinthed out of his mind voluntarily or not — I don't know and don't want to — erection subject to the whims of centrifuge and the object of much collective amusement. At some point in all this someone presses into my hand a shot of 'sinthe and instead of drinking it down right away I stand there looking at the shot glass in my hand thinking about it and considering whether to drink it — that is, do I *want* to remember, after all? Face to face with the prospect of actually knowing what came before, I balk. What if it's something terrible? What if there's a very good reason I'm not remembering? So I just set it there on the small table next to me trying to decide, and it's very distracting. In a lot of ways it's the best time I've ever had, the best time of my life, well the best I know of anyway, cracking the whip and dancing with the women like I'm Queen of the Zed Night like they used to call the Mistress, all of them worshipping me and cheering and wanting to touch me as I stand over them on the platform and getting paid for it on top of it, what can be better, except the whole time all I can think about is whether to drink that little shot of the sepia-colored liqueur.

The strange thing now is, I don't remember whether I drank it or not. Don't remember, I just look at the glass in my hand at one point as dawn's coming up over the hills and the medicine is gone — did I drink it, spill it, try to seduce some woman with it? I swear I don't remember. Perhaps that in itself means I must have

itself, how far I might have gone with him rather than, through a strang

drunk it — is that one of the side effects, not even remembering you've taken it? I suppose I should ask someone sometime, next time the Freek Recherche or another of the big-time lunatiques passes through.

It's been a decent business and it's allowed me to repay the Mistress and help support our lives in the Chateau. Sometimes the client he offers to pay in bottles of the "evilixir" but I don't accept,

I don't want it in the Chateau with the Mistress or perhaps I don't want it 'round for my own reasons, so usually he pays in cash and sometimes foodstuffs and material, transportation coupons which in this town are preferable, or something I can trade at Port Justine or the outpost over in Los Feliz. At first some clients they come expecting the oracular aspects of the sessions as the Mistress used to perform them but by now the word is out I'm not Mistress Lulu but Mistress Brontë, and instead of fortune-telling what they get from me are long gold hair and colossal boobs. Now when there's an appointment the Mistress retreats behind her own closed doors. She knows most of the clients would find her presence more disruptive than welcoming, and those who might actually want her there, well, that would be a whole other kink we're not into. The Mistress is already about to retire the night the young boatman who brought the flowers appears at the grotto door of the Chateau with not nearly enough cash for a session — though who knows where he got what he had: It's not enough, I say looking at the currency in his cupped hands in the light of the doorway lantern. He ponders the money and closes one fist over the pitiful bills and coins too proud to say anything. "Oh come in then," I say impatiently and pull him into the entryway, closing the outer door behind him, "wait here."

It's all completely irregular, I never just take a client on like that, there's a process, an interview like I said before, nothing spur-of-the-moment. I leave him in the entryway. I go through the

hance-meeting with a Japanese boy who robbed graves at the time-capsule

transitional chamber that leads to the room where I sleep, and from there into the outer room where the fire roars. The Mistress, she's standing on the terrace like she often does, as though always looking for someone — Lu, I say. She turns and I say, "I've got one out in the entryway."

"Tonight?"

"I know. I'll send him off. He doesn't have enough to pay anyway."

She nods and I'm about to leave when she says, "It's all right, I'm going to bed," and she comes in from the terrace moving very slowly, she seems suddenly old, "I mean if you want to send him away. . . " shrugging ". . . but not on my account."

"Come here," I take her arm helping her. "Are you all right?" helping her into the back bedroom. I haven't seen her look so old. I think she's in her forties and on this night she seems twenty years older. "Lu?"

"I'm all right." She lies on the bed.

I sit on the bed beside her and we lock eyes. "None of the 'sinthe tonight," I say. She shrugs again, a small smile, and while I sit there on the bed close to a quarter hour holding her hand, waiting for her to go to sleep, my eyes search the room for the little sepia-colored bottles. When I think she's finally fallen asleep and I let go of her hand, she murmurs something. "What?" I lean my ear to her mouth, and when I still can't make it out, I ask again. "What kind of life?" she whispers.

"Shhh."

"For a mother to give a daughter," she says.

"Go to sleep."

"What if I *was* your mother?" she whispers.

"You are."

She smiles for a moment and then shuts her eyes again,

cemetery now under water on the west side of town, winding up in Tokyo tha

"Your client. . . ."

"Gone by now," I kiss her forehead — but in fact he's still there when I turn off the light by her bed and go back into the outer room and through the ceremony room and the transitional chamber to the entryway. "You're still here," I say and he just looks at me and I say, "Do you talk?"

"Yes."

"Do you know what I do?"

"I think."

"All right. Do you know what I *don't* do?"

"I'm not sure."

"Well we're not going to have sex. Do you understand that?"

He seems to consider this a moment and nods.

"I'm not a prostitute, do you understand?"

He nods. He sticks out the fistful of bills.

"Next time — if there is a next time — you have to bring more than that, and you can't pay in flowers either." I take the cash and take him by the empty hand. "What's your name?"

"Kale," he says.

"Come here then." I take him into the dressing room. "Take off all your clothes" — and he begins to pull the white shirt off over his head so I stop him — "wait till I finish with your instructions. Take off all your clothes and hang them here on the door" — I point at the hook on the door — "and then go through this door and you'll be in a room where you'll see another open door, and go through that door. Are you paying attention?"

"Yes."

"Did I give you permission to look at Me?"

"No."

"'No, Mistress Brontë.'"

"No, Mistress Brontë."

iirror-city of L.A. where east and west are smeared and where I eventually

"Go through the open door you see and you'll be in a large room with a fire. In the middle of the room will be a black circular rug. Kneel on the rug and wait for Me. When you see Me, lower your face in the rug till I instruct you otherwise." Usually this is all prearranged with the client. The grotto door would be left unlocked and the inner doors open at the appointed hour so that the client, he doesn't see me at all till he's in the main room awaiting my entrance and command.   That way a strictly defined relationship exists from the first, I'm already in my role as Dominant and he's already in his as submissive before his training begins.   I leave Kale in the dressing room, take my apparel from the ceremony chamber and go into the outer room which I make dark except for some burning candles.   Then I change into the black leather garter-belt and stockings and heels and the red silk robe I was given by another client to replace the old black robe the Mistress gave me my first night at the Chateau, and I take the riding crop and wait out on the terrace.

When I fit him with a collar and ask him what his favorite color is, he says blue and I strike him lightly 'cross the face. "Is the kale-toy being impertinent?" I say, "you know there's no blue anymore," choosing a velvet purple collar for him.   From the outset he's the most compliant stoic sort I've ever had, while at the same time being the least truly submissive.   This unspoken defiance comes into his eyes even while he's doing everything I tell him.   The more compliant his body is, the more his spirit is somehow beyond enslavement.   Drifting outside himself the way he seems to, there's no self to be humiliated.   During that first session I keep asking him if he feels humiliated and he says no, and a week later when he shows up again, still holding out in his cupped hands the cash that's not enough, I don't know why I don't just tell him it's insufficient and make him leave — it would be a very legitimate reason not to see him.   But somehow it feels like a

worked as a memory girl in the revolving memory hotels of Kabuki-cho ami

defeat, and so instead during the second session I change strategies, applying a more rigorous discipline; but when I ask again if he's humiliated he says no, and though I strike him 'cross his back when he says it, I know it's true, he's not. I beat him harder than I've ever beaten a client, till I have to stop myself. Are you humiliated now, slave kale? I say, and he keeps saying no no no, and he's not. It's obvious it's not his true nature to be either submissive or dominant. He's one of those rare few whose true nature is to neither follow nor lead — more like a woman in that way, I should say. Or perhaps I mean more like me.

Which means what attracts him isn't the idea of submission, which is what attracts the others. *I'm* what attracts him, so I know from the first there's a potential problem. Really I don't want to encourage him. I know he's here for the wrong reason, I know he's taken with me, and if I didn't know before, sure I know it the night he sails me to shore when I get another outcall, after the one I did for the Freek Recherche, up at one of the houses on the Hollywood Peninsula. It's my biggest offer ever and something tells me from the start to stay away from it — these very unpleasant sorts in a powerboat show up in the Chateau grotto one afternoon with a handful of cash and I'm not keen on the looks of them. But though cash isn't the easiest currency to deal in 'round here anymore, well it's a *lot* of cash, and they want me to come up that night to some house on the peninsula owned I guess by whoever sent his messenger boys with the proposition: There's going to be a party, they say. I say to this one guy in the powerboat, I'm not a hooker.

"It's OK," he says flatly.

What sort of answer is that? "Do you *understand*," I say again, "that I do *not* have sex for money?"

"It all right," he says, counting out there on the grotto steps more cash than I've ever seen, and so, really, it's my own fault

s surrounding bars and brothels and strip joints and massage parlors and

isn't it, looking back on it. I know that. All my intuition is saying no don't do this, here I'm trying to explain the *situation*, what I do and what I don't, and they're just giving out with this vague it's all right it's OK — but I'm dazzled by the money, and perhaps I've gotten over-confident about being able to take care of myself. So that night at the agreed hour I sail out to the cove behind the

Chateau where a car is waiting to take me up to the house, and Kale, he's the one who takes me.

In the boat he doesn't say anything, not that he ever says anything anyway. But he can tell from my bag of tricks I have with me and the way I'm dressed under my long green cloak that I'm working. It's dusk and the light's fading and halfway from the Chateau to the cove a fog drifts in and as the fog gets heavier a car onshore begins flashing its lights that get hazier and hazier. Are you sulking? I finally say to him and regret it right away, it's a question that instantly makes us more familiar than I want to be. What? he says and by now I've already learned with Kale what? might mean anything. What? might mean I didn't hear you, it might mean I heard you but I didn't understand you, it might mean I understood you but I don't know why you would ask that question, it might mean I understand why you're asking but I don't want to answer. Somehow all the things that what? might mean coming from anyone else, with Kale it's just multiplied, because he's this boy that you *just don't know at all*, he's unknowable and I don't think it's just me. I realize, moments from shore, that in this boat our roles are reversed, what with him navigating — my most compliant but least submissive client in control and me, the woman in control, at his mercy though who knows whether he thinks of it like that since there's no telling what he thinks even when it's the other way 'round. Other than the one thing about him I know that I keep trying to ignore, that he's totally taken with me, there's not

porn shops, in a city of no order where streets have no names or addresses o

any telling about Kale about anything at all. Walking up the shore to the car I find myself turning 'round to look over my shoulder at him back at the lake behind me, another concession to some strange connection or familiarity I'm not too happy about. I find myself turning 'round to look at him behind me — and he's not looking at me at all. He's pushing the boat away from the shore with the oar and, for a moment, panic wells up in me, I feel stranded, I want to call him to come back and take me back to the Chateau. But I fight it and go on.

The car is one of those old stretch limos from the turn of the century. In the back is a bar with crystal bottles of the lovely-looking sepia liqueur, and suspended from the ceiling of the limo there's a little television turned to probably the only channel that can still pick up a satellite signal, from some station out beyond the Mojave. I haven't seen a television since I swam up out of the lake but I know what it is anyway and while I have no idea what's going on — a man and woman are arguing — I can't help watching with fascination as the car winds up the mountain road to the house. I have no idea where we're going or how far but I'm in the car a good fifteen minutes. Beyond the dark limo windows, one old abandoned mansion after another rolls by dark and hulking, sometimes I see a light go out in one window or another where squatters hide from the headlights of the car. When we get to the house where the party is, it's buried in black palms and cypresses and darkness, walls invisible in the night and the only thing I can see is a small glowing rectangle in the distance, a yellow doorway in the night, and we get out of the limo and I can see the driver is the man in the powerboat who gave me all the cash that afternoon. Roughly he takes me by the elbow and directs me to the door.

The house, it doesn't seem all that impressive inside, not that much bigger than the Lair — the light is dim as though to hide

ny sequence that makes sense in space, rather it's a sequence of time,

general dilapidation. The grime of the walls, the carpets. It must be seventy, eighty years old, from the middle of the last century, the left wall of the open living room lined with bookshelves with latticed doors but no books, and in the right wall of the living room a hearth that's not burned a fire in years though some wood is stacked on one side of the fireplace and on the other side is a poker and instruments for stirring embers, cleaning ashes. 'Cross the

room from where I stand windows run from the ceiling to the floor
and past those I can make out in the moonlight a pool no one has
swum in a long time because in the moonlight I can see the surface
of the pool covered with leaves, and past the pool is a mega view
of the lake and all L.A.'s islands, not that you can really see the
lake itself in the dark. But in a way that's the impressive thing, the
panorama of islands all glittery in a way I've never seen L.A. You
can almost get a sense of the *whole* of the thing, of the city and
lagoon, the way you never do in L.A.

Inside the house there are about a dozen guests not
including the gorillas hired to stand in front of the doors with their
arms crossed, like the ones in the powerboat who came to see me
that afternoon. Of the dozen there are three men and the rest are
women, and I'm relieved to see other women here but they all look
at me with bored suspicion. By now naturally I know this is some
sort of mistake and the only question is how big it is and how I'm
going to get myself out of it. One of the men comes up to me, this
fiftyish Eurotrash sort who's apparently the host, not bad looking
but not pleasant either. "You're the one from the Chateau,"
he says.

"That's right," I murmur.

He turns to the others, the men and all the women reclining
on sofas, and says, "This is the one from the Chateau," and it's
hard to tell just how interesting they find this. There's almost no
conversation between anyone, music in the background so faint

structures numbered by their age and memories, and commuters ride the

it's as though no one really wants to hear it but someone thinks
it's obligatory, everyone is drinking and I can see on the table
disheveled traces of a white powder that got used up hours ago. If
they all got stuck in this moment forty years ago, no one has had
the desire or energy to get out of it. "Have a drink," says the host,
and one of the women appears at his side with a drink for me.

"No, thank you," I say — another rule. Believe me I'm as happy as anyone to have a bit of wine or whisky now and then and I could use one given the situation, but it's a rule, you don't drink on the job *especially* given the situation. You just lose control of things which naturally is exactly why the man is trying to get you to have a drink. "Have one," he demands.

"Not," I say, "when I'm working."

"Who says you're working."

"You did. You paid me, remember?"

"Exactly. I'm paying you and now I want you to drink." He shoves the drink at me and I take it with the hand that's not holding my bag of playthings. The gorgeous woman next to him, she watches me, half smiles, raises an eyebrow, she's tall — though every woman seems tall to me — five-eight, five-nine, long and sleek looking, her hair black and there's something exotic about her eyes, some mega-combination of Scandinavian and Mediterranean. Her name is Monica. "Mmmmmmmmm she's delightful isn't she," purrs Monica running her eyes up and down me as though the long green coat conceals nothing, "boobalicious little pixie," she says, "are they real?"

"They're the realest thing in this room," I say looking 'round me, and she laughs and takes me by the arm that's holding the bag and leads me to the sofa. Truth be told, at this moment I'm happy enough to go with her, because the host he gives me the creeps and now watching us walk away he has this slightly

ubways in a neverending loop and cabbies wander pell-mell spiraling

flummoxed look like I've just slipped from his clutches for the moment and that's bought me some time. Also, well, truth be told again Monica is as close to being my fantasy woman as I've met, she looks exactly like I would want to look if I could look anyway I wanted to, long and dark and sleek like a sexy cat. We sit on the sofa awhile and Monica asks me this and that about who I am and where I've come from and about my past, and when I don't know the answer I make up something. Sometimes she puts her hand on my thigh. Taking a whiff of my drink to make sure it's not 'sinthe, pretty soon I'm aware of having drunk a bit more Scotch than I planned, but I'm still sober enough to know it's time to slow down, and Monica puts her hand under my long green cloak and runs it over my breast in this lazy sort of way like it's no more or less diverting than anything else and I have the feeling she could be as much into me as she's ever been into anything if she ever saw the point of having to decide one way or the other. Every so often I think she's going to fall asleep. "I would offer you some candy," she nods at the white residue on the coffee table in front of us, "but they've used it all. The pigs." She talks in this slow sensual way like she might be drunk or drugged except that she doesn't otherwise act drunk or drugged. Depravity becomes her.

This goes on at least a good hour perhaps longer, nothing much changing in the room or the cast of characters except when someone disappears a while and then returns. At one point one of the men takes one of the women, a Persian, by the hand and leads her off though it must not be that far away, anyone can hear it going on on the other side of the wall, anyone can hear her crying, then he comes back in alone and when she returns, a few minutes after him, her eyes look deader than they did before. I've stopped drinking, just raising the Scotch to my lips now and then to make a show of it. My hope is the whole evening will eventually just get mired in its own ennui long enough for me to slip away, though

boulevards and people drive freeways in search of phantom exits and where i

I have no idea how I'm going to get down the mountain or back to the Chateau. I'm very aware the host is looking at me and I'm trying not to look back. Finally he's standing in front of us. He waits for Monica and me to look up at him and when we don't he gives out with this hoarse bark. "Dance."

"Sorry?" I say.

"Get up and dance."

"I'm not a dancer."

"Take off your clothes."

"I'm not a stripper. You should have hired a stripper."

"I paid you a lot of fucking money."

"I explained to your men what I do and what I don't."

"Do you want to make it with her?" he says, pointing at Monica. "You can make it with her and we'll watch."

"Oh Armand," laughs Monica in that not-quite-intoxicated way of hers, "why don't you just let her do whatever it is she *does*? If you just wanted some little trollop to strip or dance or bang," waving her arm at the other women, none of whom protests, "you wouldn't have had to hire *her*, would you? She's an artist isn't she. She's a *professional*. Like you said, you paid her a lot of money so why don't you just let her do whatever it is she does and see what happens."

Dully Armand reflects on this awhile and says, "All right."

"Where?" I say.

"Here."

"Here?" looking 'round at the others.

"Here." So I stand and open my bag and take out half a dozen candles and some matches, and go 'round the room setting the candles here and there and lighting them, then turn off the one or two lamps so everything is candlelit, then take off my cloak and that surely makes an impression, everyone sort of flickers to life for a second at the sight of the white stockings and white lace

Jeno Park the trees shed their cherry blossoms and, for only a rare moment in

corset, the white being my own recent touch, a departure of sorts from the Domme's traditional black. I open the bag and out come several pairs of the fur-lined cuffs and the crop and whip and paddle and several blindfolds and ball-gags and all of this really gets their attention. "Strip," I tell Armand.

"What?"

I smack him 'cross the face with the riding crop. It's not a hard smack or anything, because like I've said I'm not into the heavy corporal stuff, but it's probably fair to say no one's done anything like this to him in a long time because now the party is definitely alert. They couldn't be more alert if I turned a fire hose on them. Armand's henchmen in particular standing by the doors, they look back and forth at each other like they don't know what they're supposed to do, and me, I figure playing this out, taking control of the situation in a way true to my nature, is my only real shot at perhaps getting out of a fix. "Are you sure you want to do this here, or elsewhere?" I say to him.

"Oh, here, by all means," Monica insists from the sofa.

"Yes, here," says someone else.

"Uh," Armand looks 'round, "all right, I guess."

I strike him with the crop 'cross the face again and now the bodyguards look at each other in consternation. "you'll address Me as Mistress Brontë."

Bewildered, Armand nods. "Yes, right." I strike him a third time; a bit too dull to know exactly how he feels about it, he puts his hand to his face and rubs his cheek. "Right, Mistress Brontë," he says.

"Then strip."

Slowly he begins taking off his shirt, still looking at everyone 'round him. When he gets off the shirt, he looks at the bodyguards and says, "I want them to leave."

the hail of dying blossoms, yesterday and today and tomorrow are clearl

"That's up to you," I say. He snaps his fingers at the bodyguards and motions them to the front door; they look at each other and then begin filing out, one by one. "Lock the door, slave armand," I say.

He nods. "Sure," he mumbles, and I give him another good crack 'cross his back.

"'Yes, Mistress Brontë.'"

"Sure, Mistress Brontë," he corrects himself and goes to the door and locks it.

"Now take off the rest of your clothes. I'm not going to say it again." He takes off the rest of his clothes except for his undershorts, and then he takes off the undershorts. Now he's standing naked in the middle of the room. The other guests are squinting at him as though they're hallucinating. "Take this," I say and hand him one of the pairs of cuffs, "put it on your left wrist and lock it shut."

"Uh, You've got the key, right?" he says, and I snap the crop so hard and loud against the arm of the sofa next to me that he and everyone else in the room jumps. Armand, he puts on the left handcuff. I give him one of the blindfolds. "Put this on." Quietly he puts the blindfold on over his eyes. I wave a hand in front of his covered eyes and then, taking the empty cuff in my fingers, pull him toward the bookcases. I slip the cuffs through the handles on a pair of the latticed bookcase doors and then put his right wrist in the empty cuff and lock it; he's now chained to the wall. "Hmm," says Armand. From the sofa I take one of the ball-gags. "Open your mouth," I say, and when he does I strap the red rubber ball in it. "Mmwrnf," he says.

The other guests, particularly the two males, are enthralled. "Hey, what about us," one of them says.

Men. Can they be more stupid? Is there anything they won't do to get naked with a woman? I snap the crop against

delineated by the explosion of trees, I arriving there not only in a blizzard of

Armand's bare butt and say to the one who spoke, "Crawl, slave," and the man gets down from the sofa and crawls to me. The third one, feeling left out, he gets down and crawls over too. "Beg Mistress Brontë to give two miserable slugs like you the honor of being Her slaves."

"Please, Mistress Brontë," they whimper, "allow us be Your slaves."

"Unworthy as you are."

"Unworthy as we are."

"Strip," I say, and they can't get their clothes off fast enough. Out of my bag come two more pairs of handcuffs and two more blindfolds; soon each of them is chained to two more pairs of bookcase doors like Armand, the three of them lined up next to each other. "Thank You, Mistress Brontë," one says. "Be quiet," I say and strap a ball in his mouth, and then one in the other man's.

Looking back on it, this is where I made my mistake. Having taken control of the situation, I should have assessed things and figured out how I might now get past the bodyguards outside the front door, but instead I get carried away. It's Monica, I know that — I'm infatuated. I'm even turned on by her silly little endearments that from a man I would despise. There's something about the audacity of her, the way her desires are all right there on the surface, just like they would be with a man, and the way one of those desires is me. There for a moment not only do I have under my control these three halfwits who have willingly chained themselves naked to a wall but, in a way, Monica too, sitting there on the sofa looking at me as though she's having a religious vision. The other women haven't been this excited since puberty. I walk 'round slapping the men with the crop and telling them how pitiful their erections are and how women just laugh at them all the time, and Monica sitting on the sofa watching all this finally can't stand it anymore and gets up. She comes over next to me as close as she

blossoms but atomized time, in a land still traumatized by the confession half

can, holding a finger to her lips as though to say shhhh not a sound: "May I?" she whispers softly in my ear, her warm breath against my neck, and that's when I do what I shouldn't do. It's just utterly unprofessional — I'm supposed to be in charge. Instead I give Monica the crop.

She looks at it deliciously, licks her lips, then lets into Armand with a blow I think will bring down the ceiling.

"Rnngswft!" says Armand.

"Oh," Monica coos, "this is too good."

The other women on the sofa burst into laughter and start clapping. "Uhm," I start to say, but Monica's not near finished. She begins giving Armand the thrashing of all time, sort of chortling at first but then laughing more and more with every thwap 'cross Armand's backside till she's so convulsed with laughter she can barely hit him at all. Armand is practically climbing the wall. "Here, here!" cries one of the other women, jumping to her feet, "let me," and rips the crop from Monica's hands. In the meantime another girl goes for the whip I've taken from my bag and another for a paddle, and pretty soon they're all wailing away and I'm Spartanatrix leading chicks in revolt against the Empire. Rage, humiliation, all the times they've been used and treated like dirt, it's all coming out now isn't it, whips and paddles and crops flying while the naked men chained to the wall are in a sort of seizure, twisting and struggling at their cuffs and making all sorts of sounds. "Now girls," I try to calm them down, but there's no calming them down, I was in control but now the whole thing's out of control till the Persian girl, the one who was taken out of the room earlier and who we all heard crying, stops and looks at the paddle in her hand and, finding it not nearly lethal enough, gazes 'round the room till her eye falls on the iron poker next to the fire place.

She throws down the paddle. She crosses the living room

entury before by the emperor whose people believed was God that he wasn't

and grabs the poker from the fireplace and is coming back with it for the man who did whatever he did to her, and I say, "Oh, hey, wait," and even Monica comes to her senses, "No no no," she laughs, holding the Persian girl back, "no no no no," restraining her but still laughing. Meanwhile the bodyguards outside are now banging on the front door, "What's going on in there," while Monica and I, we're trying to hold back the girl with the poker and the other women are still flailing away, beating the naked bodies of the groaning men to a rather glowing pink. The bodyguards are banging on the door and it's clear they're going to break it down any second. "I have to get *out* of here," I say to Monica, grabbing the poker from the other girl's hand and I've just enough presence of mind to take from my bag the keys to the handcuffs when Monica says, "This way." Turns out the whole back wall of the house with the floor-to-ceiling windows can be moved like a sliding glass door though not any too easily, and we're squeezing through the opening into the dark back yard where the pool is when I hear the front door come crashing down behind me. I hear the other women screaming in flight, some of them pushing at me from behind, all of us scattering out into the night and into the hills with Armand's boys behind us.

I kick off my heels and throw the keys to the handcuffs out somewhere into the dark 'round me, and follow Monica who's running past the leaf-covered pool to a small wooden gate you would have to know about to find. The gate doesn't really open the whole way and we have to squeeze through like we squeezed through the sliding wall of the house, and there I am in my corset and stockings splinters catching on the lace, pushing through and feeling glad for once I'm little. Except for the fact I think she's part cat, I don't know how Monica gets through. Past the gate are steps down the hill, and at one point I trip and tumble down the steps and pick myself up and keep running down the path with the

God at all, and I was the agent of chaos in a way I'm only truly aware of now

steps zigzagging this way and that, and before zagging I keep bouncing off hedges at each zig. I have no idea where I'm going except it's definitely down the hill. I'm surely not heading the way the limo came up, or toward the beach cove where I started, and I don't know when I become aware Monica is gone or that there's some heavy breathing behind me from one of Armand's gorillas right on my tail. I keep thinking I'm smaller so I should be able to outrun him but he keeps coming. It's funny how even when you're running in blind panic through the dark, a bit like when you're swimming in a lake, your brain goes on furiously thinking anyway, what can I do and how can I get away from this person, what will make him stop. What will make him just give up. I just keep running down the hill toward what I know has to be — somewhere in front of me — the water, wondering where on the lake I'm going to wind up and how far I can swim. I remember how hard I swam that first night I came to the Chateau X and almost not making it, and I really don't want to have to go back in the water again.

We reach a small glen that's all white and lit up under the moon, me and the one still chasing me, and I know the white of my corset makes me very easy to see, a little bouncing white moonbeam. He doesn't have a gun does he, I think to myself. I think to myself if suddenly the sound of his breathing stops then I'll fall to the ground and into the grass of the glen because that might mean he's stopped running long enough to take out his gun and shoot. I glance over my shoulder which is a mistake because it slows me down, and he's still right there behind me and it's the man who originally came out to the Chateau grotto in the powerboat and drove me up in the limo.

I've gotten all the way 'cross the clearing when his breathing behind me *does* stop, I don't hear him anymore, I hear nothing except this loud crack and think oh jeez he *is* shooting!

ere in the birth canal of the lake, suspended in this moment between chaos

And stupidly instead of falling in the grass like I planned I just sort of stop and turn and look, expecting to see him there on the other side of the glen aiming at me — but he's not there, at least not that I can see at first, then there's something lying in the grass like a big wounded buffalo or bear and it's him, and I hear him moan. I have no idea what brought him down but I start to turn and run into the trees to the south when a hand reaches up out of the grass and takes hold of my wrist and pulls me down.

It clasps my mouth and I don't make a sound. I'm not sure when I know it's him, whether it's when I turn and actually see him or if something just tells me. But I swear something in Kale's eyes, they light up like I've never seen in any person — in the night you think they're fireflies darting above the grass. We're hunkered down in the grass and his head moves slowly from side to side while the rest of him doesn't move at all, almost like his head sort of swivels on his neck and then it stops and his ears pick up the sound of something.

I can't hear anything. "Heart beat," he says.

I can't hear anything. I can't see anything. He still holds my wrist in his hand and I don't move at all. And then out of the trees on the northern side of the clearing where I've just come from are two more of Armand's boys, stopping long enough to check out their fallen pal and then turn our direction.

I look at my wrist. It's free, though I never felt him let me go. He's gone from where he was right next to me in the grass, and I think I hear something move through the night before me but it's the sound of the wind, I think it's the sound of the wind. I don't know what it's the sound of. But Armand's other henchmen are heading toward me in the grass when there's another loud crack like I heard just a few moments ago, and then one goes down like the first one and then another crack and then the other

and God, a point-misser on this matter I must admit, arriving in Tokyo already

one. There are two more cracks and then no movement in the grass at all, the three men just lying there when I finally stick my head up to look 'cross the glen in the moonlight. I look and there are just the three of them lying there motionless in the grass — and then right in front of me there's the momentary glow of those eyes like fireflies in the grass and Kale, almost like he's taken form out of nothing, he comes to me as though gliding, not making a sound, not the rustling of grass or anything. With one hand he's holding one of the oars from his boat, none the worse for wear for having leveled three men as far as I can see, with the other hand he pulls me to follow.

I follow him down through the trees of the hillside beneath us and to a cove different from the one where he left me off a few hours ago. I don't recognize it at all, I have no idea where we are — it will turn out we're about five miles of shoreline west of where I last saw either Kale or the lake. "Talk about being in the right place at the right time," I say stupidly when I see the boat in the water. As though, you know, it's a complete coincidence he happens to be there. As though it's a complete accident that, at this moment, he happens to be in this one cove out of a thousand. As though some instinct I'll never understand hasn't led him here, as though he's not followed the sound of my heart from the moment I left him.

I'm freezing out on the lake as he rows us south and then east. I want to go back to the Chateau but he's not taking me there and I don't argue. I freeze all the way out to the island where he takes me, the top of one of those old West Hollywood hotels rising from the water where he's set up a little nook between the stairs and a rooftop storeroom of dead telephone lines and elevator cables. There are some mattresses and blankets that have been lying 'round more years than I want to think about, and a little place where someone built a fire once. "I get the feeling you've

▸regnant but not yet knowing I carried inside me a question that I asked once

done this before," I finally say about half an hour into thawing out. To the northeast I can see lights I'm pretty sure are the Chateau. I worry about the Mistress, I don't like having left her alone. I'm angry at myself about the whole evening.

He sleeps next to me. If he had wanted to get in under the blankets with me I would have let him, as long as he kept his hands to himself. I think he doesn't want to put me in the position of saying yes or no, you see? He wants to take the decision out of my hands, into his, so there will be no question of the night being anything other than what it is. And I'm relieved and looking back perhaps I should have told him it was all right to get under the blankets with me, but I don't because I'm not sure he'll take it the right way and I'm too tired to want to think about it — but you see I think he knows that too so that's why he doesn't ask. And it moves me about him, that he wants to spare me having to be in control of anything for that moment when I don't want to be in control of anything, I want to give up all control and be able to trust it's going to be all right, I want to be able to trust him, to trust the night will pass without event or misunderstanding and I'll wake the next morning and he'll already be awake walking 'round the edge of the island looking out at whatever, and I get up and start looking 'round too, wrapping the blanket 'round me because there I am still in my corset and stockings which are pretty trashed from the night before, but there's nothing else to wear till I get back to the Chateau. I'm stumbling 'round the rooftop in the gray morning sun checking it out and trying to get warm, and there I have another distinct memory of something from before: of sleeping on another rooftop somewhere like this one, beneath an enormous sky.

Back in the little gutted room with the elevator cables I turn and he's standing there in the doorway blocking it. For a second all my defenses go up the way they do when a woman is cornered

as a little girl, running one afternoon into my uncle's bar and crying ou

and a man is blocking her way out. All my defenses go up and suddenly he looks crestfallen, he's seen it in my face, seen the way I got a bit afraid of him, the way I hate him just a bit after everything he's done, after the way he's slept next to me and hasn't even tried to get under the blanket with me; for me to suddenly get wary and afraid of him, well, I can see how it hurts him. As though he would ever do anything to me. As though he would ever threaten me in any way. He's hurt by my collapse of trust in this moment and something else, I know there's something else, I knew from the first night he came to me. "Sorry," I half murmur, half snap, and that comes off a bit defensive too.

He nods. He backs out of the doorway to let me by.

In the doorway I take his face between my hands. "I'm sorry," I say again, gentler.

He nods again.

"Jeez," I say, "what is it Kale. Are you in love with me, is that it? Do you just want to fuck me, is that all this is about?"

"Those are two different questions," he answers.

"Why," taken aback, "that's the most complicated thing I've ever heard you say." I take his hand and pull him down in the doorway and we sit together our legs entwined. I reach out from beneath my blanket and take his hands in mine and hold them. It's not like that with me and boys, I try to explain. I know a man always thinks he can change a girl like me if he only gets the chance but that's not going to happen. Really, at this moment I'm not trying to be a bitch, if anything I'm sort of begging him to understand. You're pretty though, I'll give you that, I say to him looking at his water-green eyes that light up in the night and putting my hand in his brown feathery hair that smells like tall dry grass — but it's more than that. Somehow I feel it's more than that. Later, back at the Chateau and lying in my own bed, I think about how it's more than that. Part of me thinks well I can't see

hat's missing from the world? and years later from L.A. to Tokyo there

him any more, because it just torments him, but the other part of me isn't sure I can stay away, because there's a connection for sure. Not like we're lovers but. . . something else.

Over the next couple of weeks I go out with him again to the island called the Hamblin because it's truly mega out there even if there's no blue anymore, even under the gray sky and looking out over the gray water, and also because of that connection. Because I can't help wanting to spend time with him. But after a few times I know I can't anymore, that it means too much to him to be with me and it hurts him too much not to make love to me. Like the first night out on the Hamblin he never imposes himself on me in any way except one time standing next to him looking out at the lake I put my arm in his as the wind comes up and then he puts his arm 'round me and his fingers brush my breast ever so slightly like it's an accident — boys will be boys, eh? One night he comes to the Chateau with some food and money to be my slave again but we're somehow too far past that scene anymore, and there in the Lair before the fire he tries to tell me, I know what he's trying to say and I'm thinking oh no don't, don't say it, and he can't, it catches in his throat or he can't come up with the words or something, and he starts talking with his hands. His eyes coming at me fixed, relentless, he starts talking in this sort of sign language, his hands making these urgent elaborate pictures in the air, and he becomes more and more frustrated, his eyes closed tight, hands darting in front of him faster and faster till finally I just take them in my own, "Hey, hey," to try and calm him. He relaxes and his hands rest in mine and he opens his eyes and just looks at me.

I wait for Armand and his boys to show up. I figure it's a matter of time, that they're not going to let that night go unanswered for, so I gather up all the cash they paid me and keep it handy on the off-chance that somehow returning the money will

inside me that question was beginning to grow into its own answer, What wa.

satisfy them though I don't believe that at all. My only concern now is that no harm comes to the Mistress. I've almost convinced myself it's all been forgotten when yesterday afternoon I finally hear the approaching sound of the motor of the powerboat, and get the money and go out the back, down the stone steps into the grotto. The boat approaches and it's my friend who drove me in the limo and chased me into the glen — on his forehead he has the scar of a pretty good gash where Kale leveled him with the oar.

He's about as happy to see me as I am to see him. For a moment the boat just bobs on the water in the afternoon shadows of the grotto. "Cunt," he finally says.

I let that one pass. "Look," I say, "here's the money back," thrusting it in front of me with both hands.

"What do you mean?" he says.

"Here's your money back. Tell your boss I'm sorry."

Well what can I say. You're not going to believe this, but — Turns out Armand doesn't want his money back, and he's not sent his boys out to beat me up or kill me or ransack the Chateau. Turns out he wants me to come back up to the house *and do the whole thing over again.* Without the other girls joining in this time but all the rest of it: the blindfold, the cuffs, the little red ball in his mouth — he *especially* liked the little red ball — the whole thing except we'll do it in private or, if I feel safer, he'll come out to the Chateau and send his bodyguards away and we'll do it here, all night if I'm agreeable and he'll pay me double what he paid the first time, up front. I have to wear the white lace corset and stockings, though. That's the only stipulation.

Men! Fucking unbelievable, what? I just stand there with my mouth open and finally stammer I need a bit of time to think about it, because I don't want to say yes and I'm afraid to say no. Back 'cross the lake goes the boat to Armand, from the grotto steps

missing from the world, and although I didn't yet know it was growing inside

I watch it cross the lake, trying to think what I'm going to do. I don't want to go back to that house, I tell the Mistress, but I don't want these boys out at the Chateau either. There's a lot I don't tell the Mistress. I don't tell her everything that happened that night in the hills because every time I see her now she just looks older, she seems to come out of her bedroom less and less, and to move more and more slowly — and I'm onto the business with the lapsinthe. I've figured out what that's about, to the extent it makes sense at all, she thinks one night she's going to finally take one too many that's going to put her over the edge once and for all, whatever the edge is. But I figure the last thing she needs to hear about is what happened that night at Armand's, just so she can worry about me. I tell her a bit about Kale, not really so much except, you know, There's this boy — because there's not that much I know to tell, is there? except he's strange and sort of sweet and he's in love with me. Yes she whispers they all fall a little in love with you, and I say no, this boy's *in love* with me. And what do you think about that, she asks, and I say well it's not something I can reciprocate, is it (perhaps she's checking for some weakness in my lesbian resolve), but he's sweet I say and very strange and I don't want to hurt him (I haven't really told her how he saved my little pixie behind) and the last time I saw him, I saw it in his eyes, this hurt, and I just wanted to run because I had never seen a boy hurt like that over me, not like that. I thought I was happy making the men cry a bit, what with a good healthy thrashing that would get a few tears flowing and the blood moving — but not like that, and it shocked me. And the Mistress she says well then you know you should send him away. It's only right. You should send him away. And I say, I know.

Then we're quiet in front of the fire. What is it, I say, and she smiles thinly, It's death, she says, "spreading through the baseboards and ceiling," and I can't really say what that last bit

me and my son was growing with it, still I somehow knew, *and everywhere tha*

means but I guess I know anyway, and I suppose I'm not that surprised. But how? I ask, and she answers, It's not always easy to say, sometimes it's something unbearably sad you never recover from. . . sometimes when a woman dies, it's an act of sacrifice.

One thing I know, though, she says after a few more moments. One thing I know — and she says it with more force than I've heard her say anything — I know I don't want to die on this lake.

I go to bed not long after that and, lying in bed and struggling to fall asleep, is it a Lapse I have, like everyone else on the lake used to have all the time when the lake was sinking? Or a dream? Or a dislodged memory. That night of the Freek Recherche lunatique, did I drink that shot after all and now I'm having a 'sinthe flashback? Whatever, there I am back on that night I first swam to the Chateau and the Mistress, back on that night I first came up out of the lake, back under the water not so much floating up to the surface but *expelled*, by something below me, *born*, out of some other life, the placenta of a previous consciousness trailing behind me as I make my way to the surface. Bits and pieces of whoever I was before, falling away from my naked body, and then bits and pieces of distant recollection falling away as I swim upward, flashes of a remembrance washed away in the cold of the lake, a horrific flash of rubble and fire and confusion and terror and chaos and of having been hurled through the opening of the lake in a full-force gale of ash and obliteration. Control and its loss assert themselves as the parameters of my new psyche, right there in the water. And somehow I know now, returning to this moment in my Lapse or dream or memory or whatever it is, that this passage is different for everyone isn't it, that it's a passage without time, a passage that might have taken me a moment or a hundred years, from somewhere that was a

went then I went as the bearer of chaos, with everything coming apart around

moment or a hundred years ago, and that whatever was on the other side of the hole at the bottom of the lake is different for each of us, that whatever it is this birth-passage brought me from was not necessarily where anyone else comes from, or where anyone else would go to if she were to try and go back, if it were even possible to go back. This particular passage through the opening of the lake, from wherever I came, it was my own, my unique journey from a unique place and moment, and more than that, from my own personal moment of unique chaos, whatever that was, for unique reasons having to do uniquely with me, beyond all control. And that's all I understand about it other than that somewhere in my rise to the surface I have a vision of the Mistress or someone much like her, swimming right past me except going the other way.

I also have a vision of Kale I don't understand: chaos' son. Or perhaps it is that I'm chaos' daughter. And it's not till finally the Lapse finishes that I sleep, my sound sleep from which no one and nothing can stir me, the sleep of the dead. . . .

These are the memoirs of Brontë Blu, dungeon-mistress of the Chateau X, white avenging angel of the Hollywood Hills, God's little joke on the male gender.

The afternoon before, Kale watches the powerboat with Armand's men heading for the Chateau. Sitting in his own boat under the eaves of the shoreline trees, he takes his oar in hand ready again to go to Her rescue; he waits because he doesn't want to interject himself too soon and agitate the situation unnecessarily. When he sees Armand's boat leave, he begins rowing hurriedly toward the grotto and gets there in time to see Her disappearing back into the Chateau through the door at the top of the steps; for a while there on the lake he waits, watches, to assure himself everything is all right before he starts back out to the Hamblin. Halfway to the Hamblin he turns to look back at the Chateau and

me, upheaval and confusion in my path, radios going haywire and subway.

see if perhaps She has come out onto the terrace to wave to him, but She doesn't appear and he realizes he doesn't want to go to the Hamblin, that now it only reminds him of Her. So he turns west and makes his way along the shoreline. The boat drifts awhile and he finally beaches it about a mile from the Chateau, at yet another small cove where some of the trees are still black from a fire almost a quarter of a century before. The lake there seems blacker too. he gets out of the boat into the black water and pulls it up onto shore and ties it to one of the black trees.

kale lies on the ground and stares up through the black leaves at the gray afternoon sky and has a childhood memory of when it used to be blue. he doesn't know that what he feels in his chest is the deflowering of a virgin heart, because until not so long ago it was as much the heart of an owl as a man. he doesn't want to think about Her but he cannot, i cannot *not* think about Her. i lie awhile then get back in the boat and go back out to the place in the water where i can see the light where She lives. i wait for Her to come out and see me and wave to me and call. i would sleep next to Her and not touch Her but just watch Her while She sleeps if She said to. i would touch Her long gold hair only if She said. i cannot *not* think of Her gold hair. Why can i not *not* think of Her smile. i would be Her slave all the time, Her best true slave i who have led armadas of owls. i who have multiplied and divided tides and winds. i who Big Agua has never ruled. Slave to no one and nothing else. i try to remember out on the water in my boat what it was not to have known Her. i wish it could be that way again but i don't wish it. i want to not remember Her but i don't want it. i want to have never known Her but i don't want it. i want to forget Her but i don't. i would rather die about Her than live past Her. What does it mean that i feel this. i must be sick some way. Divide the times i think of Her by the gold strands of Her hair, multiply that by the light of Her mouth — but i can't figure the

reaking down and glass buildings shattering and cherry blossoms from the

numbers of it. It's math i don't know. Why does it hurt me to have known Her. Why can i no longer hear the sound of my own heartbeat, or any heart on the water but Hers. If i was a girl would She want me then.

i cry for Her like a girl please, isn't that enough.

Next day i wait again for Her sign, there is no sign. Next day and the next and next, and then one day i take the boat out to

Her steps and Her door and knock, i wait in the boat for Her sign, there's no sign. i go back and knock on the door again. She doesn't come and i wait longer before i go inside.

i've never been inside in the day before. i think i should take off my clothes like night-time and so i go through the rooms without my clothes and think when i see Her i'll get down at Her feet, through each door i think She'll be there and i'll get down at Her feet. But She isn't there. She isn't there and standing in the afternoon sunlight in the middle of the empty lair he realizes she's gone. Realizes she's gone not just for an hour, not just for a single sun or moon, not just for a single room but gone with who was here with her; clothes are gone as well, there's that feeling of place when it's been abandoned, and it's the feeling of his existence because he's been abandoned too.

Not for the first time.

He goes out onto the terrace of the Chateau and says, more to himself at first, where are You. He barely knows what it is, his own crying. He tells himself he hates her now but knows he doesn't. Standing there on the terrace, over the sound of the lake he listens for her heart, but wherever it is now, it's too far away. Standing there on the terrace, looking out over the lake listening, it occurs to him for the first time they're all gone too, the disciples. The faithful who for years worshipped at the waterline of the Chateau X are gone and it occurs to him that in fact now that he thinks about it, he hasn't seen them for a while; and that's when he

trees set loose in a special panic, and the question What's missing from the

knows for certain she isn't coming back.

Turning his back on the lake he walks back into the Chateau from the terrace and through the main lair, back out through the transitional chambers into the grotto where he edges along the small stone walkway that circles the water leading to an old door with a brass ring for a knob that he used to know very well. He finds the door slightly ajar and opens it and steps in, gazing over the shelves that once held in captivity thousands of melodies from a thousand snakes expired in menstrual blood, but now the shelves are empty as if ransacked although the webs in the corners indicate the Vault was already vacated long ago, the songs having escaped of their own accord or having been set free by someone who couldn't stand to keep them anymore.

He thinks maybe he might find one in particular but when he doesn't he leaves the Vault and, one more time, goes back up into the Lair to stand gazing around him in a daze, seeing nothing for a moment until, blinked clear of tears, his eyes lock on the mantle above the hearth. He walks over to the hearth: i don't remember this he thinks — but it had always been night-time before, his eyes cast down in subjugation. Be a man who never looks up and you're likely to miss something.

i don't remember this here. He holds the toy monkey in his hand then goes back out through the transitional chamber into the entryway, back out onto the stone steps of the grotto to his boat. Still naked he begins to row back out onto the lake, and rows for a while east by southeast then veering slightly northward from the single coordinate drawn above him by the line of a collapsed skytram from many years before. After a while he comes to the place. This is the place he's rowed by and past and over many times as though it meant nothing to him, as though it held no recollection of anything at all for him; but that was night-time and this is day, and maybe he's known all along anyway. All along

vorld? calling up to me from that womb of mine that already predated me, that

he's known, ignoring this place as if it couldn't hurt his heart, but now everything hurts his heart, and he rows here and stops and stares down into the water, leaning over the boat and putting his face as close to the water as he can without capsizing, wondering if god lives down there and might explain something to him at long last. Out on the wide open lake at the place, above the spot, without her, abandoned again and his heart feeling not only what it's never felt but all the things it's felt but denied, breaking beyond what he can stand, he believes he's drifted into the fourteenth room of the Hotel of Thirteen Losses. When god doesn't talk to him from beneath the water Kale finally begins to row back along the shoreline he followed the last time he saw her disappearing into the Chateau doorway. He's stopped crying, rowing relentlessly until he reaches the black cove of burned trees and black water where he climbs out of the boat and lies where he lay before, with the red monkey in his hand on the black Zed shore.

This crucible of loss now only makes him realize how lonely he's always been. It only makes him realize that although he might not have had a name for desolation it was there anyway. He's now aware in a way he's never been how he believes no one cares for him, and what it means to be this untouched by another human heart. He's now aware in a way he's never been how the deflowered heart has an altogether other kind of music, a music altogether different from the percussion of blood. He's now aware in a way he's never been of how seared into the retina of memory are the echoes of all the questions he never got to ask someone, all the great questions of life and love and death that begin to occur to you when you're a small boy, maybe in the night just as you're about to fall asleep; he's now aware in a way he's never been of how there was never anyone there to answer these questions for him. Feeling forsaken as he hasn't felt since he was a small boy in

womb of mine already older than I was, the question calling up to me amid the

a silver boat, he's about to slip off into the sleep of the void when, like a voice speaking out loud to him, like someone right there at his side, there floats up from somewhere deep in his mind something that was left there years ago, planted in his ear one night while he slept and having sunk deep into him, and now opened like a time capsule that was waiting for precisely this moment of

loneliness to unlock it, there in the darkening hush of the trees
                    your mama loves you
and he sits straight up to it. Like someone right there at his side
has whispered it. He sits straight up to it and it's still there, the
thing he just heard, it hasn't disappeared like a dream. It hasn't
vanished into memory like one of the Lapses of the Lake. It's still
there in the air and, seeing it, his eyes light, like fireflies darting
above the grass.

istorical rumors and little spasms of collective memory ripping outward, and at twilight I would look out toward Tokyo Bay from the window of the ryokan

2001–2089

here I stayed when I first got to Japan and I would watch the pixilated black waves rolling in and with them they brought that memory I had forgotten, o

He gets out late winter. He's off on the exact day by thirty-some
hours, which isn't bad calculations. He made a decision when he
went in to keep track of the days, because he knew it was the
intention of his jailers to   jettison his sense of time;
they brought him in   **2037**   in a metal truck with
no windows. The rumor   is that the penitentiary is
somewhere in the plains of the Montana-Saskatchewan annex.
When he's released, a metal truck takes him back to Seattle;
they open the doors of the truck and the glitter of the afternoon sea
is like glass in his eyes. He sits back in the truck until someone
says, Move.

tanding with my uncle as a little girl on the banks of the river and seeing the

They put him on a boat going down the coast to Los Angeles. For
five days and fifteen hundred miles he doesn't see anyone except a
soldier here and there, like the guards at the Northwest-Mendocino
border. The boat sails into L.A. mid-dusk, past the smoky moors
of the Hollywood Peninsula, navigating the outlying swamps
where the Hancock Park mansions loom in ruin, water rolling in
and out of the porticoes. It crosses the rest of the lagoon

into downtown, then up the main canal. Cale can see the smaller canals trickling off between the buildings that are black like the mansions behind him, and there's a sound of bubbling music from the Chinese storefronts along the water. It comes out of the buildings, a distinct and different melody from each one; addresses on the doors are scratched and defaced, and there are no signs on the street corners anymore. Ask someone how to get to this place or that, and she'll sing you the directions.

Two women on a train. Their destination is the end of an argument. They've been riding the argument all night since they got on the train originally and carelessly bound for. . . what? dinner? a movie. . . they almost can't remember, they have been riding **2001** and changing trains so many hours now. Each knows something more is at risk in this particular argument on this particular evening than just its resolution, than one woman conceding to the other if only to placate the moment. This particular argument has always been just a little too profound to call merely a lovers' quarrel.

woman on the other side, and it was only there in Tokyo staring out over the

To others riding the train with them, the two might appear to be mother and daughter. One of them is close to fifty, with a recently cropped mane of increasingly silvery hair and serenity woven in the air around her like a web; the other is barely a woman at all, nineteen years old. The older woman, who doesn't like to think or speak of the age difference, has to acknowledge to herself that indeed it makes their argument more complicated. They've had

some version of this argument many times now in the last several
months, and this time each senses that they won't, as in the past,
just move on when it's over. Or rather: they'll move on, but
without each other. Although the older woman seems the less
agitated of the two, the less heated in her words, that's more a
function of maturity; in fact she feels more is at stake for her —
but, you know, try telling the younger woman that. Thinking about
it in the many silences that fall between each of the argument's
flare-ups, the older woman realizes that to the younger woman,
with her entire future still ahead of her, the decision has
consequences that much more resounding. So maybe, Sara admits
to herself, it's not so fair to say she has more at stake. I have too
little time, the girl has too much. She admits this to herself but not
out loud; admitting it out loud, she would lose everything.

They've just gotten on the subway line heading south. It's become
a ritual of this argument, in the way all arguments have rituals, that
every time a cessation of hostilities coincides with a subway
station, the women get off the train and change to another. At this
point they're not paying attention to which train or which station.
Somehow as long as they keep moving — as opposed to going to a
café somewhere and thrashing things out for good — perhaps some
rubicon can avoid being crossed. Lately the younger woman has
begun to feel things are out of control, a feeling she hates. She
doesn't want to bring up the age thing with Sara. It's always been

vater that I finally realized it had been my mother on the other side of that

a psychological obstacle for the couple to surmount, particularly
for the older woman who's that much more keenly aware, the
younger realizes, of everything such a divide in years represents.
By now the girl accepts there's something maternal in her
attraction to the older woman, and doesn't understand why this is
any less a basis for love or a romantic bond than anything else.

Women are drawn to father figures all the time so why can't I be
drawn to a mother figure.

That this probably says something about her relationship with her
real mother, the girl understands. Ironically it was this that
brought her to Sara as a patient in the first place. Somehow,
though, they never got into it in any of their sessions, and she's
trying to remember if she was always the one avoiding the topic or
if, now that she thinks about it, it was Sara who avoided it, once
the attraction became apparent. Rather quickly it seems, now that
the girl thinks about it, they wound up talking more about Sara
than her. "You'll spend your whole life," Sara said that first
session, "making peace with your own true nature," and every now
and then Sara repeats it as though to imply she understands the
girl's nature better than the girl does. The girl still isn't sure what
it actually means, the business about one's true nature, or whether
it's just something Sara says to sound superior. But at this moment
it seems to her perhaps it says a lot more about Sara than about her.

True to the cliché about therapists, Sara's past seems its own sort
of mess when it's not a blank altogether, and the girl realizes the
divide in years is more remarkable for all the experience Sara
never had. Whereas the girl's first sexual encounter — with
another girl — took place at eleven, Sara's had been in her
mid-twenties with an emotionally fetal man she wound up dating

river staring back at me, her shoulders sagging in defeat when she couldn'

thirteen years, never marrying, never living together. After this
relationship didn't so much collapse as trail off into nothingness,
with the man simply moving on to another job in another city,
Sara's next was with a woman, also a client like the girl, lasting
eight months and then followed by a chasm of nearly ten years in
which, as far as the girl can tell, Sara had no intimate human
relations of any sort. So talk about spending your life making

peace with your own nature. When you get right down to it, then, who's really the senior partner here, the girl asks herself on the train now.

So as to establish some control in the relationship, the girl always made it a rule never to make the first move in these things. She broke the rule in Sara's case, figuring it was the only way anything would ever happen. Now she wonders if this was a mistake. In any other situation she can't help thinking a nineteen-year-old would never come on to a woman nearly thirty years older but perhaps that's naïve; after all, nineteen-year-old girls come on to older men all the time. Within six months of their first doctor/patient session, the two moved in together. It's been a year since, and was a lovely time up till the whole baby obsession that, the girl can pinpoint exactly, began one night four or five months ago. They went across town for dinner at the brownstone of another lesbian couple, who disclosed that without much luck they had been investigating ways of having a child. All the talk that evening of eggs going back and forth from one person to another boggled the girl's mind so much it gave her a headache.

On the train now the girl feels trapped by how often and fervently she's insisted to Sara the difference in age means nothing to her. Now, subway track rattling beneath them, that argument restrains her from giving voice to the fact that, in her view,

ind the courage to face her small abandoned daughter who not so long

the daughter/mother nature of their relationship renders what Sara wants a bit bizarre. But is this really what troubles her most? the girl wonders. Leaving aside everything else — leaving aside even how it would be her body, after all, serving as laboratory, incubator, assembly line in the processing of some anonymous male sperm just so Sara's long latent, now suddenly urgent maternal drive might be satisfied — what strange new dynamic would be loosed not only between them but within the girl herself? If, consciously or not, defined as such or not, on some level the girl plays the role of daughter in her relationship with Sara, then would a baby in some way be a grand-daughter? A sister to her own mother?

Like all those eggs being bandied about over dinner, this makes her head hurt. Perhaps she should get off the train. And naturally, she realizes, we keep talking about this baby as though it goes without saying it would be a girl: what if it's a boy? Do we know how to raise a boy? Do *I* know how to raise a boy, if it should ever fall to me to do it alone given — muttered under the breath of her mind — how much older Sara is? Somehow the notion it could be a boy, it just makes the whole idea, monumental to begin with, that much more overwhelming, although the younger woman has to confess there's something irresistible about someday reminding the young teenage barbarian, fumbling with girls in car seats to heavy metal on the radio, that he's literally the son of a jerkoff; it wouldn't be nearly so satisfying with a daughter.

You couldn't have thought of all this ten years ago could you, the girl says to Sara in her mind, with such force of resentment that for a moment she's sure she said it out loud. But then she realizes the illogic of her own bitterness: of course if Sara had thought of it ten years ago, in all likelihood she would be with someone else

afterward asked What's missing from the world? and who then never dreamed

now and they wouldn't be together at all. "What was that last stop?" the girl finally says in one of the pauses between arguing that now have become longer than the arguing itself. A man sitting across the aisle stares at her; she pulls her coat to her but not too tight, folds her arms across her chest. Actually she really doesn't hate men. Actually, sometimes they can be easier to deal with than women because everything's so straightforward in terms of what

they want, and it's true, no getting 'round it, that women are often confounding labyrinths whereas men, they're always simple sidestreets just calling themselves boulevards. Plus it's one of the few advantages of the gender that almost none of the men always checking her out is especially keen for her to have his baby.
"Chambers," Sara answers.

"What?"

"Chambers was the last stop."

Really? We're that far downtown? The next station won't be open this time of night. If she gets off at the stop after that, the girl thinks to herself, should she announce it to Sara, or just do it and see if the other follows? A power play of sorts, the act of just deciding to get off the subway: a way to get Sara to tip her hand, Sara who never tips her hand, who hides everything behind her veil of doctoral calm. A power play — but also an opportunity for the therapist to point out the girl is being unduly, provocatively petulant, even for a nineteen-year-old. So she does the grown-up thing. "I want to get off at the next one," she says. Sara doesn't answer; so much for mature behavior, the girl snorts to herself. But at the next stop, when the train doors slide open and the girl grabs her radio and walks off, Sara follows, slipping through the doors just as they close behind her.

never dreamed in all her nights of childhood, in all the nights of childhood

It makes the girl feel a bit more in control and she likes that. She knows they've been on the train a long time but she's momentarily surprised anyway, as the two women walk up the steps from the subway, how dark it is and that it's not still early twilight as it was when they got on. They're not saying anything now, Sara just following as they cross the intersection and head for the open plaza. There's an incongruity between the loveliness of the balmy moment and the women's heavy tension. Sara won't continue to follow silently much longer if I don't concede something, the girl thinks, even if it's nothing more than a kind word of regret; but even that would sound contrite and the girl realizes she's beyond contrition, beyond concession — that in fact she's angry: is it over then? Entering the plaza square, her head is filled with things it's never been filled with before: the sense of betrayal, the sense of having been taken advantage of — she was my *therapist*, the girl thinks, but perhaps that's not fair is it, in as how I made that first move, pursuing the romance with the naked aggression of need. Nothing's more aggressive than need. But there's that superiority of Sara's that makes her so insufferable sometimes, that —

"Where are we going?" Sara finally says almost snappishly, Sara who never snaps, Sara of the endless empathy but no true sympathy. Sara who believes that, beyond the point of logical self-exhaustion, sorrow is only an illusion, a collapse of fortitude on the part of the afflicted.

"I want to go up," the girl answers.

"Up?"

"To the top."

when a girl dreams all the possibilities of her life in a way she'll never do

The older woman looks up. "At this time of night?"

For a moment the prospect seems a salvation to the girl. For a moment the girl is convinced their relationship will survive if Sara just comes with her. Sometimes a moment presents an unexpected, inexplicable test; the girl says, with a sudden burst of enthusiasm, "I know someone who can take us."

"Who?"

"This man I know."

"This man you know? What man you know?"

No, the girl thinks, this isn't the way the conversation is supposed to go. "Someone I've been doing some work for at the library. I told you about him."

"No. . . . "

"I *did*," the girl says, almost furious now.

Sara doesn't answer for a moment. That means she remembers. "I didn't know you and this man were such friends," she says with something almost resembling envy; has Sara ever sounded jealous? Is this a positive sign, or the last straw? As though lost in thought, there in the square the older woman begins to walk in small circles, each taking her off somewhere between the fountain and the buildings beyond. "Who is he?"

"I don't know his name," the girl says, "Sara, the men are the ones with the penises, remember? Not my sort, and he's way older than I am — " and stops herself but too late. In the dark Sara

gain, and for that reason after he was born, back from Tokyo and living in the

doesn't even raise her head to this, just laughs one of her quiet, superior little laughs. The girl has no idea what to say now, feels futile about everything. Actually she has no idea how old the man is, but he's surely younger than Sara. Now the two women have managed to make their way to the edge of the square and Sara leans up against one of the massive walls.

They don't talk for a while and now it's all seeming impossible to the girl. She suppresses an urge to turn on her radio, knowing it will be taken as a sign she's finished, when she's surprised to hear Sara, looking up at the buildings — and in that voice one can sometimes barely hear, it seems so calm — ask, "He can take us up there?"

"Yes."

"How far?"

"All the way."

"Really?"

"Yes."

"What, does he own it or something?"

Now the girl looks up, leaning back farther until it frightens her and she almost topples. "Really I don't know that much about him. He's someone who came into the library and asked me to run a search for him, and in return said he could take me up any time." Beginning to inwardly fume, she insists, "I *know* I told you about him."

Hotel Hamblin about the time the lake first appeared, part of me was actually

"Yes," Sara admits quietly, "I remember. Well," she says, "not the part about going up. Have you been up before?"

"Naturally not."

"Well. You might have. It's not like you couldn't have."

"Well, I haven't. Have you?"

"I don't know him, this is your secret friend."

"He's not a secret friend. I meant have you ever been up *before*."

"No."

"So let's go then," the girl says hopefully.

"Where do we find this person?"

"Well — " and she has to confess he may not exactly have had this time of night in mind. She looks around. The fountain with the bronze frankenstein world in the middle is empty; she thinks of it as a frankenstein world because it looks like parts of two or three worlds stuck together. Now she tries to figure out where he told her and realizes the square is bigger than she expected and that finding him will be more daunting than she anticipated. "Let's just go over — " and then notices Sara doing it again; it would be just like Sara, the girl thinks, to regard healing buildings as a step up from healing people.

Running her fingers along the wall, Sara has her ear pressed to it, listening.

lad for Kirk's nightmares, part of me was glad for Kirk calling to me in the

Now that the girl thinks about it, the baby thing and the whole business of listening to sick buildings, they started about the same time. It's a bit cracked isn't it? she thinks. Sara who's otherwise so supremely composed and logical — what's it really about anyway? A melodramatic affectation to justify a pretentious profession that's just highly lucrative listening at its most harmless and, at its most intrusive, a violation of the psyche's inner machinery. . . some semanticist was on to something, the girl muses to herself, when she introduced to each other the words "the" and "rapist." At this moment of crisis between them, the girl wonders if Sara is having a breakdown of some sort, if listening to women's voices in walls is the first fracture in the imperturbable façade of a woman who's made indominability an identity. Watching Sara now the younger woman is about to ask, Isn't this the sort of thing they do on the West Coast? but says instead, "Don't tell me *this* building is dying."

But she's never seen a look like this on Sara's face before, the look she has now, not ever. It actually frightens the girl, makes her back away from the other woman; and she realizes one of the things she's loved Sara for is the promise that she'll never have on her face a look like this. Sara answers, something in her voice, "Let's go home."

The girl finds it in herself to insist, "I'm going up."

Sara steps toward her in the dark. "Let's go home," she says again, a tension in her voice the girl has never heard. Backing away from the wall, Sara looks up: "Come home with me now," like a mother — and the younger woman can't stand it. No more mothers, she thinks, I'm done with mothers and that includes ever being one;

night from his crib Mama? as though he feared I was the thing missing from

and she turns where she stands, "I'm going up," and clutching her radio weaves her way through the concentric rings of symmetrically staggered stone benches surrounding the enormous fountain. I'm going up she keeps telling herself, listening for the other woman's footsteps behind her and, when she doesn't hear them, almost turning to look. But there's no point to it. I'm not going back. Either Sara is still back there at the wall waiting for me or she's gone, but either way —   The girl sees the dark form of someone sitting at the edge of the fountain in the waning light of a moon that's halfway between menstruation and fertility; at first she thinks perhaps it's him. "I want to go up," she says before realizing it's a stranger to whom her instinctive response is the same as always, pulling her coat closer to cover and protect herself. A stranger: the ghost of someone she's supposed to have known, she thinks, when he says so quietly and invisibly in the dark it could almost be the fountain speaking, "The Age of Chaos is here."

Jeez, it *is* getting to be like the West Coast 'round this place. "What?" she says but doesn't wait for him to repeat it; now she does turn back to look, but Sara is gone. Unsettled, the girl stumbles off into the shadows of the square: It was ridiculous to think I might just wander 'round and run into him; I had no idea it was so big. Probably it was never a serious offer anyway, a polite gesture of thanks to a young researcher in the uptown university library who agreed to help in a wild goose chase. Probably he was just hitting on me? — even if a girl develops an instinct for such a thing and, instinctively, she doesn't think so. Now it all appears so preposterous, doesn't it. So it seems something of a miracle when, there in the other building's outer lights, he says, "Hello," just as she's practically broken into a frightened sprint. "Oh," she says.

is world, as though his very life might grow into the answer to the question I

"Are you all right?"

She gazes over her shoulder at the fountain behind her. "I, uh. . . I'm a bit surprised I found you."

"I wasn't expecting you."

"I know. It's late. Impulse. Spontaneous and all."

He's a man who's spent half a life meditating on the laws
of impulse, only to reject them. "Did you want to go up?"
he says.

"Can we? Still?"

He says nothing but motions her to follow. They circle around
the corner of the building to a side door he opens with a key
from a ring of more keys than she's ever seen; closing the door
behind them, he turns on a light in a concrete stairwell and
they make their way through two more doors until
they're inside crossing the dim lobby. He stops for a moment,
mulling.

She almost asks, Is something wrong? and then, I'm sorry, it's so
late, this is an imposition — but really her thoughts already have
returned to Sara. In her head she keeps seeing Sara listening to
that wall outside, then Sara gone and the wall empty. On the other
side of the lobby, at a row of elevators, the man unlocks one.
Looking around at all the flags she absently wonders how he
knows which key goes to which elevator; she says, Do you live
here? and he says, In the elevator? and she answers, No — and
then realizes Oh, it's a joke. He makes jokes. I keep a little room

had carried inside me, part of me was glad he was having his nightmares o

with a cot, he explains, although I'm not supposed to, "they don't
know," nodding at the omnipresent *they* outside. Seeing him for
the third time, after twice at the library, she finally notices he's
good looking. More attuned as she is to the looks of women, she
finds the phenomenon of lovely men interesting in the abstract —
something she sometimes notices even before straight women,
who often are distrustful of and on their guard against lovely men.

She has the luxury of being awed by such men; she makes a
conscious effort not to look at his hand. How many are there? she
asks, and he says what? and she says elevators, and he says a
couple hundred, more or less, between the two buildings, counting
the freight lifts; he's not exactly sure. The Emperor of Elevators,
she says, and when he doesn't immediately respond is mortified:
was that a slur? she wonders. Is it the Japanese or Chinese who
have an emperor?

She's not sure which he is anyway. She's thinking frantically
when he nods, "The Emperor of Elevators," with that slight smile;
he seems genuinely amused. "It's an aversion to ground-level,"
he elaborates. In the elevator she's warm in her light coat and
almost takes it off, and checks herself: a self-conscious pair we
would be, she thinks, me trying not to look at his hand and him
trying not to look at my tits; but she does free from her coat her
long gold hair that's been tucked under. "You should be a pilot,"
she suggests.

"That would be an aversion to gravity," he answers, "which is
different." Staring at the ascending numbers above the doors,
he says firmly, "The square outside, for instance: I don't like it."
After they've gone seventy or so floors, changing elevators on one
of the sky lobbies, she says, "I'm sorry I haven't had any luck
finding what you're looking for."

he lake or lost monkeys, because it meant at least he was dreaming and

"It's all right," he answers. "I didn't give you much to work with."

"I've done a search on everything before and up through June '89,
for anything with 'higher light' or, in case you misunderstood,
'higher life.' You're sure none of the ones I've found is — "

"I'm afraid not."

"It's not some sort of hymn, or gospel — "

"No."

"But you would know if you heard it, right?"

"Yes, I would," although over the years he's become not
so certain.

"They need to develop a software," she jokes, "where you can hum
it into the computer."

"I doubt it would help. I'm not much of a singer." The elevator
stops and the doors open. They step out and, overwhelmed, she
almost faints: Mega, she mutters to herself, tottering a bit where
she stands and reaching for the wall beside her, almost dropping
the radio. Before her a quadrant of the world lies in moonlight;
she's convinced she can see the curve of the earth in a white
shimmering arc against the black of space. The river far below to
the west glitters, and a lunar gale howls somewhere in the night
sky beneath them. Looming overhead is a towering transmission
mast three or four hundred feet high. "Sorry," he says, "I should
have prepared you. Actually," he says, "no one ever comes to the

therefore I knew he hadn't inherited his dreamlessness from me as I must have

top of this one, except for workmen or. . . that's why we used the
service lift." About ten feet from them is some bedding, a mattress
and a sleeping bag. "Sometimes I even sleep up here when
conditions allow. A night like tonight," looking around him, "you,
uh, sleep above your dreams."

"Is that good?"

"Depends on the dreams." Thinking a moment, "In my case,
it's good."

"I'm not going to get blown off, am I?" she says, beginning to
walk around a bit, wandering the roof and circling the spire that
glows above them. He doesn't say anything for a while, lets her
just walk around in the moonlight as he watches. He's not in any
great rush to take her back down and she's not in a rush to leave.
He's aware she's chosen not to ask too much about what he does
or how he lives or, for instance, why the song for which he came to
her for help is so important; as the rationalist he likes to think he is,
generally unconvinced by the existence of intangibles, he probably
couldn't explain, even if he wanted to, his theory that if he could
locate and fasten down in some way more permanent than the
humming in his head, if he could take apart and reassemble the
melody that's been haunting him for twelve years, inside could be
found (since all music is mathematic) the helix of freedom and
desire, transcendence and oblivion, even (if he believed in either)
god and chaos. And that this would explain his life and the great
event that transfixed the world, and its secret the world never knew
and that he knows but doesn't understand. Now being up here
with this girl makes him look around anew at what he's seen many
times. His gaze settles on the west river and the blasted gardens of

nherited it from my own mother who couldn't even cross the river to come see

smoke beyond and, three thousand miles beyond that, the woman
he loves.

For a wild impetuous moment, a man who's spent half a life
meditating the laws of impulse only to reject them thinks about
phoning her. It's not too late, three-hour time difference — but
he's just not ready yet, he tells himself, not having communicated

with her for a while other than in letters. So he can't just pick up the phone and call thoughtlessly unless, of course, thoughtlessly is in fact exactly the way he should call, the only way he'll ever bring himself to call. Not ready yet, no. Since there's no changing the fact of her child then there's only changing the sense of betrayal — *beautiful betrayer, killer of my trust* — something he thought he got over long ago, something he thought he let go of long ago, only to wake each morning and find it still in his grip or perhaps, more precisely, to find he's still in its grip. Maybe if you can't get over it then it's just not going to get gotten over. It's been six years now since the boy was born, with the father long out of the picture — he was barely in it except to make a son, which somehow only made her infidelity worse — so you just ought to get over it and if you can't then it's not going to get gotten over because she can't undo it and you can't expect she would if she could, it's her child after all.

But not *our* child. And he should have been.

He turns to look another direction, anywhere but west. The girl turns her radio on low, tries to find the right soundtrack for a darkling world before her; but perhaps the only soundtrack that's right is silence. She settles into the base of the transmission mast. She never asked why the song was so important because it wasn't her business and, getting right down to it, she doesn't really care.

me, because the very first dream I ever had in my life wasn't until that night

With most women, she tells herself, curiosity is an unchecked reflex; perhaps I'm not the inquisitive sort. Perhaps I have an overly developed male sense of privacy — that is, for a female. Perhaps that's why it's women not men who have babies, because as a gender women are predisposed not only to not value privacy so much but to unconsciously abhor it like nature does a vacuum,

because it's women who are capable of that generous voluntarily
surrender of profound privacy, the privacy of the body,
the privacy of the heart.

I have nowhere to go tonight, it suddenly occurs to her. She
watches the Asian man pacing the rooftop and then changes the
station on the radio again: Are you a musicologist? she asked
when he first showed up at the library, and he said no and then
sometime later in the conversation revealed he had been a
mathematics student in college before "history had its way with
me," by which she assumed he meant he became a history student
instead — which doesn't exactly explain, she thinks, what he's
doing operating elevators. Did you go to school in — ? and then
had stopped herself, checked her curiosity reflex, as much because
she didn't want to insult him. Japan? Korea? China? Thailand?
can't tell them apart, can you, she muses to herself. Well it's true,
you just can't. The Emperor of Elevators, he's musing to himself
as he paces the rooftop not impatiently but aimlessly; he's not yet
become a man who never looks up.

To the contrary he's a man who looks up as much as possible, who
would look anywhere but ground level. East he can make out the
lights of the harbor; from there his eyes follow the river north and
count the bridges, contemplating the twinkling suture of the
boroughs where, just at this moment, he can almost hear raven

iscarried him in Tokyo, waking and stumbling in terror through the dark to

navies surfacing from the floors of islamic oceans. Something
about the night has already become familiar to him before he ever
feels the tail-end of the gust, funneled hot memory brushing his
face. And as he lifted his burning hand back in the Square twelve
years ago to look through its new wound at the sky behind it, now
he lifts the same hand not to feel the gust, since there are no nerve
endings in the hand anymore to feel anything, not even so much to

look at the night through the hand's tiny window, but almost as
though he expects that the lens in his palm will refract the gust and
then burst into a vision, or as though perhaps the light of the moon
above, shining down through the small round prism, will catch him
in its spotlight. Or maybe even her. What it does cast is a
moonbeam on the gust's source — or maybe he would have shifted
his gaze anyway, noting the vent in the low rectangular storage hut
near the rooftop's east edge.

By the time he reaches the vent, his mind feels about to explode.

The gust hasn't subsided. In how many dreams in the last
twelve years has he felt it blow across his face as it does now?
Up here, he told her just a few minutes ago, you sleep above
your dreams; so how is it his dreams have reached this altitude?
How high do I have to go, he thinks to himself angrily, to rise
above them once and for all? Once he wondered if this gust was
an ally meaning to rescue him, or a weapon of the State meaning
to remove him; but it's really an anarchist without conviction
either way, without interest in either rescue or attack. Once he
stood his ground and the gust subsided, but now as he nears the
vent it comes roaring out. Taking from his belt his ring of keys,
he uses one to begin prying the vent loose around its rim, before
he takes the vent cover in his one good hand and tears it from
its space.

the toilet down the hall and making it just in time to see the glistening white

He peers inside.

He looks so deeply — although he can't fit in his whole head as
he did into the tank's gun that morning twelve years ago — that
when he hears the song, of course he thinks it's coming from the
other end of the dark to where the vent leads, from where and
when he first heard it twelve years ago. Same strange distant

Moorish drums, same dreamy Middle Eastern melody with the
soft spanish horns in the background, and the same woman's voice
of another century's turn: excited, he turns to call to the girl
who's been trying to track down this very song, astonished that
the song should happen to present itself at this very moment just
as she happens to be here — only to realize the song isn't
coming from the vent at all but her radio. "But that's it," he says
to her. What? she says sleepily, and he says, "That's it," pointing
at the radio.

She looks at the radio a moment. "Are you sure?"

"That's *it*."

"Well that's odd isn't it," she finally says. She listens awhile.
"You're sure." She listens some more. "I don't think this is that
old a song."

"Do you know it?"

"No but I think perhaps I've heard them play it before and I don't
think they would play an old song like this that often, if it was that
old." She says, "It doesn't sound that old."

"How can you tell?"

ain of my boy run from my body, and at that moment I thought of all the

"Well, I suppose I can't," she confesses. He turns back to the vent
and from deep down out of the darkness feels as he did twelve
years ago the same gust in his face; it smells of that same morning,
the vent a tunnel to that very morning and that very place, at the
other end of which is the portal of a gun barrel. This is when he
realizes that, twelve years ago, what he actually heard was *this*
very moment now, in *this* time and place, up here overlooking the

world on this very night — that somewhere at the other end of this tunnel he's there standing on the Square, his Other Self at an irrevocable moment, a young man of nineteen alone before the tanks with his head in the barrel of a gun, listening to a song coming from a girl's radio twelve years and twelve thousand miles away. That what now blows through this tunnel is the Oblivion Wind back and forth across the shadowyears between the end of the Twentieth Century that morning, and this night — although he can't imagine why this particular night, when nothing would seem to be happening of any importance at all.

He turns to see her lying there on his bedding, gold hair around her head ablaze in the ovulating moon. He walks over to her; she dozes at his feet. He has this distracted impulse to lie next to her, only because he's suddenly so tired, but of course she would only take it wrong. If she could see him now, he wonders if he would appear to her as he feels: a man caught mid-transport. Uh, he whispers, we should go down now I think, but she doesn't answer and he just nods in the dark and mumbles I'll come back for you in the morning then, and turns to the dank light of the elevator, doors closing on his bewildered face. Briefly her eyes flutter to the sound of the closing doors, having somewhere in her semiconsciousness heard him speak, and now she answers from her sleep, But I have no place to go. She stumbles up from the bedding because she has to pee, and stripping off her jeans she

nights after I first learned he was inside me that I had stood in window.

half-registers the tsunamic vista of dawn's armada in a far enflamed east. Then she slides back into the sleeping bag on the mattress at the base of the throbbing antenna above her.

In her head she keeps seeing Sara listening to that wall down below. One of the last conscious thoughts she has is that her life has veered wildly out of control lately and she likes to be in control, even if it means assuming the well-defined role of slightly subservient daughter, its definitions threatened only by her role of lover. But Sara is gone now or perhaps, she thinks at the end, I'm the one who's gone. Not long before the crash of morning light she sleeps the sleep of the dead, as Sara always put it, and dreams of her own birth, her mind ticking down all her memories like the last hours of summer.

Two women on a train. Their destination is the end of a lie, although they don't yet know it's a lie. The older woman has truly convinced herself that in her last days she wants to get as far from the lake as she can, that   she'll die free of it at last; and thus the   **2029-2031**   younger woman arranged for them to leave   the Chateau X in the dead of night by boat, although not sailed by the young man who loved her so unrequitedly and to whom she couldn't bear to explain she was leaving. Rather the two other women Brontë met months earlier from the Freek Recherche lunatique drove her and the Mistress along the serrated shoreline in a beat-up thirty-year-old

xposing my pregnant belly to the city and the outside world in order to try

Jag that barely had room for them to the port at Los Feliz, with its abandoned observatory looming in the hills above.

From there, over the course of twenty-two slow hours a ferry sailed the two women further inland to San Gabriel. Lulu is sick. On the ferry deck bundled in a large coat and scarf and swathed in the gray of the wind, black late-autumn countryside and the solar casbahs of outer zedberia passing by and white waves on the lake like the veils of a hundred drowned brides, she seemed to Brontë only intermittently conscious of the journey. On the train now Brontë reproaches herself for bringing Lulu. But it's too late, they can't go back; they're traveling on Armand's money and, at that moment, Armand is shackled blindfolded and naked in the Chateau dungeon with the little red ball in his mouth, delirious far beyond any thrilling contemplation of the cracking of the walls around him and the lake beyond, delirious even beyond wondering when his Mistress Brontë is going to return. His henchmen wait in a limo on shore. In thirty-six hours it will begin to cross the narrow landfill of their minds that perhaps something's amiss, at which point they'll begin calling a cell phone that lies on the stone dungeon floor two wicked inches beyond the farthest expanse of Armand's chains. Sometimes Armand can hear the footsteps of his Mistress in the Lair upstairs, or so he supposes. What he actually hears are the steps of another man searching the Chateau for one woman he knows of, and another he won't admit to himself he knows of.

By early morning Brontë and Lulu reached San Gabriel port. They missed by twenty minutes a train that comes through only once a night, when it's on time at all, and winds up in Chicago. Unsure how stupid she could count on Armand's boys to be, or how far they might come to find her once they retrieved their boss, Brontë didn't much care for the idea of sitting around the station

and prepare him for its chaos, and in that minute there in the toilet when I wa

another twenty-four hours. In the small waiting room of the terminal, she found a kid who just put his girlfriend on the train, eating a sandwich out of a vending machine; she offered him one of Armand's hundred-dollar bills if he would drive them to the next station and beat the train there doing it. Is she all right? the kid said looking at Lulu, chewing his sandwich in deep thought. She's sick, Brontë answered. I need to get her on that train.

Forty-five minutes later the three were careening through the San
Berdoo badlands into the rising morning sun. Slipping in and out
of an ecstasy of sunlight through the windows, trying to remember
the color blue, in her mind Lulu added greens to grays to see if
they made blue together.

All she knows she remembers is red. Two hours after having left
San Gabriel, they beat the train to the Barstow station by ten
minutes. After moving Lulu slowly up the stairs of the train and
down the aisle to a seat, Brontë was bringing up the luggage as the
train pulled out; the conductor came by and sold her two tickets.
In the concessions lounge several cars down, Brontë buys water, a
sandwich, fruit salad from a can. She's alarmed when Lulu won't
eat. Lulu surfaces consciousness long enough to look out the
window and say, Where are we? Seven or eight other passengers
are scattered throughout the car; a couple of other women several
seats up whisper between them. You have to eat something,
Brontë insists, tearing off some more bread. "Where's the lake?"
says Lulu.

"At least drink some water."

Lulu takes a sip of the water Brontë gives her. "Where's the lake."

"Behind us. We're going to Chicago." Chicago? Lulu asks; for

osing him all I could do was hate myself for not having taken him back to the

however much it means to either of them, Brontë might as well
have said China. All Lulu knows she remembers is red. In her
mind she's been on this journey a long time, with its rails of green
and yellow and its tracks of orange and purple (*Tyrone the Train!*
I want to ride away with you. . .) as they rumble through the
Mojave marshlands. After nearly forty-eight hours without sleep,
Brontë sleeps until the train jolts her awake and pitches her

245

upward; she's momentarily disoriented, and for an instant she thinks Lulu is dead. Jeez, she cries softly touching the woman's cheek, to which Lulu opens her eyes and turns to look at her. By this time they've been on the train all day. It seems to be moving slower and slower, crossing landscape more and more barren although, looking out the other side of the train, Brontë notes snow on far northern mountains. Every ten or fifteen minutes a tiny house glitters in the distance. Twilight falls in blueless magenta; a spreading red sky from the west is scratched with livid vapor trails, like God trying to claw his way in. Plutonium sagebrush blows south.

Lulu mutters in her sleep. Brontë gives her more water, trying again without success to get her to eat; then the younger woman dozes again and the next time she wakes, the train has stopped completely. In the night outside their window, symmetrically staggered in concentric circles around them and stretching out for miles like battlefield bunkers, single abandoned railway cars are lit by the lightning of a desert storm. The lightning is so fierce that the flash of it across Lulu's face, as well as the tremendous thunder that follows almost immediately, wakes her as well. Brontë sits up looking around them. No one else is on the train except, at the far end, the conductor in his own seat; when he sees his last passengers have awakened, he saunters up the aisle.

silence of a dreamless delta, while at the same time I also believed it wa

Pueblo d'Elektrik, he announces idly.

"Is this Chicago?" asks Brontë.

"Pueblo d'Elektrik. Last stop."

"I thought this train goes to Chicago."

"You have to transfer here. Nothing between here and Occupied
Albuquerque and that's another two hundred miles."

"When does the Chicago train come through?"

"You'll have to check with the station." He leans down to look
out the windows on the other side of the train. "Couple of days,
I think. Station may be closed for the night."

"A couple of days?"

"Might be open in the morning," he says, "you can find out then.
In the meantime you can probably get a room here at the pueblo.
Yes," he laughs at something he finds extremely funny,
"you probably can. Yes," he goes on laughing, "I would think so."
Brontë helps the older woman to her feet and moves her down the
aisle. Down the stairs and off the train, she scurries Lulu to the
shelter of an outside corridor that links the station to the railroad
hotel next door, then moves the bags as the conductor watches.
With Lulu and the baggage huddled against a wall, the younger
woman darts from one dark window of the pueblo to the next,
trying to see in. She finds a door and raps loudly; the rain and
lightning and thunder grow. The conductor still watches from the
top of the car as the train pulls out, heading down the track. Brontë
has almost decided to break one of the windows when a light

ecause he was starved of his own umbilical dreams that the glistening yolk of

comes on and a freckled man with cropped red hair opens the door.
We need a room, Brontë says.

In the shadow of the light behind him, the man with the red hair
considers this. "It's late."

"Yes, well, please explain that to the train that left us here," Brontë snaps, pointing down the track. The man squints at the train disappearing in the distance. He seems to find the situation confounding until a particularly vicious crack of lightning catches his attention. He opens the door and Brontë hustles Lulu inside and brings in the bags. At the front desk she pays the man a deposit and the man gives the young woman a key to a room upstairs at the farthest end even though, as Brontë will learn, all the downstairs rooms are empty and there's no other guest in the hotel except one whose light seeps out beneath the door three down from theirs. Slowly Brontë moves Lulu up the stairs, then hauls up the bags one by one as the hotel manager watches. She's gotten the last suitcase up to the landing at the top in time to see an Indian girl a year or two younger knocking quietly on the door of the other occupied room; the light goes out and the door opens, and the girl glances over her shoulder at Brontë before slipping in through an electric white rip in the dark.

From their room in this section of the pueblo that juts out from the top floor, Brontë can see in almost every direction a molten desert bubbling with silver racket and tumbling from the navajo plateaus to the north. Outside the western window a grove of incinerated trees struggles skyward in black webs, and surrounding rings of single railway cars divert the storm from trains that slither through the countryside. The light and clamor are so relentless that all

Kierkegaard Blumenthal broke and emptied from me, and that night dropping

Brontë can do is huddle in her bed trying to decide whether to cover her ears or eyes; she wishes they had never left the lake. She's only seen such fire and noise once before but can't remember it. The next morning she finally gets Lulu to eat some cereal cooked by the manager's wife; next door she finds the station still closed, and when it's still closed that afternoon and the next morning and the next afternoon as well, she gets this feeling.

Oh any time, says Roy the manager with red hair when Brontë asks
what hour the station opens. Deep in the middle of the third night,
 in the middle of a dream she hears a rumbling and rushes to the
  window in time to see the light of a train disappearing down the
track. Yes, replies Roy the following morning when she asks, any
 time now that train ought to be coming back through here: maybe
tomorrow or the next day. You said that yesterday, Brontë finally
stops answering after a while.

After a while longer she stops asking. Built in the Nineteenth
Century as the grandest estancia in northern Arizona by a Spanish
  aristocrat who fled San Sebastian in disgrace with his fortune,
   then eventually handed down to his great great grandson,
the pueblo was finally lost by the family in the Wall Street crash of
ninety-nine years ago. Serenely the great great grandson walked
  out through the adobe porticoes into the desert never to be seen
   again. Taken over by the Santa Fe railway, the mansion was
converted into a railroad hotel. In the fourth and fifth decades of
  the Twentieth Century it bustled with travelers to and from the
   Midwest stopping for a meal or the night; with its sweeping
  entryways and arched passages and suspended staircases, the
pueblo was all blue tile and hacienda-deco then. A quarter century
ago the electrical storms blew in from the Juarez wastelands to the
  east, and both the railroad and hotel began to die. The tile isn't
blue anymore, and besides Roy and his wife Wanda there's no one

ɔ my knees I moaned for him to come back, come back come back, dropping to

else in the hotel except Barbrasita the Navajo girl who delivers
meals and cleans the rooms and mops the wide black-oak
hallways, and Rollin the other guest three rooms down.

Moving from city to city selling shady weather reports until
stranded by a west-bound train a few weeks before, Rollin is a
traveling meteorologist in his mid-fifties. Soon after Brontë and

Lulu's arrival he takes to rapping on their door day and night, posting himself there for hours on end, chatting up the younger woman. He's too unabashedly stupefied by her breasts to even pretend interest in anything else about her. If his knock goes unanswered, he invites himself in regardless. Ceaselessly he recounts the itinerary of his life and expounds with great expertise on the caprice of lightning, talking about anything and everything except — as Wanda dryly points out — his wife and daughter back in St. Louis. Brontë finds him too ridiculous to be threatening, but when he accosts her one night in a darkened corridor, she can't help wondering where's a whip and a good pair of handcuffs when a girl needs them. As the nights go by, the moody Barbrasita who Brontë saw slipping into Rollin's room the first night becomes more sullen, lingering outside his door to less and less attention, as the music of a radio can be plainly heard on the other side.

Whenever she sees Brontë, Barbrasita's expression grows darker. Delivering dinner from the kitchen downstairs, she practically hurls it in the other's face, and when she refuses to help change Lulu's bed a week later, the two young women have a blistering bilingual argument in the hallway that neither understands. "I think," Brontë finally tries to confront things head-on, "perhaps you've the wrong idea about me and your weatherman — " to which Barbrasita grabs the soup spoon from a meal tray and lunges at the other woman to scoop out her eyes, before Wanda pulls

my knees I retracted every stern admonition I had already given him, I scooped

her away. Walking the hotel corridors at night, Brontë takes to rounding darkened corners at a wide arc in anticipation of ambush. When she's not waking to the sound of trains, it's to the expectation of the Indian girl standing over her, lethal spoon in hand. Somehow Rollin is oblivious to all this. He assumes everyone basks in his bonhomie. Day after day then week after week, as Barbrasita lurks outside his room, he lurks outside

Brontë's, telling again and again the same stories he's told before, each time embellishing wildly as though no one ever would notice the variance with earlier versions. Sometimes Brontë thinks he's forgotten about seduction altogether, so satisfied is he by his own regalement. It occurs to her to set him straight on her preferences but she's got the feeling Rollin would just find further inspiration in ever preposterous reveries of the two women in all their possible permutations.

A couple of weeks stretch into a couple more. Only after Brontë and Lulu have been at the pueblo almost a month does Rollin — previously in no great hurry to leave a hotel so conveniently remote and teeming with comely Indian maidens and pneumatic golden-haired pixies — suddenly become very anxious himself about the next train. For several nights Brontë hears the sound of terrible fights coming from his room. Whatever Barbrasita is saying, Rollin seems to understand very well.

One afternoon Brontë sees from her window a distant car, snubbed and blunted like a discharged bullet, weaving its way toward the pueblo through the storm, daring the lightning to take it out. Driving in thirty miles from the northeast, a family of four has come for the train. When dark falls they roam the lobby waiting, an older man and woman and a younger man who dozes on one of the wooden monastery benches strewn throughout the foyer, and a

im up in a puddle and held him in the cup of my hands just as I did up there a

boy of about eleven who plays games on an ancient laptop. It's not clear to Brontë how the four are related. "Here to bury her son," the old man shrugs at the woman sitting quietly alone, "killed in the fighting up in Zion. Going back home now," but not east it turns out, rather back the way Brontë and Lulu came. Graying hair pulled back, the woman sits on her bench for hours saying nothing, staring ahead of her and only lifting her eyes and nodding slightly whenever the old man whispers to her. She never settles into the bench, rather she sits at the edge in anticipation of something she's already too late for, as though so flabbergasted by her grief she doesn't feel it, as though distilled in this moment is the tenor of her entire life. For a while Brontë waits up to see with her own eyes if a train actually rolls through, heading any direction.

Finally around midnight she goes back up to her room where, after cooling Lulu's fevered brow with a damp cloth, she sleeps.

She's awakened by yet another argument between Rollin and Barbrasita. This is by far the most violent she's heard, coming not from the room just a few doors away but downstairs. From the darkened landing of the stairs she can see Barbrasita below with a furious grip on Rollin's arm, pulling him from the family that, apparently, has given up on the train and now means to drive back through the storm and the night; over her screams, desperately Rollin beseeches them to take him. The family seems stricken. Somewhere Roy and Wanda hide beneath their covers. Finally shaking themselves free of their bereaved inertia, the older man and woman, the young man and the boy dash madly for the bullet car; and confronted with the choice of the storm before him or Barbrasita behind him, Rollin bolts in pursuit past the same adobe porticos through which the great great grandson of the San Sebastian aristocrat vanished almost a century ago — as though

few minutes ago on the lake, or down there, whichever way the lake is now, in

he thinks he can charm the lightning.

In the following weeks, Barbrasita watches from the pueblo's front window for signs of how far Rollin got — but out here, Wanda tells Brontë, even the vultures don't fly. Soon the Navajo girl gives up her vigil and instead takes to sitting every day for hours on a stark high-back chair in the hallway outside Brontë's door,

not unlike the way the woman who lost her son in the fighting up
in Zion sat all night on the bench downstairs. With no rooms other
than Brontë's and Lulu's to make up, no other clean towels to be
delivered, no other lunches or dinners to be served, she stares at
her growing belly and rains on it the same black curses she rained
on the child's father the night he left. Sitting at her own window
staring out at the desert stonehenge of railway cars surrounding the
pueblo, Brontë realizes she no longer knows for sure whether she's
waiting for a train or for the woman in the bed to die; on the
frontier of a kind of catalepsy, from time to time Lulu arouses
herself to an uncognitive waking, drinking and eating only enough
to endure but never to speak or, as far as Brontë can tell, truly
know. Brontë herself cannot know, for instance, that, beyond the
windows, Lulu sees — as no one else sees — the melody-snakes
crawling up out of the parched dust long enough to rattle a few
notes before lightning cuts short their songs in a throttled shriek.
Female screams fill the charged air. Lulu hears them even as she
slips back to sleep, the way Brontë hears trains.

Brontë has no idea why it's important to get to Chicago. Actually
she doesn't think it's important at all, Chicago's just the place the
train happens to go to. She doesn't really suppose it will make any
difference to Lulu. But this hotel seems to her an intolerable place
for someone to die — better the Chateau. On the pay phone
downstairs, she tracks down a doctor in the territory who drives in

he gondola where I came from, when his answer to my call came bubbling up

two days later. Half Indian, half white, he's never diagnosed
someone dying of sorrow, dying not of physical dissolution or
even a fatigue of body and spirit as triggered by sorrow, but sorrow
itself: Isn't there somewhere to take her, Brontë asks, a hospital or
rest home? The doctor answers that there's something about this
dying that's beyond the peace of hospitals and rest homes. When
she tries to call him again a week later, the phone is out of order.

The weeks become months. Outside, the storm is unmoved by the change of seasons, and the arrival of spring.

Brontë discovers a television one afternoon in one of the back suites on the first floor, but as she might have expected, there's nothing on it except a faint broadcast from Flagstaff, buzzing out of the clouds to the west. Constantly awakened by trains taunting her, constantly gazing out the windows for signs of a light coming up the track, at night she takes to drifting through the dark hacienda and cold cinderblock foyer, past the bare newsstand and forsaken gift shops and faded Indian murals and the bar lined with tequila bottles and cracked martini glasses drunk on their own dust. She scours the stray pieces of hotel literature as well as the volumes of local lore on the shelves; after a while she knows more about the pueblo and the families that built it and lived here than she does her own life. When the storms originally came, the first part of the hotel to have been closed was the dining room, once the finest in the territory. Now for the pueblo's rare guest Wanda cooks in the hotel kitchen a traditional soup half spicy black bean and half sweet corn, sending it up to Brontë along with lemon slices.

Boarded up after the dining room was the cavernous ballroom, its once-blue ceiling that's flecked with silver now gray like the overcast sky outside. The small tadpoles of silver flicker like the

from the bottom, so in the same way the night I miscarried him I splashed

lightning's stray offspring. One night Brontë peeks past the slabs of wood that barricade the ballroom entrance and pulls one away, stepping through; because of how the silver flashes in the dark ceiling, there in the black of the old ballroom she can almost believe there are no ceiling or walls, that there's no pueblo at all. She can almost believe the massive Navajo carpet across the ballroom floor is a great rooftop floating high above the earth.

Actually tottering a bit where she stands, she reaches for the wall to steady herself; before her, a quadrant of the world is ablaze with lightning. It curves in an electric white arc against the black of space. A lake glitters far below to the west, lunar gales howl in the sky below, and pacing the eye of the storm Brontë contemplates the shimmering suture of the northern mesas. For a moment she can almost believe that here one sleeps above her dreams — for good or ill, depending on the dreams.

Lately Brontë has been having dreams of a small boy. Only after she found a crumbling old book on a remote shelf did she learn the story that the official literature of the hotel doesn't tell: that on the afternoon the great great grandson of the Spaniard who built the pueblo walked out its porticos into the desert, he left behind a sole inheritor of his ruin. This was a three-year-old child who he so refused to acknowledge as his own son that the forsaken mother, a local Indian woman, died giving birth in a ravine just beyond the western garden. Even when the infant boy was taken in by the hotel servants, his cry was regarded by the father as simply a stray sirocco blowing through the abandoned ballroom. Thus three years later, with the hacienda empty of everyone else, on his nonchalant stroll into the desert the newly destitute patrician walked right past the child as though he was invisible, and for hours the little boy stood in the open doorway first watching the disappearance then awaiting the return of the father who had never

myself with him then, splashed him on my face and neck and breasts until I

held or kissed or spoken to him.

Brontë goes back through all the other old books of the hotel to try and find out what happened to the son left behind. But as the forbidden history of the pueblo would have it, he's still standing in the doorway waiting for his father, and at night sometimes Brontë wakes to his small sirocco-cry from somewhere in the hotel.

She presses her ear to the walls listening for him, convinced the
brown-haired brown-eyed child scampers up and down secret
passages between the rooms looking for his father who's hiding
from him, as though his abandonment has been only a game.
Outside, the storms seem to stop moving over the mesas, rather it's
as though the earth continues turning its way into a single endless
storm that rolls on and on and on into the coming years.

As Barbrasita gets bigger, she begins lumbering slowly up and
down the hall snarling at the growing child inside her in ever
blacker language. Even to someone who doesn't understand the
Spanish, it's awful. In her sleep Lulu hears the girl cursing her
unborn baby and murmurs for someone to make her stop. Brontë
stands at the window staring for trains and thinks that between the
dying woman in the bed behind her and the pregnant girl outside in
the hall, perhaps she'll go insane: Perhaps I will. Then what will
they do, she rages silently, what will they do when I'm crazy. As
her belly grows in the passing months, Barbrasita curses it more
and Lulu curses back, and this exchange continues until the night
Brontë finally wakes to find the Mistress sitting straight up in bed,
streaked with the electric frost of the storm outside, eyes wide to
the sound of something Brontë can't hear through the cracked
euphonium of the storm, until it trails off in a baby's cry.

Brontë rushes into the hall of the darkened pueblo. Searching for

couldn't distinguish the tears of my eyes from the discharge of my uterus, unti

the sound of the crying, she finds Barbrasita who, like a cat, has
taken her labor into the linen closet, producing a bloody baby
between her thighs, umbilical snake singing between them;
the young Indian mother seems in shock. Down the dark deserted
halls Brontë runs knocking on doors until Wanda appears. Calmly
taking a flashlight hanging from a hook, grabbing from the kitchen
the knife used for slicing Brontë's lemons, she follows the crying

to its source and, with a single swipe, slashes the cord. Its song howls into silence. Brontë reels. "Can you warm up a pot of water, miss," Wanda says, "not too hot?"

Barbrasita doesn't curse her baby anymore after that. In the days after that, she sits in her bed so rapt at the sight of the little boy that she almost has to be reminded to feed him, his small hands pawing her breast. Trying to explain it's not a good idea for the two to sleep together, Wanda has to gently pry the child from the mother's arms: You could roll over on him dear, she says, wedging the baby on his side in a small makeshift cradle a few feet away. Commissioned to keep an eye on the infant while Barbrasita sleeps, Brontë fumes. It's very convenient for everyone isn't it. It's very convenient that a train abandoned me here so I could baby-sit a dying woman *and* a newborn. Brontë feels no affinity for babies. She believes she has a man's sense of privacy that doesn't accommodate babies. But as more weeks pass and she tires of watching for trains in whose arrival she has no more faith, she finds herself looking in on the baby anyway, even when the mother is awake. "Just thought I should check," she tells the Indian girl. "Force of habit."

Later, almost four hundred days after coming to the Pueblo d'Elektrik, standing out on the station platform one night and seeing at long last, long after faith's exhaustion, the small distant

oth had seeped into me and I was bone dry, profoundly unmistakably empty,

light of an approaching train, Brontë will note it's not so much like a full moon at all. But one night a few months before, before she can even imagine let alone know what's to happen, out on the station platform one night she sees a globe of light emerge down the line over the far ridge and for a moment thinks it's a train before realizing it's the moon growing larger and larger like a plummeting airplane, its nose a burning bomb. That's when she doesn't believe in trains anymore. That's when she thinks that she and the Mistress have as much chance of riding the moon to Chicago — assuming the moon ever traveled from west to east. But of course this moon like all others travels from east to west, back the way they came from. There in the pueblo station, what Brontë doesn't yet know is that, as the four hundred days of the Pueblo d'Elektrik tick down, the two women come nearer their destination than she thinks: the end of the lie that they can or ever could leave the lake, or live beyond it.

Enthralled by her child, Barbrasita is paralyzed. In the weeks after his birth she can't even bring herself to name the little boy, so afraid is she that her first maternal act will be a mistake, setting everything thereafter wrong. What if I name him something bad? she asks Brontë in broken English. She's consumed with guilt about having cursed the baby when he was inside her. She's convinced he heard every word, so now she pets his brown hair and begs his small brown eyes to forgive her. She seems to Brontë in a trance. One night when lightning strikes one of the railway cars outside, the reflection of the flaming mausoleum through the window makes the Indian's face appear on fire, ecstatic, purged by love; that's the night Brontë checks in one more time on the Mistress three doors down, turns down the lamp by Barbrasita's bed, closes Barbrasita's door behind her, and then takes off her clothes. Is the look on the Indian girl's face just a variation of the

and then it was after that that I dreamed, for the first time in my life, no

one she always wears now as a mother, or a response to Brontë's naked body next to her? Never with another girl before huh, Brontë whispers, careful should the wound of birth still be tender. Vixen, Brontë accuses herself, I'm no better than Rollin. Afterward, as the young Navajo woman sleeps in her breasts, wrapped in her long gold hair, out of her sleep Brontë reaches over in the dark and slowly rocks the cradle.

But in the ensuing days, the fire that's been cast in Barbrasita's face doesn't die, rather ecstasy burns down to the diamond of a fixed notion. In her heart, her nameless little boy has opened the door to a vast plateau of fear, stretching out beyond her young years when mortality is supposed to be so inconceivable. In the beginning, perhaps her dread was attached to nothing she could name but now she can name it, pyre of the railway car outside flaming in her face: it's the way she cursed him made manifest that's coming for him. Like it was a thought wandering the desert waiting for her to rescue it, she's come to know in no way she can explain even to herself that it doesn't matter where she goes, it doesn't matter how far she tries to get her little boy away, the lightning outside will keep coming for him, moving through the labyrinth of railway cars ring by outer ring, striking closer and closer, and that she can't be paralyzed anymore. Out in the storm, out where the sky curses the earth in sound and light, lurks her son's doom and she must stop it. She has to shake herself loose of the love that holds her down and find inside her the love that will save him. She has to go to war with the sky that would take him.

In the room three doors down, Brontë is alarmed by Lulu's moans in her sleep. Oh jeez she's going to die now, Brontë thinks to herself; she sits on the woman's bed holding her, trying to calm her, but Lulu's rant — stop her no no no stop, stop her, stop (in

ealizing at first I was dreaming since I had never had a dream and didn't

dreams of red) — grows from the depths of something else. Finally, not knowing what else to do, Brontë hurries from the room in search of Wanda only to find Barbrasita standing in the dark hall with her unnamed baby in her arms. Brontë can no longer see the fire in Barbrasita's face but Barbrasita can, it's right there in front of her eyes, getting closer: "What are you doing?" says Brontë. She pulls the young mother back to bed. Then she starts back down the hallway knocking on doors like the night the baby was born, but this time Wanda doesn't answer: "Where is everybody?" Brontë actually says out loud in the dark at one point. When she turns back to the room, Lulu's ramblings growing louder and more agitated, Barbrasita is in the hallway again, with her baby in her arms again.

Brontë takes hold of the girl's shoulders. "Go to bed," she says.

Barbrasita answers, in what sounds to Brontë like remarkably good English, "I know what I know, and I must do what I must do," and with that shoves the baby boy into Brontë's arms. "Hey," Brontë says, Barbrasita striding past her, and in the porticos of the pueblo the Indian girl pulls open the doors that then seem to blast apart in the storm.

"Hey, hey!" Brontë calls again, holding the child and running in confusion after the other woman, who stops only for a moment in the doorway. Only for a moment in the doorway, everything about Barbrasita's ravaged life comes to a halt. She's riveted by a calm that's still secret to her. She's riveted by a resolution beyond rationality, by some wisdom forgotten as soon as she's seen it; for a second, she lives in the red gazebo of her heart, standing at its placid center where her life surrounds her like a diorama. Brontë can hear her say very clearly, very calmly over the sound of the

know how to identify one or distinguish it from consciousness, rather in tha

thunder, "Give him a good name," and then the young mother runs out into the lightning.

"No!" Brontë screams after her. But Barbrasita runs for the burning railway car, not to meet the fire but to head off the storm's advance and conduct up into her, between her legs, through the place she gave birth, all the sky's electric rage. Just outside the

blowing, slamming doors of the hacienda, Brontë is pelted
by rain and wind, stopped in her tracks as she turns her back on
the wet and cold to protect the baby; at her side Wanda has
finally appeared, eyes wide, and Brontë goes on crying "No!"
over her shoulder at Barbrasita now far beyond earshot in the
dark distance splattered with wet light — until there streaks
from the black sky a bolt that suspends the girl in a momentary
glow. Then she's gone. She's stepped through a white rip in the
sky to some other desert on the Other Side where mothers don't
fear for the loss of their children. Brontë thinks it's her own cry
that she hears until she realizes it comes from the other end of
the pueblo, Lulu sitting up in her bed in her room tearing at the
sheets around her.

Will they make a saint of her? Lulu wonders, collapsed back
into her pillow and red dreams. Will they all come out and gather
on the mesas surrounding the electric desert, revering the place
where she went up in smoke, Saint Barbrasita of the Loud Light?
Wherever she is now, on the Other Side of the cracked sky,
does she wonder to herself, What have I done? What mad love
made me abandon him, in order that I might believe I could save
him from all the vagaries of life? Does she find herself burned
into some place between chaos and God, neither within reach?
Does she sing to herself *if there's a higher light, let it shine on me*
when it's a higher light jagged like a knife she meant to take

irst dream I believed that the small flicker of light I saw on the other side of

up into her womb and snuff out? Wherever she is now in the
Other Desert, staring around in bewilderment in a place where
the same storm seethes and everything is the same except that
her child is gone, missing him she doesn't even know what to
call him.

For a while, all she knew she remembered was red. Here's Lulu's lie: that she would not die on the lake. It's now been so long since that day when some other naked version of her left to sail back where she left her small son in that silver gondola that she can't be certain anymore it really happened at all. She can't be certain it wasn't a dream or hallucination, she can't be certain of anything she ever did or didn't do, she can't be certain of her own life except: the one thing she knows for certain was ever real is him — *that* she knows — and she also knows she wouldn't die anywhere else but on that lake even if she could, as if she could leave her heart behind and forget where it was and then, having lost it, forget there ever was a heart. So as the lake stopped draining, because it would wait to die with its mistress, so the Mistress in return has laid suspended on the edge of death four hundred days waiting for the lake to die: Well no kidding, Lulu says to herself in her fever. Who's the point-misser now. She waits for the lake, the lake waits for her. But now in the first vision she's had in a long time, like those she used to have going back to her very earliest, when she would sit on her bathroom floor reading the patterns of her periods in the porcelain toilet, now as if she's conducting one final ceremony and as if a melody-snake has wound its way up out of the desert from the ashen place where the lightning took Barbrasita, Lulu has a new epiphany.

In it she runs after Barbrasita to stop her, into the wind and the

the darkness, on the other side of unconsciousness, was the very dream itself

rain. As she almost catches her, the girl stops and turns and the lightning rips the sky in two and, inside the radiance that Barbrasita becomes, the red that's been the only thing Lulu could remember finally takes form: and she sees him standing there in the Chateau lair with the small red toy monkey in his hand, wondering how it is he's been abandoned again. First confronted by this vision, she can't face the question of whether she left the toy behind accidentally or, so to speak, accidentally on purpose, but once the memory of red takes the form of the red monkey, then in this ozone between living and dying, for the first time since motherhood, Lulu fights to live. . .

. . . and opens her eyes, and he's gone. Opens her eyes and she lies in her bed in the pueblo and, outside, after four hundred days, the lightning has finally subsided. It flashes just enough that the snow falling glitters like glass — but that isn't what she notices. What she notices is the bird beyond the window of her room, in the high black branches of a charred tree, very calmly unperturbed by the falling ice, as though the tree's surrounding wisps might actually shelter it. "Look," she says.

Rocking in a chair at the foot of the bed, resting with a brown baby in her arms, Brontë opens her eyes at the sound of Lulu's voice, a little astonished. "Hello," she brings herself to say.

"Look," Lulu says again, weakly raising her arm to point through the window, and Brontë turns to look.

It takes a moment for Brontë's eyes to communicate the color of the bluejay to her mind, or perhaps it's the other way around: "It's not a trick of the light, is it," says Brontë. "That is, it's not really just some strange shade of green and gray mixed together.

which I approached across some limbo between consciousness and sleep, and

It's really blue?"

"All color is a trick of the light," Lulu explains.

After a moment, "It's New Year's."

"Really?"

"Day before yesterday, actually."

Lulu looks at the baby in Brontë's arms. "How long since. . . ?"

"Five weeks."

"Five weeks?"

"You would come to just long enough for me to get some soup in you. You don't remember?"

"No."

"Some part of you must have wanted to stick around awhile."

"Have you named him?"

"Not yet," Brontë sighs, shaking her head. "Want to hold him?"

Lulu has a pang at the sight of him. "His mother: she chose you."

"No," Brontë argues, "I was just the one who happened to be there, that's all." She doesn't mention the night she and Barbrasita slept together. "Who else was she going to give him to? Wanda I suppose, but. . . . "

it was like the flicker of a gunshot in the distance, a small flash on the far

"She chose you," Lulu insists, as vehemently as her weakness allows, "with boobs like those, she figured you were the woman for the job."

"Well aren't you feeling better," Brontë says. "They're not exactly baby-ready."

264

"Tell him that. Put a bottle between them and he'll never know the difference."

"He'll just grow up to be another breast-blinded man like his father."

"He'll grow up to be that anyway. The male wangie at its most basic."

"Hold him while I go get you some soup," and Brontë gets up and gives the baby to Lulu. While she's gone Lulu barely brings herself to look in the little boy's brown eyes. She holds him pretending he isn't there. She hears his gurgles pretending she doesn't; the soft brown of his hair, she pretends she doesn't feel that. The small hand that waves in the air for her finger, she pretends she doesn't see it. She pretends she's not thinking of names. Brontë comes back and sets the baby in his cradle nearby and feeds the other woman some soup, then when she's finished she lies in the bed next to Lulu and picks up the little boy as he starts to cry. Brontë pretends she's sick and fucking tired of crying babies. She pretends it was the unluckiest day of her life when Barbrasita pushed this child in her arms and ran out into the storm. What I get for seducing her, she thinks. She looks at the baby in her arms who's stopped crying. "Why does he make me afraid?"

horizon, until I finally identified the sound coming from it as crying, and when

"Because there's nothing a mother fears more," Lulu says closing her eyes, "than the chaos of the world." Before she sleeps, she looks once more to see if the bluejay is still in the black tree outside; together, the two women on the bed watch it with the baby asleep between them. "Brontë. . . ."

"I know."

"I have to go back."

Jeez, Brontë wonders, you don't suppose Armand is still chained up in that dungeon, do you? "I know."

It's the fur. There's something about it that makes his flesh crawl. He would vastly prefer the cold hard metal of regular handcuffs cutting into his skin. With every twist of his body, with every struggle against his   constraints, then the
more the fur of   **2018 (2004-2089)**   the cuffs softly
caresses his wrists.   A wave of disgust
washes over him. There's something depraved about it; it's like a strange animal, mutated and hermaphrodite, curling between Tapshaw's hands. Oh God don't even. . . . He actually thinks he's going to throw up. "Can't you use rope or something?" he says.

"I don't have rope," the other man says. "I thought you would find those comfortable."

I finally reached it I saw it was a baby sitting on the ground waiting for

For a moment Tapshaw stops struggling. "You're a sick. . . ."
I'm definitely going to throw up, he thinks, drenched in sweat; another long moment goes by before the feeling subsides. "You've taken leave of your senses," he croaks. Sitting on the other side of the room, Wang considers this: That's it, he thinks. He turns it over in his head, deliberating it in all its meaning: *I've*

taken leave of my senses. Regaining his composure, Tapshaw
growls, "You don't even know how to use that."

"Uh," Wang says, studying the gun in his hand, "I point it at you
and a bullet comes out and hurts you?"

"How in God's name you ever became the hero of a revolution,
I'll never understand."

"Well, I'll admit it was from staring into guns rather than firing
them." Wang gets up from the chair and walks to the window.
"Anyway I never said I was a hero. And is that what this is,
a 'revolution'?" Leaning in the sill, he's noticed lately the sky
is less and less blue. In the nearby hills, the observatory above
Los Feliz glows in the sun like a skull. "I thought this was a
'crusade,' and I'm the mystic — I who don't have a mystic bone
in my body — divining messages that come singing out of the sky
or floating up in boats in the form of children's toys. Which is
really more a crusade-thing than a revolution-thing. What sort is
this anyway?"

Tapshaw snorts in contempt.

"Oh, all right," Wang shrugs, "it's a nine-millimeter. You see?
I'm not as hopeless as both of us like to suppose."

ne, and he stopped crying and looked up at me blinking, and now in the

"It's an *old* nine-millimeter that will probably. . . ." Tapshaw
stops a moment for the nausea to pass, ". . . that will probably blow
up in your hand when you fire it."

"Yes, well," Wang goes back to the chair where he was sitting,
staring at the captive man on the floor, "there's one way to find
that out, isn't there."

"These things are going to make me puke," the bound officer gasps, swallowing frantically.

"Tapshaw," Wang answers gently and not completely without sympathy, "if you'll permit me: that may say just a little more about you than it does about anything else. Anyway the handcuffs are all I have and they're not coming off, not for a while anyway. So if I were you, I would calm down."

After a moment Tapshaw says, "Where are we?"

"Actually," Wang sets the gun down on the old table next to him, "I used to live here." He gazes around the tiny one-room wooden house. "When I first came to Los Angeles, this part of the city wasn't even under water." He gets back up and returns to the window. "There was a park over there," he nods, "right down those banks, at what used to be the corner of Alvarado and Sixth. A nice park once, I think I heard, back in the earlier part of the last century, 1930s, '40s. I got here at the end of '1, from. . . well, by way of that proverbial slow boat from China but in a roundabout fashion, let's put it like that. I would sit here at this same window at a table a lot like this one and smell the Mexican bread baking, I could never figure out where exactly, and. . ." In the northwest, the sky is definitely less blue than it used to be. ". . . write letters, lots of letters." He says, "Each right

memory-stream of the lake's birth canal, remembering it so distinctly, I car

after the other. Hadn't mailed one before I started the next."

"In code, no doubt," says Tapshaw, leaning back against the wall taking deep breaths, "to the other side you were spying for."

"Yes, that's right," Wang snaps impatiently, "that's the way
we top agents send all our secret messages — by the postal service.
Now you're just being *irrational*. This was seventeen years ago,
remember such a time? Before there *was* another side for me
to spy for, if in fact I *were* spying for anyone, now or then or ever."
He sighs, paces back to the chair. For a while neither of them
says anything. "You know," Wang finally decides to try again,
"you can believe what you want of me. You will anyway. And
when your men catch up with us, as I know they're bound to,
persuasion brought to bear will undoubtedly get me to say exactly
whatever it is our superiors — well, *your* superiors — want said.
But right now, before the truth becomes so opportunistic,
I'm telling you two things, assuming the truth means anything
to you at all. The first is this. I promise you, I absolutely
guarantee you, that most of what we call, oh, history, happens
for reasons that have absolutely nothing to do with why we think
it happens. The second is, that kid had nothing to do with
anything. You want to tell yourself I'm whatever it is you want
to believe I am, go ahead. But all that boy ever did was row
me in that boat." He runs his hand through his hair. "He was
barely verbal."

"Yes, well maybe he was a little more verbal than you know," and
of course now, unwittingly, Tapshaw has revealed he's not really
so sure about Wang's complicity after all. Both men realize this as

ell it was obviously him, I can see it so obviously in a way I couldn't then

soon as Tapshaw says it but Wang lets it go because it's a little
beside the point, and also because part of him has always suspected
the same about the boatman — not that he was part of any plot,
which is absurd, but that maybe he wasn't exactly the idiot savant
of the lake he pretended to be. "Are you going to tell me he wasn't
broadcasting those messages?" Tapshaw says.

"I'm telling you," Wang answers evenly, "they were meaningless," which to Tapshaw, Wang understands, is the most dangerous prospect of all, the most subversive of all possibilities, the possibility that polemicists and ideologues, political spokesmen and militarists alike reject down to their core, not to mention rationalists: yes, Wang ruefully reminds himself, let's not forget rationalists. "I'll tell you what," he says to the other man. Tapshaw glares up at him from the floor. "I'll let you go," Wang nods, "if you can answer one question. "

"I'm not playing your games."

"Tribulation II, or III?"

"What?"

"Tribulation II or III. That shouldn't be so hard. Haven't you been keeping track? Haven't you been able to tell when one ends and one begins, and then when the next ends and the one after that begins? You answer that and I'll unlock those cuffs right now."

Unconsciously Tapshaw begins chewing his lip. Wang can practically see the gears turning in his head.

because I didn't really know him then, now I can see it's Kirk with flashes of

"Come on, III or IV? Or, wait a minute, I said II or III didn't I?" Wang taps the gun on the table next to him. "Well, we'll throw in IV too. Give you more choices, more chances to get it right."

Tapshaw exhales. "III."

"Wrong."

The other man's shoulders sink in defeat. A moment of silence passes before Tapshaw finally thinks to ask, "How do you know?"

"Actually," Wang says, "I don't. But apparently, neither do you."

"Then it was a trick question," Tapshaw says.

"You're really not getting the gist of this, are you."

"What do you care about that kid anyway?"

Another trick question, Wang thinks, because he doesn't know the answer, just as he doesn't actually know for a fact what the young boatman was involved with or wasn't, it's just intuition — a little late in my life for intuition, Wang muses. A little late for instinct. That's what bondage queens are for, instinct. There's no mathematics for intuition, even for someone who was a student of mathematics once, but then mathematics isn't always necessarily the language of reason and sense; you can stick numbers after anything, including a tribulation or two or three, and pretend everything adds up. He doesn't really know for a fact, moreover, that what he's told Tapshaw is true, that what the boy was broadcasting those nights from out on Hamblin Island was truly meaningless. The broadcasts didn't mean anything to Tapshaw or Wang, or maybe even the boy, but that doesn't mean they didn't

Brontë in him maybe, as if she was the shadow of his resurrection, or maybe

mean something to someone, or that they didn't have a meaning
no one knows.

And at that point, of course, well then what's rational and what isn't? At that point there's no saying anymore what chaos is, there's no saying anymore what "meaning" means. At that point. The broadcasts were meaningless, Wang said to Tapshaw, as though that was the rational explanation — which only means sometimes randomness is rational and meaning isn't. Then you're lost in the dark heart of god or the void, whichever you've decided you believe in: when there are no accidents, is chaos chaos anymore? And if everything is an accident, is order an accident as well? One man stands before a line of tanks. Another crashes an airliner into a building. One ends an Age of Reckoning, the Age of the Sky; the other begins the Age of Chaos, in which the sky melts to earth and becomes a lake. On one or the other or both, those who record the times and those who interpret or use the lessons of what's recorded — and especially those who love power first and last and only, and use such interpretations to their own ends — will impose a rationale. But ultimately and interiorly, the reasons belong not to those who watch and record and interpret and use, but those who do.

Which isn't to say that, because the man standing before the tanks and the man crashing the airliner each does so for his own secret reason, they're the same. It's not to say there's no difference between them, or that good and evil aren't real. To the contrary — thinking about this now, although he doesn't know it Wang crosses a point of inexorability, on his journey to the center of his life's enigma — it's men's secret reasons that best testify to good and evil, which are as real as love and hate, which in turn are the world's only incontrovertible things,

he was the manifestation of hers, and I woke then or rather was awakened in

empirically incalculable as they may be. In his self-loathing there's part of this proposition even Wang won't accept yet, even as he now, yes, intuits it: he won't accept that because he may not have stood before a line of tanks solely for whatever reason the world believes, the act was no less noble, no less heroic. Sometimes an act means something unto itself. Sometimes it has a heroism unto its own. That boy who rowed him in the boat back

and forth to the Chateau, well, Wang didn't even know him; and
he's going to live only long enough to begin to intuit the way a
child — above and beyond any other creature or thing — explodes
all notions of meaning and rationale, chaos and god, because it's
one's child who makes such things matter beyond one's own self.
And if Wang can't really answer the question of why the boy in the
boat matters to him, or even *if* the boy matters to him, what does
matter is that *she* had a boy, not *my* boy no; no not mine, not ours,
but one perhaps who could have used a father anyway, if there had
been a man around big enough to overcome his pain and pride: so
this, Wang thinks, this is for lost sons, and Tapshaw will never
understand that.

A sudden dusk descends.

In China they would have found me by now, he thinks to himself
sitting at the table; and then, turning to the increasingly frayed
ribbon of blue in the sky through his window, rationale fractures to
its fundament — and he catches his breath, thunderstruck.

She never got the letters.

His jaw actually drops a bit. A hot wave of his own absurdity
washes over him; a moan only he can hear rises from the pit of
him. Never having remotely crossed his mind before, this sudden

wave of nausea by the bubble of him breaking the surface of my dream and

realization out of the, well, gray if not blue, now has a stunning
clarity: she never got the letters (*labial jewel, riverine rapture. . .*);
and suddenly he sees the last fourteen years for their grand error,
the greatest hubris of which has been not simply how reactively
and immediately he concluded she had spurned him, without even
considering the possibility that chaos might have intervened to
thwart his attempts to reach her, but that he then called this

conclusion "rational." The rational processes of mathematics aside, one chooses what it is he wishes to consider rational about his life; and now if Wang could simply find a way to begin breathing again, if he could simply find a way to loosen himself from the revelation that grips his chest at this moment, he might ask himself not only how it is that rationality minus chaos equals not rationality but chaos, but also why he chose to believe in her rejection of him rather than in the intercession of chance. He might ask himself how it is he could have not taken into account a lake that appeared in the center of a city, and that cast into such pandemonium the age before him and all its correspondences.

Then he might ask himself who he is. The Emperor of Elevators, he whispers. What? asks the man handcuffed on the other side of the room; but Wang takes no notice. He raises his hand to the sky as though, viewed through the prism of his palm, its rare blue might be located. Wang? the other voice says again from the floor a few feet away, what's wrong with you? but holding his hand up to his eye, staring through, Wang is transfixed, and finds himself back fourteen, fifteen years ago in this same house, sitting in this same place at a table much like this one, pen and stationery spread out where, just a moment ago, there was a gun, the waters of the lake not yet having risen as high up the banks outside the window. Oh this is one of those spells, he tells himself very lucidly, one of those "lapses" that have been reported around the city lately,

reclaiming his place in my womb, and it wasn't long after that I came back to

that he's dismissed out of hand as outbreaks of mass psychosis even as he himself experienced such a thing one night a year ago, after returning from the Chateau for what proved to be his final visit there. Possessing both "present" and "past" consciousness, now he's back in the days of '4, back before the crusades and his days as a dockhand at Port Justine, hurled back to this time by force of either trauma or triggered recollection, to this memory on

which a life turned — several lives, as he's about to learn. He
feels it all again, his rage at her silence then and, beyond that, at
her old infidelity that produced the son that was not his, and at the
forsaken years between them, and at his simultaneous
imprisonment by and exile from the polar events of great moment
through which he lived without her so anonymously: and once
again, as he was fourteen years ago, he's paralyzed by, what?. . .
my love for her? or my fear of it. . . and then a man who has from
time to time meditated on the laws of impulse only to reject them
does the second profoundly impulsive thing of his life, and the first
since he was nineteen years old.

Having been cast by his Lapse back into this memory, now he
breaks free of its destiny. He turns from his window to gaze at the
small empty house around him, stares at the pen and stationery on
the table, and takes in his one good hand the umpteenth furious
unfinished letter that another Kristin would receive by accident if
he ever sent it — and instead crumples it up; then he takes leave of
his senses. He walks quickly from the house and breaks into a run,
hurrying to a boat moored on the banks, gets in the boat and,
binding his bad hand to one of the oars with his belt, begins to row,
undaunted by the four or five miles he has to cross.

Other than the smattering of lights coming on in the Silverlake
casinos to the northeast, he takes little note of the slightly altered

he city where he had been conceived, and if once I was convinced that no

not yet submerged scenery around him. The ghost of history,
he feels himself grow more corporeal by the moment. He glides
through the watery sky of the lake an hour and a half without break
until the weak arm of the bad hand throbs with pain. In this
moment on the lake, everything about Wang's absurd life comes to
a halt; he's riveted by a calm still secret to him. He's riveted, as
when he was nineteen years old in the Square, by a resolution

beyond rationality, by a wisdom forgotten as soon as he's seen it. In this moment he has more than passing acquaintance with his own strange courage. After a while he turns to look over his shoulder for where he's heading; he sees her hotel, not far from the Hamblin where he and Tapshaw, following the sound of a song, once sailed out thirteen years from now. He grows closer to her hotel as twilight grows darker and, just as though his life was exactly timed for such a thing, his final approach coincides with the cry of a child from the waves around him.

He hears her wail for her drowning son from a hotel window. He hears again the boy's desperate call and turns the boat to the sound; just as though his life is exactly timed for such a thing, he unties his hand from the oar and reaches into the water — and small fingers reach up and grabs his throbbing arm. With his other good hand, Wang pulls the boy up from out of the lake into the boat. In the boat, holding close to him the nine-year-old soaked and terrified but, as of this new moment, alive, Wang thinks to himself, Someone try telling me this isn't my son.

The next morning Wang, the woman he called K in his letters, and her son Kim leave the sinking hotel and move to shore. A day later, Wang buys a used car that needs new tires. On their way up Highway 1, Kim rides in the front seat with Wang as the woman sleeps in back; they stop at a shop in San Luis Obispo and get the

matter where I went a lake would have followed me there, now I don't know,

boy some new animé posters to replace the ones left behind in L.A. His room is the first they decorate when they rent the new flat in San Francisco that rests at a fork in the fog and overlooks the bay. On their first night in the apartment, staring out the large windows at the blue bay, Wang doesn't think of Lake Zed but only this, his most fulfilled moment; the next morning, when he makes a quick run to the market for chocolate milk — Kim's favorite — and his used car that needed new tires suddenly spins out of control on Van Ness and crashes into the oncoming bus, in those final moments before his neck snaps Wang wonders how it is that he, of all people, personally bore witness to both the very moment the Twentieth Century died and the very moment the Twenty-First was born, separated by the twelve shadowyears between them. He's a little surprised in those final seconds that it should be the young girl with the long gold hair he remembers, who he saw only a few times and whose name he never knew. In those final seconds he would like to believe he's been redeemed somehow, something about which he would give more thought if he had the time, but in the few seconds he has, the only thing he can be sure of is that the view of the San Francisco Bay from the new apartment the night before was worth everything.

Orphanhood is the bond, then, when Kim meets Saki more than fifteen years later. By the time he's twenty-five years old Kim is an orphan three times over, having lost first the father who was there only long enough to make a son, then Wang, then his mother to ovarian cancer three years ago in Toronto, where the two of them fled before the Bay Area's occupation in '9. Returning to liberated San Francisco in '18 following the siege of Monterey, Kim sees Saki for the first time when she mysteriously emerges from a condemned hotel at Chinatown's Dragon Gate looking coolly and fully capable of casting a spell on every man before her.

don't know, even as I feel like there are so many things now that I do know,

Part Japanese, Saki was orphaned by her mother, a former stripper from Las Vegas who vanished early in the girl's life — into a religious cult, unconfirmed and dubious rumor has it — and by her American father she's seen only in her dreams, a strange man who once charted a huge blue calendar that completely reordered history according to the chronology and logic of apocalypse, and from whom the daughter got her electric blue eyes. Kim can't believe his luck to have a woman so beautiful. He and Saki move in together. When he receives a position at the university as a professor of musicology, Saki goes to work for a map maker, walls around her floating with brightly colored places of indefinite borders, oceans of uncertain shores; although it would make more sense for the couple to live in Berkeley where they work and the rents are cheaper, Kim can't bring himself to leave a single-room flat not far from where he grew up near Van Ness. If he leans from the upstairs window as far as possible and turns his head sharply north, he can see a blue sliver of the view of the bay that the adopted father of one week who saved Kim's life saw on the last night of his own life.

Kim marries Saki two months after she becomes pregnant. Angie is named after her grandmother even if it wasn't the grandmother's real name but the one she took from an old rock and roll ballad she loved while dancing underage in a Vegas strip joint back in the 1970s. So it is that two generations later Kim and Saki's daughter has more music in her genes than she knows. When Angie is eight years old, long before he's entitled to a midlife crisis her father has a ludicrous and cataclysmic affair with a student not nearly as beautiful as Saki; far from only a passing distraction, even after it comes to light the affair becomes an ever more disastrous obsession. It's as clear to Kim as to everyone else that he's taken leave of his senses. One afternoon Saki marches Angie to a hotel

even as now I know not only that Kirk's father is dead but that my own mother

room and bursts in on the rendezvous at a particularly debauched moment, a scene that profoundly traumatizes Angie more than whatever indignant satisfaction on Saki's part can compensate; in the years to come, she'll hate the mother for it more than the father. Two years later, the relationship between daughter and father is finally reduced to Kim — now without job or family or lover, and in defiance of a restraining order — suddenly appearing one morning before Angie and her mother on the sidewalk outside the little girl's elementary school, in rags and pleading for a single embrace, sobbing the little girl's name as Saki curses him.

Angie never sees him again. He disappears, either to enlist in some distant crusade of some undetermined roman numeral or to fulfill a family tradition of disappearing fathers and mothers. Given this, on some level it doesn't really make sense Angie would go to the same university as her father and, like her father, study musicology — or it makes complete sense. Perhaps it makes sense for all the reasons it doesn't. The rational processes of mathematics aside, one chooses what it is she wishes to consider rational about her life; and in fact Angie is not one to set rational processes aside even if, Wang not being her true grandfather, technically his blood doesn't run in her veins. She works hard in school to the exclusion of everything else. Except for one extremely perfunctory dating relationship that lasts five months with a young computer programmer, her life is consumed by combinations of music and math (since all music is mathematic), and her theory that as there's a basis for physical matter so there is for psychic matter, that within a deconstructed and reassembled melody there's to be located the helix of freedom and desire, transcendence and oblivion, even — if she believed in either — god and chaos. She spends her life searching for this helix. By the late '40s and early '50s, called a genius by some and a crackpot by

is dead too, even as now I know that my own father was dead before I was

others, and utterly nonplused by either distinction, Angie has pursued her musical grail throughout Europe, the Middle East and America as the diminished skirmishes of what's no longer called by anyone the "tribulation" but rather the Unrest have receded to the last bastions of certifiably insane Americans, Wyoming and Utah. For two years she conducts her research in lower Manhattan, for five years in the two hundred miles of desert west of formerly occupied Albuquerque, using as her headquarters an old Spanish hacienda once converted into a railroad hotel.

In wire glasses and dour attire, adopting an increasingly severe appearance in the way of women who believe no other physical identity is possible for them, Angie has neither her mother's beauty nor her father's handsomeness. If she did, it's possible she wouldn't marry anyway. But in the early '70s, as she nears her fiftieth birthday, to her own surprise she finds herself seized by a compulsion.

This is the compulsion to adopt a child. She listens for the compulsion's melody so she might analyze its mathematics, but all she hears is a fugue not of numbers but indecipherable runes. She pores over pictures of motherless children from all over the world, waiting for one to strike a chord. They all strike a chord. Her head fills with an awesome and heartbreaking symphony. For more than a year she wrestles with the decision, finally waking one morning in a strange ecstasy from a dream about her father; when she finally files the application, she's stunned to be turned down, due to institutional doubts as to her "domestic stability." Thousands of children in the world without mothers or fathers and she's turned down? She appeals the decision and is turned down again. She applies to go to China where she might find one of the countless infant girls abandoned by their parents, but ironically is

born and it's just as well, and in a way here in the birth canal of the lake none

denied not in spite of her Chinese heritage but because of it, as though there's some subversiveness about it she doesn't know. For months afterward she sits at night in her endless stream of hotel rooms poring again over the pictures of children, of sons or daughters who might have been. She runs her finger over their small faces. She holds the photos up to the light and peers into them as though some flicker in their faces, something in the backgrounds of their lives in Africa or Appalachia or the Andes, will offer clues as to why she isn't worthy of them. Like all children who assume responsibility for their own desertion, she becomes convinced this is her punishment for leaving her errant father outside her school that morning she was a small girl when, in rags, he cried futilely for her arms in the company of the mother who cursed him.

She returns to looking for the helix. She privately despairs of ever redeeming her life with a purpose when, in the late '80s at the far end of her career, she's called to Los Angeles, the city that takes leave of men's senses.

Arriving late afternoon, she asks to be taken to the site immediately but is convinced by excavation officials to rest first. She spends the night in one of the new hotels that have gone up near the old airport razed and rebuilt in the last five years after being closed more than seven decades. As dark falls, from the highrise window she can see a hesitant galaxy of lights growing across the basin, though still far less than the dazzling overturned jewel box that was night-time L.A. a century ago. The next morning, her driver explains that while the last of the freeways has finally been reopened, none takes Angie where she's going so they make their way instead up Old La Cienega Road, one of the city's major thoroughfares before the lake and now a narrow two-lane,

f it matters and in a way there's nothing that matters more, and am I still

part paved and part mud. They keep the windows rolled up due to the black clouds of mosquitoes that descend suddenly from swampier parts of the city. From the backseat Angie can see the permanent watermark on warped buildings that haven't been demolished yet, like the permanent shadows of mid-Twentieth Century Hiroshima: How long since this part has been submerged? she asks halfway across the lake bottom, and is

stunned when the driver answers almost twenty years, as much by
how quickly her own life is passing; it doesn't seem so long ago
she was hearing the stories about the "new L.A." being built — as
the civic phrasemakers had it — "from out of the shale," when the
lake was finally declared officially dead. "Recovery's been slow,"
she notes.

"Yes," the driver, not wanting to venture too far into politics,
answers carefully, "well. . . some never saw the point." Then,
becoming bolder, "After all, it's not like there ever was supposed
to be a city here in the first place. Even back before the lake,"
the driver goes on, "everyone knew it was doomed."

It's two hours before they reach the site. As it looms into view
she's astonished at the size of it; her sixty-six-year-old heart beats
harder and faster than it has in a long time. The car stops and the
driver helps Angie unload from the car a large case of instruments
and equipment. She's greeted by two members of the excavation
team, one of them the director of the project, a man in his early
thirties with tired watery gray eyes who fairly exudes skepticism.
He asks if she would like some lunch first. They're not in a rush
about this, she thinks — a battle of bureaucrats: the government
wants me here, these guys don't. She says she would like to take a
look at what she's come for but the director insists on lunch and,
given how her heart is racing, she relents. Over tacos she heads off

sinking? am I still drowning? am I still descending? am I still falling down

his questions with her own, and studies in the near distance the
outside scaffolding that props up part of the recovered structure.
At this point, he explains, we've cleared almost everything but the
western wall that was the most deeply embedded when that part
of the hills collapsed from the water.

On a long path of planks that disappear under the complex
of scaffolding, Angie, the project director and the driver with
Angie's instruments head into the site. Workers stop to watch.
When she emerges into what appears to have been once a grand,
now decayed lobby, the workers inside stop as well. Across
the atrium, two wide stone stairways spiral up one side and
the other, as well as long corridors that glint with a dead
blue residue; above, much of what was the roof has been washed
away. Almost immediately she hears it. It's very faint and high,
almost beyond human hearing; her ears, once extremely attuned
to such sounds, aren't as sharp as they once were. "A hotel?"
she says.

"That's what we figure," the director answers, "hard to think it
could have been anything else." They climb the stairs and
continue down one of the corridors, cutting through a small,
comparatively barren room and then what might have been a
sitting room beyond that, with a large window. Sodden
overstuffed sofas and high-armed chairs lie overturned against the
walls. In every room through which they pass, workers stop what
they're doing: She's here, she hears them whisper, that's her.
"There are a couple of things," the director says, "that make this
site more interesting than some of the other structures we've
excavated in the area." As they make their way down a long
corridor into a room overwhelmed by both a massive fireplace

down down? or am I rising? up up up, and how did I get turned around then?

and a melancholy Angie feels almost immediately, the music she's
heard since they entered the unearthed hotel grows. "First,"
he says, "there's no record of a hotel being here."

"What do you mean?"

"I mean we go back into old references to try to find some sort of entry, old travel books, old hotel guides, we go back into the city archives and pull out old geological surveys, zoning ordinances. . . and find no record of a hotel here at all." He stops and gazes around them. "Look at this. This wasn't a truck stop. This wasn't a motel on some back road to nowhere. There are plenty of records of another hotel about half a mile southwest of here, but not this."

"Maybe this is that other hotel. Maybe the records aren't exact."

He shakes his head, "We found that other one. It never went all the way under and actually was pretty famous, the Chateau Something with rock musicians and movie stars back in the last century, and then in the '10s and '20s some sort of religious-mystic fortune-telling bondage. . . uh. . . hey," he shrugs when he sees the way she's looking at him, "it was L.A., even if it *was* under water. But this," he sighs, sweeping his arm at the floor beneath them, "was just the middle of a road leading into an old canyon that led to a valley beyond that. Records show homes, a neighborhood, a corner gas station. . . no hotel though, and nothing like this."

"What's the other thing?" Angie says. They come into what appears to have been a huge ballroom, or several ballrooms

or have I really gotten turned around at all? and now I feel my first real panic,

conjoined; a few patches of wall still have shards of old mirror, and from the ceiling sway the stems of chandeliers plucked by the lake long ago. "The other thing?" says the project director.

"You said there are a couple of things that make this site interesting."

"The other thing," he answers, "is that. . . what our records do
show is that. . . well, this was it."

"This was what?"

"This was where it came from."

"This was where what came from?"

"The lake."

"The lake?"

"Yes."

"The lake came from here?"

"Yes."

"The lake came out of this hotel."

"Well of course we don't have any official indication there *was*
a hotel."

"Well there was, obviously, officially or not."

hat I've gotten turned around, that maybe I'm returning up up and up to the

The director takes a deep breath. "I can't explain the hotel,"
he says, "but the whole reason for digging here in the first place
was a pretty formidable amount of evidence, ranging from the
anecdotal to the geological, that the source of the lake was
somewhere right under here. Look," he takes another deep breath,
"*I* don't know. . . and the stories surrounding all this you wouldn't
believe. . . . " They cross the plundered ballrooms into two small

transitional rooms that appear to provide the only passage to the rest of the building. In one stands the remnants of what may have been a large pillar; if there was such a pillar in the other, it's gone now. Out of these rooms Angie and the director exit into the hotel's mezzanine, once obviously spectacular and lavish. Now the music, still high and vague, is close; once again, at the sight of Angie the workers stop. There's a buzz in the mezzanine as they turn from their work.

By itself, in the middle of the mezzanine that dwarfs it, under lights that have been set up around it, stands a rough wooden table, with high legs and a small surface-top; the table has been roped off. On top is a closed metal box.

"That's where we first found it," the director says, "crawling across the floor where the table is now."

"Do you know where it came from?" the woman says looking around the mezzanine.

"Not really," he answers, pointing, "we assume one of these suites."

"I would like to take a look there first, if it's all right," she says, "before the box." She follows the director through one suite then

wrong lake, to the version of the lake I came from, and I almost turn back

the other. They wander among the strewn beds and loveseats in a rounded blue chamber beneath a light fixture that's managed to survive all the water and years; another suite is circled by doors, a couple still with their original mirrors. "We looked through all those," the director nods at them, "there are passages running to some of the other rooms and we went through those too." Angie walks over to the wall. Running her fingers along its side, she

presses her ear to it, listening; the director peers around at the
workers watching.

They go back out into the mezzanine that's filled with sound.
"All right," Angie says, nodding at the box. All the workers
watching back up against the surrounding walls. The director
moves the rope that cordons off the table while Angie pulls from
her case some gloves and two long-handled stainless steel forceps,
one large and one smaller. Everything has so long led to this
moment that now, for her own reasons, Angie realizes she's afraid
of it too, like the rest of them; she's about to ask either the driver
or project director to open the box but decides it's something she
should do herself, as though her hands aren't shaking and her heart
isn't thundering in her chest. The workers circling the edge of the
mezzanine shrink back even though there really isn't anywhere
else to back into; some flee the room. Although the music is
much louder now and — as she reaches the large forceps into
the box and picks up the glowing snake — grows louder still,
it isn't cacophonous exactly. It's hardly a din. Some of the time
it even exists at a level barely anyone can hear, spiraling into
itself, devouring first its own tail and then the rest of itself,
at the place where terror becomes beauty before it becomes
terror again.

It writhes brilliantly at the end of the forceps. Then suddenly the

downward, but I go on up up and up rising like the bubble of him that rose in

snake's body sizzles into nothing, and in its place is a vapor,
leaving only the snake's head in the forceps' grip.

By now most of the excavation workers have fled the mezzanine,
along with Angie's driver. The project director is stricken, fixed to
where he stands. Almost spellbound herself, gripped by an ecstasy
she's felt before but can't identify, Angie tells herself she must

work quickly should the snakehead vanish too; with the smaller forceps she invades the snake's mouth and then, when the tool proves useless, throws the forceps to the floor and sticks her fingers in the snake's open mouth roughly pulling the helix from its throat. An answer? she wonders, the Question? holding it up before her, one moment a black bubble the next moment collapsed light, neither reducible nor mutable by chaos or god

this
is the
loss of
one's
child

and then in the blink of an eye it's gone as well. Completely alone in the mezzanine now, the director having unfixed himself and run, Angie spins in her place before rushing into the first suite turning one ear then the other to the walls, then rushing into the next suite and then the third, listening to the walls of each. She runs back into the mezzanine and slides herself along the walls listening with one ear then the other until she stops, cocks her head, and then turns her gaze to the mezzanine's far end, and a single small pantry door. She crosses the length of the mezzanine. Reaching the small closed door, she places her fingers to it, putting her ear to it and immediately pulling back. She presses her ear to it again and,

my dream that night I miscarried him, up up and up rising to break the surface

opening the door, can practically feel the oxygen leave the room; leaning into the small dark pantry, it seems like minutes before she can see in the black gorge beneath her, far inside the birth canal of the century; the small boy in the water, both unknown to her and more familiar than she can stand, flailing and grasping for someone's hand, a mother's that's too far from him or, perhaps, a man's with a glint of glass in it — except there is no man there.

The boy descends. Angie feels rise behind her the nullifying tide
of a life never lived.

Then this is for lost fathers, she thinks. Then this is for lost fathers
and lost mothers, and the Measure of the Real, the bond forged by
lost fathers and their daughters, mothers and their sons, against
which all else is dream. Knowing she has only moments in which
to fulfill a life, she gazes over her shoulder just long enough to see
hovering overhead the wave of the null, before she vanishes, along
with everything around her, into the unremembered.

Divide the mist on the grass by the sway of the trees. Add the still
of the water's surface and multiply the result by forty vineyards of
loam. Subtract the burning masts of seven boats while factoring
in the cosine of smoke,   then add all the rooms
of loss times the suites   **2031**   of sorrow divided by
half the somnambulist   highways outbound.
Compute the barges of the wind multiplied by the total of
fire-robots falling within the radius of rain, adding twenty-one

f the dream of the lake, as something that's once more being born to the lake

spacemonkeys with a variable of black bridges cubed, subtracting
the unmelted icicles of the moon plus the gaslights of night-time,
then dividing the result by the whips of love minus the collars
of devotion. Taking into account, of course, the square root of
snakes times one boat of missing mothers for each year of his life,
he's calculated how and when to make his way to the Chateau

which, as darkness falls, he can now see from where he hides on
the lakeshore.

He doesn't ask why they're after him. He has no idea why but he's
been living the life he lives too long to think that why matters;
twelve, thirteen years ago it was soldiers then it was gangsters in
the Hollywood Hills, now it's soldiers again. He recognizes one of
them, wonders whatever happened to the other, the one he would
row back and forth to the Chateau in the dead of night many years
ago. He knows they're going to catch him, because sooner or later
everyone gets caught by something. They're closing in, all over
the hills with their lights and dogs, they're all over the lake in their
boats, swarming everywhere; he tallies the inevitability of his
capture; his aren't the mathematics of freedom but time. An hour,
a few minutes. Just long enough to talk to her.

He's wondering why she came back, although maybe that's just
another why that doesn't matter. After watching the Chateau dark
and silent for more than a year he had finally given up, leaving the
lake behind and heading for the sea; he was sleeping on the beach
one night when he woke, his ears — which don't hear very well
anymore the sound of heartbeats — picking up one's faint
telegram. Making his way back from the coast past soldiers,
moving in the shadowy perimeters of the mulholland highway
inland, he tracked the approaching heartbeat from the mojave

that thinks it miscarried me, up up and up to reclaim my place in its womb, and

marshes growing closer, reaching the port at San Gabriel about the
time he reached the sepulveda channel. He's been hiding on shore
for a day now, in the trees and watching the lights in the Chateau
out on the water. He hears the barking of dogs grow nearer. Thus
he's figured his best moment of opportunity, and with aggregates
of light and sound in his head he makes his move and slips into the
lake. He swims to the Chateau grotto and, when he reaches its

stone steps, lingers for a while in the water to rest, at the place
where years ago he used to find food and wine in a basket. Having
caught his breath, he climbs out of the water and up the steps,
turning out the old lantern that hangs at the top by the door. Either
someone, he thinks, will have seen me, or will notice the light is
out; in any case he doesn't have long.

He opens the door and slides into the dark of the entryway.
He waits for a moment then walks quietly in through the outer
transitional chamber into what was once the ceremony room, then
her sleeping quarters, then goes through another door and he's
in the Lair's shadows.

Brontë sits on the divan before the hearth where a fire burns. He
notices she's cut her hair and that maybe it's darkened just a bit,
not quite as brilliant gold as it was. Not yet having seen him, she
gets up and crosses the Lair holding something in her arms; then
Kale realizes it's a baby. He's baffled for an instant, then nods to
himself oh that's why she left then. Guess some man changed her
mind after all. In the kitchen on the other side of the Lair she heats
some milk; he's stood there almost a full five minutes before —
crossing back the way she went, steadying the bottle in the baby's
mouth — she looks up, astounded for a moment before she decides
she's not, really. He looks at the baby's brown hair and eyes. He
thinks maybe the dogs outside have gotten louder.

ar above me I see it, I see it as I dreamed it, and maybe the lake sees it too in

"You shouldn't have come," she finally blurts, "they'll find you."
She shakes her head. "I'm not worth it."

Over Brontë's shoulder, through a door ajar, is a glimpse of
someone lying in a darkened room. He says, "It isn't you I've
come to see."

its own dream of me, that flicker of light in the dark, up up and up an

2031

maybe the lake believes as I did that night that the flicker is the dream itself, growing closer and larger, a small flash on the far horizon, up up and up and

Someone in the doorway. Who's there. Another slave come for his discipline? no I don't do that anymore. Who is it then. . . Brontë? Do I hear lightning? we haven't heard the lightning for a while now. . . are we back at the lake? yes in the Chateau, I'm. . . . Listen to these walls and tell me what they sing: I know what they sing. They sing goodbye. They sing goodbye to me. They sing goodbye to all of us and the bedlam of our ecstatic days. They're in such a hurry, the voices in the walls. . . I've hung on, well, it's been awhile now, I won't pretend to know how long but it's been awhile. Long enough to leave Zed and return. . . but I may hang on for a while longer, you watch. So keep your songs to yourself

maybe I'm the first dream the lake has ever had, as Kirk was the first dream I

until it's time. I may have one or two memories left. I may have one or two things to remember. . . so keep your songs to yourself until then. I may yet have some particularly poignant recollection that's particularly unbearable. . . like the way I used to see other children with their small open faces and couldn't stand it. . . so there are more memories I'm certain. More to torment me before

I go. . . . *If there's a higher light* and I'm still waiting. I'm still
waiting for it to shine on me. Who's in the doorway, come here.
Whoever you are, come closer to the candle so I can see. Don't
mind the singing walls. Come closer closer closer. . . who is it.
Let me look at you, let me take a. . . . Well well, if it isn't. Well
well, what do you know. After all this time. Finally worked up
the nerve did you. Come for your discipline, have you. Here you
are. Come for your humiliation: oh we must think of something
special for you. Come for something special I'm sure so we must
think of something special, for the ultimate slave, the ultimate
submissive. The ultimate humiliation. Something far grander than
the banal sadisms. Something that could lay so low someone so
high. . . let Me think. I'll think of something. I never pissed on
anyone in My illustrious career but I must say it's hard to think
of something more appropriate for the likes of you: I think I could
work up some piss for the likes of you. I've never made anyone
bleed other than Myself of course but I must say it seems fitting
now. So much blood the rest of us have bled for you over the
years, a little bleeding back on your part hardly seems unfair,
hardly seems asking so much. Did I say you could look at Me?
you don't look at Me until I tell you to look at Me, do you
understand? your discipline begins now, your training begins
here, at My feet. you don't regard Me until I tell you. you don't
stir until I say stir. you don't exist until I say you exist. you don't

ever had, and now of course as I rise up up and up to break the surface of the

do anything or say anything until I tell you. Nothing about you is
yours anymore, everything about you is Mine. Everything you
feel, if you feel anything, everything you think, or think you think.
Get on your knees. Lick the stone of the floor. Let Me put around
your neck this collar of thorns, around your neck, you remember
thorns don't you. you're familiar with thorns. you in particular,
you of anyone. you most of all. No one's ever done thorns like

you, right? Don't mind the blood. What's a little blood. Don't
mind the flow from your neck now. What's a little flow from
the jugular. Here's a leash for your collar, woven from the flesh
of children, stained and soaked in lapsinthe, to remind you who
you belong to. Tell Me, because I've never been straight on this:
which is it that's always best proved your existence? That you
give children? or that you take them away? I think you and I made
a bargain once but it's occurred to Me lately I've never seen a bit
of evidence you ever kept your end. I think I kept My end. Yes
I believe so. I think I did. I think I did and then some. If it was
our bargain that I would give up all the happiness of a mother in
order to save My son from the chaos of the world, well then I have
to say I think I kept My end. First you sent him to make Me so
tender. Then you drove Me mad with it. So now lick the drops
of your blood that fall on the stone beneath your knees, lick it, lick
it. Lick it up. Lick lick lick. Suck it out of the pores of the stone.
Did I say look up? Did I say to? There! that's for looking up
without permission. I'm the god here and you're the woman this
time, don't think you aren't. Don't think the god-cock means
anything within these walls. you're the woman and w(W)e're
going to prove it soon enough don't you worry. turd. sack of
divine shit you. Here let's see what you think of the point of My
high-heel in your side, what do you think of that. How do you feel
about that. Here's another good kick for you, and another. Roll

ater, I can see, I know that the silver flash above me is the gondola waiting,

over so I might consider grinding your balls to dust under My heel.
Get up. Get up! What a stupid slave! There! that's for being such
a stupid slave. There and there and there. Now get up. you're not
even amusing now. you're not even a diversion. Come here now,
w(W)e're going down to the dungeon. Come on or I'll yank you
down. W(w)e're going down now. Get up off the floor, you
disgust Me, come over here. Put this shackle around your foot

and lock it. Now the other. Now one wrist, now the other. There. That's more like it. It's so you. Here, your collar's loose, let's tighten it, there. Pale is such a nice color on you. Raise your arms now: there. Slip the cuffs that bind your wrists up over this hook above your head. There. Now w(W)e swaddle you in latex, start at your head and leave just enough exposed that you might barely breathe, wrap you tight so you see nothing, wrap you tight so you hear little but the muffled moan of the world coming up behind you, the world you've made moan for so long. So that every sense is bound, deprived. . . wrap you from head to your feet leaving the almighty god-ass exposed bare for the sake of the lash of course, crank up the hook a little and hang you from your cuffs and hoist you until your toes barely touch the floor: there. So that when I flog you, you'll spin in the air like a black cocoon, twirling above all the dead bluejays covering the dungeon floor around you. Let the god-toy try to imagine, for only a moment, what it might be like to spend eternity suspended in the Uncertain, as the rest of us have. . . and while you consider that, I think it will entertain Me to whip you for a while — there and there and there — before w(W)e get to the good part I mean, the best part where w(W)e make you a woman. As best you can through the latex, listen to the lake outside the walls, listen while you can before it dies. Hear the lake? or is it the blood pounding in your ears from the blows of My crop and the crown of thorns around your throat. OK then.

but since I've gotten confused in my way and can no longer be sure to which

That's enough. That's enough of that. you've become tedious, as you've always been tedious in your fashion. Let's lower you from the ceiling and feminize you now, make a woman of you now. No I'm not going to cut it off: please. It's so trite. I was many things in My life but not trite. It's rather an unimpressive specimen anyway if I may say so, for supposedly being the Ultimate Specimen. No let's lower you from the ceiling and slip

the cuffs off the hook while I dig something out of the old tool
chest here. . . get back down on your knees. you'll get used to it.
The rest of us have. The rest of us got very used to it a long time
ago. Tell us, what's it like from the other angle? How is it gazing
up for a change? *Don't look at Me.* Did I say you could look at
Me? I asked what it was *like*, I didn't tell you to *do* it. . . what a
very stupid slave. . . I guess it's all just a little unfamiliar for you
though. I guess it takes some getting used to. Well tell Us about
it. Yes tell Us all about it. Where's My evidence? is what I want
to know, that you ever kept your end of the bargain. Where's the
evidence except a vision or two. Was that supposed to satisfy Me,
a vision or two? where's the evidence. That he was ever OK. That
he was ever safe. That he was even loved, maybe. That he wasn't
so painfully lonely in the night. That's what I want to know, I who
gave him up. I who haven't gone a day without seeing his small
face, hearing his small voice, every little thing he said, polite little
dictator with all his whys and answers to the chaos of the world.
Oh here's what I was looking for. A little large but appropriate
I would think for a god-toy, suitable I think for the ultimate slave,
here it is. . . then bend over. Bend over now. Bend over and put
your face in the ground. Arch your back and open yourself behind.
A little large but you know, this is what it is to be a woman in your
world. This is what it is. This is what it's always been. There.
What do you think of that. How do you feel about that. What

ake I've returned, then swimming up up and up to break the surface I can

ridiculous female could ever have suggested God is a woman.
What ludicrous bitch could ever have thought the viciousness of
God anything but male. Are you God for the way you give us
children, or the way you take them from us? that's what I still
want to know. Here, a little deeper I think. Here, here, here, yes.
What's the matter. Yes. Here. you don't like it so much? Here,
yes. This is for, you know, all of them. Isaac and the carpenter

kid and all the eldest sons of an Egyptian night, and, well, for the
little wildman too. For him too. Here then. Here! and. . . I. . .
here, and. . . oh. Oh I. . . . No. No I swore to myself I wouldn't,
no. I swore to myself I wouldn't let you. Swore to myself you
would never make me cry like this again. . . but You have. Swore
You never would but You have. . . oh no. Oh no. Let me die now.
What are You waiting for. Let me die now. Let this dream be
over now. i've only been waiting for it since the moment i lost
him. Since that moment i. . . since that moment i returned to the
boat and he was gone; so let me go now, so i can hope on just the
merest of chances there *is* somewhere else Over There where he's
waiting right now, waiting for me, and i'll hold him to me again,
pull him to me, smash his soft hair in my hands and press his
small eyelids to my lips. Let me go. There's nothing here for me
anymore, no other delusion to make me believe in my own life
anymore, if only for a minute: no Domination or submission to
give me purpose: no method for going on. i don't care about Your
subservience or Domination, i don't care about Your humiliation
or Glory. This is the ritual no mother can win, when God gives
a mother her child just so she might go mad with love for him.
There's nothing here anymore so i want to go now. You there in
the doorway, come and take me then. What are You waiting for.
Come on then. Come here. Come on. Please. Please i beg You.
i'm begging You. Is that what You want, is that what You've been

therefore as well no longer be sure to which gondola I've returned either

waiting for, to hear me beg? then i'm begging You. i'm begging
You now. Please come take me. . . please i'm begging. The walls
can sing now, it's time for their song. i don't know what more i
can do than beg You. i'm begging then, i'm pleading. Come on
then, please. Yes please. Come on. Please. Please. Please.
        *Someone in the doorway. Not yet fifty years old but ancient
in her grief, she rises up on her elbows to try and see in the dark,*

falls back, eyes wandering the ceiling looking for the way out of her life. In the dark she hears his footsteps, waits for some explosion of final pain or deliverance or both, not really bracing for it because she doesn't have the strength to brace; and when a hand falls on her forehead to calm her, as if she were a child having a bad dream and talking in her sleep with her fingers, it takes her a moment to think to herself maybe it's not God after all, maybe it's someone else.

In her bed, she turns to the shadow beside her and, reaching out, puts her own hand in his hair, and remembers from long ago a smell of tall dry grass. At first it catches in her throat but she finds the will to ask it anyway: "But who is it," she murmurs in the dark, "are you. . . ?"

"I'm Nothing," says a voice she knows, that she knows she knows, transformed by all the years though it is, "a Bright Light."

r whether there truly is another gondola, or ever was, or whether there was ever even Another Side at all except in my red hysteria, or whether I truly

2XXX

wim from personal chaos to collective god or from personal god to collective chaos, or whether they're the same chaos, the same god, the same lake, the

The night before it happened, she had a dream about her father. *She was crossing a square in the dark, making her way past a huge fountain through concentric rings of symmetrically staggered stone benches. Hovering over the fountain was a bronze world patched up from the pieces of other shattered worlds. Particularly since it was dark she didn't recognize him at first, as though he was only the ghost of someone she was supposed to have known; when he said, so quietly and invisibly in the dark it almost could have been the fountain speaking, "The Age of Chaos is here," she woke thinking, What, it's just arriving now?*

ame empty gondola I left just a minute ago, and I don't know but that as I rise

At first she didn't even think to call him. *They had been estranged for several years anyway; the last time they had talked was right after her mother's death, although she would get cards*

from him along with the occasional, tentative e-mail she never answered.

Even that day, she picked up the phone and put it down several times before dialing. Then naturally the call wouldn't go through and in a way she was relieved. But it nagged at her, the feeling she had, and grew stronger in the months since her dream, until it became something much more than a distraction from her studies and her confused deliberations over her sexuality and everything else going on in her life; it got to the point when everything reminded her of her dream and this feeling about it for no reason she could figure: walking her West Hollywood neighborhood, passing the classic old movie-star apartments with their turrets, the little Italian eateries and xerox stores and travel agencies and mailbox rentals and gay fetish shops and video outlets and cappuccino stands, and especially the sight of the Century City towers when she took the bus down Santa Monica Boulevard to the university. Over the next six months she might have expected to have more dreams about him, or perhaps the same dream over and over, each elaborating on the previous; but instead she stopped dreaming altogether. Instead she woke from each night as though it was a void, as though she had slipped into the night's very womb, dark, still, swaddled in the unseen and unlistened; this she found more ominous.

up to break the surface of the water whether, even if I make it, even if I ge

Even the winter twilight when she *finally found herself in a cab heading down Hollywood Boulevard as it made its way through*

traffic before finally turning south on La Cienega, after it had been all she could do just to decide to go, she still resisted the temptation to ponder the true nature of her feelings about him.

Deep down, she really wasn't so sure her resistance was completely about anger. If she was honest with herself, she wasn't even sure most of it was about anger. When she discovered at the airport that she had left her ticket back at the old hotel where she lived, she was relieved, like when her phone calls wouldn't go through those first few days; she thought perhaps random accident was letting her off the hook. But she knew it wasn't random accident. In her mind she could see the ticket in plain sight on her bookshelf: she had "forgotten" it accidentally on purpose, naturally, which was a bit pathetic, since it was an electronic ticket and she didn't need the hard copy anyway. Checking in and making her way through all the new security, in her seat on the plane she finally resigned herself to the trip. It was a red-eye, so she was glad she had cashed in the miles for an upgrade.

Arriving at dawn, she took a cab into the city. It was too early to check into her hotel room, so she left her bags behind the front desk and took a walk outside. But it was too early and cold for walking too, and she was exhausted, upgrade or no. She gave herself permission not to have to deal with anything today. She lingered in the hotel coffee shop eating a muffin and drinking tea and reading the newspaper; at eleven, after she had been waiting three hours, she was able to get into her room, although going to

here, even if my lungs don't burst first not even having taken a gulp of air

sleep now didn't seem a good idea. She spent the rest of the day reading and watching the news cable, looking out the window — she had a nice view of the science museum across the street and the park only half a block east — passing the hours before she decided it was late enough for her to order room service. The dinner was all right but she didn't like the way the waiter looked at her. Afterward she pushed the tray out into the hall, called

*housekeeping to let them know it was there, then took a hot bath.
By now she was almost too tired and — she had to confess —
emotionally wrought as well, and it took her awhile to get to sleep.*

She woke the next morning in dread. *Trying to read the morning*
Times *she was entirely unsettled; she dressed and, as she left the
hotel, turned to the park rather than flagging a cab. She spent*

before my descent, I don't know whether I'll have the courage, I don't know

*several hours walking in the park then went to a restaurant and
had for lunch something she forgot even as she was eating it. Then
she went back to the room. She couldn't even bring herself to go
to a museum or movie; instead she lay in bed stunned by the
afternoon. By around five o'clock, when it was too late to do today
what she had come for, she was furious with herself. She didn't*

*sleep all night, and by morning was both exhausted and wired.
She skipped breakfast, skipped the newspaper, dressed and went
downstairs and caught a cab heading downtown.*

*Thinking she was too early and she should kill some time
walking around, she made the mistake of having the taxi drop her
off on Seventh Avenue where the streets of the West Village got all
crazy like in L.A., shooting off in diagonals. When she finally
found the address, she looked for the manager among the names
posted outside, buzzed him and they had a garbled conversation
over the intercom in which she tried to explain who she was;
finally he let her in, more out of frustration than anything else.
Inside, he was standing in his office doorway . When she saw her,
he brightened a bit like men always did. "Yes?" he said.*

*"We spoke last week," she said, "remember? About my
father. I called you from Los Angeles."*

*The realization sinking in, he nodded somberly and
motioned her to follow. They climbed the stairs; at one point he
turned to look at her over his shoulder as though to say something,
but whatever it was may not have seemed sufficient, and instead he
said nothing. On the third floor he unlocked a door and opened it
for her. For a moment they just stood together silently in the
hallway before she went on in ahead. The manager watched as the
young woman roamed the empty apartment and then, again as
though he was going to say something, left her.*

whether I'll have the courage to open my eyes if I get there, because I won't be

Nothing about the apartment was *particularly remarkable. She supposed it wasn't really necessary for her to have come rather than just arranging for it all to be shipped back, but perhaps she just needed to actually see it; that was possible. Perhaps she just needed to see it for precisely all the ways she told herself she didn't. Don't suppose we would have needed to ship this, she said to herself, pulling a vodka bottle from the trash and wondering when he switched from tequila. Piled on the shelf were books and magazines and movie videos, tacked to the walls were notes and newspaper clippings. There was a photo of her from when she was fifteen, and one of her mother; that one was the most unbearable.*

able to bear the possibility that the boat is empty again, like the last time I went

The photos leaned against the wall cocked at a slant, as though he had trouble deciding whether to turn them face up or down.

Over by the computer and printer was the unkempt stack of a manuscript curling at the corners. On the top page was the ringed mark of where he had set a glass; for a while she circled the

manuscript as though pretending she didn't know it was there. But after she had surveyed everything else, it was all that was left

these are the memoirs of Banning Jainlight, failed novelist, dabbler in chaos and connoisseur of self-pity, dilettante in husbandry and misbegotten father. . . .

and then for several hours, in the morning shadows of his apartment she sat reading. For most of it she didn't cry at all. She felt she didn't have the luxury of crying, at least until

and in the darkest moments, I've made my peace with the failure of my life by believing that, sometime in a future I'll never see, I made a deal with God. This wasn't a vision, it wasn't a dream. It was an unshakeable notion that whatever good things might have ever been in my future, I made a deal with God trading all of them for the well-being of my little girl, because I knew that, however much I've ever wanted all those things, I would make that trade without hesitation or deliberation. I would exchange every moment of fulfillment and accomplishment, success, fame, glory just for her to be all right. . . my failure then became only the very small price I paid for God's guarantee that my daughter would somehow be saved from the chaos of the world

until she got to that part, then she didn't read anymore. She sat alone in the apartment the rest of the day. When she finally left, the manuscript was all she took with her, stuffed in a large padded envelope from a literary agency, in which something had been returned, perhaps the manuscript itself; at the hotel,

in the lake and returned to the gondola, I won't be able to bear the possibility

in spite of how poorly she slept the night before, she constantly woke to passages from the manuscript in her head. Finally she got up from bed, called the airline, changed her reservation to an earlier flight, and carefully packed the manuscript in her suitcase among her clothes. Setting the room key on the hotel's front desk, she left just a bit before daylight, waving down a cab that took her to the airport where she found that, despite having booked it just a couple of hours before, there was no flight back to Los Angeles after all. For some reason she didn't find this perplexing. Rather she calmly booked another flight for later that evening and returned to the hotel. The key was still at the front desk where she left it. When she went back to the airport that evening, again she found there was no flight to L.A., nor were any scheduled.

None? she said to the attendant at the ticket counter. She caught a taxi back into the city where the driver took her to Penn Station; a train was leaving for the West Coast the following afternoon. Due to a cancellation she was able to get a sleeper. She checked into the Hilton on Sixth Avenue where she ordered room service and took a hot bath and an over-the-counter pill to sleep; the next morning she phoned the front desk for a late check-out and watched cable movies on the TV. She checked out of the hotel and got another taxi to Penn Station, where she waited until it was time to board the train.

On the train she worked up the nerve to ask for a glass of wine, and although he had a knowing, suspicious look in his eyes, the porter brought her one without asking for verification of her age. A few hours later the train was in Washington, moving south through the night. When she woke in the morning and peered out her window, she was in Atlanta. She was becoming more aware of an undeterminable urgency, a feeling there was some rendezvous to keep at an appointed hour; it grew in her with every passing mile. At twilight the train crossed a very long bridge, pulling into

of opening my eyes and seeing nothing and no one before me but the awful

New Orleans at nightfall. She slept through Texas. The next morning she woke about two hundred miles west of Albuquerque outside what, in the flashing light of a storm, appeared to have once been an old railroad hotel; the porter was knocking on her door. This is where you change trains, miss, he announced.

No, she answered.

What?

No thank you, she corrected herself.

The porter blinked at her a few moments and disappeared. When he returned, the conductor was with him. We change trains here, miss, he told her, more authoritatively than the porter.

No, thank you, she said, I'll wait. I would prefer not to get off the train.

The conductor and porter looked at each other and then disappeared, and the next fifteen minutes she was aware of various attendants whispering outside her door. When the porter didn't return, she made her bed up into a seat and sat. After a while, the train suddenly shuddered and the lights went out. She dozed in her seat and when she woke the lights were still out and the train was still outside the old railroad hotel; she opened the compartment door and looked out into the aisle of the car. Neither the porter nor conductor was to be seen. She made her way down the aisle of the train and found the car empty; the next car was empty as well. She returned to her compartment and, when another hour or two passed, got up again and went exploring the dark deserted train looking for the concessions lounge in particular. Foraging for food, she found nothing. Returning to her compartment with an empty water bottle, she filled it with tap water from the restroom. Looking out the train at the old hotel there by the track, sometimes she thought she saw a flicker of light in one of its windows.

She slept in her compartment that night and woke the next morning to find she was still outside the hotel. Ravenous and

emptiness, like the last time, and now in this new fear all I can do then is go

finally frightened, still she didn't get off the train. She was convinced that as soon as she stepped off to see if there was food in the hotel, the train would depart. By now she had gone up and down the length of the train looking for anything that might have been left behind by someone, a candy bar or part of a sandwich. In the afternoon she began to feel faint.

The day was darkening into evening and she was seriously considering a dash to the hotel when instead, in a slight delirium, she opened her suitcase to pull out her father's manuscript, carefully packed among the shoes and underwear. It wasn't there. By now she wasn't quite lucid enough to be sure whether this surprised her. She tried to think of when she last looked for the manuscript but, dazed by her time on the train, having lost track of exactly how long she had been traveling, she couldn't remember seeing it since New York. Trying to think the situation through as rationally as possible, she was beginning to doze again when she was awakened by a lurch; as lightning fell, the train slowly began pulling away from the old hotel. Soon the storm was behind her and tiny houses glittered in the distance. Sagebrush blew south. Snow was on the far northern mountains.

The aisles of the train remained dark and empty. After being awake most of the night, watching the Mojave marshlands outside her window glisten in the light of the full moon, not until the early morning hours did she finally sleep. At dawn the train slowed again, finally pulling into what she now believed was indeed the end of the line. At the port of San Gabriel she tore into a sandwich and some fries, then waited for the afternoon ferry that sailed her further up the lake into Los Angeles; stretched out on a plastic bench on the lower deck, she actually slept. The ferry continued through the night and by dawn the next day pulled out onto the greater lake, which she found instantly familiar. Around

on, all I can do is keep swimming up, all I can do is swim on up and up to it,

noon she reached Los Feliz. The abandoned observatory loomed in the dark hills above. Any number of men were happy to offer her a ride but she held out for another woman, an older psychotherapist who drove her along the serrated shoreline from canyon to canyon as her passenger tried to explain with some difficulty exactly where she needed to get to. On the winding dirt road through the hills it was nearly an hour to the mouth of Laurel

Canyon, not far from where the end of Hollywood Boulevard had been when she left; given the transformation of the landscape she had to get her bearings quickly, her eyes searching for whatever reference points she could still recognize. Now she knew she had no more time. With nothing else to do but leave her bags there at the side of the road, she rushed down the southern knoll in the direction of where her old West Hollywood neighborhood had been, crashing through the thicket and searching for a path she somehow knew would be there. She could make out the lake through the trees. As she hurried down the banks to the lakeside, the sound of loons echoed around her in the growing fog; in the wind on the banks of the lake she could see flapping the tents from an abandoned fair. Empty tents billowed and collapsed in a long dark row, black mouths blowing out over the water. Reaching the

end of the path
out of breath
she emerged
out onto the
shore of the
lake just in
time to stop,
look around
and raise her
hand to wave
. . . and then
to see Kristin

n up up and up to finally *break the surface of the water and, in a strangled gasp for air, take hold of the boat. . . and for the moment Kristin doesn't open her eyes. She feels the wood of the gondola in her arms, feels the evening air around her. The last bit of sun to the west splashes across one side of her face, throbs through the lid of one eye — and she won't look. She keeps her eyes closed because, for that moment, as long as her eyes are closed, then, just as she clings to the very boat itself, she can cling to the possibility that he's there.*

*For that moment she can believe he's there inches from her; for
that moment, there half in the water clutching the side of the
gondola with her eyes closed, she fixes herself to the possibility of
him. She can't bear the possibility the gondola is empty. She can't
bear the possibility of opening her eyes and seeing nothing and no
one before her, like the last time. As long as her eyes are closed,
it's possible he's there now next to her, small head in the sun,
sea-green eyes flecked with amber and the sanguine mouth of the
mad monk: it's possible. In the dark cathedral of her closed eyes,
she summons her best prayer, promises her best promise, to never
be paralyzed again by her love for him, to leap blindly into hope,
to stride boldly the border between terror and beauty. She
reconciles herself to the whim of God or chaos or both, she finds a
way to just* be, *there in the heart of the most desperate and cruel of
sure things: that sooner or later, one way or another, whether she
departs this earth first or he does, a mother will lose her child and
feel the most unbearable of losses; and that until then she has no
choice but to accept his life and hers in all their possibilities. So
now, there in the lake, clinging to the side of the gondola, she
doesn't want to open her eyes yet because it stops the moment at
the fork of all the lives that can still be lived, with the helix of
eternity glittering before her.*

*For this moment, in the dark of her eyes shut, she listens. For a
sign if not a song; and then*

*feels a small hand on her wet hair, a small hot breath in her ear,
and hears a small voice. "No Big Agua for Mama?" and she*

*pulls herself into the gondola, tumbling over the side and, lying
in the bottom still gasping for air, feels his hand on her brow as if
to calm her, as if she were a child having a bad dream. She pulls
him to her as if to crush him into her. She pulls him so hard to her
that he's a little afraid and, besides, she's getting him all wet.
Slowly she sits up.*

As she wipes the water from her eyes, he says, "Kulk," and as she runs her fingers over his face, the boy points at the lake where he dropped the spacemonkey that floated to her a moment ago on the other side. She remembers now leaving the toy behind in the other gondola. "Kulk is OK," she nods, "he has his own boat now." Kirk thinks about this. Kristin picks up the oars as if she has the slightest idea where to go. "Wait," Kirk says.

Somewhere in a century of rapture, a red wind rises off a midnight sea. Kirk points to the lake's edge where the girl with long gold hair to her waist waves to them again; the two young women look at each other across the water. "Yes please," the boy insists, ever the little dictator, and so, turning the boat in the other woman's direction, Kristin rows to shore.